COVET

Book 2 Vegas Sins Series

Rosanna Leo

COVET

Crave Publishing, LLC
Kailua, HI 96734
http://www.cravepublishing.net/

Formatting: Crave Publishing, LLC

ISBN-13: 978-1-64034-407-5
ISBN-10: 1-64034-407-1

DEDICATION

For Anise Eden.

Thank you for being such a good friend
and kind soul.

Chapter One

"Let me get this straight." Dana Hamill stopped stirring her coffee. "You're breaking up with me? In a hospital cafeteria?"

Her fiancé Tommy Parker picked at his muffin. "I just think, given the circumstances, we should maybe take a break."

Given the circumstances. "A break. So you're not suggesting we book a vacation to Jamaica. You mean we should take a break from each other."

"Just to, well, re-evaluate our priorities."

Dana laughed. She couldn't help it. This situation was ridiculous.

"You're taking it better than I thought you would."

"I'm not. I'm really not. If I'm laughing, Tommy, I guess it's because of the way you decided to end our one-year engagement. Instead of breaking it to me gently in a private location, you decided to do it in a chintzy hospital café, over cold coffee and a stale bran muffin."

"I only ordered the muffin because I missed

1

lunch."

"Fuck the muffin, Tommy. Just *fuck the muffin*."

The other customers in the café turned to look at Dana. Had she raised her voice? She didn't care. Her world was crumbling, just as surely as the bits of dry muffin in Tommy's hand.

"Let's take a breath and talk this through."

"Oh, you want to talk? Sure thing. We can talk. How about we talk about your tragic sense of timing?"

"Dana, please try to understand."

She lay her hands flat on the table, in an attempt to stay grounded. "We just got out of the doctor's office. She gave me a life-changing diagnosis. Five whole minutes later, you're calling it a day."

Tommy seemed to wither under her gaze, shrinking lower in his seat. Good. She hoped he'd grow so small he'd disappear completely.

Maybe he was acting on impulse, blindsided by what Doctor Batra had said. After all, this changed everything.

In truth, for one crazy moment in the doctor's office, Dana had seen this coming. She'd felt Tommy start to pull back the moment the doctor uttered the words she never thought she would hear.

Premature ovarian failure.

Three little words. Before today, she never would have even strung them together. Taken on their own, each word seemed innocent enough, but used in the same sentence, in the description that would forever define her, they were cataclysmic.

Tommy's retreat wouldn't have been obvious to anyone other than her. It was just a shift in the

2

atmosphere, a gradual movement. A sliver of rejection irritating her skin, even though she couldn't see the point of entry. His posture had angled ever so slightly away.

From her.

As if she was now a thing to be avoided.

She'd known in that moment but had hoped she was wrong. She'd definitely never expected him to act so quickly.

He was clearly trying to dodge a bullet.

No. She gripped the edge of the table. *You are no man's bullet. You are better than he is. This is Tommy's loss.*

"I'm sorry."

"Are you?"

They were quiet for another couple of minutes. She could tell he didn't know what to say. Hell, she barely knew what to feel. A year ago, she'd just been a woman suffering from missed periods, night sweats, and the odd hot flash. Strange for her age, but she'd attributed her symptoms to work stress. Tommy had been the one to urge her to call her doctor.

"Dana." Tommy reached for her hand. "You know me, probably better than I know myself. I can't lie to you and tell you this…*situation* isn't a deal breaker for me."

"This *situation* has a name. Say it with me. Premature ovarian failure."

His lips compressed.

"You can't say it, can you?"

"If I thought we had options, baby, I'd be all in, but you heard what Doctor Batra said. Only a small percentage of women like you can conceive."

Women like you.

Did this make her a different category of woman?

Tommy continued. "Even IVF is a crap shoot, and I just don't think I want to go down the road of adoption."

"What's wrong with adoption?"

"Nothing, but I want a child of my own."

"Any child we adopted *would* be our own."

Their friends Ginger and Maria had recently adopted a little boy, and if anyone dared to tell them they weren't "real mothers," or that Glen wasn't their "real son," they might very well get a fist in the face.

Only this wasn't about Ginger and Maria.

Dana understood Tommy was coming from a different place, she really did. He was desperate for a family. Having grown up an only child, he'd been honest from day one about wanting to raise a sizable horde. *I don't want our child to feel lonely like I did growing up. I want to have at least three kids. As a parent, I want to be totally outnumbered.*

His enthusiasm for family had been infectious. He'd always made Dana laugh when he talked about taking their gaggle of children on outings and trips.

She just had no idea he'd made a distinction between children.

In fairness, she'd never really considered adoption either. She'd just always assumed pregnancy would happen.

"I love you and I would like nothing more than

to spend the rest of my life with you, but we need to be honest here. I've always been clear about what I want from life."

"And it's not a *woman like me*."

"I want to do the right thing. I want to support you. Believe me, I do, but I don't think I have what it takes to go through this. All those things the doctor was talking about…I can't face it. I'm not strong enough, Dana. In some ways, I think you've always been the strong one."

He wasn't far off the mark. There had been times when she'd doubted Tommy's fortitude. Even at her grandmother's funeral, he'd been the one to fall apart. Dana had been the one to greet the mourners, the one who'd kept her head. And when she'd looked to him at the end of that exhausting day, hoping to cry on his shoulder for a while, he'd disappeared. She'd found him outside the funeral home, avoiding the situation with a couple of her idiot cousins.

She'd ignored that red flag, even though it had waved at her like the flagman at the stock car races.

Was she supposed to be the brave one now too? Was this what brave felt like? This sense of repugnant inevitability?

"I'm scared I'll have regrets. I'm scared I might resent you ten years down the road."

"You're just scared, period."

He turned his cheek as if he'd been slapped. When his pale skin reddened, she fancied she could see the imprint of her fingers. If she thought it would make her feel any better, she'd slap him silly.

"It's true," he admitted in a small voice. "I wish I

5

was a better man for you. I wish I could say this won't create a wedge between us, but I know it will."

For the first time in her life, Dana was unsure of what to do next. She'd always been the steady one, the one who had her life carved out. So far, she'd followed it to a tee.

She'd gone to college on a full scholarship, had done a Bachelor of Commerce, specializing in hospitality and tourism. She'd landed a plum job with the tourism board right out of college and had moved up the ranks.

It hadn't been easy either. As a Black woman, she'd had to contend with her share of good old boys, most of them very old and very white. However, she'd built a reputation on being a solid worker and she was now responsible for booking some of the biggest conventions to Las Vegas.

When she'd met Tommy Parker, falling in love with his deep voice and Jason Statham looks, she'd known they would build a life together.

Only they wouldn't now.

At college, Dana had had a friend named Melanie who wanted to be a novelist. Any time life threw Melanie a curveball, she merely threw her hands up and shouted, "Plot twist!"

That's all this was. A plot twist. It didn't mean Dana's story was over. She just had to write a new ending.

So she'd never conceive. It wasn't the end of the world. She could adopt one day. She didn't share Tommy's aversion to it.

Or maybe she wouldn't adopt at all. Lots of

people chose to remain childless. She had no doubt they were perfectly happy.

Only she would have preferred to make the choice for herself. Her choice had been taken from her and now Tommy wouldn't be there to help her adjust.

She was on her own. This was her new reality.

"I get being scared," she said, "but this isn't like you. The Tommy I fell in love with wouldn't end it like this. The Tommy I fell in love with would have shown some consideration. When did you stop being that man?"

He looked away. "Maybe this is who I've always been."

"Well, then shame on me." Rage kicked in. Sneaky and sour, it insinuated itself into her core, making her taste bile. "What if I'd gotten this diagnosis two years into our marriage? What would you have done then? Divorced me?"

When he didn't respond, she knew.

"You're a selfish pig."

"Dana, I'm just trying to be honest without wasting your time. Please don't hate me."

"Hate you? This isn't *about* you."

"Isn't it?"

"Not nearly as much as it is about me. Tell me something. At what point during the doctor's appointment did you start planning your escape?"

"That's not fair."

"Life's not fair, clearly. You didn't even have the decency to sleep on it. You've given me no time to process what's happening. You're just taking care of your own agenda. Here I am, in a goddamned cafeteria of all places, still reeling from the news, and you hit me with this now."

"I know you have the strength to get past this. It's one of the things I've always loved about you. Besides, it could be worse. You could be sick. You could be dying."

"I can't bear children, Tommy! What part of that don't you understand?"

He sat still. The harsh cafeteria lighting accentuated every hollow in his face, creating new ones as well. "I'm so sorry. I don't want to break your heart, baby."

"I am *not* your baby, and you don't get to comment on the state of my heart. My heart will be fine without you."

It had to be.

She held her breath, waiting for the first *chip chip chip* of the invisible chisel, the one that would cause her heart to shatter. But that wasn't what she felt. Instead, the beating organ inside her began to expand and harden, sitting like a weight in her chest. It was as if someone had just started pouring cement inside her chest cavity. Little by little, it took hold. It set like a newly-poured sidewalk in the sun. The heaviness pressed against her ribs, threatening to crack them.

Tommy couldn't break her heart with his flimsy apologies.

It was unbreakable.

He reached for her hand and fingered her engagement ring. Tears filled his eyes. His lip wobbled.

The asshole had the nerve to cry?

"I remember picking this ring out for you. It took me two hours. When you said yes, it was the happiest moment of my life."

Memories of his proposal flashed through her brain. Him, kneeling in the restaurant. All the other patrons clapping when she accepted him. The wonderfully snug bubble of warmth and security that surrounded her.

"I want you to know I love you. I always will."

"Just not unconditionally."

He hung his head.

She would not allow him to play the victim here. Dana wrestled her diamond engagement ring from her finger and set it on the table. The paler strip of brown skin underneath made her finger look so bare.

"You can keep the ring if you'd like."

"Take the damn ring. I don't need any mementos of this moment."

He slid the ring into his pocket. "Will you forgive me?"

"Are you for real?"

It was official. She would not pine over this man. She'd dodged the bullet instead.

Tommy stood.

"Oh, no, you don't." Dana stood and pushed away from the table. "You do *not* get to walk out before I do, do you hear me?"

Channeling her musical idol, the great Ms. Diana Ross, Dana sashayed toward the cafeteria exit.

Don't look back.

Her eyes stinging, she hurried down the hospital hallway and found the nearest stairway. Trying the door, she found it open. Escaping into the stairwell, she sat on one of the cold, concrete steps.

Women like you.

Dana waited for the tremors and the tears. They were coming. She knew it. Head in hands, she braced herself.

Only the tears didn't come.

They would, of course. Eventually.

When they did, the deluge might very well sweep her away.

But not today. She wouldn't allow it.

"Breathe." She rested her palms on her knees. "I'm not dying. This is not the end."

It was just *an* end.

***

This was a night for forgetting.

With that thought alone in mind, Dana opened the door to Joe's Tiki Bar. She didn't choose the spot because it was her favorite Vegas hangout. She chose it because it looked like it hadn't been anyone's favorite Vegas hangout in about thirty years.

All five people inside turned to look at her, but she didn't let that stop her. Forgetting was best done in a dark, dingy place that wouldn't attract scores of tourists like the sleek, popular bars down the Strip.

Ignoring the glowering wooden gods on all the posts and the cheeky hula girls smiling down from every piece of crap artwork, she chose a seat at the far end of the bar. It was darker in that corner because one of the overhead lights had burned out.

It didn't matter anyway. Darkness suited her mood right now.

One man haunted her end of the bar, but he seemed more focused on his drink than on her, so she positioned herself two chairs down from where he sat.

Although he was hunched over his drink, he appeared tall and had long limbs. She knew he had muscles because the fabric of his clothes strained a bit over his biceps and thighs. As she adjusted herself on her seat, she took a discreet look, but not because she was interested in his muscles.

Her brain craved a distraction.

He was white and had tawny hair, almost blond. He was handsome, at least from what she could tell of his profile under the muted lights. Although she hadn't seen him head on, no man with that kind of defined jawline could be homely. He wore jeans and a t-shirt, but there was something regal about his appearance. Then again, maybe it was because he looked so distant and removed. If she hadn't known he was sitting on a kitschy bar stool made out of fake bamboo, she would have thought he was a lonely king, perched high on his throne in his mountain kingdom, forgotten by his subjects.

Girl, you need a drink. Yesterday.

The bartender approached. "Hey, pretty lady. What can I get you?"

"Just a glass of white wine, please."

As the bartender walked away to pour her drink, the blond man next to her spoke. "I wouldn't, if I were you."

At first, Dana wasn't sure he'd spoken to her

because he continued to stare into his glass. "I'm sorry. Did you say something?"

"I said, I wouldn't order the white wine here if I were you. They don't exactly serve vintages." He turned on his creaky stool and faced her.

Heat swarmed Dana's cheeks. He *was* handsome.

Frat boy handsome.

Disney prince handsome.

No. He wasn't clean cut enough for either of those. There was something rugged in the cut of his chin, a hint of danger in his cat eyes.

Disney princes would cower in front of this man.

She cleared her throat. "Are you a wine expert?"

"Not officially, but because of my work, I've picked up a few things."

"What do you do for a living?"

"A bit of this. A bit of that."

"That doesn't sound mysterious at all."

"I'm not trying to be mysterious. I just don't want to think about work right now."

"I understand." The bartender returned and set down a glass. She paid him right away. There was no sense in starting a tab. She could only tolerate one drink anyway. "And luckily, I'm not concerned about the vintage tonight."

"Don't say I didn't warn you."

As blondie appraised her, she took her first sip. It tasted like piss, or so she assumed. Frowning, she set her glass down. "I think that might be the worst wine I've ever tasted." Despite the unpleasant aftertaste, Dana sipped some more. "Yup. It's official. They should put that on the label as a warning."

"Now you know." He spun around and wrapped his hand around his glass.

"Okay, Mr. Sommelier. What are you drinking?"

"Just a Coke. It's kind of hard to screw it up."

"I'll make note of that for next time."

"You do that."

They both stared at the mirrored bar for a couple of minutes, lost in their separate worlds and woes. Eventually, his eyes met hers in the mirror, one lost soul seeking communion with another. A glimmer of interest made his light eyes shine, but it was quickly doused when he blinked.

Feeling alone, she decided to make conversation. "I'm Dana, by the way." She held out her hand.

He shook her hand. "Alex."

"It's nice to meet you, Alex."

"The pleasure's all mine."

When he let go of her hand, his fingers slid against her palm in the faintest of caresses. His touch was light and oddly familiar. She'd been in situations where strange men had held her hand a little too long during introductions and it always made her feel awkward. Not this time. Alex's touch was gentle and respectful, despite feeling somehow intimate.

He ran his hand through his hair and looked up at her from under his lashes.

Something about those eyes seemed familiar. "Have we met before? I feel like I should know you from somewhere."

"I don't think so. I never forget a face, and I definitely would have remembered yours."

Hmm. If he didn't look so lonely, she would have sworn that was a pickup line.

She searched her brain, trying to place his face. He wasn't one of her clients. "You sure do look familiar."

"I guess I just have one of those faces."

And what a face it was. If a marketing executive put his cheekbones alone on the front of a men's magazine, they'd sell millions.

He drank some of his Coke and then picked up a swizzle stick. The green plastic stick was in the shape of a curvaceous hula lady. Alex shook his head and sighed. He stuck the swizzle stick in his glass, swirled it around and let it go, making the hula lady dance.

"So. What brings you here tonight? I know it's not the wine."

The slight compression of his lips was meant to pass for a smile. "I'm celebrating, actually."

"Really? No offense, but this doesn't look like much of a party."

"I guess it's more of a private affair. I just moved to Vegas."

"Congratulations on the move. What brought you to Sin City?"

"Business. It's also a chance to start a new life."

"I see." Dana dared to take another sip. The wine wasn't as offensive this time around. "You didn't like the old life?"

"All in all, I can't complain, but I made mistakes. Handled some things badly."

"Don't feel too guilty. We've all been there."

"Have you?"

"Oh, yeah. Don't be fooled by the image of perfection you see here, drinking alone in a cheesy tiki bar."

"You're not drinking alone anymore."

"I guess not."

"Tell me something, Dana. Do you have any regrets in life?"

"That's a loaded question."

"It's that kind of night, I guess."

"It's safe to say I have some regrets."

"Big ones?"

"Sure. We can't let them shape us, though."

"Wise words. You're a smart woman."

"I don't know about that." She tossed her head. "What about you? I'm guessing you have some regrets."

"Like I said, you're a smart woman."

His reply made it clear he wasn't willing to do a deep dive into his motivations with a stranger. She couldn't blame him. She wasn't looking to make friends tonight either.

What am I looking for? She wasn't sure, but she was starting to wonder if it might be wrapped in a tall, tawny package.

Other than losing herself in a glass of wine, she hadn't really planned ahead. Mostly, she just wanted to forget.

"So," he said. "What brings you to Joe's Tiki Bar?"

"I guess you could say I'm starting a new life too."

Alex slid off his bar stool and moved over to the one next to her. His new proximity made her inhale in anticipation. "How so?"

"Do you want the true story? It's very sad."

"I can take it."

"I was dumped by my fiancé just a few hours ago."

He had been about to take another sip of his drink but put the glass down. "I'm sorry. Here I am, moaning about my situation, and you've had a truly shitty day."

"It's okay, but thanks."

"Wait. Please tell me you didn't come to Vegas to get married and he bailed."

"No, we both live here. Now that you mention it, I suppose I should be grateful he didn't ditch me at the altar. Knowing what I know now, that could have been a distinct possibility."

"That sucks."

"Yeah. You're the first one to hear the news."

"Don't you have anyone you can talk to?"

"Oh, I have family and friends. I'm just not ready to let them know. My parents are all over this wedding and they think Tommy is the Second Coming. My sister lives out of town and she's going through a divorce right now. I don't want to upset her. Besides, she and I have a prickly relationship. We're very different. And anyway, sometimes it's just easier talking to a stranger." She raised her wine glass.

"I get it." He clinked his glass against hers and they drank.

Once again, their gazes met, this time over the tops of their glasses. Alex's eyes narrowed in appreciation.

Nah. The cheap wine must be affecting her vision.

"Your ex-fiancé, his name is Tommy?"

"Yes."

"Tommy is a fool."

"Aren't you sweet? I might need to call you the next time I need a pep talk."

"You can call me any time you like."

"Well, well. Sweet and agreeable."

"Not at all. I just have excellent taste."

She smiled. "Right. The wine. I should have guessed."

"I wasn't talking about the wine." When her face heated up with what must have been the mother of all blushes, he took pity on her and averted his gaze. "Do you mind me asking why he ended it?"

Momentarily distracted by the gorgeous man one bar stool over, she'd almost forgotten she'd started her day in Dr. Batra's office. Once again, the doctor's words came back to haunt her.

I would advise you to seek counseling right away. Most women in your position experience a period of grief. I can refer you to a therapist.

"Actually, I don't want to talk about it."

"Fair enough. How about I just buy you another drink?"

"I'm good. Three sips of this stuff is enough, thanks. I have a lot to think about and I need to keep a clear head."

Alex stirred his Coke again, seemingly fascinated by the whorls made by the stir stick. Dana watched the movements of his wrist until her eyes began to glaze over. Neither of them said anything for a few minutes, but that was fine. Something about his presence soothed her. She wasn't sure whether it was because a gorgeous man of mystery was taking an interest in her or because they both had shit on their minds. Either way, her burden seemed lessened.

Unable to finish her wine, she pushed the glass away. The evening opened up before her like a chasm. She didn't want to go home, where everything would remind her of Tommy and the dreams they used to share. She didn't want to call her sister, Anise, either. Besides she'd be seeing Anise soon enough.

Once her divorce was finalized, Anise had announced her intention to come to Vegas with some friends to see Dana. She wanted to commemorate her newfound freedom. When she had first mentioned the idea of a week-long divorce party in Las Vegas, Dana had almost spit up her lunch. However, as an account manager for the Las Vegas Convention and Visitor Association, she knew people visited the Strip for all sorts of reasons. If one could hold a stag party here, why not a divorce party? In fact, divorce parties were big business. Just last week, the papers had been buzzing with the exploits of a certain soap opera actress as she hit the town to celebrate the destruction of her marriage.

Dana had just never expected her big sister to buy into the hype. Personally, she thought it was tacky.

However, if that was what Anise wanted, Dana would give it to her. It was the least she could do.

The sisters might not always see eye to eye, but Dana's heart went out to Anise and her ex-husband.

Thanks to her connections in the tourism world, Dana had been able to arrange a week-long extravaganza at Vice, the best hotel on the Strip. Anise was so excited to stay in the famous casino hotel.

How was she supposed to host a divorce party now? She was meant to be the ringleader, showing off the best of Vegas to Anise and her friends, Bea and Jessica.

Instead, all she wanted was to crawl into a hole.

Or maybe stay right here, quietly drinking next to Alex.

"So," he said, "would you like me to badmouth Tommy some more?"

"You could."

"Because I can invent all sorts of interesting crap to say about him and I know some colorful words."

She laughed. "I bet you do."

"I even know a few curse words in other languages if we want to give our badmouthing an international flair."

"It's tempting. Or maybe we could talk about why you look so sad."

"I'm not sad. Like I said, I just have one of those faces."

"Right, and my ex is a wonderful man who loves me more than anything."

"So now you want to give *me* a pep talk?"

"Would it help?"

"Nah. Pep talks are overrated. In my experience, they help the people giving them much more than the people receiving them."

"You're probably right. I'm not in the mood for friendly encouragement either."

"Oh, yeah? What are you in the mood for?"

"Is it too much to ask that Tommy gets sucked into a black hole?"

Alex sat up. "Say the word. I'll make it happen."

"Ah. So you're friends with the guy who runs the black hole?"

"Maybe I *am* the guy who runs the black hole."

"As much as I appreciate your offer, on second thought, I guess I don't really want him destroyed. You know, completely. That seems harsh."

"What do you want?"

"I have no idea." She lowered her head as sadness overwhelmed her again.

Alex touched her chin. Once again, she didn't shrink from the stranger's touch.

It was all she could do not to lean into it.

He looked her deep in the eye. "I think you know exactly what you want."

Under his intense scrutiny, Dana giggled out of nerves. She cast a glance over his appealing form, and didn't worry about being discreet this time. "If only you knew."

He cocked an eyebrow. "I would love to know."

Do it. Just do it. "I want…to forget about things for a while. With someone."

"Is that so?" Alex stood before her, his voice a deep rumble. "What if I told you I want the same thing?"

She ran a finger over the taut bulge of his arm. "If that was the case, then I'd ask you to follow me

20

into the ladies' room."

"I can get us nicer accommodations."

"Believe me, right now I couldn't care less about satin sheets." This was all about the moment, and the moment was telling her to seize him and do very dirty things with him.

"Are you sure?"

Made courageous by the cheap wine, Dana stood and whispered in Alex's ear. "Do you have a condom?"

"Yes."

"Then I'm sure. I'm going to head into the ladies' room and I'd like you to follow me. Don't leave me hanging."

"I wouldn't dream of it."

Her heart rattled in her chest. Amazed at her own bravado, she grabbed her handbag off the bar and walked toward the washrooms in back. Keeping her head high, she entered the ladies' room, grateful there were no other women in the bar.

What are you doing? This isn't you, her inner voice railed.

Exactly, she countered. *This isn't me*.

When Alex followed her into the washroom two minutes later, Dana didn't stop to question her actions any longer. He reached her in two strides, took her mouth in a savage kiss, and backed her up toward the sink.

He adjusted his clothes, removing key pieces. As he rolled on the condom, his gaze flicked toward her. "I understand if you want to say no. I don't want you to have any regrets because of some cheap wine."

His hand was shaking.

So were hers.

"I didn't even finish my wine. I'm completely sober and I want this." She pulled up her skirt. "Am I being clear enough for you?"

"Fuck, yeah."

He drew close and his clean scent swarmed her. His touch was so warm on her thigh. Already lost to sensation, she gasped. When his fingers slid between her legs, pushing aside her panties, she was wet and ready for him.

They fumbled, knocking noses as they kissed, but when he hoisted her legs up around his waist, his movements were strong and sure.

She was sure, if only about this one thing.

Alex entered her with a deep thrust and rocked against her.

Such sweet, aching fullness. *Yes, fill me*.

Dana closed her eyes. And forgot everything.

***

As Alex Markov disposed of the condom, wrapping it in a paper towel, his heart was still racing.

What have you done?

If Dana recognized him and went to the papers, it would only add to the speculation that had been hounding him for over a year.

The thought made him break out in a cold sweat.

He waited for the lights to go on, for that glimmer of recognition that would make her shout. *Oh, my God. You're Alex Markov!*

But it didn't.

She was too busy adjusting her clothes and wasn't even making eye contact.

It was a probably a good thing. He was tired of seeing his humiliation reflected in other people's eyes.

He'd just broken one of his own commandments. *Don't get involved.*

One could argue he was hardly involved with Dana…what was her last name, anyway? Even still, their conversation, short as it had been, was probably the deepest one he'd had in ages.

Alex didn't do deep, not anymore, and yet something about Dana had coerced him out of his shell.

It had been over a year since he'd had sex, unless he counted all those nights of lonely masturbation when he'd needed to alleviate his sorrow.

To think it had happened in a dirty bar bathroom with a perfect stranger.

He washed his hands, wishing he was alone so he could splash some on his face. He looked over his shoulder at Dana as he reached for another paper towel.

The cheap paper was scratchy, so unlike her skin.

Would it be weird to ask her out after what they'd done? Probably.

Besides, he didn't date.

At the same time, for the first time in ages, he was tempted to try. Tempted to break more of his rules, tempted to prolong this…whatever this was.

Dana wouldn't thank him for it, not in the end.

All sorts of questions raced through his head, making him wonder if he'd been wrong to hole himself up. Uncertainty and shame had been Alex's reality for so long. He second guessed himself a lot, even if he never showed it.

For a few, sweet seconds, balls deep inside Dana's sweet body, he'd never been as sure of anything. As soon as he withdrew, he was filled with doubt again.

Better to end this. He would only hurt her in the end.

It's what he did.

She fixed her outfit, taking care to smooth down her skirt, avoiding his gaze the whole time.

"Are you okay?"

Her head bobbed in a tight nod. "It might be hard to believe, but I've never done that before. You know, in a bar with a stranger, up against the bathroom wall."

"I hope I haven't added to your regrets."

Her silence told him she hadn't decided one way or the other yet.

"If it makes you feel any better," said Alex, approaching slowly and reaching for her hand, "I haven't done that before either."

She gave him the side eye.

"I've done many things, but not that. I don't know what it is about you, Dana. I think I could forget myself around you."

"Maybe forgetting's overrated."

"Look, do you want to go grab a coffee somewhere and talk?"

She removed her hand from his. "Um, do you

think you could give me a few minutes?" She nodded toward the cubicles. "To freshen up."

"Yeah. I'll just be in the men's." He headed to the door, but when he turned around, all he saw were downcast eyes. "I'll wait for you in the hallway."

She disappeared into a cubicle, so he left. Shaking his head, Alex walked into the men's room. Thankfully, it was empty as well. At the sink, he turned on the taps and ran the water on the coldest setting. Once it was nice and frigid, he splashed some on this face and toweled off.

Bracing his hands on the basin, he stared into the mirror.

A tired man stared back.

However, there was a new light in that man's eyes, one Alex hadn't seen in himself in a while.

It was all because of Dana, the beautiful woman who'd asked him to screw her in a tiki bar bathroom.

Shit.

She could barely look at him now. She regretted the moment, anyone with eyes could see it, and he couldn't blame her. When she'd made her move, after confessing how her ex had broken her heart, Alex should have been the one to step back and keep a cool head. He should have known better, should have realized their quick fumble might have added to her pain.

Unfortunately, when she'd whispered in his ear, he'd lost all sense.

He just wanted to forget his own pain.

Now Dana would think he'd used her for some

cheap bathroom sex. In a way, maybe he had been using her. He'd done it because, even in their short time together, Dana helped him feel something other than the numbness he'd carried for so long.

He needed to prove to her that he thought she was worth more than bathroom sex. If he didn't make that clear, it would bother him.

He liked their banter and the intelligence shining in her eyes. She intrigued him.

To say nothing of the fact she was so fucking beautiful. Her cocoa skin was smooth and warm. Her light perfume made him want to breathe deeply. He wanted to bury his fingers in her curls and stare into her midnight eyes all night long.

He was getting ahead of himself. *That's what happens when you remove yourself from the world. You get carried away.*

Maybe it was time to join the world again.

He'd known it was time when he'd bought Vice from Liam Doyle. The casino hotel would be his lifeline. It would force him into the land of the living.

Was he ready? Probably not.

He'd felt ready when he was holding Dana in his arms. A man could get used to holding a woman like that. Although it had lasted mere minutes, he'd tasted her fire. She'd clutched at him, her fingernails scratching the skin under his shirt. When she came, she made the sexiest little noise he'd ever heard. It was something between a sigh and moan, and he became hard just thinking about it.

Tommy really was an idiot.

Checking himself in the mirror once more, Alex

left the men's room and waited for Dana in the bathroom hallway, just outside the ladies' room.

After a couple of minutes of waiting, he poked his head back into the bar area. Perhaps she'd gone back to their seats.

There was no sign of her in the bar.

Maybe she was still freshening up.

He returned to the hallway and paused for another few moments. When his gut twitched, he knocked on the ladies' room door and cracked it. "Dana? I'm just in the hallway."

There was no response.

He entered. "Dana?"

The cubicle doors hung open. Her handbag was gone.

She had left.

As a sick sense of desperation assaulted him, Alex ran out of the washroom and out of the bar. He looked up and down the street but couldn't see her.

She must have ditched him, thinking he was about to ditch her.

After everything she'd been through today, it was the last thing he wanted her to think.

When it became clear she wasn't coming back, Alex grabbed his car keys and headed to the lot. Maybe he could find her and make it up to her.

Only then did it hit him.

He didn't even know her last name and she didn't know his.

He'd been trying to protect his heart in remaining anonymous and he'd only succeeded in making things worse.

Idiot.

It seemed he had more in common with Tommy than he thought.

Better this way.

Dana would want a long-term relationship with a stable man, someone with a good heart.

Alex was in no position to offer her any of those things.

Chapter Two

Two months later

It had been over a year since Shannon's death, but the newspapers wouldn't let him forget.

Hot shot developer seeks to escape his sordid past in Sin City.

Sordid.

No matter how many times Alex read the description, he still tasted sulphur.

Maybe this was a mistake.

Unfortunately, there was no going back now. As the Escalade approached Vice, Alex folded up the newspaper. A small cluster of reporters huddled at the door of the casino hotel, like a murder of crows waiting on a platter of carrion.

Waiting for him.

A trickle of perspiration materialized at the back of his neck. As the lone bead dripped into his shirt collar, he swatted at it, but another followed it.

Photos flashed outside the car, causing bubbles of light to appear before his eyes for a moment. As he had been so accustomed to doing over the past year, he put his hand up, shielding his face.

Stop it. You have no reason to hide. You've done nothing wrong.

Right. The devil on his shoulder laughed. *Tell that to them.*

This was supposed to be his new beginning.

His driver Pierre glanced at him in the rear-view mirror. "Are you okay, Alex? You look like you need a stiff drink."

Ha. That was almost funny. No more stiff drinks for him.

And no more hiding.

Gritting his teeth, he dropped his hand and sat up straight. "I'm okay."

Hotel security guards corralled the paparazzi. Front and center was a wall of a man. If one didn't know Wade Kennedy was head of security, one would guess it from his sheer bulk. His mere presence caused a couple of the less intrepid reporters to pale. Those who were daring enough to push forward immediately took a few steps back when he stared them down.

Alex reminded himself to increase Wade's salary.

He should have guessed he'd arrive to this scene, should have known some would continue to doubt his motives. When the opportunity to acquire his new hotels had arisen, first and foremost, he'd seen it as a solid business decision.

He'd also seen it as a sort of relocation therapy. Moving from New York to Vegas felt right.

It wasn't that he was trying to escape his past.

He just couldn't handle the constant reminders of Shannon anymore.

Unfortunately, because Shannon's family had tried to assassinate his character, a door had been opened. The Dean family had been vocal in their criticisms and speculations from the start, trying to lay blame at Alex's doorstep. Their angry grief had allowed trashy reporters to pounce. If there was anything the paparazzi appreciated, it was the chance to obliterate a man's reputation.

God only knew the New York crew had already tried. Alex wouldn't let the Las Vegas vultures finish him off.

However, once again, he was confronted with the stark reality. There were people in this world who thought he was a cold-blooded killer, one who'd gotten away with his crimes.

During his darkest moments, he wondered if they were right.

Pierre slowed down. "Alex, I could pull into the underground garage instead."

"No. This is my hotel. I'm not skulking from anyone."

Pierre drove the Escalade up to the entrance. The reporters once again clamored, but Wade puffed out his chest and they backed down.

Alex took a deep breath. His dad used to say, "When you're nervous about walking into a room, pretend you own the building." The philosophy had served Alex well.

And, in this case, he did own the building.

Pierre got out and opened the door.

"Alex! Alex!" The reporters chanted his name,

each one hoping to get his attention. "Over here, Alex."

Another trickle of sweat dripped down his back. His heartbeat sounded in his head.

Wade stepped forward and held out his hand. "Mr. Markov. Welcome to Vice."

Alex grabbed Wade's hand as if it was a lifeboat and he was about to go down in freezing waters. Somehow, he managed to return his firm shake. "Wade. Good to see you again."

More flashes. It was amazing Alex hadn't gone blind yet. He blinked several times and angled his face from them.

"I apologize about the welcoming committee. They just arrived."

One of the reporters threw up his hand. "Mr. Markov! Shannon Dean's father says you're trying to run from justice by moving to Las Vegas. Any comments?"

"Jesus Christ." Wade glowered at the man. "Show some respect, you pack of hyenas."

Sticking close to Alex, Wade escorted him into the hotel lobby. A couple of guards from Wade's team hovered at the door to keep the press out.

Once they got inside, Wade apologized again.

"It's not your fault, Wade. The headline just broke. I figured it might bring the termites out of the woodwork. I'm used to it." Only he wasn't. Not at all.

"Still, it's your first official day here and you shouldn't have to deal with that crap." The security expert peered at him. "Are you…okay?"

"Yeah."

"You're really pale." He handed him a plastic bottle of water from a nearby counter. "Here. Take mine. I haven't cracked it open yet."

Alex nodded in thanks, opened it and drank half the bottle. His heartbeat steadied with each gulp. The coolness of the water calmed him.

"Gotta love the press," said Wade. "They're bastards, aren't they?"

Alex managed a chuckle. "Not all of them. Just the ones who follow me around. Legitimate reporters don't seem to be interested in my story anymore, just those pricks."

"What the Dean family has been saying about you...it's awful."

"They've been saying the same things for a year now."

"You should sue for libel."

"I can't do that, Wade. They're grieving. I just wish they could move on. Thanks for the concern, though. And the water."

"Sure. No problem."

Alex blinked away the last of the light bubbles. "I appreciate you giving me the grand tour today. Do you mind if we start in my office? I could use a minute to stop sweating before I meet the staff."

"You bet."

Sweat or no sweat, they still had to walk through the massive Vice reception area to get to his office. Faced with the prospect of being on display, he tensed. However, the tone of the greetings changed once they were inside the casino hotel. In fact, Alex was met with numerous warm smiles and handshakes from staff members as they welcomed him aboard. In his first few minutes, he pressed the flesh of several front desk staff and their managers. He imagined he'd be shaking hands on an almost constant basis for a while. Even the wait staff at the bar across the lobby stopped in their tracks, colorful drinks poised on their trays, so they could bob their heads.

It was nice. After the onslaught at the door, he felt a little more at home.

Home.

Could he really make a new home here? He certainly couldn't go back.

Several tourists pointed him out, unabashed. A few snapped photos.

"That's the guy," one of them said out loud. "The one who bought this place from Liam Doyle. They say he offed his girlfriend."

Hearing the comment, Wade put himself between Alex and the tourist.

For crying out loud. Every time he thought he'd left the insanity behind, the Deans thrust it back into his face. He'd been trying to take the high road for some time, but it was getting harder to keep his feet from falling into the ditches.

Just don't dignify the rumors. Once again, Alex's father's calm voice guided him.

As he and Wade passed a couple of female tourists, the women checked him out.

"Hmm," one woman said, her gaze trained on his body. "Hey there. You're even prettier in person, Killer."

Killer. Nice. He hadn't heard that one in a while.

Put it out of your head.

He didn't have time to wallow in the unfounded opinions of strangers.

He was here to start over and he wouldn't let anyone stop him.

As far as Alex was concerned, his sole reason for living right now was his hotels. It was time to start making some improvements around Vice and he couldn't wait to get started.

Of course, one could argue Vice, the newest and grandest of his three Las Vegas casinos, needed no improvement. Neither did its sister properties, Sin and Luxe. In many ways, the former owner's tastes matched Alex's. His friend Liam Doyle had done a fantastic job, but that didn't mean Alex didn't want to put his stamp on the three hotels. After all, it reinforced the sense of ownership. Every new homeowner gave his house a fresh lick of paint.

Alex had a few licks of his own in mind, which was why some rebranding was in order. Nothing drastic, but a clear shift in a new direction.

His.

As proprietor and operator of Vice, Sin, and Luxe, he was now in charge of the Strip's busiest casino hotels. There were moments when he still didn't believe it. The deal with Liam had been so quick and easy. Granted, he'd never known such a motivated seller as Liam.

He hoped his old friend would be happy with his girlfriend, Kate. Alex didn't know exactly what went on between the two, but it had been important enough that Liam had changed his entire life around.

Being a good businessman, Alex had come in

with a reasonable offer for the casinos, knowing there were other offers on the table. Friendship or no friendship, he'd expected a shrewd man like Liam to force him to up the stakes.

But he hadn't. He'd taken Alex's first offer.

Even as their lawyers completed the paperwork, Alex had called Liam on it. "You know you could make more money on these properties. Why didn't you counter my offer?"

"Because it was fair and because I trust you," Liam had said. "I know you'll take care of them. Besides, I just want it done. The casinos are my past."

"And Kate is your future?"

"If she'll have me."

Amazing. Liam had completely transformed his life and business, all for the love of a woman.

Alex had been seeking his own sort of transformation when he'd taken Shannon on that trip to Bermuda a year and a half ago. Unfortunately, life had other plans for them.

His transformation would begin today instead.

Liam's change of heart had worked to Alex's advantage. The casinos would provide financial security. Liam had been clear about that. Alex would have to fuck up in a major way to end up in the red. However, bad things happened all the time. Businesses closed every day, even Las Vegas businesses, and he'd be a fool to think himself immune.

Still, as Liam had made clear, the house always won. Alex wasn't used to that concept. A nightclub owner and developer, he'd always lived with the

36

reality of financial instability. There was always a new club springing up, new competition. His customers, as a species, grew bored easily. They were always in search of the newest, brightest diversion. Like kittens with ribbons, they could be led astray.

Casino customers were a different breed. In this business, there was a sort of brand loyalty, even if much of it stemmed from the fact gamblers liked to sit at the same slot machine every time they played. All he really needed to do was keep the gamblers happy and provide entertainment for the non-gamblers.

As it happened, Alex knew all about providing entertainment.

Wade led him down the administrative hallway toward the executive elevator. "So this place has been buzzing with the news of your arrival."

"Oh, yeah? I hope the buzz hasn't all been bad."

"You know how it goes. New boss and all. I think some staff members have been nervous."

"I'm glad the change in ownership hasn't scared you away."

"Who, me?" Wade scoffed. "I'm not scared of anything."

"Really?" Alex teased. "Liam told me you were afraid to kick Kate off the property."

Wade rolled his eyes. "Mr. Markov, if I had kicked Kate off the property, Liam would never have lived happily ever after. Besides," he said, grinning, "she's his problem now."

"That she is. Oh, and didn't I tell you to call me Alex last time we met?"

"Yeah, you did." Wade blushed. "Liam always insisted on first names too, just not in front of the guests. I'm glad you're sticking with it. That was one of the things we all liked about him."

Going into this sale, Alex knew he would have to deal with the cult of Liam Doyle. His friend had been the toast of Vegas for several years. In addition, he was adored by his employees, even though he had run a tight ship. A sense of nostalgia over Liam still pervaded the place. Alex respected that but he would have to make it clear he was not Liam Doyle. "Liam speaks highly of you too, Wade."

"Thanks. He was a good guy. *Is* a good guy. I gotta stop talking about him like he's dead." Wade hit the elevator button. "Can I ask you something?"

"Sure."

"A lot of folks around here are worried about layoffs. Should they be?"

The elevator arrived on the fourth floor with barely a whisper, opening directly into his new office space.

"I like you, Wade. You speak plainly," Alex said as they got out. "Look, I'm not planning any massive reorganisations. I know how Liam operated. We learned the business from the same people. If anything, I want to make a few improvements."

"That's good to hear."

"The casino business might be a whole new adventure for me, but in running my nightclubs, I've learned a thing or two. It's time to tweak a few things around here." He turned and opened his arms toward the fourth-floor office. "Starting with this."

Liam's former office space was also his home away from home. A workaholic, Liam had designed his office to incorporate a luxurious living space as well. Alex knew his friend had spent many a night in his casino sanctum, rather than going home to his own condo. It had led to burnout.

Alex preferred to live offsite and had been renting a luxury property in the nearby community of Summerlin. However, now that work was to begin in earnest, he figured it was best to live onsite. The workload was bound to be intense for some time, and it would be helpful to be in the thick of things. Still, Liam's vision for the flat was nothing like his own.

"I respect Liam," he said, gesturing to the sumptuous office before him, "but this isn't me."

Wade laughed. "I always thought it was a bit much myself."

"If I'm going to be living here, I need something more zen-like."

"Zen, huh? That doesn't sound like Vegas at all."

"Maybe not, but simplifying my life has helped me get through the past year."

Wade caressed the overstuffed Italian leather couch. "So all of this is going to go?"

"All of it."

"You're different."

"Change is good, Wade. Embrace it."

Alex walked over to the enormous window at one side of the office, the one with the view of the Strip. In the daytime, it reminded him of an amusement park. The other casinos resembled hulking carnival rides. It came alive at night, the entire area pulsing with activity and desire for sensation.

Everyone in this city wanted something, someone. In most cases, they found it. Sometimes it was as easy as calling a number on a card. He had no doubt, however, that other visitors to Vegas sought something they couldn't identify. A magic moment that would either change their lives or help them escape the life they knew.

Either way, they all sought pleasure in one form or another.

Alex would provide that pleasure. He would create the perfect escape, a refuge so addictive they would have no choice but to return again and again.

All he ever wanted was to be a success, to make his parents proud. Maksim and Natasha Markov had given him everything. Unconditional love, a first-class education, and space to make lots of mistakes.

He'd certainly made mistakes with Shannon and the whole world knew it, even if they didn't know the extent of it.

Guilt gnawed at Alex's insides as his former girlfriend's voice spoke to him from the grave.

You did this to me, Alex. It's all your fault.

He clutched the windowsill, closed his eyes, and forced calm into his being.

Wade approached Alex from the side. "You okay?"

"Yeah. Just thinking."

Regrets wouldn't serve him well now. The best thing he could do was keep busy. Being industrious had carried him through the trials of the past year and his ability to focus would help him become more successful than ever before.

When he'd opened Champagne and Liberty, his New York clubs, he'd tasted a dollop of true success. With Vice and his two other casino hotels, that success would be cemented.

Right now, this was Alex's time, and he would make a difference.

But he would do it his way. Not Liam's, not anyone else's. By the time he was done with Vice, it would be the most popular casino hotel in the world.

Alex clapped Wade on the shoulder and led back him to the elevators. "I have great plans for this place, Wade. Wait and see."

"Sounds awesome."

"First things first. I want to meet as many staff members as possible. You know this place better than anyone." He summoned the elevator and they got in. "Lead the way."

As they descended, another woman's face flashed in front of his eyes and Alex indulged in a quick daydream.

Dana.

He'd barely spent an hour in the woman's company two months ago and he still couldn't get her out of his head.

Dana, the one who'd made him forget himself.

He just wasn't sure he deserved to forget.

He'd flirted with the idea of searching for Dana, but with nothing more than a face and a first name to go by, he hadn't bothered. What good would it do, anyway? They may have shared a raw sexual encounter in a tacky bathroom, but she'd left him high and dry.

Clearly, she hadn't wanted a second round. It seemed stupid to waste time thinking of her now. Even if he did happen to run into her, what would happen? She'd probably take one look and run.

There was nothing quite like getting rejected by the same woman a second time. He wasn't sure he had the stomach for that kind of embarrassment. There was no way he could tolerate a put down from Dana, the stranger whose fragrant skin and quiet moans had soothed his soul for an evening.

She might be his favorite daydream, and a memory that caused his mouth to run dry, but that was all she would ever be.

Besides, he had work to do now.

His Dana fantasies would have to come to an end.

It was time to create some new fantasies.

***

Shortly after arriving at Vice, Alex realized he was being stalked.

Badly.

The paparazzo wasn't even trying to hide the fact he was trailing Alex. If Alex had business at reception, the man would stop at one of the lobby bars and strike up a conversation with the bartender on duty. If Alex walked through the casino, the man followed, always at a distance.

It was starting to get on his nerves.

With the walls of Vice surrounding him, Alex

felt more at ease. This guy had dared to set foot inside his safe place. Alex didn't want to have to keep looking over his shoulder.

Now, as he walked to the site of Vice's former piano bar, invisible fingers teased the back of his neck. A backward glance confirmed the paparazzo once again followed him.

"For fuck's sake." As much as it made him feel sick, it was time for a confrontation. When he reached a quiet hallway, he turned around. "What do you want?"

The man aimed his camera, took a picture and shrugged. "You're an interesting guy. I'm just waiting for you to do something…interesting." He took another photo.

"You're going to be waiting a long time. Now get that camera out of my face."

"Got something to hide, Killer?"

"Killer, huh? That's inventive. I've *never* heard that one before."

"You know what they say about the shoe fitting." *Flash, flash.*

"Look, I'm pretty sure your readers, although I use the term loosely, aren't going to want to shell out their hard-earned cash for pictures of me standing in a hallway."

"We'll see, Alex. We'll see."

"It's Mr. Markov to you."

"Ooh, formal. A stickler for etiquette, are you? Is that why you killed your girlfriend? Because she dared to use your first name?"

"Get the fuck off my property."

"I'm not bothering any customers. How do you

know I'm not just a tourist who lost his way in the hotel?"

Once his blood pressure started to race, Alex figured it was better to call in the experts. He dialed Wade on his cellphone. "Wade, he's back."

"Where are you?"

"Near the entrance to Decadence. I'm meeting Marissa in a few minutes and I'd rather not expose her to this filth."

"I'm on my way."

Knowing Wade, he'd be moving at a good clip. He'd been on the lookout for the man ever since Alex first noticed him and his hands must be itching with the need to escort him to the door.

"Ah, come on," said the paparazzo. "Be a good sport. The world wants your story. I'm giving you a chance to share it."

"There's no story."

"That's not what the parents of Shannon Dean keep saying. They have some definite ideas about you, mister. Did you hear the latest? They're saying that even if you didn't kill Shannon, you drove her to suicide."

Even though every muscle in Alex's body was screaming at him to use them against the man, he stood still, hands clenched. "She didn't commit suicide. It was an accident. Ask the coroner."

"Right. Because coroners are infallible. They never get anything wrong, do they?"

Rise above it. If you react, it'll be all over the papers.

"So tell me the truth. We know you argued with Shannon before she died. You admitted as much yourself. Did you tell her to commit suicide?"

Where the fuck was Wade?

Just like that, heavy footsteps echoed down the hallway. Wade appeared around the corner, his face red. "Oy! Patterson, you son of a bitch, didn't I warn you to stay away?"

"Wade," Patterson drawled. "My old buddy. We really need to grab a beer and catch up one of these days."

Wade snarled.

"On second thought, maybe some other time." The paparazzo broke into a sprint. "See you, *Killer*!"

As the pursuit steered away from him, Alex tasted blood. Shit. He'd been biting his lip and hadn't even noticed. He swiped his mouth with the back of his hand.

The door to the old piano bar opened. Marissa Flores appeared, her shrewd eyes narrowed. "Hey, Alex. You okay?"

"Yeah." He cleared his throat. "Sorry for the excitement."

"Come here. I know you're my boss and hugs are probably not professional, but I'll take that risk."

They embraced. Alex held her at arm's length. "It's nice to see a friendly face from home."

"You too." Marissa nodded toward the spot where Wade and Patterson disappeared. "What happened?"

"Just another rag reporter. Only Wade has a grudge against this one. They have history. Apparently, he used to hassle Liam when he owned the place as well. He's the sort of dirt bag who likes to invent stories."

"Nice."

"You got settled okay?"

"You bet. I've already been here for an hour, double-checking some measurements."

"Of course you have. You look good, by the way. Life's treating you well?"

"Oh, you know. Life's busy."

"It's hard creating trends everywhere you go, isn't it?"

Marissa rolled her eyes. "Yeah. I'm such a style icon."

Despite the self-deprecating tone in Marissa's voice, she spoke the truth. In New York, she was regarded as a trendsetter in the design business. She had been the creative genius behind Champagne and Liberty, Alex's two New York clubs, and had been overwhelmed with contracts since.

"I'm lucky I was able to lure you away."

"Alex, you gave me a chance when no one else would. The Queen of England could ask me to give Buckingham Palace a makeover and I'd drop her for you."

He gave her a look.

"Okay. Maybe I would just reschedule her." She landed a soft punch on his arm. "I've been thinking about you. How have you been coping?"

"I cope. That's all that matters."

"Stoic as ever."

"You know me."

"Yes, I do." She sighed and waved toward the entrance to Decadence. "Let's go inside."

46

"You bet." Alex didn't want any hassles today. This was a big day for Vice, a day to initiate change.

Granted, he'd already made a few changes.

His renovation team had been working day and night to transform Liam's former home into a suitable abode for Alex. The office no longer held any trace of its former lavishness. Some might call it plain, spartan even.

To Alex, it was perfect. When a room was free of clutter, he could think better, breathe deeper.

Every time he detected a whiff of the fading fresh paint, he smelled satisfaction. The walls were now a calming dove grey. The heavy light fixtures had been replaced with pot lights in the ceiling. All of Liam's plush pieces of furniture had been removed and donated to local charities. A basic desk area had been set up in the corner overlooking the Strip. To the right of the desk lay a casual seating area with minimalist furniture. Several green plants transformed the space into a mini-oasis.

As for the private area that housed his bedroom, that had been scaled back as well. As much as he appreciated the luxury of Liam's built-in gas fireplace along the bed footboard, he didn't imagine he'd have much use for it in the Las Vegas heat. Alex had heard through one of his team members that a women's shelter was looking for financial assistance so they could begin some much-needed renovations. After making a donation, he'd asked if they might like the fireplace and they'd happily accepted it. It would bring some cozy ambience to a place that held so little cheer.

Things were coming together.

It was now time to embark on his first major project. Liam had planned to open Decadence, a piano bar, but he'd never gotten around to it. The site remained the one vacant piece of real estate in the hotel complex.

Marissa would help him change all that.

He opened the door for her and they walked into the empty bar. "Now that you've seen it in person, what do you think?"

"I think it's beautiful, like a jewel box in the heart of Las Vegas."

A group of men in hard hats were already in the midst of dismantling the jewel box, ripping out upholstery and furniture. Marissa grabbed two hard hats, handed one to Alex, and they put them on.

"It is beautiful, just not what I had in mind. It doesn't exactly scream 'nightclub.' Decadence is ethereal. I want Covet to be a place of primal energy."

"Ah. You've landed on a name for your nightclub, I see." She hummed in appreciation. "Covet, as in wanting what you can't have."

"And that's exactly how people will feel if they don't get in. We're going to keep them coming back. Covet will be the ultimate escape, a place of total excess. I want my customers to be transported, taken out of themselves for a few hours. I want them to forget their troubles. Hell, I want to make them forget their names."

"No concerns with my design?"

"No. It's brilliant."

When Marissa had first shown him her plans for the club, it had taken him all of two minutes to buy into the idea. With sleek furnishings and rich colors throughout, it was welcoming without being quaint. Metallic fittings gave it an edge. Heavy stone plinths and columns stood around the room, balancing out the industrial feel with a touch of antiquity. Red velvet curtains would hang near some booths, transforming them into private nooks. Reproductions of religious icons would hang on the walls. Blasphemous, but he liked it. State-of-the-art LED lighting would create hypnotizing effects, tempting revelers onto the massive dancefloor and toward the swimming pool outside. The outdoor area would be stocked with its own bar and cabanas, and guests could swim if they wanted.

Total excess.

"Are we still on track to open in a month's time?"

"Absolutely. I had less time to turn around that old steakhouse in Miami."

"I knew you were the right person for the job."

"Thank you." A flash of color brightened Marissa's cheeks. "I assume you still want to host a big opening night party."

"Of course."

"You don't have to host it yourself, you know."

"And disappoint all my friends?"

"I'm sure *your friends* would deal with their disappointment."

Alex was taken aback. Marissa had never questioned his choices before. There was a certain pinch around her eyes, a tightness that was all too familiar.

He'd seen it in Shannon's face a hundred times.

These people aren't your friends, Alex. They're using you. Maybe you should spend less time catering to them and more time with the people who actually care about you.

He bit back the response on his tongue. "What's going on here?"

"You've been through a lot this past year. You told me you wanted to start over in Vegas. If this is a fresh start for you, then why not hire someone to host your parties?"

"There are VIPs who come to my events, people who pay a premium for our services and unique touch. There are expectations, and one of those expectations is that I'll be there to welcome them."

She took a moment to choose her next words. "Alex, your VIP customers are wealthy people. They can snap their fingers and someone will amuse them. I know you like to think they rely on you for their entertainment needs, but they can easily find entertainment elsewhere."

"Exactly. I don't want them to find entertainment elsewhere. I want them to spend their money in my clubs. If that means I have to cater to them, then I will. They provide a lot of free buzz for me and all I have to do is take selfies with them so they can say they partied with Alex Markov. Without them, I wouldn't be as successful. They're my bread and butter."

"That's a crock of shit and you know it. You just bought three casino hotels. You're doing all right."

Once more, she took him off guard. Their

working relationship had evolved into a good friendship but Marissa had never been this blunt before. He wasn't sure he liked it.

"Besides, you're not personally hosting events at Champagne and Liberty anymore. You have people to do that now that you're in Vegas. You can't be expected to attend all your events. You'll be a vampire, living at night. How are you supposed to function? How will you handle the other demands of the business? Alex, I'm going to be honest with you. Over the past couple of years, I've seen this lifestyle wear you down. This job, it used to energize you. Little by little, you've grown jaded and tired and stressed."

"It's just the press."

"It's not just them. It's the grind. I've seen you work all hours of the night and then show up again in the morning. It's not healthy. Besides, you don't even enjoy your own parties. I know you're not happy. Not really."

"Wow. Anything else you'd like to share?"

"Don't be mad."

"I'm not mad."

"I'm just worried about you overextending yourself. You can't run three casino hotels and party into the wee hours with Hollywood actors who don't have to worry about waking up at dawn."

"I appreciate what you're saying, but you don't need to worry. I'm a big boy, Marissa, and I've been doing this a long time. I have it down to a science. If it gets to be too much, I'll take a break."

Marissa scrunched up her mouth the way she did when she was concentrating. She took a deep breath. As her face relaxed, her professionalism was restored. "Okay. I've said my piece. I'll get back to work."

"I leave it in your capable hands."

"I won't let you down, Alex."

"You never have."

"Covet will be special."

"If you tossed broken peanut shells on the floor and put up a mechanical bull and called it 'fresh and exciting,' everyone would still buy it because *you* said it. Once word gets out that you designed the new club at Vice, everyone will want in."

"You flatter me." She started to walk away but turned back. "We're okay, right?"

"We're okay. And thanks."

She nodded. "I promise you, by the time we're done here, even the ghosts of the Brat Pack will be trying to get in."

Ghosts.

He could do without those.

One was more than enough.

Chapter Three

If Dana had to repeat herself one more time, she would scream. Swallowing her outrage, she looked the blond hotel desk clerk in the eye and forced a smile. "Yes, I understand Vice is fully booked. What I need *you* to understand is that I booked two double rooms months ago."

Even though every one of her hairs was in place, tucked into an elegant chignon, the clerk smoothed a hand over her updo. She clicked the keys on her keyboard one more time. "I'm sorry, Ms. Hamill. I don't know what to say. I can't find your booking anywhere in the Vice database. Are you sure you didn't book some other hotel on the Strip?"

Dana's pulse sounded all through her head. "No. My sister wanted Vice for her divorce party so I booked Vice. I have a confirmation number."

"But your confirmation number doesn't pull up anything in our system."

"That's unfortunate. I also have a confirmation email." She pulled up the reservation on her phone and showed the clerk the email. "See? I'm not making this up to get a free room. I'm not a scammer."

"I never suggested you were making it up. I just want to get to the bottom of this little issue."

Little issue? "With all due respect, this isn't little to me. My sister and her friends are on their way from the airport as we speak. You're asking me to tell them there's no room at the inn. This is unacceptable."

"Of course, and I do apologize if the error was on our part."

If the error was on their part? *Stay calm, Dana.*

Her temper had been getting the better of her ever since the day of the hospital fiasco. Tommy hadn't called once, not once, to see how she was coping with her diagnosis and his ignorance infuriated her.

What did she expect? The man called off the wedding. He was out there somewhere, rejoicing in his freedom.

She still hadn't told anyone what happened, and she knew it was wrong, but every time she opened her mouth to tell a friend or family member, the words wouldn't materialize. When a couple of friends had recently announced their pregnancies, it had taken everything in her just to congratulate them.

Nothing like being a total downer by mentioning her condition.

As for her parents, they were starting to show signs of concern. Her mom asked why Tommy hadn't come to recent Sunday dinners, and she'd fobbed her off with excuses about his work and new projects. Although her mother often peered at her, questions in her eyes, she hadn't pushed the matter.

Yet.

Luckily, her dad was a little more oblivious. And then there was her sister Anise. Dana had managed to keep the topic at bay with her as well.

There was only one other person in the world who knew about Tommy dumping her. Alex, the stranger from the tiki bar. She doubted he'd blabbed it to anyone.

Alex of the sexy cat eyes and the amazing core body strength.

Damn, she'd taken that image to bed with her several times.

Maybe she shouldn't have bolted that day. It hardly mattered. There was nothing she could do about it now.

"Let me check again," said the clerk. "We have had a lot of calls lately. Ever since Mr. Markov opened Covet, it's been insane here. Everyone wants a room."

Dana had heard about the new club and had even told a few clients about it. It was supposed to be like something out of a dream. A contact in the industry had visited once and hadn't stopped talking about it.

You should see it, Dana. At the end of the night, everyone jumps into the big pool. They have floaties made for couples and the best drinks in town. People line up around the block to get in.

She had to admit, she was curious to see it, and clearly so was the rest of the world. Still, it wasn't her issue if Vice was having trouble coping with the demand for rooms. She had booked her room way before the new owner showed up. *Not my problem.* "You're telling me you're sold out because of a new nightclub."

"We sure are. It's an amazing place. It was designed by Marissa Flores. She does outstanding work."

"Wonderful."

"Now everyone wants a room."

Dana was in no mood to discuss the design. "Please, check again."

Just then, a child's cry caught Dana's attention. Over to her right, a young couple was checking into the hotel. Hopefully, they were having more luck than she was.

A squirming toddler clung to the mother's leg, wanting to be picked up. "Mommy." The little girl did a dance of impatience. When the child realized she wasn't succeeding at getting her mother's attention, she reached for her father's leg. He paid her no attention, too busy focusing on the desk clerk's description of the buffet.

Waiting for resolution on her reservation, Dana kept an eye on the toddler.

The parents continued to ignore her. The girl began to back away from the check-in counter. She moved by degrees, with the sneaky concentration of any toddler who'd just decided to make a break for it. As she continued to back away, she almost bumped into a group of rowdy men passing through the lobby. Too busy drinking beer from enormous glasses, the men didn't even notice the child and didn't seem to realize they were about to plow into her.

Dana scurried forward and directed the little one back to the desk. "Come this way, honey. You don't want to get lost." She tapped the mother on the shoulder. "Your child almost ran off."

Neither of the parents said a word of thanks. The mother just rolled her eyes and grabbed the girl by the arm. "Lily, how many times do I have to tell you to stay put?"

Sure. Blame the child.

"Ms. Hamill?"

Dana bit her tongue. It didn't seem fair that some people who had babies ignored them, while others couldn't have them at all.

Stop that. She'd been living with her diagnosis for three months now. The key word was *living*. She'd moved on. The diagnosis of infertility might break some people, but she wouldn't let it break her.

"Ms. Hamill?"

"I'm sorry. What were you saying?"

"Just that we do work closely with a number of the other hotels on the Strip. It's a busy week in town, but I've heard there might be openings at the Flamingo and Excalibur. I would be happy to see if we can find you something at one of those properties."

Okay. The time for calm was officially over. "Excalibur, huh? We booked Vice, the most sophisticated hotel on the Strip, and you want to send me to a place that has a fire-breathing dragon in the lobby?" Dana checked the clerk's name tag. "I'm sorry, Cecilia. That just won't do."

"But we have no rooms."

"Check again. I bet if you try really hard, you'll find a couple."

"You don't understand—"

"Oh, I understand, believe me. Did I mention I work for the Las Vegas Convention and Visitors Association? I've spent the last few years bringing major conventions to the Strip. I have worked with every hotel and have sent a great deal of revenue in Liam Doyle's direction."

"Mr. Doyle no longer owns Vice. Mr. Markov is the new owner."

Dana's frustration erupted in a crazed laugh. "You're missing the point, Cecilia! I'm trying to tell you I have done this before. Now I'm not blaming you. Let's say, for the sake of argument, someone else *mislaid* my reservation. Mistakes happen. Systems go down. I get it. I'm just asking you to fix it. Maybe you could bump someone else and send them to Excalibur."

"Ms. Hamill."

"Look, we're wasting time here. I want to speak to a manager."

"I'm sure my manager would be happy to talk to you but she's in a meeting."

"Great." Dana's voice cracked. "Please. I don't like causing scenes. I've had...a lot on my plate lately. Woman to woman, help me out here."

A deep voice sounded over Dana's shoulder. "Maybe I can help."

Dana froze.

That voice.

The last time Dana heard a voice like that, it was cursing softly in her ear as its owner fucked her into oblivion.

Help me, Jesus.

She turned, degree by degree. It couldn't be.

And yet, everything she remembered was there. The cat eyes, the sun-kissed hair, the long, hot body.

This Alex looked different, though. The stubbled, jeans-clad creature from Joe's was gone. He'd been replaced by a man who held himself with an easy authority. Dressed in an expensive grey suit, he looked as if he'd be just as much at home on a catwalk as in a casino. His short hair shimmered under the hotel lights, a deep golden color that would make most trophy wives salivate. His lips compressed as he took in the shock on her face.

Various emotions flickered in his pale eyes. Disbelief, concern, even anger. She understood them all and would have felt them too.

It was the last emotion that caused her heart to sink.

Indifference. The Alex from her fantasies now looked at her with indifference.

She supposed she couldn't blame him after abandoning him in a tiki bar bathroom.

As everything became clear, his name slipped from her lips in a whisper. "Alex."

He was Alex Markov. No wonder he'd looked so familiar that night. She'd seen his face in trade magazines a few times and also in the newspapers, ever since his girlfriend died at that resort. She just hadn't connected the man from Joe's with the man in the headlines.

Of course, she hadn't been at her best that day,

caught up in her own woes. She could have run into Prince Harry and she probably wouldn't have recognized him either.

Cecilia paled. "Mr. Markov, I don't want to trouble you."

The famous Mr. Markov. Unbelievable.

"It's no trouble." He extended his hand to Dana, his face blank. "I'm Alex Markov."

She resisted the urge to say "Oh, yeah. I know who you are." Instead, she just shook his hand and played along. "Dana Hamill."

He held her hand a moment too long. As his fingers touched hers, something in her belly twitched in cruel anticipation.

She'd felt that touch on her thighs, her hips, between her legs, and had spent most nights since reliving the moment.

Let it go.

He asked Cecilia to bring him up to speed but his gaze remained trained on Dana. Those eyes. She hadn't been able to ascertain their exact color the night at Joe's because the lights were dim, but she recognized the shade now.

They were the color of green amber.

Her mom had a green amber pendant years ago. When Dana was little, she used to hold it and stare into the stone, imagining fairy worlds in its flecks of brown and gold.

Alex Markov's eyes filled her with the same sense of wonder.

She'd thought him enigmatic a few months ago. Now, he was surrounded by more mystery than Agatha Christie.

When the clerk finished explaining, he spoke to her in a lowered voice. "I understand we have some fifth-floor suites set aside."

Cecilia angled away from Dana and spoke in the same hushed tone. "The penthouse level? But Mr. Markov, those suites are for VIPs. Mr. Doyle always liked having a few suites available for impromptu visits. High rollers sometimes drop in unannounced."

Markov's jaw clenched. "Mr. Doyle no longer owns this hotel and I don't see a reason to hold rooms for guests who may or may not grace us with their presence." He turned to Dana, his face a mask of emotionless professionalism. "Ms. Hamill, I'd like to apologize for the mix-up. We have a few new systems and everyone is getting used to them."

"These things happen."

"Yes." He looked her up and down. "They do."

"I work in the industry too, but as I mentioned to Cecilia here, my sister is counting on staying at Vice. She's had a rough time lately and I don't want to disappoint her."

"Of course not." He commandeered the clerk's keyboard. "Bear with me. I'm new at this."

Another flash from those green eyes awakened something inside her, feelings she'd suppressed since leaving Alex behind in that bar. She hadn't meant to run away that night and certainly wouldn't have run from him. But after asking Alex to give her some privacy, the impact of her actions had weighed on her.

What she'd done in that bathroom had been so uncharacteristic of her. Hell, she'd practically begged him to take her. She'd been consumed with guilt the moment the deed was done, even though she owed Tommy no allegiance whatsoever. She could sleep with whoever the hell she wanted. Still, shaking with unfamiliar emotion, Dana had bailed.

Ever since, she had been numb. She knew it was just the diagnosis wearing on her. She'd get over it eventually, no matter how it clawed at her.

Or so she told herself every morning upon wakening.

It was still hard enough facing people when she felt as if they could somehow see into her, and understand she was different. She had barely made eye contact with anyone since the day at the hospital, worried they'd see something horrible reflected in her eyes.

But that's not what she'd seen in Alex Markov's eyes. At Joe's, his eyes had glittered and narrowed in appreciation, flitting back to her again and again.

Not anymore.

He probably couldn't bear to look at her now.

He made a few tentative clicks on the keyboard. "I understand you were supposed to have two standard double rooms."

"Yes."

"Four ladies in your party?"

"Yes."

"I've taken the liberty of upgrading you, booking you into four VIP suites. No additional charge."

VIP suites? "That's very generous of you but we don't need big suites," said Dana. "Any standard room will do. We're happy to bunk together. I only want what I reserved. I don't want to make insane demands."

"And you haven't," he replied. "I'm offering them, as a 'thank you' for sending so many convention delegates our way."

Or a bribe to keep her mouth shut?

"Did I hear you say the occasion was a divorce party?" he asked.

"Yes." Did he remember their conversation from that night? "My sister's."

"Right." Another flash from those eyes told her he remembered. "I'm sorry to hear it."

"Thanks."

He considered her for another moment. Her face heated under the scrutiny. He'd looked at her the same way at the tiki bar, right before she'd asked him to follow her into the ladies' room.

Once again, she squirmed.

"Well," he said. "We'll put a complimentary bottle of champagne in each room. To help make a difficult occasion a bit better."

"Mr. Markov—"

"It's Alex."

Sure. No sense being so formal with a man who'd been inside her. "Alex—"

"It's already ordered."

"Thank you."

"You're welcome. Sorry for your trouble. You'll handle the rest of the details, Cecilia?"

"Yes, Mr. Markov."

"Thanks." He walked out from behind the desk and shook Dana's hand again. "Enjoy your stay."

"We will. Thank you."

Without so much as a grin, Alex headed off in

the direction of the casino.

"I'll just need your credit card please, Ms. Hamill."

"Huh?"

"Your credit card?"

"Oh, right. Sure thing." Dana burrowed in her purse and pulled out her Visa card.

"You're getting quite the steal," said Cecilia.

"It does seem that way. Look, thanks for your help. I wasn't trying to be difficult."

"Don't give it another thought." The woman finished up the reservation. "Everything's confirmed. I'm happy we could make it better for you."

Alex had made it better. He'd made it a whole lot better.

Suites at Vice. One for each of them. Amazing.

The clerk presented her with several key cards. "Your party is on the fifth floor. Because it's the penthouse level, you will have access to a private set of elevators."

Private elevators too? "Sounds exclusive."

"Oh, it is. You'll find the elevators to your right, around the corner. To activate them, just swipe your card. Enjoy."

"Thank you." Dana gathered her things and looked over her shoulder to get another glimpse of Alex's retreating figure.

She wasn't sure what she was looking for. Another glimpse of that fine suit or perhaps a spark in those eyes. Maybe just some insight into what he was thinking when he'd put her up in the most expensive room in town.

Whatever she was looking for, she didn't find it. Alex had already disappeared.

Would she see him again?

A part of her hoped so, if only to thank him.

And to apologize.

She didn't imagine she could do that sort of thing on Trip Advisor.

***

Keep walking. Just keep walking.

Alex had to keep telling himself this. If he didn't, he'd do something stupid like hurry back to Dana and pull her into his arms.

It was actually her, right here, in the last place he'd expected to find her.

He hadn't even meant to stop when he heard a snippet of the conversation between Cecilia and their new guest. But after hearing Dana's plea, he'd hoped to help in his professional capacity.

Then when he saw her, all the memories from that night came flooding back. At first, he had himself convinced she was just a Dana lookalike. His conviction lasted all of two seconds, if that. There was no denying it once he got a good look at her. In that split second, he'd catalogued all the attributes that had fascinated him at Joe's. She was taller than the average woman, standing about five foot nine. Of course, because he was six foot three, she still looked cute and compact to him, even though her smooth legs seemed to stretch for miles.

She'd wrapped those legs around his waist not long ago.

Her hair was thick and black, a happy turmoil of curls. Soft and rounded, her body put the bronze goddess statues in the lobby to shame. She also had a girl-next-door quality. It was probably the dimples in her cheeks. He'd seen those dimples a few times at Joe's.

They'd remained hidden today.

It had taken all his willpower not to lean over the counter to stroke her face. He wasn't sure why the urge to touch her was so strong. Maybe it was the fact her pretty brown skin looked so soft. Although they'd only spent a few moments in each other's company, he knew enough to know he wanted to touch her again.

Dana had stopped him in his tracks, the same way she'd commandeered his senses at the bar. That night, when she told him what she wanted, he'd become a slave to his senses.

Now, she was under his roof, so to speak.

He'd taken a good look at her reservation. One week.

They could get up to all sorts of trouble in a week.

Yeah, right. As if she'd have you. The woman walked out on you, minutes after you fucked her.

Not a good track record.

And yet the way she looked at him across the counter made his palms sweat. Her eyes had widened with something more than shock or even remorse.

There was an awareness there, so palpable it was almost physical. Her lips had parted and she'd licked them. She'd twisted her finger in one of her

66

curls, tugging in such a way she probably didn't even realize she was doing it. Her gaze had wandered, noting the details of his suit and the body beneath it.

Total awareness.

Alex may have handled himself poorly at Joe's, but he'd never been naïve when it came to women.

He just wasn't sure he had the presence of mind to remain detached around this woman. He'd tried, God only knew he'd tried at the reservation desk. His sense of pride had demanded he act aloof, at least until he knew where he stood.

Maybe he should just talk to her and find out why she left that night.

It was the path to heartache and he couldn't afford it. It had been hard enough digging himself out of his hole the past year. He was only just starting to regain his equilibrium.

Dana had already toppled him once and he'd been reliving that moment since it happened. Her sweet breath in his ear had lured him out of the doldrums. Her perfumed skin had bewitched him. And the luxurious glide into her body was so good it ought to be outlawed.

Oh, yeah. He'd been reliving that night.

Had she?

You don't have time for this.

He already had enough on his plate. Launching Covet on such a short deadline had been a challenge, but he'd done it, working long hours. Aside from the launch, he'd had to master the rest of the business. There had been endless meetings with his marketing team, casino pit managers, and everyone from housekeeping to catering. Luckily, he was the head of a stellar team, all of whom knew their jobs very well. They'd all risen to the occasion when he'd suggested small improvements and had taken time to educate him about matters he'd never handled before.

Since Covet had opened, reservations had increased, both for tourists and residents alike. He'd expected that with enough hype, the locals would be circling. Sure enough, they had been. The best part of all was the fact they were booking rooms for the night, so they could party as late as they wanted.

His plate was as full as it could get.

Unfortunately, his brain wasn't receiving that information. It was too busy thinking of Dana and every thought sparked activity in his lower half.

Shit.

That hadn't happened in a while, not since his early days with Shannon. Since her death, he hadn't even been able to muster up an ounce of interest in another woman. In some ways, he felt guilty about noticing Dana's soft skin.

He shouldn't. His relationship with Shannon had been over for a couple of months before she died, even though they hadn't advertised it to family and friends. If he started dating again, some would undoubtedly think he hadn't mourned her long enough, or might even wonder if he'd mourned her at all.

He had, during those dark, lonely nights. He'd mourned her with the fury of ten men. Only he'd realized afterward what he missed most was the Shannon he'd always kept at arm's length. She'd begged him to let her in, but had he? No.

He'd always handled his relationships the same way he managed his clubs.

With cool detachment.

He portrayed a persona. It served a purpose. No one got too close so no one got hurt.

Until recently.

Did he feel anguish over Shannon's death? Of course.

Was he still angry at her for running that night? Yeah, but he was angrier at himself for letting her run.

Despite his guilt, Alex was tempted to sneak another look at Dana. He cast a glance over his shoulder. In the distance, he saw a flash of denim and dark hair. Everything in him tensed.

You're acting crazy. She made it clear you need to forget her when she walked out of that bar.

Alex knew he had too much baggage to be wondering about Dana's perfume or the length of her legs. He knew for a fact she carried her own sizable baggage.

The best thing for both of them was to remain detached.

There was just one little problem.

She was on his turf for a week. They would be sleeping under the same roof for seven nights.

The back of his neck grew hot.

Crazy or not, he might not have it in him to stay away.

Chapter Four

An hour and a half later, Dana was still reeling at seeing Alex again, and still kicking herself for not recognizing him at their last meeting.

She'd asked one of most influential men in Vegas to bang her against a dirty wall.

So the man's rich and famous, so what? Does that mean you wouldn't have asked him to screw you in the john?

Yeah, probably.

Well, maybe she would have, although she probably would have asked him to screw her somewhere else, like Vice.

She couldn't process this right now. There was no use visualizing Alex screwing her in any situation. If there was anything Dana was good at, it was compartmentalizing things. It was one of the keys to her success at work. She understood when to prioritize a project and when to shelve one.

Alex Markov was one project she definitely had to shelve.

She *had* shelved him, for all intents and

purposes. His face may have insinuated itself into her dreams and fantasies, but she understood the attraction for what it was. She'd run into him at her most vulnerable moment. If he'd been any other man, the outcome would have been the same.

You're kidding yourself.

There had been several men in the bar that night. Something had led her to Alex.

Rattled, she tried to push him out of her head. This week was supposed to be all about her sister.

Anise Davidson and her friends had arrived shortly after Dana's encounter with Alex. After a long greeting full of hugs and a few tears, Dana had led them to the fifth floor to their penthouse suites.

She would have expected the penthouse level to be higher up, but as she discovered, the floorplan for Vice meandered. What the building lacked in height, it made up for in its mazelike structure. It seemed every corridor led to another set of corridors. Left to her own devices, Dana knew she would have lost her way in no time. However, because the penthouse floor had its own elevator, they were deposited close to their set of suites.

Anise's gobsmacked reaction upon seeing the luxurious accommodations had made Dana's earlier unpleasantness worthwhile. "A suite? Dana, the bed's bigger than my house! And is that champagne? You spent too much money. What the hell have you done?"

"I didn't do it," Dana had said, grinning for the first time in a while. "The owner of the hotel did. They messed up our reservation so he bumped us."

Anise had shaken her head. "Remind me to mess

up more of my reservations."

Now, as they caught up over cocktails in the lobby bar, seated next to a bronze statue of the goddess Artemis, they compared their rooms.

"Did you see what they put in the mini-fridge?" asked Anise. "Those gourmet ice cream bars, the ones that cost ten dollars in the store. I'm going to sneak them all home in my purse when I leave."

"Don't do that!" Her old friend Bea Allen piped up. "They'll charge Dana's credit card. Anyway, never mind the ice cream bars. Did you touch the bed linens? They're so soft. When I die, I want my coffin lined with those sheets."

"Oh, my God," said Jessica Gonzalez, another friend of Anise's from high school. "We're in Vegas. Stop talking about coffins and drink your Manhattan. Did you guys see the bathrooms in the suites? Black granite everywhere. The shower stall is insane."

"You can fit a football team in there," said Anise.

"This is the Vegas Strip," said Dana. "I guarantee you there have been entire football teams in there."

"Ooh, girl," said Bea. "That's hot."

Jessica started a discussion about the walk-in closets, marveling at their size and shelf configuration. She said she had half a mind to get her husband to install a similar walk-in closet once she got home. As for Bea, she mused aloud about getting her gorgeous young girlfriend into that humungous bed. Even though Bea was only thirty-six, she had just started dating a younger woman and liked to joke about how Sasha exhausted her on a regular basis with her "millennial drama."

Dana tried to join in the conversation, she really did, but she was too busy scouting the lobby for signs of Alex. Would he have an office close by? Not likely. Being the head honcho, his office was probably tucked into some quiet corner away from the action. Still, she'd managed to run into him in the lobby already. She supposed it was possible they might bump into each other again.

A faint flush made her head swim.

What's next? A full-on swoon?

Somewhere or other, she would run into Alex. She just knew it. What better way for the universe to torture her?

At the same time, thoughts of Tommy intruded. She hated that. It wasn't fair the man could still claim her thoughts, even after he'd treated her like dirt.

In some ways, her situation with Tommy seemed unresolved. Even though she'd basically told him to go to hell, she still had more to say.

The worst part was every time Tommy popped into her head, her diagnosis did as well. She hadn't arranged to meet up with the therapist Dr. Batra had recommended. Life had been too busy, although she knew her hesitation had less to do with life's obligations and more to do with her own fear.

If she met with a therapist, she had to talk about her inability to conceive. Even though it made no sense, talking about it felt like regressing. She'd been trying hard to stay positive and focus on the future.

Talking about it meant opening herself up to pain.

She didn't want this to be a painful transition. Dana wanted to embrace her womanhood, even though in the eyes of others, it might be flawed. She wanted to be a force of nature, brilliant and strong.

At the same time, just as in real life, nature could be unpredictable. Dana was aware some very difficult emotions hovered in the distance, threatening like a storm, ready to unleash their elements.

She wasn't ready for the onslaught, even if it meant getting help in the end.

During those rare moments when she could forget there was a neon sign flashing over her head that said *Barren*, life conspired to remind her.

At one point while in her suite, she'd thought she heard a baby crying out in the hallway.

Ridiculous.

This was the Vegas Strip and she was on the penthouse level at Vice. Why on earth would there be a baby crying in the hotel hallway? Even though she'd told herself not to, she'd checked, just in case. Of course, there had been no baby. Someone probably had their TV on too loudly in another suite.

It didn't matter. She'd been walking around in a daze ever since.

Just like that night at Joe's, she needed a distraction. If she didn't find something else to occupy her mind, she'd travel to all the dark places, the ones that seemed so eager to welcome her.

The women would all want updates on the plans

for her wedding. She'd already asked Anise to be her maid of honor and Anise took her role seriously. She wanted to start planning her own events, showers and the like, and now Dana had to stall for time until she found a way to explain there would be no wedding.

She should have told her family about the breakup by now, but every time she spoke to Anise on the phone, the conversation centered on her sister's divorce. Dana didn't want to add to her troubles and bring up sad feelings. There were bound to be enough as it was.

It wasn't that she didn't want to tell her family the truth. She just wanted to do it in her own time. Her parents had always been so focused on the thought of potential grandbabies. They doted on her cousins' kids, and barely a month went by without Dana's mom reminding her to *make some bundles of joy*.

According to her mother, having children was her greatest source of fulfillment.

Dana had never questioned whether her fulfillment might have to come from another direction.

Even before Tommy, if anyone had asked if she was happy, she would have said yes. She had a great job, great friends, and an active social life.

Tommy was the one who'd first said they needed something more. After a while, she'd believed him.

What was Tommy doing right now?

Was he out seeking fulfillment of his own, searching for another baby mama?

That's not fair. You know, on some level, it hurt

him too.

Oh, yeah. He was probably in tatters over her, the one who just wasn't enough for him on her own. No doubt he was gnashing his teeth over dumping her in a chintzy hospital café, five seconds after the doctor told her she'd never conceive.

This anger...it festered inside her, inching through her body, scoring her flesh. Eating her up.

She wasn't sure what made her angrier—the diagnosis or the way Tommy ended things.

It was enough to make her sick.

Maybe you need some Alex medication.

As if that would help anything.

Despite not wanting to dwell on her memories, images from the night at the tiki bar flashed before her eyes. Alex checking her out in the bar mirror, his face half in shadow. The intensity in his eyes as he asked, "Are you sure?"

Worst of all, she couldn't forget the way he cradled her against that bathroom wall. For a cold, anonymous sex act, his touch had been full of heat. Each thrust had filled her with surprise. His clawed fingers had demonstrated his desire, and a need as potent as her own.

In that one moment, they'd needed each other.

Did he still need her?

Bea and Jessica went to the bar and Anise took that moment to draw Dana into a private conversation. "Hey, you okay?"

"Why do you ask?"

"You're more, I don't know, subdued than usual."

"I'm fine. I just can't believe it's over between

you and Roman. The papers have been signed. You're actually divorced."

"Onward and upward, baby."

"Sounds positive. I'd be devastated." Dana chose her words carefully. She already suspected her sister was masking her pain. "It's okay if you want to feel sad."

"This week isn't about being sad. It's about being free."

"I didn't realize Roman was holding you prisoner."

"It's not that. Look, I know this is a big change, and not just for me. But, believe me, it's for the best."

"Roman's a good man, better than most. I hope you realize that."

"I never said he wasn't." Anise stirred her Bloody Mary with vigor. "And why does everyone assume *I'm* the one who called things off?"

"Because you were."

"Yeah, well, there were reasons. Dana, Roman may look good on paper. He has a nice job, he's responsible, people like him. Deep down, I still love him, I do. But, in our case, love wasn't enough."

"What do you mean?"

"Let me rephrase that. *I* wasn't enough." Anise sighed. "He cheated."

"What?" Dana had to shut her gaping mouth. "You never said anything!"

"I know. I just don't like admitting it out loud."

Dana grabbed her sister's hand. "I never would have guessed. I'm so sorry. Who was it?"

"A former co-worker." She rolled her eyes.

"Honestly. How predictable is that? I think I would have been more impressed to find out he'd been giving it to the woman who delivers our mail. Anyway, may they be very happy together."

"I'll kill him."

"No, you won't. Believe me, it's not worth you going to jail."

"Let me be the judge of that."

Anise's mouth quirked into a semi-smile. "If you're going to waste away in a cell, let it be over something more important than Roman's straying dick."

"This is awful." Dana nodded toward Jessica and Bea. "I guess you'll have to tell them at some point."

"They already know."

"What? You told them but you didn't tell your own sister?"

"I know. I'm sorry, but when everything was going down, I was so tired and they were there with me in LA. I just wanted to vent to someone local. And besides…never mind."

"Tell me."

"You're my sister and I love you, but you know as well as I do we don't always look at things the same way."

She wasn't wrong. Dana waited for her to continue.

"If I'd told you the real reason, you would have dropped everything and grabbed the first flight out of McCarran. You would have fussed and worried and treated me with kid gloves. You might be younger than I am, but you've always been the nurturer, the babysitter. You would have made me sit in a room with Roman and tell him how he hurt my feelings and that's not what I wanted. So I made you believe it was sort of my idea."

Dana tried to keep the defensiveness out of her voice. "I would have supported you however you needed it."

"No, baby. You would have made me sit on the couch, wrapped me up in soft blankets and would have fed me homemade chicken soup. You would have treated me like an invalid. What I wanted was someone to take me to a bar, encourage me to hook up with a stranger, and hold my hand while I went off the rails."

It sounded vaguely familiar. "Did you…hook up with a stranger?"

"See? You're already doing it."

Maybe Anise had a point. "You could have told me. I would have tried."

"Dana, you frown if I ask for a second drink."

"You make me sound like a prude."

"You are, but you're *my* prude."

Prude. Hmm. If only she knew.

Anise rubbed her arm. "I'm sorry I kept you in the dark. If it makes you feel better, I'd really love some of that nurturing this week."

"Of course. Whatever you need. Wait. Do Mom and Dad know?"

Anise grimaced.

"Shit, really? Everyone knows except me?"

Jessica and Bea returned to the table with a few snacks. "I see Anise finally told you," said Bea.

"We told her she should," said Jessica.

Dana crossed her arms and then uncrossed them. She didn't want to pout, but it was hard not to when her sister thought she was some sort of rampaging schoolmarm.

"Will you forgive me?" asked Anise.

"Yeah." If Anise hadn't come to her for support, then clearly Dana had failed her as a sister. She supposed she could be a little judgmental at times. God knows she'd been judging herself ever since that night with Alex.

That would stop today.

This week was for Anise and she would make sure she got whatever she needed. Besides, Dana could hardly blame her for keeping secrets. "I guess we all keep secrets from time to time."

"No more," said Anise. "I promise."

Dana's secret burned a hole in her gut, but she swallowed in an attempt to ease the burn. She definitely couldn't unload that shit on Anise now. "What now?"

"Now? I just want to forget about Roman for a week and I'm counting on you to help me with that. And maybe look the other way if I decide to bring a football team back to my suite."

"You wouldn't!"

"That was a joke and you're doing it again."

"Oh, sure, blame the prude, but I was the one who had to help you home after a few too many wild college parties."

"I know and I appreciate it. You kept track of me in my wilder days." Anise looked around the bar. "Hey, there are some fine specimens around here. Maybe I'll meet my next husband."

"You don't need another husband," said Bea. "And you certainly don't need to look for him in Las Vegas. See those men at the bar, the ones flirting with the bartender? They all have wives at home, guaranteed."

"You're probably right," said Anise. "Still, it would be fun to feel some sizzle again. Some chemistry. I think that was part of the problem with Roman. We grew too comfortable with each other. We had no spark."

Dana shook her head. "Your issue with Roman wasn't chemistry. Your issue was him keeping it in his pants."

"Yes, but even before that, we had problems. I think I traded romance for security. I don't ever want to make that mistake again." Anise paused, deliberating. "If I ever remarry, it has to be because I feel passion. Fireworks."

Dana remembered the way her belly flopped around Alex Markov. Pure chemistry.

Don't be silly. You were just excited because he caught you off guard and gave you a suite.

"Fireworks, huh?"

"Is it too much to ask?"

"No." Dana patted Anise's hand. "It isn't too much to ask at all."

"I thought about it long and hard one night. Do you know what I realized? I couldn't remember the last time Roman and I kissed on the lips." A soft sound emerged from Anise's throat, the faintest of sad giggles. "How sad is that?"

"I'm sorry."

"Don't be. What's done is done. Make sure you

treasure what you have with Tommy. Not everyone has that kind of love."

Oh, yeah. Enduring love. That's what she had with Tommy.

This was probably the ideal time to spill her own secret, but she couldn't. If she started talking about Tommy, she'd have to tell them about what Dr. Batra said, and there was no way she was opening that can of worms. Their week of fun would turn into seven long days of misery.

"How is he, by the way?"

"He's fine."

"Still trying to move up the wedding date?"

It was hard to answer her sister's questions without actually lying. "Listen, enough about Tommy and me. This week is for *you*." She appealed to the other women. "Isn't that right?"

"Yeah!" Jessica clapped her hands. "When can we go see the male strip tease? I brought lots of coins to weigh down their G-strings."

"Speak for yourself," said Bea. "I want to hit the casino. Mama's got a lot of bills. Maybe I can get Alex Markov to pay them off for me."

"Maybe he will." Anise laughed. "Hey, I hear lots of celebrities stay at Vice. What if we run into Idris Elba?"

"No, *mija*," said Jessica. "I'm keeping my eyes peeled for Chadwick Boseman."

"You never know." Bea smiled "This week is all about letting loose and having new experiences, right?"

"We're in Vegas, ladies," said Jessica. "No inhibitions, no regrets."

Dana stood and raised her glass. "To Vegas and to letting loose. All of us. Even the prude."

Anise followed her lead. "To Dana. I shouldn't have called you a prude. You're just careful and I love that about you. Thank you for arranging this week, and thank you for being such a good sister." Her eyes misted. "I'm sorry I haven't been there for you very much, and I'm really sorry I kept the truth from you. You've always been my champion and my superstar, and I'm so proud of you. You're a wonderful woman and you're going to make a great mom one day."

"To Dana," Jessica and Bea echoed.

"Thank you." Dana swallowed the lump in her throat, clinked glasses, and motioned for them to sit down. "We're going to have a great week. Lots of fun. No sadness. No judgment. Those are the rules."

"I like those rules." Anise sipped her drink. "If it feels good, let's do it."

"Let's do it," echoed Dana.

As the women finished their cocktails, Dana's words came back to haunt her. As much as she tried to dislodge the ball of sandpaper in her throat, it continued to itch. She excused herself. "I'm going to get a glass of water. Anyone else want one?"

Jessica rose. "I'll come with you."

Dana tried to crack a smile as they walked to the bar. "I would have thought you were tired of water. You've been drinking Perrier since we got here. Don't you want something more exciting?"

Jessica lowered her voice. "I can't." She tugged on Dana's sleeve and pulled her to the far end of the bar. "Oh, Dana. I'm bursting to tell someone but I don't want to steal Anise's thunder this week. I can't have any cocktails. I'm pregnant."

"Pregnant. Oh. That's wonderful. Congratulations."

"Thanks." Jessica's cheeks turned a bright pink. "We weren't even trying. My mother says the women in our family are blessed with baby-making genes. Men just need to look at us a certain way and, *bam*, out comes a baby."

Dana tried to think of a response but couldn't.

"Hector and I are so happy. We had planned to wait another year or so, but now's as good a time as any. Anyway, like I said, I don't want to monopolize the conversation with baby talk, but the girls will notice I'm not drinking alcohol. I was hoping you might run interference for me. You know, help me change the subject if someone brings it up."

"Of course. You can count on me."

"Thanks. It's still early in the pregnancy so I don't want to jinx myself by telling everyone. I'll let Anise and Bea know soon."

"Sure. Makes sense." Dana's eyes began to burn. "Um, are you okay going back on your own? I need to use the ladies' room."

"Yeah. Thanks for listening, and for *you know*." Jessica rolled her eyes toward her stomach and giggled. She grabbed their waters and headed back to the table.

Dana walked through the lobby, keeping her head high. Her eyes decided this was a perfect time to betray her and filled with water. Moving quickly, she rounded a corner and slid into a quiet alcove by one of the shop entrances. Facing the wall, keeping her face turned from prying eyes, she bit her lip and breathed in and out.

I will not cry. I will not cry.

She hadn't cried yet and didn't want to. She had been managing to hold it in, but between her own situation, Roman's betrayal, and Jessica's pregnancy, her emotions refused to be contained.

She couldn't fall to pieces now. Anise needed her support. The least she could do was toe the line for a week.

Just one week of putting on a brave face.

She could come apart later.

You can do this.

Just as she convinced herself she was in control of her emotions, another gurgle sounded from her belly. Dana touched it, amazed and angry and horrified at the same time.

Men just need to look at us a certain way and, bam, out comes a baby.

Jessica was Tommy's kind of woman.

"I fucking hate you, Tommy," she whispered. Once more, the tears threatened. "Stop it. Keep your shit together."

There was no room on her agenda for tears and regret. God help her, she would somehow find it in her to have the best goddamn week of her life. She would take every opportunity, would seize every moment, drink every drink, and experience all the pleasures the Strip had to offer.

Even if it killed her.

With a discreet swipe, Dana wiped her eyes and turned around.

Alex stood before her, a respectable distance away. His brow furrowed when he saw her face. "Dana, are you okay?"

Oh, my. This is it. Breathe. "Yeah. I'm fine."

"You don't look fine."

"It's just…allergies. I'm not used to being around so much cigarette smoke."

"Allergies. Right." He took a step toward her. "The smoke can be thick in places."

"Exactly. Anyway, I'll see you around."

"Dana, wait."

She stood still. "Alex, before you say anything, I should apologize."

"You don't need to."

"No, I have to. That night at Joe's…I wasn't in a good place. I've never run out on anyone like that. Hell, I've never *done* anything like that."

"I know. You had a rough day. It got intense. I get it."

"I didn't mean to leave you hanging. Everything overwhelmed me. I needed some air, so I went outside for a minute. Once I went out, I couldn't go back in. I ran."

"It's okay. Things happen. I was just worried it was something I did or something I said."

"No. It wasn't you at all. In fact, in a strange way, I think you were just what I needed."

"Okay."

"I don't mean to sound like I was taking advantage. I just wanted to—"

"You wanted to forget."

"You remember?"

"I remember everything." He took another step

toward her. "As much as I've tried not to."

Her lungs stopped functioning for a moment. Heavy and useless, they hung in her chest.

"Look," he said. "There's no need to feel badly. We can be friends, right?"

"Sure. Friends."

"Good. As your friend, and your host for the week, I should probably ask if your suites were okay."

"They're beautiful. Thanks again. My sister and her friends are really happy about them."

"I'm glad." He paused, considering her face. "And yet you're crying."

"I'm not—" There was no sense lying. He'd seen through it. "It's just been a long day."

"Anything I can do?"

"No. If only it was that simple."

"I'd like to try."

"I appreciate it, but there's nothing you can do. This is one problem that can't be solved by bumping me to a fancier room."

Alex stood still, gnawing on the inside of his cheek, as if he didn't like her answer. "Is it Tommy?"

"Boy, you really do remember everything." Unlike some men she'd known, whose eyes glazed over when she talked for more than a minute at a time.

"I pay close attention when I'm interested in something."

Interested, right. He was probably just hoping to get lucky again. Any other man would be. Perhaps he thought he could take her for a spin in one of the

Vice bathrooms too.

"I thought about you. A lot."

"Our time at Joe's was very nice."

"*Very nice?*" He put a hand over his heart. "Wow. Are you trying to wound me?"

"I'm sorry. This is surreal."

Why was he still standing there? Anyone else would have seen her crying and would have run for the hills. In her experience, most people didn't do heavy emotion well.

Come to think of it, she was having a bit of trouble with heavy emotion herself. Maybe she was the one who should be making a run for it.

Alex saw into her somehow, but there were things she didn't want him to see.

"What's surreal?"

"When we hooked up, I had no idea who you were."

"I know."

"You could have told me."

"I was laying low. Besides, what should I have told you exactly? Neither of us seemed keen on giving out information that night."

"I guess you're right."

"Should we start over?"

"I guess it depends what we're starting."

He ignored her quip and held out his hand. "I'm Alex Markov. Nice to meet you."

"Dana Hamill. Nice to meet you too."

"There. That wasn't so bad, was it? By the way, how's your sister doing?"

"As well as can be expected, considering we're celebrating the death of her marriage."

"Did you know the guy?"

"Yeah. I liked Roman. I mean, I only see him about twice a year, but we always got along." She paused, not wanting to reveal too much to a stranger, and yet wanting to unburden herself at the same time. "He cheated, the son of a bitch."

"I'm sorry."

"Me too. I just found out. I'm still wrapping my head around it. I don't understand why he'd do it. My sister is a good woman, a total catch. She's smart and attractive and fun. What did he see in this other woman that he didn't see in her?"

"I wish I could answer that."

"There probably isn't an answer." Dana threw up her hands. "Why do men do that? Why is it they can't be happy with what they have? He has a perfectly good woman in front of him, someone dedicated to his happiness, and he throws it all away. Men are pigs." When Alex's face darkened, she realized she might be lobbing too much verbal diarrhea in his direction. "I'm sorry. *Some* men. Not all of them. That came out wrong. This whole situation sucks."

"It's okay. You have a right to feel that way. As for your question, I don't know why some people cheat. There's no excuse for it. I suppose they do it because they can."

"Your honesty is refreshing."

"I don't like lies. They don't serve anyone."

"It sounds as if you've been lied to once or twice."

"Haven't we all?"

Tommy had said he'd love her forever. He'd

lied. "Boy, I bet you never expected to have this conversation when you saw me."

"Maybe not, but I'm glad we did. Frankly, after the past few weeks, I'm happy to have any conversation with you."

This man. Who *was* he? Every word out of his mouth felt like a hug. She crossed her arms, trying to fend off the imagined embraces.

"So I guess I shouldn't be keeping you from your party."

Dana sighed. "I really should get back to my sister."

Alex stepped aside so she could pass.

"Thanks for listening, Alex. I didn't mean to spill my guts like that."

"I don't see any messes here."

He must need his pretty green eyes checked. She started to make her way down the hallway.

"Dana?"

"Yes?" She turned about quickly, probably a little too quickly.

"If you ever want to talk, I'm here. Literally, I'm always here."

"Aren't you busy running a hotel?"

"I'm never too busy to help my guests."

"Is that so? You must be dedicated to your work."

"What can I say? I'm a people pleaser." Even though his face remained serious, merriment made his eyes sparkle.

"And you feel a need to please me, huh?"

He stood very still, like a wolf whose keen nose had just detected the scent of a doe with a broken leg.

She cleared her throat. The comment had sounded innocent in her head, but when it spilled out of her, it was accompanied by images of Alex gripping her hips as he thrust inside her.

His eyes narrowed but he didn't respond. Instead, his gaze dropped toward her collarbones and then slowly traveled back up. "Have a good day, Dana." With that, he left her in the alcove.

Once he was out of earshot, Dana grunted. "What's wrong with you? *And you feel a need to please me?* Where the hell did that come from?"

Her mortification, though searing, didn't last long.

It was the other fire that bothered her, the one that burned in Alex's eyes.

***

Alex didn't run into Dana until the next night, but their conversation had played on a loop in his head the whole time. Considering he'd been in and out of meetings all day, it was frustrating. They were in the process of hiring two new directors, one for cage operations and the other for revenue management, and Alex had wanted to meet all the candidates for these high-profile jobs. The last thing he needed as he shook hands with potential directors was to be imagining all the ways he could please Dana.

He knew her question had been blurted innocently enough, but it was hard not to give it some naughty subtext.

He never thought he would hear her sexy moans again, but a few minutes in her presence told him he had a chance. Maybe, if he handled things right, he could convince Dana they had a connection worth exploring.

What are you doing?

Their only connection was a few minutes of hot sex. If he honestly thought it was the basis for something more, he was a fool.

Besides, he didn't want anything more, not until he sorted himself out. Dating just wasn't in the cards right now. After buggering up his relationship with Shannon, the woman he'd initially pegged as his partner for life, did he actually think he could achieve more with Dana? He knew nothing about her.

That didn't stop him from wanting to know everything.

Put her out of your head.

Emptying his brain of the carnal imagery, he focused on his last task of the long work day. On his way to his apartment, he stopped in to talk to the night manager at the reception desk. He'd asked the manager to provide an update on how the staff was handling the new reservation system. Now that the IT department had worked out a couple of the bugs with their online reservations, everyone was much happier and less stressed.

When he finished speaking with the desk manager, he turned and made a beeline for his private elevator.

The sound of feminine laughter caught his attention. Four women crossed the lobby, three

Black women and a Latina. They were dressed for a night on the town. A soft perfume cloud surrounded them, making him want to breathe deeply and be part of their world.

It was Dana and her friends.

She and two of the others held "mile-high" slushie drinks from the bar.

Although all four of the women looked glamorous, it was Dana who trapped his gaze. She looked amazing.

Her short, pale pink dress might actually be considered modest for Vegas standards, but it fired up his imagination just fine. The dress itself wasn't tight or revealing. In fact, with long sleeves and a neckline that sat around her collarbones, it showed little skin above her thighs.

But those thighs.

It came to rest a few inches below her ass. A line of sequins dotted the hem, drawing his gaze to those incredible legs. She wore sparkly silver heels with little straps around her ankles.

So fucking sexy.

Something roared to life inside Alex.

So much for putting her out of his head.

Although she made for a pretty picture, it wasn't just the dress that attracted him. She laughed at something one of her friends said and her face was the picture of happiness. It was the first time he'd seen this carefree side of her and it made him greedy to see her like this again. He wanted her smiles and laughter and happiness, but he wanted them all to himself.

Most troubling of all, he wanted to inspire her

joy.

Stop looking at her. You look like a stalker.

Shaking his head, Alex looked away. It didn't matter. Her throaty laugh reached his ears a couple of times and then he thought he heard his name.

His fantasies were getting away with him.

"Alex!"

He turned around.

To his surprise, Dana grabbed one of her friends by the arm and led them over to him. She waved, said something to one of the ladies, and giggled. Perched on her high heels, she tripped on her own feet, righted herself, and laughed out loud.

Now he understood why she was so carefree. She'd had one too many slushies.

"Alex," she said when they reached him. "My buddy. I was thinking of you today."

Good. Hopefully he'd driven her as mad with curiosity as she'd driven him. "Hello, *buddy*."

"Don't tell me you're still working. It's ten o'clock." She took a sip of her slush drink through the tall straw, flipped her hair over her shoulder, and grinned.

She was definitely tipsy.

"I'm afraid so. No rest for the wicked, as they say."

"Wicked, huh?" Her dark eyes warmed. She patted his arm, squeezing his biceps. "All work and no play make Alex a dull boy."

Her friends traded looks.

One of them, a woman whose dark eyes had the same shape as Dana's, pulled her arm back. "Don't mind my sister. I think she snuck a couple of extra slushies when we weren't looking."

"Who's counting?" said Dana. "You're in Vegas now, honey. No one counts the drinks here. Isn't that right, Alex?" She cleared her throat. "Where are my manners? Ladies, meet Alex Markov. Alex, this is my sister Anise, and our friends Jea and Bessica." She snorted. "Oh, my God. I mean, Bea and Jessica. Alex is the nice man who put us up in those glamorous suites."

The other women thanked him and took turns shaking his hand.

When Anise shook his hand, her eyebrow arched. "That was very generous of you."

Alex recognized a fellow skeptic when he met one. "Just trying to make a bad situation better."

Dana inhaled the last of her drink.

Anise lifted the long cocktail glass out of Dana's hands and set it on a nearby table. "You're cut off."

"Hey, the prude is just trying to have some fun. Don't be such a stick in the mud." She let out an exaggerated sigh.

Tipsy Dana appreciated a bit of drama. So unlike her sober counterpart.

"We're hitting the Strip, Alex," she continued. "You should come out with us. You look like you need a break."

"That's nice of you to offer, but this is your party, not mine."

"Oh, come on."

His face heated. "Where are you going?"

"The House of Sin." Bea grinned. "You know, the male revue at the other end of the Strip. Their idea, not mine."

"Ah. I might have to take a pass on that one."

"Don't be a drag, Alex. We're gonna get busy with some hotties. You could be one of them." Dana threw up her hands and began to shimmy next to her sister.

Yeah, she had definitely had one too many slushies. The woman standing in front of him was nothing like the woman he'd spoken to yesterday.

Alex bristled when he thought of an inebriated Dana at a male strip club. She could get up to all sorts of trouble. He knew for a fact many of these establishments turned a blind eye when it came to sex between their clients and the dancers. And if she had an amount of cash with her…

His pulse quickened.

He couldn't very well accompany her. He really would look like a stalker. Even still, the thought of her in a compromising position made his stomach lurch.

"I apologize for my sister," said Anise, as Dana continued to dance to a song in her head. "She never gets carried away like this."

"I figured as much," he said, pulling out his cellphone. "Let me arrange a ride for you. I'll get one of my security people to take you to the club and he'll stick around to bring you home later."

"Oh," said Anise. "That's kind of you, but you don't have to do that."

"I want to." Before Anise could argue, he called Wade. He'd just finished up a shift and had made it clear he was up for a bit of overtime. "Wade Kennedy is one of my best men. He'll be here in just a couple of minutes and will make sure you get there and back safely."

Alex would also ask Wade to keep an eye on things at the House of Sin. If anyone tried to take advantage of Dana's state, Wade would put a stop to it.

"Thank you, Alex," said Anise.

"It's no trouble."

Although Dana hadn't been listening to the tail end of their conversation, she latched onto this last part. She grabbed his arm and hugged it. "Alex is such a sweetheart and such a good listener. He remembers *everything*. And look at the way he fills out his suit. Alex, honey, you're like a six-foot piece of candy. I bet all the girls want to lick you."

The other women gawked.

"So that's why I keep seeing random tongues." Still hot in the face, Alex gently extricated his arm from Dana's clutches. "Have a great night, ladies."

Dana held out her arms. "No hug?"

When he spotted Anise's frown, Alex refrained. "Good night, Dana."

She mimicked his stern tone and pretended to salute like a soldier. "Good night, Alex, *sir!*" She burst into laughter.

His pulse continuing to misbehave, Alex headed toward the private elevators.

Something told him he'd be up all night, fighting the urge to text Wade for updates every five minutes.

***

Clack, clack, clack.

97

Every time someone spun the roulette wheel, Dana winced. Why did they make those devices so goddamned loud? She wouldn't have thought such a tiny ball could create such a clamor in her head.

The commotion escalated when some lady shouted in triumph as her number was called.

"I can't watch anymore. It's giving me a headache."

"The roulette wheel is giving you a headache?" Anise patted Dana's back. "I could have sworn it was the drinks last night that gave you that headache."

Dana grunted.

"Someone got mighty happy at the House of Sin," teased Jessica.

"Are you kidding me?" said Bea. "Someone was pretty happy before she ever stepped foot inside the place."

"Yeah, yeah." Dana groaned. "So you all keep telling me."

"You can't blame us," said Bea. "That was the first time I've ever seen you like that. You're a silly drunk, Dana."

"I wasn't drunk. I just overindulged a bit." She wandered away from the roulette wheel and into another section of the Vice casino, the others following her.

"What exactly did you drink before we got our slushies?" asked Anise.

"I had some wine in my room while I was getting dressed," replied Dana. "It must have been strong. Are we honestly keeping score?"

"The tables have turned, little sister." Anise

smirked and wagged her finger. "You lectured me a lot during my misspent youth. Consider this payback."

"Payback, right. Only I thought we were supposed to be having fun. Isn't that part of our manifesto for the week?"

"We are having fun," said Anise. "Some of us more than others, that's all. If only Tommy knew what you were getting up to in that private room with Rico."

Tommy, Tommy, Tommy. Why did Anise have to keep mentioning Tommy?

Jessica laughed. "Don't forget, Anise. His full name is Rico Maximum."

"As in maximum girth." Bea cackled. "He wasn't lying."

"I don't care what he said. That thing was not real." Jessica shook her head. "You touched it, Dana. Did it feel real?"

"I didn't touch it. How many times do I have to tell you guys? He just gave me a lap dance. Besides, with Wade watching over me, poor Rico could barely perform. I think he scared him."

"Poor Rico."

When Anise repeated her words, they all burst out laughing again, which only made her head hurt more.

"Ah, Wade was adorable," said Bea. "Such a sweet man."

"He looked so uncomfortable." Jessica bit her lip. "All night long, he kept averting his gaze so he wouldn't make eye contact with any of the penises."

"We need to bring him out more often," added

Bea.

"It's a good thing Alex asked him to join us," said Jessica, elbowing Dana. "God only knows what sort of trouble you might have gotten into, Miss Thing."

Alex.

Dana's memories of the evening had been foggy, but Anise and her friends had taken great delight in regaling her with every detail that morning. They said she'd been all over Alex, begging him for hugs and calling him "a six-foot piece of candy."

She wasn't sure if it was her hangover or her embarrassment that hurt worse.

"I can handle myself, you know."

"Really?" Anise laughed. "Last night, you were like a teenager with her first wine cooler. You kept inviting strange men to make you 'feel like a woman.' Thank God Wade was there to act as your personal bouncer. I don't think the three of us could have corralled you."

Anise may have dismissed Dana's antics with a laugh but there was an undertone in her voice. She wasn't sure why Anise was so ready to pass judgment on her for having a couple of drinks. Hadn't she accused her of being a prude the other day? She should be proud Dana had let her hair down. Anise had no right to talk. She'd driven their parents to distraction in her college days. When she had, Dana had never judged her.

Okay, maybe a little, but she'd always been there for her.

There was no sense bringing up ancient history, but her sister's attitude still pissed her off. "I thought this was our week of yesses."

"You're right. I'll stop teasing. I've just never seen that side of you before. I have to admit it made me a bit nervous."

"It was a one-off. I'm fine." Her head was pounding and she was sure Alex would flee the next time he saw her, but she was fine.

"Let's try the slots." Bea led them toward a bank of bright machines.

A new cacophony exploded in Dana's head as they neared the slots. The ever-present clink of coins being inserted into the machines warred with the computerized music. Every so often, someone won a chunk of change and the thunderous evacuation of coins made Dana lightheaded.

"Now," said Bea, "the trick is to find a slot machine someone just vacated. Because you know how it goes, the minute you leave a slot machine is when it pays out."

Their walks around Vice had led them through the casino several times now. Despite not having played the slots yet, Dana had seen lots of others doing so and was beginning to recognize patterns. She had yet to anything resembling the phenomenon Bea described. "What do you mean, a slot machine someone just vacated? No one leaves their slot machines. Have you noticed? I'm seeing the same faces over and over again."

"These slot people are hard core," said Jessica. "I think I'm going to try my hand at Twenty-One. Better odds."

"Me too." Anise looped her arm around Jessica's. "It's less complicated. I just have to remember how to count to twenty-one. Some of these slots look way too advanced. I don't want to lose too much money at once."

"See you two later." Jessica waved.

Anise blew Dana a kiss. "Don't do anything I wouldn't do."

As the others walked away, Jessica gave her tummy an absentminded stroke. Dana had seen many expectant women do the same thing. The quiet secrecy of the moment, the strengthening of the bond between a pregnant woman and her unborn baby, threw her for yet another emotional loop.

She touched her own belly. It looked the same as any other woman's, and yet it would never operate the same way. It would never shelter another life.

Right now, all it housed was a roiling mess of acid.

"Hey, you okay?" asked Bea. "You look stunned."

"It's the lights here. They hurt my eyes."

"Regretting those slushies, are we? Come on. The slots await."

Dana and Bea found a couple of slot machines next to each other in an alcove that was somewhat removed from the main part of the casino floor. Muted lights made the place appear cozy. It was relatively dark, just as every other casino was, with not a single window. Although the gaming devices were bright and sometimes kitschy with their depictions of mermaids, Greek gods, and roaring animals, the casino itself was more sophisticated than any other she'd seen. The walls were ornamented with a scrolling silver wave design that traveled throughout the entire room. Backlit with soft purple lights, each piece of artwork gleamed. Plush violet chairs invited one to sit for long periods of time. Echoing the Greek goddess statues that graced the lobby, another set of goddesses stood at intervals throughout the casino.

"Help me out here." As Dana considered the panel of buttons and images of fruit on her slot machine, an imaginary gong sounded in her head. "This thing has a more controls than the dashboard of my car. What am I supposed to press?"

Although she'd lived in Nevada all her life, she'd never been tempted to play any casino games. She'd heard too many stories of tourists bankrupting themselves and didn't care to follow their examples.

"I'll show you. You'll get the hang of it in no time." Bea's cellphone rang and she excused herself so she could answer it. "Sasha! Hey, baby. How are you? I miss you. Yeah, I have a minute. I always have time for you." She motioned to Dana that she needed to take the call and walked out of the alcove and around the corner.

"There goes my tutor." Dana looked around. In the same alcove, sat a cute little old lady, playing on a device a few feet away. She approached her. "Excuse me, ma'am. You wouldn't happen to know how the slot machine across the way works, would you? I'm hopeless with these things."

The cute little old lady looked over her shoulder and scowled like a demon. "Don't interrupt me! I'm on a roll."

"Okay, then. Pardon me." Chastised, Dana returned to her machine. "Sorry I asked."

She put a few coins in the machine and pressed a couple of buttons but nothing happened. Maybe that was how casinos made so much money. She wondered how many of the people on the floor actually knew what they were doing and how many were simply hitting various buttons in the hopes they were the right ones.

There was a panel with some instructions on the front of the machine but the font was so small it made her head dizzy reading it. She decided to take her chances and press a few more buttons.

By the time she'd lost twenty dollars, she was annoyed. Rather than waste any more of her hard-earned cash, she abandoned her machine. She texted Bea and let her know she was going for a short walk and then did her best to find one of the casino exits. It wasn't easy because the place meandered, discouraging gamblers from leaving.

She spied an open doorway in the distance. Two huge displays of lilies and greenery indicated a shift in energy as the intensity of the casino gave way to something more ethereal.

"That looks more my speed."

As she walked toward it, a sign became visible. It said, "Paradise Chapel."

Dana paused.

So this was where couples came to get married at Vice. She'd never seen the chapel in person before, only in online photos.

A new throb began taunting her above her right temple. It was probably just the lights in the casino playing havoc with her eyes again. It had been a few hours since she glimpsed anything resembling natural sunlight, and she knew for a fact those slushies were still messing with her system.

When she tasted bile, she knew it wasn't just the slushies coming back to haunt her.

Memories of Tommy intruded, specifically of the night he asked her to marry him. She'd known something was up from the start. He was a terrible actor and had been sweating. He'd taken care to dress in his best suit, the one he only hauled out for weddings and funerals. He'd brought her flowers too. When he'd begun to suffer palpitations over their appetizers, she'd known. She remembered feeling such excitement and had done her best to contain herself so he could have his moment.

The more she thought about their engagement, the more her head hurt. Pulsing with a beat that refused to be ignored, it seemed to have a voice.

Tom-my. Tom-my. Tom-my.

She rummaged in her purse, hoping she had a bottle of Tylenol in there. Unfortunately, the only things she found were her wallet, a wad of unused tissues, three shades of lipstick, a Minnie Mouse pen sent to her in a Walt Disney World tour operator press kit, and a few Band-Aids in case she got blisters from walking the Strip.

Tom-my.

She gritted her teeth. "You're better than this. Mind over matter."

Despite the increasing pain in her head, she wandered toward the chapel.

The hallway leading to it was long and quiet, taking her far away from the constant thrum of energy in the casino. The purple color scheme of the casino lightened, transforming into soft neutrals and pale flocked wallpaper. Enlarged photos decorated the corridor. Some were close-ups of diamond rings. Others focused in on clasped hands or intricate pieces of lace. Huge bouquets of flowers stood sentry every few feet. There wasn't a single wilted bloom among them. She couldn't imagine how much it cost to keep the arrangements looking fresh.

Alex must have a battalion of florists at the ready.

She hadn't even entered the chapel yet but the atmosphere was peaceful and soothing, very nice as far as Vegas wedding locations went. No cheesy photos of Elvis here.

If only its tranquility had an effect on the tumult in her head.

Figuring a few minutes in a quiet chapel would help her feel better, Dana passed through the open door.

Alex stood at the top of the aisle with a woman.

What the hell? Everywhere she went, she ran into the man.

She couldn't face him now, not after what happened yesterday.

She turned, hoping he hadn't seen her. At the same time, she couldn't help being curious about his female companion. A beautiful Latina, she was well-dressed, held herself high and had an amazing head of black hair.

No doubt she was fertile too.

Stop it, just stop it. Keep moving.

"Dana."

She stopped in her tracks and slowly turned around. "Hi, Alex. I didn't mean to interrupt anything. I was just snooping."

"Snoop away." He headed toward her, fire in his eyes. "It's nice to see you. Are you having a good day?"

"Yeah. I just tried my hand at one of your slot machines. The machine won."

"I'll let you in on a secret." He leaned in and whispered, winking. "They usually do."

His pleasing scent teased. It wasn't overpowering like some men's colognes. With herbal undertones, it reminded her of the scents men wore in the old days.

"How was your evening?"

"Oh, that. It was fine. At least, what I remember was fine."

Gentle creases formed at the outer corners of his eyes. "And how are you feeling today?"

"A little sick. And mortified."

"Don't be. We've all been there. Come. Let me introduce you to someone."

He put his hand on the small of her back and walked her down the aisle, in a weird parody of the wedding march she would never have with Tommy.

Only it was hard to think of Tommy with Alex's hand on her back. Heat shot into her body and into all her extremities. All from one innocent touch.

If he put his mind to it, he was likely capable of incinerating a woman.

As they marched down the aisle, for one crazy moment, she thought of her aborted wedding plans.

She would have carried roses, scarlet roses, and

she would have worn a stark white gown…

Yeah, you need to throw that fantasy into the trash.

"Dana Hamill." Alex gestured to the other woman. "This is Marissa Flores. She's head of design here at Vice. She's the brains behind Covet. I've asked her to give our wedding chapel a makeover."

"Nice to meet you." Marissa shook Dana's hand.

"Likewise. I wouldn't have thought the chapel needed a makeover. It looks brand new."

"In this line of work," said Alex, "not only do we have to keep up with trends, we have to invent new ones. Weddings are a huge part of our business."

"Of course." Even though Dana dealt with business travel in her work, she was just as familiar with the numbers when it came to leisure travel.

"Marissa wanted my opinion on color schemes but if she left it up to me, I'd probably just paint everything builder's white."

"Alex, you've never given yourself enough credit. You have a great head for design." Marissa laughed and touched his arm.

The brief contact made Dana bristle.

They seemed to know each other well. She never touched any of her co-workers like that.

Alex and Marissa clearly had history but what kind?

Really? Girl, you're too messed up to be jealous of this woman.

"Can I ask your opinion on the paint and fabric swatches?" asked Alex. "Marissa has already made recommendations, but I could use a second opinion before I sign on the dotted line."

"Sure."

Marissa spread out a number of coordinated swatches. Some featured bright, eye-catching colors but Dana's eye went straight to the more classic, muted shades. They were all laid out on a small table.

"What do you think?" Alex's hand made contact with her lower back again.

Dana edged away from him. She couldn't think with his fingers anywhere near her skin.

He cleared his throat and put his hands behind his back.

"I, uh, I like this grey and lavender palette. It feels modern but also retro. The colors blend well with some of the other shades around the hotel."

"My thoughts exactly," said Marissa. She ran her hand up Alex's arm. "See? Your friend has great taste."

Seriously. Did she have to keep touching him?

Alex didn't seem to care about Marissa's straying fingers. "All right, then. Let's do it."

"Consider it done. It was lovely to meet you, Dana." With a nod, Marissa walked down the aisle and out the chapel door.

"Yeah, you too." Tired for a number of reasons, she sat on one of the chairs meant for wedding guests. "This is quite the place. I can see why weddings are such big business for you."

"Thanks. It's worked well for us, but I think we can do better."

He sat next to her. The chapel lights made his hair look brilliant with highlights and so touchable.

She'd always liked Tommy's shaved head and he wore it well, but something about Alex's locks invited a caress.

Stop making comparisons to Tommy.

Volley upon volley of pain made Dana's head want to explode. She didn't want to draw attention to her headache in front of Alex, but it was getting hard to hide. Hoping she was discreet, she touched her temple, gently rubbing.

"Are you okay?"

She dropped her hand. "It's just a headache. Those slushies looked innocent but they packed a punch."

"Let me see if I can find you some water." He stood and walked toward a door in back. "I think we keep some bottles in a fridge in the back room, you know, in case any of our grooms faint."

"Don't go to any trouble."

"It's no trouble."

"Alex, I'm okay. Really. I don't need any water."

What she needed was to get out of this place. What made her think she could saunter into a wedding chapel and not feel an ounce of regret? She'd been numb for months, unfeeling and uncaring. Was it any surprise her emotions were now manifesting in cruel, new ways?

I now pronounce you man and barren wasteland.

He sat back down next to her, frowning.

"What do I have to do to get you to stop glaring at me like that?"

"I'm not glaring."

"Alex, you are glaring so hard I might turn into

110

stone."

"I'm just trying to figure you out." His features relaxed, just barely. "You don't accept help very well, do you?"

If anything, she had always been the helper, the problem solver. She'd always taken pride in it and liked being the one others looked up to. In her eyes, no matter how faulty her reasoning, accepting help always made her feel diminished. "No, I guess I don't."

"That's going to be an issue between you and me."

"I didn't realize it affected you at all."

"Yeah. It kind of surprised me too."

She needed to change the subject, pronto. This man put strange thoughts in her head, ones she couldn't afford to contemplate. "So, Wade was popular with my friends."

"He's a good guy."

"A little overprotective, maybe."

He bit his lip. "Did he stop you from having fun?"

"Not exactly, but let's just say all the dancers from the House of Sin are going to be looking over their shoulders from now on."

He almost smiled. "Mission accomplished."

"So you *were* trying to stop me from having fun?"

"No. I was just hoping Wade's presence would discourage anyone from taking advantage of you in that state."

"And what state was that, exactly?"

"Come on, Dana. There are a lot of bad people

out there, ones who wouldn't think twice about putting something in your drink. Wade knows how to keep an eye out for those people so they never get a chance."

"I don't need a bodyguard."

"I never said you did. I've worked in the nightclub scene a long time. I know what goes on, that's all. I wanted to make sure you and your friends didn't have any reason to worry."

"Your concern is touching, but unnecessary."

"If you say so."

It grew quiet in the chapel, so quiet Dana was tempted to find an organ and pound out a tune. Something, anything other than having to endure the shocking heaviness between them, the pregnant pauses that seemed to say so much.

"Who hurt you?"

Those three little words hit her with the impact of a speeding Mack truck. She couldn't have felt a greater wallop from *I love you* or *Donkeys fascinate me*.

"Tommy broke up with you three months ago but you're still torn up. Something else is wrong."

"You shouldn't make assumptions."

"I agree. Why don't you fill me in so I don't have to?"

"There's nothing to say."

"Right. The thing is, Dana, the only times I've spoken with you, you've either been angry or crying in dark corners or sneaking alcoholic drinks. And then there was that time you begged me to fuck you against a bathroom wall. It's not hard to draw conclusions."

"Well, you shouldn't. And I didn't beg you. You were up for it too."

"I was. Believe me, I was totally up for it. I'm just concerned you've been hurt."

"People get hurt all the time. They move on."

"Is that what you're doing? Moving on? Because I can think of better ways to do it."

Damn. Her Aunt Gladys had a term for someone like Alex. She called them "onion peelers." She always said her Uncle Maurice was an onion peeler, that she fell in love with him because he stripped away all her layers. Well, she wasn't ready or willing to shed any layers for Alex or anyone else, for that matter. If she allowed him to see her sensitive inner core, the weeping heart of her, he wouldn't like what he saw.

"Dana?"

She swallowed past her raw throat and smiled. "So, grey and lavender for the chapel, huh? It'll look nice."

As tempting as it was to flee from his gaze, she returned it. Others might cower before Alex Markov, but she wouldn't.

He passed a hand over his face. His eyes narrowed and she thought she saw a measure of appreciation in his eyes. Maybe he liked stubbornness.

She crossed her arms. "I should get back to Bea. If I don't, she'll take over my slot machine and win my twenty bucks."

"Of course." He checked his watch. "I have to get back to work anyway. Unfortunately."

"Why's it so unfortunate? You're too new here

to be jaded about the job already."

"I like talking to you. I don't want to stop."

His voice, already deep and rich, must have dropped an octave when he said those words. She wanted to tell the rest of the world to screw off and luxuriate in his velvety baritone for the rest of the day. It even alleviated some of the ache in her head. "You know, you should think twice before saying those things to women."

"Why's that?"

"Because it sounds an awful lot like you're flirting with me."

His lips twitched and she found herself hanging on his promise of a smile. She hadn't seen Alex smile yet, teeth and all, and suddenly couldn't stop wondering what his smile looked like.

And what it would do to her.

"What if I am flirting with you?" He looked her right in the eye. "Is it working?"

She tried to articulate a response, but had none. "I really should go."

"You already mentioned that but you're still here."

Trapped in his gaze, she couldn't move.

He stood and held out a hand to help her up. Seeing as her knees were gelatin, she accepted his hand and rose to her feet.

"There. I'll put you out of your misery."

Only she wasn't miserable. Far from it.

"Before you leave, I have a question for you."

"Okay."

"Have you been to Covet yet?"

"Your new club?"

"Yeah."

"No. I hear it's impossible to get in."

"It can be, but on Thursday night, I'll be hosting a party there. I'm bringing in a new DJ and, well, I'm worried no one will come."

God bless him, he managed that entire speech without cracking a smile. Dana stifled her own grin. "You're Alex Markov. I've never been to your clubs and I've still heard about your parties. Do you honestly expect me to believe no one will attend your event?"

"Yeah, that's what I'm expecting you to believe. Sad, isn't it?"

"Oh, it's almost tragic." Her mood was starting to lighten and she suspected it had a great deal to do with him and his crazy bid for sympathy. "Don't worry. I have no doubt people will be banging on the doors, demanding to get in."

"Who knows? It never hurts to pad the numbers. Better safe than sorry." He looked up at her from under his eyelashes. "I was wondering if you and your friends would like to attend, as my special guests, of course."

"*Your* special guests?"

"Yeah."

Alex's New York soirees were legendary. If she wasn't mistaken, his last New Year's party was attended by everyone from supermodels to politicians. They got write ups in *People Magazine*. His special guests were typically the starlets of the day.

And he wanted to pass Dana and her pals off as his VIPs? "Are you joking?"

"No."

"Right." She chuckled. "Well, I'll be sure to mark it on my calendar. See you around, Alex." As Dana turned, he touched her elbow, a quiet plea that compelled her to stop and confront the fireworks exploding behind her eyes.

"Dana, I'm not joking. I'd like you to come."

He was serious.

Did she even have the right wardrobe for this kind of party?

"I don't know. I'll have to think about it."

"What's there to think about?"

"Well…I've arranged a whole itinerary for my sister and her friends." She'd even had it laminated but she left that detail out. "I made plans to take them clubbing Thursday night."

"Great. So do it at my club."

"But—"

"But what?"

"Thursday's tomorrow."

"Yes, it is."

If she told Anise and the girls about this, they'd flip. Bea would kill her if she said no. And yet something warned her away. "I hate to change our plans at the last minute."

Alex cocked a golden eyebrow. Even he knew how ludicrous that sounded. Who in their right mind would give up an Alex Markov party for some other club? "It's not the last minute."

"I don't mean to sound ungrateful. I do appreciate you asking."

He drew closer and pretended to pout. "Why don't you want to come to my party, Dana?"

116

Why didn't she?

At the very least, she could rationalize it as a chance to network. In her line of business, having Alex as a connection would be extremely beneficial. Through him, she could arrange all sorts of perks for her convention delegates and he would no doubt appreciate her sending customers his way. It made sense.

As long as both of them could manage to forget his passing acquaintance with her vagina.

Why wasn't she jumping at this opportunity?

Perhaps it was because when she looked at Alex, the last thing she thought of was networking. The man looked like sex and moved like sin. He gave her very dirty thoughts, ones she had no right having, especially in her current frame of mind.

The truth was every time she looked at Alex, she experienced the sizzle Anise had described.

And yet she'd fallen into a comfortable routine of alternately hating and mourning Tommy. Without her realizing it, her ex had taken up the bulk of her mental energy and he wasn't even in her life anymore.

How sad was that?

She shouldn't feel badly about partying with the gorgeous hotel owner. So he was nice to look at. So what? She'd taken note of his lean muscles and the sharp cut of his jaw. There was no mistaking the fullness of his lower lip and she could admit she'd already wondered how he got the little scar at the outer corner of his left eye.

He was the sort of man who made a woman wonder.

No, her reluctance had nothing to do with Alex's party.

It had everything to do with Alex.

Even now, with him standing so close, her temperature soared. She plucked at her shirt to get some air. Even though there was plenty of space around them, he seemed to absorb it all. It was hard breathing around him.

If only he still looked like the casual guy from Joe's. In the guise of Alex Markov, rich golden boy, he was right out of her league. In fact, he was so far out of her league, he was in another dimension.

It wasn't that she thought he was better. He was just so otherworldly.

She hadn't exactly been feeling like she was part of the world lately. She felt removed somehow, set apart.

Other.

She'd been trying so hard to tell herself she wasn't missing any pieces, but it wasn't always easy. Her time at Vice had been a hotbed of emotion, for more than one reason, and it was when emotion throttled her that her power flagged.

Alex looked at her as if she was pretty and whole and strong.

Not hollow.

Was it so wrong to want more of that?

"Dana." Was it possible his voice just got huskier? "You haven't answered my question."

"I…it's because…I just." She let out a puff of air. "You should really pull that lip in, you know."

"The pout's too much?"

"Maybe a little."

He relaxed his lips but they were no less full and tempting. "Please come."

"Why?"

He searched her eyes, serious once again. "I like talking to you. I like looking at you. And I want to flirt with you some more."

"I see." If she'd been chewing gum, she would have swallowed it. "I'll run it by the others but I can't promise anything."

"Fair enough. I'll still make sure you're added to the guest list, but why don't we trade numbers in case something comes up?" When he produced his cell phone, she surprised herself and brought hers out as well. They traded mobile numbers, like normal people.

The little digits on her phone display fascinated her. Alex Markov's contact information in her phone. He'd given her both his personal number and an office number.

It shouldn't seem strange. They'd done the nasty, and in a nasty place to boot. And yet having his number in her contact list seemed as plausible as having ET's.

"I guess we're set then." With a nod, he slid past her toward the chapel entrance.

"Alex?"

"Yes?"

"Thank you. I don't know why you're being so nice to me."

"Yeah, you do." With that, he left the chapel.

Dana waited a moment and then followed him outside. She watched as he walked down the corridor, entranced by the way his hard body moved under that nice suit, hoping she'd find some clarity in his wake.

She only had more questions, the main one being why he'd singled her out. Had that night at Joe's affected him as much as it had affected her?

I want to flirt with you some more.

He'd given her an opportunity to party all night at Covet, the place that was destined to become the Strip's most famous nightclub. Would it be so wrong? It was just a party, and they'd already planned to hit the clubs.

This was fate telling her she needed to stick to her plan and try to enjoy herself. The universe had clearly ushered Alex in her direction, knowing she needed a little nudge.

That's all this was. Alex was her nudge and his party would be her chance to embrace oblivion for a while.

Yes. They would attend Alex's party and she would have a blast.

No looking back. No more Tommy.

No more pain.

It was time to get her party on.

Chapter Five

"I'll need a name for the reservation."

Gordon Dean glanced around the shabby motel lobby. Where was that smell coming from? Probably a dead mouse behind the wall.

"Hey, buddy. Your name?"

"Oh, right. David. Uh, David Johnson."

The manager, whose smoke-stained mustache matched his yellowed fingers, scrawled it on a paper. "Right. Welcome to Vegas, *David Johnson*. Cash or credit?"

"Cash." He couldn't leave any records. When the clerk gave him a figure, he handed over a small stack of bills.

"So." The clerk turned his back and proceeded to rummage through a drawer full of keys. "You here for business or pleasure?"

"Neither."

"Just passing through?"

"Yup. Just passing through."

The man handed him a greasy key card. Gordon shoved it in his pocket and tried not to grimace. Of course, he could have shelled out for a room at Vice, as much as it would have killed him to add more zeroes to Alex Markov's bank account. Close proximity would have been nice but the hotel was completely full.

No matter. He didn't need a reservation at Vice for what he wanted to do.

Lots of visitors to Vegas spent time wandering through the various properties. He wouldn't look out of place strolling through Markov's new palace.

"How did you hear about us?" asked the manager.

"I didn't. I just asked the cabbie to bring me to the cheapest motel near the Strip."

The man's face fell. "Oh. I was kind of hoping you'd heard about us."

Gordon gritted his teeth. "What room am I in?"

"You know, back in the day, visitors *chose* to stay here. But now, everyone wants a fancy hotel with all the bells and whistles. In my day, tourism was simple. People were simple. Back then, tourists didn't need magic shows and oxygen bars and table service. All they needed from their Vegas vacations were chips in their pockets, a hot buffet meal or two, and a fling with a couple of topless showgirls. Now that, my friend, was the life."

"I'm sure it was. Can I get my room number now?"

"Of course, most of my best customers are dead now. Tell that to my three ex-wives, those greedy bitches."

Gordon took a deep breath. *Just give the old airbag a minute and he'll run out of steam.*

"I just can't compete anymore. It's like a new resort springs up every day, either that, or some snotty hotshot is offering up Celine Dion on a platter. Hey, did you hear that Russian guy Alex Markov just opened up a new nightclub? Did you see the picture from the grand opening? Surrounded by young honeys, he was. I bet that dirty immigrant gets all the ass he wants. They probably let him fuck them sideways too. Some guys get all the luck."

Just the mention of Markov's name made Gordon's blood boil. "I really don't care who Alex Markov is sleeping with."

"Oh, yeah?" The man waved his pinky finger. "Are you funny? Because I don't need those kinds of shenanigans in my establishment."

"My room. Please."

"Fine, fine." The man checked his ledger and made a note. "Number fifteen, next to the ice machine. Oh, and don't kick it if it doesn't work right away. You need to give it a minute."

Gordon picked up his bag and headed down the hall.

"Enjoy your stay, *Mr. Johnson*. Pleasant chatting with you."

Gordon didn't care if he'd offended him. This little sojourn wasn't about making new friends in Las Vegas, and he certainly didn't want to be that guy's friend.

This trip was about making Markov pay.

***

123

Alex sat at his streamlined desk Thursday morning and fired up his laptop so he could check his emails. He glanced once out the window but the activity out on the Strip barely registered.

Something else was on his mind, the same thing that had been on his mind all night long.

Dana Hamill.

He wanted her.

He wanted her the way he'd wanted that glass of water at three in the morning, after he'd awakened parched. It had been a long time since he'd desired anyone that way.

Considering the way his one-track mind worked, he'd get little peace until he could make his daydreams a reality.

It had been a couple of years since Alex had trained himself to keep his emotions at bay, ever since things started to sour with Shannon. It was just easier that way.

Dana brought those emotions back, as well as several others he hadn't felt before. When he'd spotted her holding back tears in the alcove that day, a cyclone of feeling had whipped through his body. Most powerful of all was the need to make someone pay for those tears.

When she'd been drunk on slushies, he'd been plagued by worry and an overwhelming need to protect her.

And now, after admitting he was flirting with her? His curiosity was killing him.

Yeah, right. You just want to sleep with her.

Who could blame him?

Dana was gorgeous, although he suspected she

124

might not agree with him right now. There was a gentle slope to her shoulders that suggested a lack of confidence, and yet she clearly had no problem speaking her mind.

It wasn't that she lacked confidence.

Someone had tried to destroy it.

That made him angry.

Surely, she wasn't pining over her ex any longer. He might not know her well, but something told him she'd exorcised those demons with him that night at the tiki bar.

Whatever it was, it went deeper than getting dumped by some loser named Tommy.

Leave her alone. It's none of your business.

If it had been any other woman, he might have succeeded. Because it was Dana, he had a bizarre compulsion to make things better. Maybe it was because when they'd first met, he'd seen her at her lowest. Their encounter, so unresolved, had caused him to become obsessed.

He had a chance to resolve things now, one way or the other.

He checked the clock on his laptop. Nine in the morning. How was it his eyes felt so heavy so early in the day?

Marissa had warned him about burning the candle at both ends. She was probably right, but with a party tonight, he had no choice but to power through the day.

Coffee. He needed more coffee.

As he walked over to the coffee machine in his office, his thoughts turned to Dana over and over again. Why the fascination for this particular woman?

Why not? There were plenty of reasons to like her.

She was smart and successful. He knew because he'd Googled her and found her professional bio listed on the local tourism board website. Dana was responsible for bringing thousands of convention delegates to Vegas every year. She'd won awards for her work. Her resume, listed on LinkedIn, read like a dream.

If they'd met in different circumstances, he would have offered her a job.

She obviously had a good heart. After all, here she was at Vice, trying to make her divorced sister feel better. He could tell family meant something to her. That, in turn, meant something to him.

And, as his cock reminded him on a regular basis, her body was a temptation he couldn't ignore.

Any man with half a brain would be interested in Dana for any of those reasons. For Alex though, it was something about her eyes. There was a sadness there, one she was trying hard to keep hidden, and it tugged at him. It compelled him to fix it for her, to fix everything for her.

Whatever the reason, he was spending way too much time thinking about her. He couldn't afford to spend time wondering about the woes of strangers, not even the beautiful ones with sad eyes.

He certainly had a shit ton of work to get through before tonight's party.

He wanted Dana to come. He hadn't just been flirting for kicks with her yesterday. He'd been testing the waters and her reactions led him to believe she might be receptive to more than just flirting. She'd had plenty of opportunities to tell him to take a hike but she hadn't. Every lick of her lips and each halted breath convinced him she was just as interested in him as he was in her.

It wasn't enough living off memories of having her in that tacky bathroom.

He wanted to get her into his bed.

Tonight, at the party, he would leave her in no doubt as to his feelings.

Shaking his head, Alex clicked on a folder icon on his screen and tried to get something accomplished. It was only then he noticed the small pile of mail left behind by his assistant. He flipped quickly through the letters. One caught his attention because there was no return address. It was in a plain envelope, his name printed on the front on a label. Figuring it was a piece of junk mail he could dismiss easily enough, he opened it.

Inside was a single sheet of standard paper with one word printed on it.

MURDERER

He reread the letter although he didn't know why. It wasn't as if the foul message might change, and the last time he checked, he had 20/20 vision. He hadn't read it wrong.

Bile crept into Alex's throat but he swallowed it.

He checked out the envelope again but nothing gave him any indication as to the sender. There wasn't even a stamp.

Someone had hand delivered it.

A familiar image sprang to mind, one Alex had wrestled with in his nightmares for months. Shannon, prostrate at the pool's edge, her hair caked in blood.

No.

The letter was some sort of cruel prank. Everyone knew his history, and the Deans hadn't stopped talking about the circumstances surrounding their daughter's death. They insisted on dredging up bad memories, turning a harsh light on his failing relationship with Shannon.

Thanks to them and their misguided sense of blame, others had jumped on the bandwagon.

He would have to check with his assistant. Maybe he would remember if someone had dropped the letter off.

Who would send him something like this?

Someone lashing out over some petty jealousy, perhaps. Liam had told Alex that when he opened the casinos, a lot of people had resented his success. That's all this was, someone trying to make him feel unsettled because he was the new kid on the block.

He knew for a fact others had wanted to buy the casinos from Liam, but his friend hadn't entertained those offers. In fact, he'd snubbed them. He could see how some might resent Alex for swooping in and taking the reins.

Unfortunately for them, he didn't appreciate pranks, especially not ones that took so little thought. If someone out there wanted to intimidate him, he should have tried harder.

Alex was about to wad up the letter and envelope and toss them into the garbage bin, but decided not to. Instead, he tucked them into an empty folder in his desk drawer.

Something told him to keep them.

As if he needed evidence of what some people thought of him.

Biting back his disgust, he returned to his work, but eventually his head dropped to his hands.

He could deal with someone trying to scare him.

His breaths grew shallow.

If anything, it was the shame that would do him in.

***

Tommy: Hi Dana. I was hoping we could talk.

No matter how long Dana stared at the incoming text, she couldn't absorb its message. She hadn't had any contact with Tommy since the day at the hospital. Seeing his name on her cellphone display was as bizarre and off-putting as finding a ghost in her closet.

He hadn't bothered to check on her once, and now he wanted to talk to her?

"I don't think so."

Whatever he had to say, it was too little, too late.

Gnawing on her lip, she put her phone down. She walked over to her suite window, hoping the scenery would take her mind off Tommy.

It didn't work. No matter how hard she concentrated on the looping, red whorls of the rollercoaster at New York-New York, she couldn't shake the crackling ball of anger in the pit of her stomach.

"Stop it. Just stop it."

She had Alex's party to attend tonight, and she still had to put on her makeup. There was no room on her agenda for wondering about Tommy.

Tonight, she would start over.

After being stuck in the mire for weeks, she'd promised herself this party would be her changing moment.

Grabbing her makeup case from her luggage, Dana marched into the bathroom and turned on the light. In her line of work, she'd seen a lot of hotel rooms but she'd never encountered such flattering lighting as in the Vice bathrooms. Instead of washing her in a sickly glow, the light bathed her in soft tones that made her skin look smoother and unblemished. It was almost as if someone had sprinkled fairy dust in there. She didn't know what kind of crack Alex was piping into the hotel bathrooms, but she should ask him if he was willing to bottle the stuff so she could bring some home.

She'd get a chance tonight at his party.

She hadn't been far off the mark when she'd expected Bea and Jessica to flip when they heard about the event. When she'd told them about his invitation, their jaws had dropped in unison. It had taken everything in her not to grab some tissue, roll it into tiny balls, and lob them into their mouths.

Bea had gripped Dana by the shoulders, giving her a little shake. "Please tell me you said yes."

"I told him I wasn't sure."

"*Mija*," said Jessica. She'd cupped Dana's cheek. "Are you nuts?"

"Call him," Bea had urged. "Call him now or we'll never forgive you. Seriously, I have a very long memory for this kind of shit."

Anise hadn't been quite as enthusiastic. As the others had bubbled with delight, her sister had remained quiet.

"Are you up for a bit of clubbing?" Dana had asked Anise.

"I'm supposed to be up for anything, right? Those are the rules."

The old Anise would have swung from the rafters. She would have become the unofficial queen of Covet.

Dana wasn't sure what to do with this new, cautious Anise.

"Because we can do something else," Dana had said.

"Dana." Bea had pointed a finger at her. "Are you calling him yet?"

"You'd better do it." Anise had shrugged. "You'll never hear the end of it if you don't."

Dana had had no choice. With a tremor in her gut, she'd dialed the office number Alex had keyed into her phone. Even though she didn't expect Alex to answer the office number, she'd stifled her disappointment when a man named Trevor answered.

What did you think would happen? Duh. He has people to do that sort of thing for him.

Alex's assistant had confirmed they were already on the guest list. Bea and Jessica had spent the next few minutes dancing around the room in excitement and Dana had been forced to accept the fact there was no getting out of this plan.

So she'd decided to own it. She would embrace this party. They would have a great time.

And if the opportunity to flirt with a certain blond hotel owner came up, who was she to deny it?

As she unzipped her makeup case, she heard a buzz in the other room. It was her phone.

Another text from Tommy. She knew it in her marrow.

She planted her hands on the granite vanity and looked herself in the eye. "Do not check your phone. Whatever it is, it can wait. He can wait."

Taking a deep breath, she applied her makeup. She hadn't worn it much lately, for fear of messing it with any guerilla attack tears. Tonight wasn't about tears. Dammit, she would apply a double coat of mascara.

When Dana was happy with her makeup application, deep rose blush, wine lipstick, and a shimmery eyeshadow to complement her new white dress, she set her brushes down. Her natural curls hung loose. They would make her mom want to reach for her flat iron but Dana had long since given up her relaxer.

"You look good." She smiled at her reflection. "Just have fun and forget about everything."

Her phone buzzed again.

This time, Dana walked into the living area of the suite and grabbed her cell.

Tommy: I know I'm the last person you want to talk to. But I'm asking you, can we talk? Please.

132

Tommy: It's important, Dana.

Important. Right.

He'd stopped being important to her. She couldn't think of a single thing he could tell her that would carry any import for her. This was probably just a case of Tommy feeling nostalgic. Perhaps he hadn't met anyone yet and wanted attention.

"No way, sucker."

Dana shut off the phone and tossed it in her evening bag. Resolved, she walked over to the minibar and opened it. There were all sorts of enticing bottles inside, samples of everything from white wine to vodka to Drambuie. She knew full well drinking from the minibar would cost dearly but she didn't care. She'd already gotten the suites at a steal. Grabbing a small bottle of white wine, she emptied the contents into a glass.

Reading the label, she noticed the vintage. Although she would never call herself a connoisseur, she knew enough to recognize it was the good stuff. Alex had talked about vintages at Joe's. It made sense he wouldn't serve cat pee at Vice.

She drank it down in three gulps. Definitely not cat pee. Dry and tangy, it doused the fireball in her belly.

The flames didn't stay out for long. In seconds, they surged again with renewed heat.

She checked the wine bottle but there were only drops left.

Tommy's voice, although reedy and thin at the back of her head, sounded like a cannonball.

Women like you.

"Women like me." She paced. "What the hell do you know about women like me?"

As the minibar door hung open, her eye was drawn to a tiny bottle of Bailey's.

She loved Bailey's.

The bottles were so small. One more wouldn't hurt.

She reached for the tiny bottle and cracked open the lid. As the creamy nectar burned a pleasant path down her throat, she closed her eyes.

Screw you, Tommy.

The alcohol might not destroy her anger but it softened it, made it tolerable.

Lo and behold. One more bottle of Bailey's hid at the back.

Another fine example of fate at work.

It wouldn't kill her. It was so sweet it was practically candy.

Dana polished the second bottle of Bailey's off even quicker than the first and disposed of them in the trash can. She wiped her mouth, brushed her teeth again, and reapplied her lipstick.

Tommy's words might have taken residence in her brain, but she'd managed to kick him out temporarily.

A moment later, there was a knock at her door. She opened it to Anise, Jessica, and Bea.

When they saw her, they let out a whoop.

"Well, well," purred Anise. "You look good."

"Thanks. I feel good."

Bea looked her up and down. "Woman, you should wear that dress every single day for the rest of your life."

"That might not fly at work."

Jessica hooked her arm in Dana's. "You look beautiful. And Bea, you can pop your eyes back into your head. This woman is taken. I'm sure Tommy wouldn't appreciate you ogling his fiancée."

"A girl can always look." Bea grinned.

"Exactly. Besides," said Dana, "Tommy isn't here."

"Hey, hey." Anise poked Dana in the ribs. "Do I need to ask Wade to keep an eye on you tonight as well?"

"Whatever." As they filed out, Dana shut her suite door, taking care to check it was locked. "Ready to party, ladies?"

"Ready!"

"Alex Markov," said Bea. "Here we come!"

I want to flirt with you some more.

As she remembered the heat in his gaze, she couldn't help feeling excited about what the night might bring.

In fact, when she and the others had gone shopping earlier that day, she'd purposely picked out a dress that would catch Alex's eye. She'd have to be careful not to drop her handbag, because if she bent over too far, the slim-fitting white mini-dress might very well catch the eyes of everyone at the club.

Even Anise had raised an eyebrow when Dana had picked it out. "Planning on wearing that for Tommy when you get home?"

"Who says I can't wear it tonight?" Dana had

replied.

"It's pretty slinky. Not really your style."

"Maybe my style is changing."

Anise had placed a gentle hand on her shoulder. "I'm going to ask you one more time and then I'll leave you alone. Are you sure you're okay? You don't seem the same."

"I'm fine. I have a few days off. I just want to be with you and forget my responsibilities for a while. Is that allowed?"

"Honey," Anise had said. "As you keep reminding me, this is Vegas. From what I hear, everything's allowed. But you would tell me if something is bothering you, right?"

"Sure thing, sis. Just like you told me." Dana tried hard to keep any remaining bitterness out of her voice, but it slipped out anyway. At the sight of Anise's downcast face, she had reached for her hand. "I'm sorry. I promise nothing's wrong. If there was a problem, I would tell you."

The lie tripped from her tongue as smoothly as the Bailey's had coated her throat.

She would deal with the repercussions later.

Dana smoothed a hand over the short skirt of her dress. If all went well, it would make a pair of green eyes sparkle.

She didn't care what Anise thought. Tonight, she just wanted to laugh and smile and forget the world.

Alex Markov, here I come.

Chapter Six

The name over the Vice nightclub marquee said Covet. It had been chosen well.

As Dana approached, she held her breath, eager to enter. She'd been a part of Alex's world for one night, not long ago.

She wanted to be a part of his world again, even if it was only for a few more stolen moments.

Others did too. At least two hundred people were lined up around the corner. However, Alex's assistant Trevor had instructed Dana to go right to the bouncer at the door and bypass the line. Everyone eyed them as they headed there, probably wondering who they were and who they knew.

The bouncer, in conversation with another staff member, held the door open. Through it, Dana spotted a celebrity. An A-list action movie actor, the man held court just inside the entrance. His arms were around two women, one of whom was nibbling his neck, and neither of whom were his wife.

Jessica grabbed Dana's arm. "Is that—?"

"Yup. That's him."

"Hmm," said Jessica. "He's shorter in real life."

"Everyone's shorter in real life," said Bea.

Anise's lip curled. "More importantly, he's married in real life."

Dana squeezed her sister's shoulder. "Do you want to go somewhere else?"

"No. It's just disappointing, that's all. I've seen all his movies but I won't be seeing any more. Imagine, playing the honorable family man on screen over and over when he's keeping a couple of women on the side."

Dana knew her sister didn't care about celebrity marriages. Anise didn't even read the rag magazines, but seeing such a flagrant display of infidelity would no doubt remind her of Roman's betrayal. "If you change your mind, just say the word."

"Okay."

The bouncer finished up his conversation and turned to them. "Ladies. Welcome to Covet. May I have your names, please?"

Dana told them their names, wondering if this was the part where the guy would laugh and show them the door.

"Very good. Mr. Markov asked me to keep an eye out for you."

So this wasn't just some weird joke.

The bouncer waved to a beautiful woman dressed in a body-hugging black dress. When she approached, he directed her. "Viola, would you please escort these ladies? Mr. Markov's expecting them."

"Of course." Viola smiled and turned on her heel like a model on the catwalk. "You're more than welcome to have fun here in the club, but Mr. Markov asked me to bring you to the VIP suite first. He'd like to say hello. I'll be your personal concierge tonight. If there's anything you need, please let me know."

As they followed, the bouncer smiled at Dana. "Have a sinful night."

Jessica and Bea squealed.

Dana didn't know where to look as they walked through Covet. Plenty of people mingled and danced, and each one looked more dazzling than the one before. Although she'd never considered herself a slouch in the looks department, suddenly she felt a need to touch up her makeup for the hundredth time.

Don't be dumb. She knew how these gigs worked. Nightclub owners routinely hired dozens of models to entice guests. No doubt, it also made the regular folk feel as if they were part of a chosen few.

The club itself was stunning. Although the focal point was a huge dance floor, there were lots of cozy alcoves for sitting, all partitioned off with red velvet curtains. Gorgeous men and women circulated, dressed similarly to Viola, distributing colorful cocktails and flutes of champagne. The red walls provided a sumptuous background to the many works of art. A lot of the pictures on the walls had religious themes. Some even looked like gold icons of saints. It made the place feel like an art gallery.

Only she'd never been in any art gallery with a soundtrack. The lighting scheme pulsed in time with the EDM, in an energetic show of illumination. The music itself was orchestrated by a familiar DJ. Although Dana couldn't place her name, she'd seen her in entertainment magazines. The tattooed woman stood on a dais, whipping the crowd into a frenzy on the dance floor. Everyone standing near it swayed in time to the groove. Wherever Dana looked, she saw flashes of silver and gold, and happy, sweaty faces.

There was something psychedelic about the place. It made her head swim but she was more than happy to dive into those waters. Her body was already begging to move to the beat of the music.

At the far end of the room, the space opened onto an elaborate pool deck. It was lit by soft light, so flattering most people wouldn't hesitate to don a bikini. Outside, partiers swam and relaxed on teak deck chairs, surrounded by palm trees and cabanas. Staff members in designer swimsuits encouraged guests to take a dip or lounge on floaties built for two.

There was something decadent about laying on a floatie, listening to dance music and sipping champagne.

After crossing what felt like an expanse, Viola steered them away from the main part of the club and turned a corner into a darkened hallway lined with more religious icons. Saints and martyrs watched their progress, as if in judgment.

Viola knocked on a closed door at the end of the hallway. A man opened it. "Mr. Markov's guests are here."

He held the door open. "Welcome, ladies. Please come in."

Trading looks, Dana and the others headed inside.

When Viola had mentioned the VIP suite, Dana had expected some sort of stuffy back room. She couldn't have been more wrong.

Where the rest of Covet was opulent and rich, the VIP suite was airy and light. Beige leather couches extended across each wall. Partiers sat and lounged on them, sipping cocktails from filigreed goblets. The great room was subdivided into smaller sections by enormous glass panel artwork that hung in various places throughout the space. The floor-to-ceiling glass partitions made each nook feel private, but still allowed one to see everything on the other side.

The lighting here was soft and neutral, unlike the brighter color display in the main part of the club. Although one could still hear the music, it was muted in this sanctuary and people could talk to one another without having to yell.

As a carryover from the other part of the club, the VIP suite also boasted private booths along each wall. These too featured red velvet curtains that could be closed if guests wanted some privacy. Dana could only imagine what some people got up to in those nooks.

An enormous bar lined one wall, staffed by more employees with perfect skin and perfect hair. This room opened onto the pool deck as well, but had its own separate entrance and private cabanas.

She had no doubt VIP guests paid a premium for the exclusivity. Bouncers stood guard on the pool deck, ready in case any of the regular guests tried to enter the private area from outside.

Anise grabbed Dana's arm and whispered. "Look. Isn't that Adam Maxwell?"

Dana did a double take. Another A-list movie star. "Yeah, that's him."

"The woman he's talking to," said Bea. "That's Sheree Tucker."

Sure enough, the Hollywood star was in deep conversation with the famous country singer.

And they weren't the only celebrities in the room. Everywhere Dana looked, she spied familiar faces, even if she couldn't place them all.

Alex had some powerful friends. She'd already known it, but it was something altogether different to be surrounded by them.

Where was Alex?

Her heart in her throat for reasons she didn't want to admit, Dana followed Viola.

She looked all around, needing to see him. Needing to have some sort of assurance that she hadn't just walked out of her regular world into some other sort of bizarre existence. Her pulse quickening, Dana suddenly felt adrift.

Untethered.

She needed Alex to be her anchor, to tell her everything was perfectly normal.

Nothing unusual here, Dana. This is just how I spend all my days. Stick around. Mick Jagger is due to arrive any minute now with a bevy of European princesses.

Within seconds, she'd spotted him.

As the others kept walking, she hung back for a moment, taking him in. Her pulse tripped to the same beat as the music.

Or was that just her heartbeat pounding in her head?

Alex lounged behind one of the glass partitions on one of those expensive leather couches. He was surrounded by a bevy of attractive men and women, all of whom seemed to be clamoring for his attention.

One of the women asked him to join her in a selfie. He shook his head and frowned, mouthing the words, "Not tonight."

What struck Dana most was the look on his face. Although he appeared to be following the conversation on the couch, there was a certain detachment in his eyes, as if he'd had that conversation one too many times. Tuned out, he rested his chin in his hand, and his gaze flitted around the room.

He had all of the approachability of a bored Bourbon king on his throne.

Was it possible Alex was blasé about his own party?

When his gaze landed on Dana, his posture changed. He sat up and his eyes narrowed with predatory focus. A twitch of his lips made his pleasure known. The brunette sitting next to him was in the middle of saying something but Alex excused himself and stood. As he walked over, everyone near him watched.

Dana's belly fluttered. An honest-to-goodness

belly flutter.

When was the last time she'd had one of those?

Maybe it was just all those Hollywood types walking around. They made her nervous.

Alex walked out from behind the glass partition and smiled.

Sweet Mother of Jesus.

Dana had never seen him smile in any of their other interactions. Now she understood why he'd kept it under wraps.

It was too magnificent.

When his lips curled upward, it was like Zeus unleashing his untamed glory upon mere mortals. There was something sly and wanton in the curve of his mouth. It made him look like a lion about to go in for the kill. Heat washed over her. Everything in the party room seemed doused, the lights, the shiny fixtures, the mere mortals who flocked around him. They all faded into the background like sad, grey shadows.

He might not smile a lot, or at least not at her, but when he did it made an impact. Sort of the way an asteroid left a gaping crater behind.

Alex's smile had the power to decimate lesser creatures.

All of a sudden, her clothing scratched and she fought the urge to drop her drawers.

He was probably accustomed to women having that reaction. *Relax, Dana. Women strip around me all the time.*

"Dana." He closed the distance between them. "You came."

"I, uh, yeah. Thanks." *Smooth, girl. Real smooth.*

144

He's gonna be putty in your hands if you keep talking like that.

"I'm glad." He leaned in and kissed her on both cheeks.

"Oh." Her breath caught. "Like a European."

He smelled good. Really good. He wore some other cologne that sparked her senses. With citrusy undertones, it had an outdoorsy appeal. If she didn't know any better, she'd swear he'd been traipsing through an orange grove.

Maybe this club had an orange grove too.

The absurdity of the image made her want to cackle, but she managed to contain it.

Another roguish grin turned her shins to mush but she held her ground. "My background is Russian, but sure." He turned to the others. "Anise. Bea. Jessica. You all look very nice."

As Jessica and Bea made small talk with Alex, he listened attentively but his eyes darted toward her at intervals. Star struck, Jessica gushed over Adam Maxwell's latest movie, while Bea complimented him on the music and décor.

Anise, on the other hand, was silent.

Dana gave her a look but Anise didn't notice.

Instead, Dana decided to check out their host in greater detail.

Alex was dressed in black trousers and a black shirt. The deep shade made the golden highlights in his hair seem even more brilliant. The beautiful fabric of his shirt caressed the curves of his arms and shoulders. The man obviously took care of himself, although he wasn't a body builder. His long, lean build was closer to that of a basketball player. His eyes shone, and Dana wasn't sure if it was the clever lighting or curiosity that made them pop.

As he chatted with the others, his deep voice imprinted itself on her. She loved a man with a cool baritone. People talked about "bedroom eyes." In her opinion, Alex had a "bedroom voice." It was the sort of voice a woman wanted to hear first thing in the morning and last thing at night.

Dirty words cried out to be spoken in Alex's voice.

"Well." He waved a hand around the room. "What do you think?"

"It's gorgeous," said Dana. "I've never seen so many celebrities. I feel like I should have had an audition to get in."

When he laughed, it boomed.

Check. One more thing that attracted her. She loved a hearty laugh.

This was not good. She was sinking like a stone.

"They're just people, like you and me."

You and me. Right.

He gestured toward Adam Maxwell. "I'd be happy to introduce you to Adam. He's a cool guy. We've been friends a long time, since he was doing theater in New York."

The Hollywood star might be the most famous person in the room but even he, with all his celluloid beauty, paled in comparison to Alex. "That's okay. Maybe later."

"You look thirsty," said Alex, grinning. "Let me get you all some drinks." He held out his hand.

Without once considering the implications or the

optics, Dana took it.

This time, Anise gave her a look.

She ignored it.

He led them to the bar. "What can I get you? Champagne? A glass of wine? Or can I suggest one of our signature cocktails?"

"Ooh, I like the sound of a signature cocktail," said Bea. She turned to Jessica. "What about you?"

Jessica reddened. "Um, just a fizzy water for me, please."

"Fizzy water?" Bea laughed. "Aren't you sick of it? It's all you've been drinking. I'm surprised you haven't floated away."

When Jessica froze, Dana spoke up for her. "Is it your stomach again? You mentioned it was bothering you earlier."

"Yeah." Jessica let out a sigh of relief. "I think I'm just fighting a bug. I'm trying to flush it out."

No one else said a word about Jessica's drink preferences. She mouthed a thank you to Dana.

Alex nodded at the bartender, a guy who looked as if he was a soap opera actor in his spare time. Within moments, a Perrier appeared on the bar, next to three identical cocktails that glistened with gold flecks. Alex distributed them to the women. "We call this cocktail Golden Oblivion."

Oblivion. That sounded good. Dana might have to have a couple.

Somewhere inside her, the voice of reason reminded her she had probably already mixed one too many drinks. However, although the wine and the Bailey's had nudged her into happy territory, she needed something stronger to push her over the boundary.

She was too on edge, too aware.

"What do we owe you?" she quietly asked the bartender.

The man just glanced at Alex, who shook his head. "It's on the house."

"We can pay for our drinks. I don't want to take advantage."

"You're my special guests, remember?" Alex winked. "It has its privileges."

"Well…um, thank you." Why did she have trouble stringing a sentence together in front of this man? "You're not having one?"

"No." He reddened. "They're pretty sweet. I try to limit how much sugar goes into my body, but please enjoy yours."

"I wish I could say I was strict about what goes into my body." As soon as the words tumbled out of Dana's mouth, she remembered what happened between her and Alex at the tiki bar. Her nerves finally manifested in a crazed laugh.

Alex's gaze dropped briefly to her mouth, but he didn't point out her slip of the tongue. "It doesn't look that way. You look like you take care of yourself."

"It must be all that running to the gourmet cheese shop."

"You could have fooled me. You look beautiful, by the way. That dress…it's life-altering."

Dana's cheeks heated. "Thank you." She tried to look sophisticated, as if she attended VIP parties all the time. She sipped her cocktail. "Oh, my God. This is delicious."

Laced with cinnamon and rum, the cocktail made her feel warm and pliable. This time, when she snuck another glance at Adam Maxwell, he looked like any other guy.

"I'm glad you like it," said Alex. "Try to nurse it. I hear they're stronger than they taste."

Dana took another sip of the sweet concoction. *Not strong enough.*

Anise finally broke her silence. "It was nice of you to invite us, Alex."

"My pleasure. I'm just sorry a divorce is what brought you to us."

Anise's eyes tightened. "That's life. Onward and upward."

"This trip is all about creating experiences," added Bea.

Alex nodded in approval. "I'm glad my party will be one of them."

As a buff man in swim trunks strode toward the pool deck, Jessica cleared her throat. "Oh, it's an experience, all right."

Alex chuckled. "Well, aside from the scenery, we have the best DJ, the best drinks, and the hottest dance floor in town. And now we have all of you."

Jessica poked Dana. "This one's a charmer."

"He has his moments."

Alex turned to look right at Dana. His questioning gaze was full of heat, one she couldn't ignore.

She looked away, but no matter where she looked, she couldn't escape the thick atmosphere or the allure of sex. She saw it in the flirting couples around the room. She definitely saw it in the bikini-clad guests out on the pool deck. And it shone clear as day from Alex's eyes.

Maybe it was time she admitted he might have a thing for her.

Just as she did for him.

The knowledge might be unnerving, but it was also exhilarating.

"So," Alex said to the other women, "tell me what you all do when you're not partying in Vegas."

Dana listened as her friends regaled him with stories about their work. When Jessica mentioned her flower shop, Alex was able to share anecdotes from his own floral designer at Vice. It was clear he had his hand in all aspects of the business, and his knowledge tickled Jessica.

Bea talked briefly about her art classes. Alex nodded, asking her opinion about a couple of hot art exhibits in the LA area. Clearly impressed he could carry on a conversation about modern art, Bea smiled when it became clear they shared some favorite artists.

Dana marveled at the way he could direct a conversation without monopolizing it. He was unlike any hotelier she'd ever met, and she'd met a few. Most of them were arrogant, wanting to talk only about themselves and their latest achievements. Alex certainly could have extricated himself from the conversation any time he wanted and sauntered off to find more "important" company but he seemed to be enjoying himself.

He certainly seemed much happier than when he was sitting on that couch, a subject of interest for the pretty people.

He kept looking her way, offering her shy grins. Each curl of his lips made her want to beg to see that brilliant wide smile again. In fact, when Bea teased it out of him with a couple of jokes, Dana secretly rejoiced.

Aside from being smart and well-read, Alex was just too beautiful.

The more she sipped her Golden Oblivion, the bolder she grew. Before long, she was able to return his heated glances. As the other women chatted, their voices faded. Locked in a bubble with Alex, she couldn't have been more spellbound if he'd spiked her drink.

Covet was working its magic on her.

Anise didn't seem to be languishing under the same spell. She'd noticed the way Alex hung close to Dana and the way he looked at her. Worse still, Dana suspected her sister had noticed the way she looked at him.

Guilt prickled the area between her shoulder blades. She should have told Anise about Tommy, but the timing had always seemed wrong.

Of course, Anise was jumping to conclusions. Dana would have done the same thing.

She had to fix this, and soon.

When Anise drank her last sip of Golden Oblivion, Alex smiled. "I'm glad you enjoyed the drink. Can I top it up for you?"

"No, thank you."

"So, Anise," he said. "What do you do for a living?"

"Sales."

Alex waited for her to elaborate but she didn't. "What kind of sales?"

"Real estate."

"Ah."

When the silence once again hung heavily, Dana spoke for her sister. "My sister is modest. She wouldn't tell you herself but she's amazing at what she does. In fact, she was the top broker in her company last year."

"That's great," said Alex. "Congratulations. You must really understand the market."

In any other situation, Anise would have appreciated the praise. This time, she merely nodded.

Bea polished off her Golden Oblivion. "I think maybe I could use a top up on that drink, Alex."

"Of course."

Anise chose that moment to break her relative silence. "Actually, Alex, if you don't mind, I think it's time we hit the dance floor. Right, ladies?"

"You bet. I want you to have fun. The DJ will be here until morning. Oh, and don't forget to check out the fortune teller while you're here."

"A fortune teller?" Jessica's voice rose. "That sounds fun."

"She's doing readings in the small room next to the entrance," said Alex. "We also have one of the top illusionists arriving shortly to do some tricks for the guests. And when you're in the club, please make sure Viola gets all your orders. I've asked her to take good care of you tonight. Food and drinks are on me."

"That's very generous of you," said Bea.

"Like I said, you're my special guests."

He looked over his shoulder. Viola appeared again.

"Viola, would you please take the ladies to the table I reserved for them?"

"Absolutely."

They excused themselves. When Dana stood still, Anise turned to her. "Aren't you coming?"

"No. I'm good."

"But…don't you want your fortune told?"

Hearing her fortune was the last thing Dana wanted, even if it was hogwash, done for entertainment's sake. "Not really."

Anise paused. She looked at Alex and back at her sister. "Are you *sure*?"

"I'm quite sure. It's quieter in here and I just want to enjoy my drink."

The look on Anise's face made it clear she was worried Dana might enjoy more than the cocktail. For a woman who appreciated a party, she was acting as she'd been invited to the fall of Sodom and Gomorrah.

Dana understood. Anise had been betrayed and hurt, but it didn't give her the right to play babysitter.

Anise pulled her aside. "I didn't think this kind of party was your thing. You know, with all the fake eyelashes and fake boobs and fake people."

"That's not very nice. You don't know they're fake."

"Believe me, honey. I can spot a fake a mile away. This place is pretentious."

"No, it's not. It's exciting and fun. And maybe I

will schmooze with the Hollywood crowd while I'm here. Is that a problem?"

"I think your friend Alex has the wrong idea."

"And which idea is that?"

"That you're available. And interested."

"He's just being friendly. *I'm* just being friendly."

"Well, it seems to me you've become good *friends* pretty quickly."

"Anise, go. The others are waiting for you. I'll join you later."

Anise followed the others out of the VIP suite.

Alex touched Dana's elbow. "Your sister isn't happy."

"She's just having an off day. I think she was uncomfortable, that's all. She's got a lot on her mind."

"What about you? Are you comfortable?"

"Honestly? I don't know. This place…it's like another world. It's a bit overwhelming."

"I'm sorry."

"No, it's not bad. It's beautiful. I like it here."

"Thanks. I'm glad you're staying."

"Me too."

Left alone with Alex, her awkwardness returned. After all, aside from what she'd read in the papers, she knew very little about him. For courage, she took another sip of cinnamon nectar.

This time, as the lovely burn hit her throat, it warmed everything from the neck upward. Like brain freeze, only much better.

A group of partiers skipped past, laughing. They made their way to the pool deck, dressed in expensive swimwear. A couple of the faces looked familiar, but she didn't ask Alex who they were. "See. I told you your party would be a hit."

"You did."

"Do all your parties have celebrity guests?"

"Not necessarily, but I do have some regulars, people I've known for years. A lot of them have been partying with me since the beginning. They have the means to travel and come to most of my events. I know them, they know me, and they understand they won't be mobbed in the VIP suites. There are strict rules about who gets in."

"So I was vetted?"

"I'm not worried about you and your friends. Something tells me you won't try to corner Adam in a dark hallway, demanding his autograph."

"I happen to be a fan. How do you know I won't corner him?"

Alex leaned in a whispered. "Because I plan to keep you all to myself."

Dana swallowed.

He gestured to one of the quiet nooks, one of the ones cordoned off by a red velvet curtain. "Sit with me."

All they needed to do to make the space completely private was to untie the cords holding the curtains back. If they did, no one would see them.

She hesitated. Right now, sitting in that nook with Alex seemed just as naughty as sliding between his sheets.

Isn't that what you wanted anyway?

She might not have anticipated this exact

scenario but she'd guessed they were headed in this direction.

He's not asking you to take part in an orgy. He just wants to talk. Alex is a nice man. Since when is having a conversation a crime?

Only, right now, with the muted lights illuminating the shadows in his face, he didn't look like a nice man.

He looked like a dangerous man.

And she was in the mood for danger.

There was also a wondrous sort of intrigue shining in his eyes. His eyes glittered with the fascination of a lost man who had just discovered a map.

A part of her wanted to see what he'd do with that map.

He led her toward the nook. It was more spacious than she would have expected, big enough to hold a black leather sectional couch and a couple of small tables. A tall vase stood next to it, filled with ornamental, feathery fronds that draped over one side of the couch. A single sconce cast a dim light over the area. She sat at one corner of the sectional, her rigid posture an indication of her nerves.

"Do you mind if I sit next to you?" he asked.

"I don't mind."

Alex sat back, his arm draped on the couch behind her. Dana angled herself toward him and crossed her legs. His gaze flickered toward them. His casual observation didn't make her feel ogled but it certainly made her feel noticed.

She couldn't help making her own discreet

observations, specifically noting the way his shirt skimmed over hard abs.

He was perfect.

The man from Joe's had all but disappeared. This man didn't show the same vulnerability, although she suspected they might share the same loneliness, despite the people flitting on the other side of the curtain. The Alex from Joe's had let most of his guard down, but this Alex had them firmly in place.

"You look nervous."

"I am nervous," she replied.

"Why?"

"You're sort of an intimidating person."

He didn't dispute it. "You weren't intimidated the first time we met."

"Yeah, well, things change."

"I don't want you to be intimidated."

"It's hard not to be." She glanced around the VIP suite. Everywhere she looked, she saw wealth and ease and perfection. Everyone was smiling, showing off straight, white teeth, the kind you buy. There wasn't a single blemish in this crowd. They all seemed to be enjoying life to the fullest, because they could. Not a single thing could stop them.

She wanted to be one of those carefree, perfect people, if only for a while.

"What are you thinking?"

"Just that everything here is so luxurious. I keep worrying I've got spinach between my teeth. You have some fancy friends, Alex."

"They're not fancy. Some of them just work in the public eye."

"So does my pharmacist, but it's not the same

thing, is it?"

"I want you to be comfortable with me."

"I'm trying, but it's sort of hard here."

"It's just a club."

"Right." She rolled her eyes. "And you're just the boy-next-door."

"In fairness," he said, moving an inch closer, "I'm probably not that guy."

Warning, warning.

Last year's headlines flashed before her eyes. The family of his dead girlfriend had tried to implicate him in her death. Although there had never been any charges or indication that Alex was guilty of anything, it was hard not to wonder.

There was clearly more to him than she realized.

Unfortunately, the air of mystery surrounding him lured her far too easily. She couldn't shake the sensation she was a mouse, distracted by a savory hunk of cheese, and that Alex was the skulking cat in the shadows.

His continued appraisal set her even more on edge. He didn't say anything else and just waited. The cat in her mind put forth its claws.

Lord, you're having fantasies now. What was the alcohol level in that Golden Oblivion anyway?

"Is that who you're looking for? The boy-next-door?"

His direct question shocked her even more than the display outside. "I'm not looking for anyone." *Don't sound so defensive.*

"Something then. Everyone comes to the Vegas Strip looking for something."

"Not me. This getaway was just something my

sister needed."

"And what do you need?"

"What makes you think I need anything?"

"Dana, I'm not an idiot."

For the first time since learning who Alex was, Dana began to feel a sense of futility. The man partied with starlets and socialites. And she thought she could seduce him just by slapping on a tight dress and some makeup?

Of course, he hadn't brought any starlets into the nook with him.

The music from outside took on a primal beat, almost echoing the throb in her chest, beat for beat.

Would any of those seemingly perfect people look at her and realize she wasn't quite right?

Would any of them glimpse the hole in her heart?

Just like that night at the tiki bar, Dana wanted to forget. So far, she'd only found one thing that helped her forget.

Alex.

So many negative thoughts had insinuated themselves into her inner dialogue and she was trying as hard as possible to combat them. Some days, it worked and she functioned like a normal human being.

Other days, not so much, and this was one of those days.

She needed to up the ante.

"Can I ask you another question?"

"Sure. Why not?"

"Why did you decide to come to my party?"

"Curiosity. Plus I figured the drinks here would

be better than at the joint down the street."

He unleashed that Zeus smile again. "I like you, Dana."

It was time to channel her own inner deity. "I like you too." She licked her lips. "But you know what would make me like you a lot better, Alex?"

"I'm all ears."

"If you shut those curtains, you'd be so much more likable."

"Well," he said, his voice scratchy, "I'd hate not to be likable."

Alex stood and walked over to the curtains. He released one curtain panel and then the other. When they met, there was only a sliver of space between them. People moved in front of them, outside the nook, but they might have been shadows. Sitting there was like being in her own world with him, one with the other partiers, but somehow apart.

Dana leaned back on the couch. She uncrossed her legs and then crossed them to the other side.

Alex's gaze followed.

"There," she said. "Isn't that better?"

He nodded, lips tight.

"You know, Alex. I often think of that night at the tiki bar. Do you?"

"It's all I fucking think about."

"Is that so?"

"I think you already knew that."

"Are you going to stand there all night long?"

"Tell me what you want me to do."

"Hmm. What would you like to do?" Dana was enjoying this dynamic. She hated playing the mouse. She was happier playing the cat.

160

"Honestly?"

"Honestly."

"I want to make you come again. I want to watch your face as you unravel. I want to hear your moans. I want to hear you whisper my name."

"I want the same things. What if I told you I wanted them right here?"

A tendon tightened in his neck. "I'd give them to you."

"Sit down, Alex."

He sat. This time, his posture turned rigid with anticipation.

Feeling a surge of power, Dana stood and moved in front of him, turning her back to him. As he spread his legs wide, she moved closer to him.

"Do you want to touch me?"

"Fuck, yes."

"Then touch me."

He traced her hips with his hands, squeezing the flesh of her thighs and ass. His fingers crept under the hem of her dress and he slowly rolled it up toward her waist.

Dana sucked in a breath.

Once her ass was exposed, along with her lacy black thong, Alex cursed again. He plumped each cheek, as if measuring how they fit in his hands. Then, gripping her hips, he pulled her close and kissed the spot right above her crack, licking her skin. He hooked one finger in her thong and slowly dragged it downward.

Even as desire pooled low in her belly, the most wonderful numbness overcame Dana. She stared straight ahead, unseeing. The interior of the nook became a wash of color. The music from the club was nothing more than a hum. All she knew was the heat of Alex's fingers and tongue. She surrendered to it, let it beat her into submission, even as she sought to reclaim her power.

As her thong reached her ankles, she stepped out of it.

Alex kissed every inch of her ass, dragging his tongue over her cheeks, stroking lazy circles on her skin. His hands moved up and down her jelly legs. Little by little, he eased her legs apart.

When his hand snaked between them, she sighed.

Yes. This.

Utter oblivion.

She didn't even care about the shadows beyond the curtains anymore. She might be almost completely exposed but she didn't have a care in the world when Alex touched her. Anyone could walk in at any time, but she wasn't bothered.

If anything, it heightened the sensation.

Alex really was dangerous. Maybe she was too.

His middle finger dipped inside her on a wave of new moisture. Spreading her juices, he circled her clit. She could come, just like this, but didn't want to.

"I want you on your knees."

His hand stopped moving. "Anything you want."

Dana stepped aside and sat on the sectional, laying back at one of the ends. She hooked one leg over the side of the couch and let the other fall open. To tease him, she touched herself.

Alex stood at the end of the couch. "Do you have

any idea how hot you look right now? You're a goddess."

"What should you be doing in the presence of a goddess, Alex?"

He fell to his knees. "Worshipping her."

Alex clutched at her hips as if receiving life from her body and buried his face between her thighs.

"Yes!"

His tongue flicked. His fingers explored. The steady rhythm of his head produced shudder after shudder in her. In a daze, she let her head fall back on the upholstery and her gaze landed on the curtains. Only a piece of fabric protected them from the outside world, but in that crazy moment, she dared the world to look at them.

Look at us! We're incredible.

His hands crept up her body to twist her nipples. Even under her dress and bra, they stiffened. Her breaths started to sound ragged, echoing the equally ragged breaths coming from him.

"You taste…" *Lick. Nibble. Lick.* "So good."

Dana wiggled, desperate for release.

He knew it too.

"What do you want from me, sweetheart?"

Abandonment. She wanted abandonment. "Make me come."

It was the only thing that would numb the pain that never quite went away.

His face set in furious determination, he suckled and suckled until her body seized. As the orgasm devastated her, it washed away her earlier reticence and softened the pain.

Her mind reeled. She wasn't sure if Alex had the

power to help her feel better, but he definitely had the ability to take her out of herself.

She liked it on the outside. Nothing could hurt her out there.

It was the inner darkness that terrified her.

He licked until her body issued its last quiver and even beyond. He licked until her deflated pile of nerves pricked into awareness once again.

Looking like a vengeful god, he seemed bent on making her come again, but she wasn't ready.

His touch had brought emotions and she didn't want any of those. They had no place here.

Dana tugged on his shoulder. "Thank you. I'm good."

Alex pulled away but looked at her sex with longing. "I'm not sure I am."

She wriggled away and reached for her thong. "Could I just have a minute?"

He nodded and moved in front of her. Surprising her, he took her thong and helped her into it, easing it over her ankles. Dana stood. With Alex on his knees before her, he slid the undergarment up her legs and over her hips. He took his time, adjusting the elastic as he went, making sure it sat perfectly on her. With gentle hands, he pulled her dress down. Only then did he look up. "Does it feel okay?"

Something about seeing him like that, catering to her, made her throat itch. The little gesture of tenderness set her off balance. Her inner goddess fled, her cover blown. All that remained was Dana. Damaged and all too mortal. "Yes, thanks."

"Can I sit with you?"

"Of course."

They sat together and he put his arm around her shoulder. Neither of them said anything for a while.

When he did speak, his voice cracked. "I liked doing that for you."

"It was amazing. I want to reciprocate."

"I want that too." Alex stared ahead, his gaze just as glassy as hers must have been a short time ago. "But not here. Not now."

In that moment, his inner god fled as well.

Had she ruined the moment by taking control? That couldn't be it. She might not know him well, but she didn't think Alex was the sort of man who had issues with strong women. Still, maybe she shouldn't have been so demanding.

His girlfriend had only been in the ground for a year. He was probably still hurting. It was entirely possible he hadn't been with anyone else since her. No doubt, Alex had plenty of women volunteering to help him take the edge off here and there, to say nothing of many men, but that didn't mean he wasn't still going through a period of grief.

What if they weren't ready for a relationship? She knew she wasn't, and yet she still wanted to feel his fire, his breath, his awe.

Whatever this was between them, she needed it.

Alex removed his hand from around her shoulder and lay it between them on the couch.

It was as if he'd taken all the heat out of the room. She wanted to snuggle against him and absorb his warmth again.

His eyes were vacant.

Was it possible he'd come to Vegas looking for

something too, something he hadn't yet found?

Dana squeezed his hand. "Alex, are you okay?"

"Yeah. Just thinking."

"About your girlfriend?"

He turned to her, his mouth open. "I'm sorry. Shitty timing, huh?"

"Grief can be like that. It has its own schedule and it doesn't usually respect ours. I never told you, but I'm so sorry for your loss."

"Thank you." His voice was soft. "I thought I had stopped missing Shannon but, in some ways, I still do. She was actually my ex by the time we went on that trip, but most people wouldn't know that. Our relationship was stormy from day one. There was so much I liked about her, but we spent all our time either arguing or fucking. There were never any peaceful moments. I could never sit here quietly with her, the way I am with you. She was always on the lookout for the next grand gesture. It was exhausting at times."

"I can imagine. Why do you think she needed grand gestures?"

"She had some bad relationships before I met her. They made her lose her trust. By the time I came around, she was ready to lump me in with the other guys. She constantly needed proof of how I felt and I got tired of having to prove myself. Things soured. Taking Shannon to Bermuda was a last-ditch attempt to make things better but it only made things worse. What we did just now...well, it's been a while since I've done that. I forgot how much I enjoyed it. I feel guilty for enjoying myself sometimes."

Maybe they had more in common than she thought.

Something shifted in Dana's chest. The fragmented pieces of her heart moved, seeking to reassemble. There was a hole there. She knew Alex would never fill it, but perhaps, given more time with him, she could throw a tarp over it and work around it.

"I want to get to know you better, Dana."

"I'd like—"

Viola's voice sounded from outside the nook. "Mr. Markov?"

Alex sighed. "Yes?"

"I'm so sorry to disturb you, but Wade is outside. He needs to speak to you. He says it's important."

"Okay. Thanks." He brushed Dana's hair from her face. "I should probably go, but I hate to leave you alone."

"I'm hardly alone here. Besides, I'm a big girl. Duty calls."

"Yeah." He stood. "I won't be long. Will you wait for me?"

"I'll wait."

"Good." Alex leaned over and kissed her on the cheek. It was quick and soft and it made her want to lean in for more. "I'll be right back."

As Alex left, her emotions crowded once again. She'd had one goal tonight, to flirt with him and feel better about herself. She hadn't planned on learning his story or feeling his pain.

She wasn't sure she had room in her soul for anyone else's right now.

And yet it sat there, like an unchecked lump, making her worry.

Dana's head swam. She put a hand to her forehead. "What is happening here?"

She couldn't deal with this right now.

It was time to return to her plan.

Her plan demanded she have another drink to forget everything that had happened. She wanted to be hazy around the edges. Another Golden Oblivion was the trick.

Rather than wait for Alex in their nook, she made her way over to the VIP bar and checked out the bartender's nametag. "Nathan, I don't suppose I could get another Golden Oblivion."

"You sure can." Nathan prepared the cocktail and moved it toward her. "Enjoy."

When she reached for her evening bag, he began to walk away.

She waved. "Wait. What do I owe you?"

"Nothing. Mr. Markov made it clear your money's no good here tonight."

"But that's not fair. I don't feel right accepting free drinks all night."

"Sorry. I like my job. I want to keep it."

Dana thanked the man and left him a fat tip. Resigned, she took another healthy sip of Golden Oblivion.

Just as sweet and spicy as the first. Nathan deserved that tip.

Happily drinking, Dana began to sway to the music but it wasn't loud enough in the private room. The DJ had just started playing one of her favorite tunes and she wanted to dance. She could wait for

Alex in the club.

Seeking another sort of oblivion, she headed down the dark hallway and joined the mass of bodies on the dance floor.

When the pulsing music threatened to sweep her away, she let it.

***

"You sure this couldn't wait until morning?" Alex fell into stride next to Wade. Although he tried to keep the frustration out of his voice, his grunt gave him away.

Why did he have to mention Shannon to Dana? He knew his relationship with Shannon had been fucked up. Did he have to act like he was too?

He still tasted Dana on his tongue. He'd never known such bliss as when he was between her legs, eating her to orgasm. After his shameful display back there, he'd likely never get another chance.

"No. You're gonna want to see this." Tight-lipped, Wade led the way back toward the massive main lobby of Vice and then across the casino floor.

"Let me guess. Are we having an *Ocean's Eleven* moment?"

"I wish."

Wade headed down the hallway leading to the dining room where the morning buffet was always held. This part of the hotel was closed off at night once the restaurant stopped serving. Away from the hub bub of the casino, it was quiet, almost eerie.

"One of my guys was on patrol in this area earlier and saw something you need to see," said

Wade. "It's usually dead here once the restaurant closes, but people still wander down here to use the bathrooms." He stopped short at the closed men's room door.

One of Wade's team members stood sentry outside the door. His face somber, he nodded at Alex.

Wade held the door open and Alex walked in, not sure what he expected to see. The smell of fresh paint hit him.

Someone had defaced the pristine white tilework. A message had been scrawled in enormous red paint letters.

Alex Markov is a murderer!

Some of the paint was still dripping, giving the message the appearance of blood. Each letter had to be about ten inches in height and the entire sentence ran across two full walls.

"It's fresh," said Wade. "Whoever did this, he can't be far."

Shannon's voice sounded in Alex's head. *It's all your fault.*

He cursed under his breath. "Call someone to clean this mess up."

"Alex, no. What we need to do is call the police."

"Because some gambler got drunk and decided to deface the washroom? Wade, come on. Don't waste their time."

"This isn't the work of a drunk. People don't exactly carry red paint around with them when they hit the casinos. Vice was targeted. *You* were targeted."

"Okay, fine. Maybe this was intentional. Still, no one's been hurt. As far as I can tell, this is just a case of mischief. You know as well as I do the cops will make a few notes, pat us on the backs, and tell us to install more security cameras."

"There aren't any cameras in the johns, of course, but there are a few outside. I've already got someone checking the footage from the ones in the hallway."

"Good. Once you see who it was, we can put this to bed."

"You're taking this calmly."

"I don't do hysterical."

"Alex, this sounds personal."

"Wade, I promise you someone's just having a laugh at my expense. I'm an easy mark and my name's been in the papers." As much as Alex tried to dismiss the message as the work of some inebriated fruitcake, his memory teased a fingernail down his back, making him bristle.

Murderer!

He'd almost forgotten about the letter.

Maybe he needed to be sensible here. "Look, I don't want to get the security team up in arms, but a letter came for me this week. Anonymous. It said the same thing."

Wade's face darkened. "I need to see it."

"Sure. It's in my office. I kept it, just in case."

"Why didn't you tell me?"

"Because I figured it was just some prick getting his jollies."

"Yeah, right. Just some prick, huh? I'm glad you kept it. It's evidence."

"Of what?"

"I can think of at least a dozen things and none of them good. How many of these letters did you get?"

"Just the one."

Wade paced the length of the washroom. "I don't like this."

"I'm sure it's nothing."

"It doesn't matter. It wouldn't be the first time the owner of Vice was threatened. Back when Liam was here, he got a few strange letters too. At the time, we figured they were from some environmental group who got their noses out of joint because he opened a third hotel instead of turning the land into a community garden. There was a lot of name calling, death threats, that sort of thing."

"Nice."

"Thankfully, that's all they were. Threats."

"Which is worse than what we have here. No one has threatened me. I'm not in danger." Alex waved at the paint job. "This is just the work of a sad, lonely troll. You know what people are like."

"Still."

"Wade, let's not get ahead of ourselves."

Wade's hum sounded less than convinced. "I can put guards on you twenty-four-seven."

"I don't want to go down that road."

"Alex…"

"I mean it. I don't need a security detail. We have guards all over the hotel and I'm always here.

172

It's a non-issue."

Wade scowled.

"I'm taking this seriously, I promise. I just don't want to make a mountain out of a mole hill." Alex peered at the painted message, shaking his head. "You'll let me know if anything comes up on the security cameras?"

"Yeah. I'd like to see that letter."

"Sure."

Wade spoke to the guard on duty. Alex then led him back toward his office. Despite wanting to believe the messages were nothing more than the work of trolls, a bead of perspiration dotted his upper lip. In spite of himself, he looked over his shoulder a couple of times.

He'd been doing that a lot lately.

The anonymous nature of the messages had him on edge. If someone had an issue with him, he should be man enough to confront him and tell him to his face.

He tried to think of who might want to rattle him like that but couldn't think of anyone who might hold that sort of grudge. As far as he knew, the only people who hated him were Shannon's family, but they'd never been shy about telling him so. They told everyone they could. Subterfuge wasn't exactly their style. The Deans, however, were in New York, not Nevada.

No, this was a hater, nothing more, and he'd already wasted too much time worrying about the pathetic loser. Now that Alex knew Liam had dealt with the same sort of deranged shit, it was easier to shelve his initial misgivings.

All he really wanted right now was to get back to Dana and make sure he hadn't ruined everything with his "woe is me" routine.

He liked her. She made him smile. She made him laugh. Not too many people managed that these days.

Back at his office, Wade examined the letter. "We might be dealing with a real sick fuck. We need to call the police."

"I don't want any bad publicity. I mean it, Wade. I'm sick to death of it."

"Alex, if this is the same person, there's a chance he's been on the property at least twice now. If that's the case, not only is he a danger to you, he could be a danger to others."

"You're right."

As Wade called the police, Alex texted Dana and let her know he might be a while. Without revealing all the details, he told her there was a situation in the hotel that needed his attention.

She didn't text back.

Maybe she had her phone on mute.

The police arrived in good time. Alex listened as Wade recounted the details.

"Mr. Markov," one of the officers asked, "can you think of anyone who might want to upset you?"

"Honestly? It could be anyone." In building his company, he probably had offended numerous people. It came with the territory when one had to make decisions. Could this be the work of a disgruntled contractor or former employee? Somehow, he couldn't credit any past or present associates with that much hate.

Only three people in the world hated him. Shannon's parents and her brother Gordon. They'd all made it abundantly clear. And yet something prevented him from mentioning the Deans by name.

Wade didn't share his misplaced loyalty. "Someone needs to talk to the parents of Shannon Dean. A year later, they're still trying to pin her death on Alex." Wade sat up. "And don't forget the paparazzi. They've been hanging around. A couple of them are real scummy. I can give you names."

Wade provided those details, making sure to spend a few minutes detailing exactly how Bill Patterson had tormented both Alex, as well as Liam in the past. It seemed Patterson didn't simply stalk the halls at Vice. He'd basically parked himself outside the administrative offices during the period when Liam was being harassed by the environmental group. Patterson had bothered numerous employees at the time, digging for dirt on Liam. Of course, he'd never uncovered anything because there was nothing to uncover.

It hadn't stopped him from being a nuisance.

Alex kept an eye on the office clock. He'd been gone for an hour, if not more.

There was no way Dana would have waited.

Pacing his office, Alex almost didn't hear the police officer when he said they were done. The cops handed them both cards, told them to contact them if anything else happened, and left.

Alex thanked Wade for his persistence. The men shook hands and Wade returned to his work.

By the time Alex was making his way back to the club, his dander was up. His shoulders tense, he reminded himself to breathe.

Whatever was going on, they would get to the bottom of it.

Rolling his shoulders, he realized he looked forward to seeing Dana even more now.

When he finally reached the door to Covet, he spotted her right away.

Two guys were grinding up against her on the dancefloor, sandwiching her. Her eyes were glazed. She barely moved and seemed to be held up by the two men, rather than by the power of her legs.

As red flashed before Alex's eyes, he dashed into the crowd and put his hands on both men's shoulders. "Back off."

"Hey, man," said one of them. "This is our party. Go get your own."

His hands curled into fists. "I said, back the fuck off."

The men scurried away.

Dana's eyes widened, barely, and recognition lit them up. "Alex! You're here." She pulled on his arm. "Dance with me."

He grabbed her by the arms. "Not right now. Look at me, Dana."

She swayed. "I love this song. Do you love this song?"

"It's a good song. Is your sister around?"

"I don't know. I never found her. Maybe she went outside. Oh! But I met Ron and Dave. They're such nice guys."

"Yeah, real nice. Listen to me. Did Ron and Dave bring you drinks?"

"Nope. I told you, I'm a big girl. I got my own

drinks."

At least it didn't appear she'd been roofied. "I'm taking you back to your suite. Where's your key card?"

"In my bag." She looked at her empty hands. "Wait. Where's my bag?"

He extricated it from around her shoulders. "It's right here. Do you mind if I open it so I can get your key?"

"Go ahead." She rested her head on his shoulder and grinned. "There was something I wanted to say to you...oh, yeah! I like you, Alex."

"I like you too."

"You have a very tight ass. Did anyone ever tell you that?"

He led her out of the club. "Not lately."

"Well, you do and you deserve to know. I would so hit that."

"I'm glad, but I think you need to hit your bed right now."

"Only if you hit it with me."

When her lips curled into a smile of flirtation, he found himself wishing she was sober. "Dana, I'm going to ask you a question and I want you to be honest with me. How many drinks did you have while I was gone?"

She held up two fingers. "The Golden Oblivions are so much better than the drinks I had in my room."

"You drank before as well?"

"A little. But I think you need to talk to your bar staff. That last one was stronger than the others." She giggled. "I'm not a very good drunk, am I?"

As they left, she stumbled. The bouncer at the door stepped forward. "Need some help, Mr. Markov?"

"No, thanks. I'm good."

"You're so, so good, Alex," drawled Dana. "You're the best."

When she stumbled again, Alex picked her up. She gave a *whoop*, like a kid who'd just boarded her first rollercoaster. With her in his arms, he carried her down one of the quieter hallways toward the private elevators for the penthouse level.

As he got closer to the elevators, she hiccupped. "Oh." She began to turn green and touched her belly. "That doesn't feel good."

"Hang in there. We're almost home."

At the elevator, he swiped her key card and hurried inside, careful not to knock her feet on the walls.

When the elevator started moving, the green tinges in her face turned grey. "You'd better put me down. I may have to make a run for it."

He gently set her on her feet, cursing the elevator. Even though he knew it wasn't moving slowly, it seemed to crawl. He reached for her arm to support her but she surprised him by falling into his embrace. He stiffened and then wrapped his arms around her. For some reason, the gesture seemed even more intimate than what they'd done at Covet. "I've got you. It's going to be all right."

She smelled so good, fruity and powdery all at once, but he resisted the urge to bury his nose in her hair.

Alex had known they were crossing a threshold

when they entered the private nook at Covet, but this outcome caught him off guard. It had been some time since he'd cared for a woman and he wasn't sure what to do with the emotions that now hammered his chest.

She mumbled against his shirt but he couldn't tell what she was saying. Surely she could hear how hard his heart was beating.

When they got to the fifth floor, he sighed. "We're here."

Her chest heaved as they left the elevator, but not with the spasms of nausea. She was quietly sobbing.

"Dana, sweetheart. Are you all right?"

"No."

It was such a small, quiet word, and yet no sound had ever hurt his heart quite so much.

Whatever she was going through, it cut deeper than he'd ever imagined. She wasn't just hurt.

She was devastated.

Her face was streaked with tears.

"Hey." He touched her chin. "Don't cry. I'll make sure you're okay."

"I'm not okay." She sniffed. "I'm defective."

"What do you mean?"

"Nothing works inside me. I'm broken."

"No, you're not. You're just feeling a little sick right now. Come on. Let's get you to your room."

She continued to cry softly as they walked to her suite. What did she mean by saying she was defective? Her strange words put him even more on edge.

He unlocked her suite and helped her inside. As soon as he turned on the light, she lurched and groaned. Knowing what was coming, Alex followed her as she raced to the bathroom. She dropped to the floor before the toilet, one high heel on and the other falling off, and vomited what looked like a thousand Golden Oblivions.

Fuck. Just how much had she had? She hadn't looked anywhere near tipsy when he left her.

Alex kneeled behind her. With a gentle hand, he pulled her curls back and made a ponytail in his hand. He rested his other hand on her upper back, slowly rubbing. "Let it out. It needs to come out."

Her sobs continued between spasms and his guilt skyrocketed. He never should have left her alone.

Just as he never should have left Shannon alone that night.

He wouldn't make that mistake again. Dana needed his help, perhaps in more ways than one.

I'm broken.

Her words haunted him and he knew they would keep haunting him until she explained herself. He might not have a right to question her. He barely knew her, but he wanted to know her. This thing may have begun as pure sexual interest, but it was changing, and he wasn't sure he had the power to stop it.

She groaned. "Oh, God. I'm disgusting."

"No, you're not." Vomit or no vomit, she was the furthest thing from disgusting. Even still, Dana was a proud woman. He didn't think she'd remember this moment fondly.

Her body calmed. She breathed in and out and eventually grew very still.

"Better?"

"Maybe. Not really."

"I'm going to get you a washcloth. Just rest." Keeping an eye on her, Alex stood and reached for a clean washcloth from underneath the vanity, dampening it with warm water. He handed it to her. "Here you go."

She took it and wiped her face. She then angled her face toward him. Her beautiful brown eyes pinned him to his spot. When her lip wobbled, he knew he was a goner.

"I'm sorry." Her quiet voice insinuated itself into his heart. "I don't know what came over me."

"It's okay."

"No, it's not. Would you believe it if I told you this isn't like me? I don't drink a lot of alcohol, I really don't."

"I believe it."

She touched her forehead with a shaky hand. "My head's spinning."

"I'm sure it is. I'll help you over to the bed. I'm going to call someone to get your sister."

"No." She moaned. "Not her."

"Why not?"

"She'll judge me."

"Dana, you're hardly a raging drunk."

"It's not that. I'm just always in control and I feel so weak right now. I don't want her to lecture me." Supporting herself on his arm, she kicked off her remaining heel and got to her feet. "Are you going to lecture me?"

"No. We've all been there."

"You haven't been where I am right now."

"We all feel weak from time to time. I know I

181

have. We're all human."

She didn't look convinced as she poked his biceps. "I don't know. This feels genetically enhanced to me."

She was definitely operating under a little buzz and it clearly hadn't worn off yet. "I promise, I'm all natural."

When they made it to the bed, she noticed the sick on the front of her dress. "Shit. I just bought this. It cost a mint."

"I'll send it to dry-cleaning for you. They'll take care of it." And if they didn't, he'd find her a new one. "I can wait outside if you want to change."

"No." She spun and almost fell.

Alex righted her, pulling her to him. His hand landed on her hip. Her very luscious hip.

She looked at him, her face full of awe and sadness. "You look like Zeus."

"Are you saying I look like an old man?"

"No, young Zeus. Glorious Zeus. You light up the sky."

His voice grew husky. "I think the drink's just making you see lightning bolts."

"Not lightning bolts," she whispered. "Stars."

Alex let out the breath he was holding. He needed to stop this before he lost track of his good sense.

Steadying her, he removed his hands from her body. Being alone with her in her room, having her in his arms, was too much of a temptation. He wanted Dana, but this wasn't the way he wanted her.

When he held her, and he would again, he

wanted her completely sober, willing, and excited. Not with tears streaking her face.

She touched his chest, trailing her finger down to his abdomen. "Maybe you could just help me with the zipper and turn your back while I change?" The look in her eye made it clear she wasn't so fussed about the turn your back part.

"I would love to, but I don't think that's a good idea right now."

"Alex, come on. You can't tell me you're not up for it. I know you are."

"I am, and I wish we'd had more time at Covet tonight." He cupped her cheek. "But it was never my plan to get you drunk, and it was definitely not my plan to take advantage of you. If I'd known you had those other drinks…."

"It was just a couple of tiny bottles from the minibar."

"It doesn't matter. Dana, you were just in tears."

"I'm not crying now."

"Will you please talk to me? I want to help you."

"There's only one way you can help me right now." She touched his cock.

Her touch was electric, stimulating every nerve ending in his body. *Goddammit*. He hardened, in spite of himself.

"Please, Alex." Her eyes watered again. "I need to forget."

Gritting his teeth, he removed her hand. "Forget what?"

"Never mind. I know when I'm not wanted."

"You are an incredibly desirable woman and I would like nothing more than to take you to bed and show you how much I want you. But right now, I think you need to talk to somebody, and seeing as you won't talk to me, I'm going to call for your sister."

Mumbling in discontent, Dana flopped down onto the bed and put her head on the pillow.

He took the opportunity to call one of his assistants at Covet and told him to look for Viola. She would round up Anise and the other women. After he made the call, he pulled up a chair next to the bed, facing Dana.

Her eyes were closed, and for a few minutes, she appeared to be asleep. But then she moved her legs, the long limbs sliding against each other, and opened her eyes. She looked right at him. "You're still here, huh?"

"Yeah."

"I've embarrassed myself."

"Don't be embarrassed."

"Right. I guess women throw themselves at you left, right, and center, huh? You're used to it."

"You'd be surprised at how few women throw themselves at me. Nowadays, I barely need to duck when they fly past my head. I just step aside."

"Ha ha." Her lashes lowered. For a couple of long minutes, she seemed to be doing nothing more than contemplating his shoe. "Alex?"

"Yeah?"

"I'm glad you're here."

"I'm glad I'm here too. I want to make sure you're okay."

"Why do you care?"

"I'd rather have that conversation when you're

184

sober."

"So you *do* want to have that conversation?"

He leaned forward, hands on his knees. "I do and we will, but right now, you need to rest."

Her eyelids fluttered closed but the skin around them pinched, as if she was trying hard to shut out a bad memory. That, or she was fending off another bout of nausea.

He began to fidget. When he caught his knees bouncing up and down, he forced himself to sit still. Instead, he passed a hand over his face. Her perfume lingered on his fingers. So fucking sweet.

He wanted to smell her up close, to touch her and taste her again and show her pleasures she'd never known before.

It went deeper than animal attraction too. He was amazed he could feel so much for someone so quickly. Her pain made him feel sick inside.

He needed to take her pain away. It was that simple.

The sound of female voices outside the door drew him from his daydreams.

There was a knock. "Dana, it's me. Can you let me in?"

Dana really had fallen asleep this time so Alex padded to the door. He opened it and put a finger on his lips. "She's asleep."

Bea and Jessica gawked but Anise's eyes hardened. "I'd like to see her," she said, pushing past him.

He stood aside.

Anise hurried into the bedroom and they followed. When she saw her sister on the bed, she

185

ran over and crouched next to her. She ran a hand over her hair. "Honey? Dana, are you okay?" Her angry gaze darted toward Alex. "What did you do to her?"

"I didn't hurt her. She just had a bit too much to drink."

"She had one cocktail!"

"Actually, she told me she had a couple of drinks on her own before ever coming to the party. I had to leave to take care of something and she had more when I was gone."

"What?" Anise paled. "This isn't like her. She can barely tolerate half a glass of wine."

"As far as I can tell, she's been drinking much more than that since she got here. She was sick and wobbling, so I convinced her to lie down."

"I bet you did."

"I can assure you nothing happened."

"Oh, right. Not a single thing happened in the VIP suite. Let me guess. You were all just sitting around, reading passages from the New Testament?"

Dana's eyes cracked open. "Stop yelling at Alex."

"I'm not yelling," yelled Anise.

"He didn't do anything wrong. He helped me. Now if you can't say 'thank you' like a normal person, you can just leave."

It meant the world that Dana would jump to his defense, but it didn't make the ball of nerves in his gut dissipate. He didn't want her to think badly of him, and the last thing he needed was to be accused of taking advantage of the situation.

Everyone got quiet. Jessica and Bea finally expressed their thanks, but Anise remained close-lipped.

It was clearly time to make his exit even though he hated to leave Dana to her sister. He doubted the inquisition was over yet. "I'll leave you to it. Good night."

"Wait." Dana rose up on her elbow. When she let out a slow stream of breath, he knew lifting her head had taken a lot out of her. "Alex, thank you."

"For what?" For leaving her alone and giving her a chance to get wasted? Hardly his best moment.

"For holding my hair back."

Her tired voice flipped a switch in him. With those few words, he was transformed from a protective man into an overprotective beast. He wanted to banish her sister and friends, claw her to him and hold her in his lap. However, he controlled his inner grizzly bear. "You're welcome. I hope you feel better."

She nodded and lay back down. He walked out of the bedroom and over to the suite door.

Anise followed. She gripped the door, suddenly more intimidating than his biggest, meanest bouncer.

"Just so you know," he said, "I didn't realize she'd had those drinks. I wouldn't take advantage of her."

"Good night, Alex."

Thanks to her tone and bitter smile, when her words reached his ears, they sounded a lot more like *Fuck you, Alex.*

"Good night."

Exhausted and uncomfortable, he headed to the elevator.

The party might continue into the early morning but it would have to continue without him.

Chapter Seven

"I don't know." Anise held up a purse in the Fendi shop at Caesars Palace the next day. She inspected the bag's intricate stitching. "It costs a lot and it's really showy. Do you think it screams, 'I just got divorced and now I'm on a spending spree?'"

"Hell, yes," said Bea. "Since when is there anything wrong with that?"

"You should treat yourself," agreed Jessica.

"I've been treating myself since I got here. Two new outfits and three pairs of shoes. Maybe the purse is a bit much." Anise put the purse back down on the display.

Bea picked it up again and placed it in her hands. "Buy the purse. You'll regret it if you don't."

"I guess you're right. It's a good thing we go home in a couple of days. I can't believe how quickly the week is flying by." Anise smiled but it faded when she glanced at Dana. "What do you think? You're awfully quiet this morning."

"That's because this is her second walk of shame

this week." Jessica laughed.

Dana slid her sunglasses up the bridge of her nose. "The only thing I'm ashamed of is having one too many drinks. It was a good thing Alex was around to help me to my room."

"Oh, right," Anise drawled. "Alex, your savior."

"What's that supposed to mean?"

"Do I have to spell it out?"

"Look, like it or not, he did help me when I was sick." Dana stiffened. "I just don't like the fact I put him in that position."

Anise put her hands on her hips. "Which position was that? The one where he put a drunken woman in bed without telling her family first?"

"Anise, you're not being fair."

"I'm being sensible. What were you thinking? Alex could have done anything to you in that room. For all I know, he put something in your drink."

"He didn't. He wouldn't hurt me."

"Um, excuse me," Anise argued. "But how would you know? You know nothing about the man."

"What do you have against him anyway? He's been good to us."

"And now we know why." Anise waved her hand in the direction of Dana's body. "He wants a piece of this."

"Just give it a rest, would you?"

"Someone around here needs to keep a clear head. I always thought you were that person but I guess my turn has come."

"A clear head, I don't mind," said Dana, "but I could do without the lectures. We're in Las Vegas, for God's sake. At any given time, there are over a hundred people in the general vicinity who are drunker than I was last night."

"I just think Tommy would be extremely worried if he knew you'd put yourself in that position," continued Anise. "What are you going to tell him? *Are* you going to tell him?"

"Why should I?"

"He's your fiancé! He'd be out of his mind if he knew. I never should have left you alone in that private room."

Dana sighed. "Anise, give it up. I promise you, Tommy isn't concerned about me at all."

He had texted her another three times before breakfast but no one needed to know that. Three more cryptic messages about needing to talk to her as soon as possible.

"Well, I just think if roles were reversed," said Anise, her voice cracking, "and you were sitting at home, you'd want to know you could trust him."

Since when was her sister so concerned about Tommy anyway? They'd always gotten along but Anise had never been the sort to leap to his defense in any matter.

The sudden shift in loyalty stuck in Dana's craw.

"Uh, guys." Bea put a hand on both their shoulders. "We're supposed to be having fun."

"And people are watching." Jessica waved at a couple of women who'd stopped to observe the argument. "Thank you, ladies. Next show is at seven. We'll pop some popcorn. Bring your friends."

The spectators walked away.

Anise scratched the side of her nose, a nervous habit she'd had since she was a kid. She reached for Dana's hand. "I'm sorry. My older sister side got out of hand."

"No kidding. I'm usually the one lecturing you."

"Don't I know it?" Anise shook her head. "Dana, I don't trust Alex. He's from a different world than we are. He's used to people doing anything he wants, giving him anything he wants. For God's sake, he snaps his fingers and everyone bows before him. Did you see all those people fawning over him? And that VIP room was just pretentious. I said it before and I'll say it again. It was fake. Everything about that whole scene was fake."

"It's a nightclub. It's all about fantasy."

"Fantasy is fine, but you have a man at home waiting for you. Have you told Alex about that little piece of reality?"

Dana was silent. Once again, she wanted to explain but she couldn't do it here, in a purse shop.

"Alex and his celebrity friends might be able to fly around the country at a moment's notice and party all night long," said Anise, "but people like us have responsibilities. At the end of this week, Alex can still frolic all he wants on the Strip. A month from now, he'll have forgotten all about you and will be in the pool, sitting on a floatie with one of those bikini-clad honeys. Not us. In a few days, we'll go back to our regular lives. I don't want you to get caught up in the fantasy and ruin what you have with Tommy."

She had nothing with Tommy. "I'm not getting caught up in the fantasy. I promise."

Yeah, right. She'd called the man Zeus.

"Are you sure?"

She'd never been more unsure in her life.

Dana understood what her sister was trying to do. Anise only wanted to save her from messing up her life.

If only she knew how messed up it really was.

A pregnant woman and her husband walked into the Fendi shop just then. As she crossed the threshold, the woman touched her belly and squealed. "John, the baby's kicking!"

Dana stared at the woman's swollen tummy.

Her husband rested his hand on her protruding stomach, his face bright with amazement. "Oh, man. That's incredible. Our little guy has strong legs."

Dana's hand moved to her belly.

No man would ever touch her with the same sense of wonder. She would never lay in bed with her husband, feeling for kicks under the covers.

The pregnant lady and her husband walked by Dana. As they passed, she heard the husband tell his wife, "I'm so proud of you. You're just amazing."

"Are you even listening to me?" Anise touched Dana's elbow. "I wish Tommy was here to talk some sense into you."

Dana yanked her arm away as all her rage finally issued in a loud grunt. "Tommy, Tommy, Tommy. All I ever hear about is fucking Tommy. You know what your precious Tommy would do if he was here? He'd make a run for the door. That man could not care *less* about what I get up to with Alex Markov, or anyone else. In fact, he'd probably encourage me to sleep with him, and you know why? Because then I'd be someone else's problem!"

"What the hell?" Anise stood shell-shocked, and so did Bea and Jessica. "What are you saying?"

"Tommy dumped me. Okay? Let's be real clear on that. He dumped my ass." She lowered her voice, running out of steam. "Months ago. I stopped being the woman of his dreams, and God help the woman who takes my place. Tommy made it perfectly clear he has a certain *type*. You can stop worrying about whether he's pining over me at home. He isn't. I owe that man nothing. Not my loyalty, not my respect, and definitely not my faithfulness. He doesn't need them. He doesn't care."

Everyone in the store fell silent.

"So I don't need your lectures, sis. Save them for someone else. I'm a free bird, and this bird has places to fly."

Before Anise or anyone else could respond, Dana turned and walked out of the shop.

***

"Hey, Patterson. Leon wants to see you in his office first thing."

Bill Patterson was just about to take his first slurp of coffee when he heard his co-worker's summons from down the hall. He lowered his cup, sighed, and turned around.

What the hell did his editor want now?

Probably to ride his ass some more. Leon Parkes had complained about Bill's quality of work for some time.

Everyday, the Strip is littered with famous people, most of them misbehaving, and you can't find me a story?

He was trying, God knew he was trying. Bill had basically tried to camp out in the vicinity of Vice, going there at all sorts of odd hours, but he still hadn't dug up any dirt on Alex Markov. At least nothing that hadn't been heard before.

It didn't help that Markov's security team was on to him. He'd tried to sneak in a couple of times over the past two days but had been escorted out promptly. They knew his face too well. There were days when he imagined they had his picture pinned up in the security office. Wade Kennedy and his fellow goons probably threw darts at it on their breaks.

He needed to step up his game.

He knocked on Leon's open door. "You wanted to see me, boss?"

Leon barely glanced up from his laptop. "Come in. Shut the door."

Bill shut it. This couldn't be good. Leon always kept the door open.

"Take a seat, Bill."

As he pulled up a chair, it squeaked on the floor, making him wince.

The editor made a steeple of his hands and hit him with his laser glare of death. "You promised me a story on Markov. Where is it?"

"I'm working on it."

"You've been working on it for months, but all you've brought me is photos of the man walking through Vice, and not even good ones at that. Not exactly incriminating evidence."

"This is the sort of story that takes time. I'm building up a relationship of trust between me and a couple of the employees."

"Bullshit. I hear you can't even get through the door anymore."

Bill hung his head. He had no real explanations for why this wasn't clicking. It never used to be this way. When he was a younger man, his journalistic exploits were legendary in this town. He was the one who'd discovered the actress Eleanor Fisher was cheating on her doctor husband with a male stripper. The woman was a Hollywood outcast now thanks to his photos, and rightly so. If you were going to flaunt your ass all over the Strip, you deserved every moment of shame that followed. He didn't take her to that nudie bar. He wasn't the one who told her to get plastered. He just took the pictures.

And what about that time he outed Dr. Mike Flanagan, the respected Vegas plastic surgeon? The LGBTQ community had been up in arms about him outing the man. Tell that to his long-suffering wife of thirty years.

Bill was good at his job and it was for one basic reason. He understood that every person who walked the planet was dirty. Scratch anyone's polished veneer and you'd see the pile of ugly secrets underneath. Everyone had a story, and most of them were vile.

"Are you seriously wasting my time by daydreaming in my office?"

His editor's reprimand brought him back to harsh awareness.

"I need you to give up this ridiculous idea that Markov is hiding bodies somewhere in his luxury hotel and get me a real story."

"But it is a real story. I've been in touch with the Dean family numerous times. They said—"

"The Dean family needs to move on and so do you. If you do talk to them, maybe suggest some grief counseling or anger management. I don't know and I don't care. I'm not in the business of fixing people here."

"But—"

Leon silenced him with a hand and then opened one of his desk drawers. He pulled out a familiar bottle of vodka.

As a terrible thirst made Bill's tongue sweat, he dragged his eyes from the bottle and played dumb. "We having a drink?"

"Bill, this was found in your desk."

"What? No. Not my desk."

"I found it myself."

When perspiration erupted on Bill's forehead, he realized playing dumb might not be the best tactic. He mustered up some righteous indignation. "You went through my stuff?"

"Oh. Did you expect privacy here? Shame. I guess you thought you were working for *The Washington Post* or something."

"Give it back."

"No, my friend." Leon put the bottle back in his desk drawer. "I need you to understand something and I need you to understand it before you leave this office. This is your last warning. Dry up, forget Markov, and get me a real story. Have I made myself clear?"

"Sure. Clear."

"Now get out of here." Leon returned to frowning at his laptop.

His hands shaking, Bill pushed back the chair, cursing that goddamn squeak again. He backed out of Leon's office, trying to think of something he could say that would salvage his dying career.

But there was nothing to say.

He would have to prove it with his actions.

He knew Markov was hiding something, and he would find it.

***

"The first set of images from your security cameras are grainy," said Detective Bell. He fanned out an array of photos on the police station desk.

Alex perused the photos. Because they were taken from a distance, he couldn't make out the facial features of the rogue painter. It was clearly a man. He was dressed in painter's overalls with a black hoodie underneath. Sure enough, he carried a can of paint. From this vantage point, he looked like half the guys in Facilities.

"But then," said Detective Bell, "we found this one."

Finally, a closeup.

Alex gawked. He knew that face.

"Do you know this man?"

"Yeah." His shoulders slumped. "It's Gordon

Dean, Shannon's brother."

Alex hadn't seen him in person in a long time, but he'd recognize him anywhere. The short brown hair, the beefy features, the crooked nose.

Gordon hadn't even tried to disguise his appearance. In fact, he seemed to have known exactly where the security camera was. In the photo, he was looking straight at the camera, grinning.

Daring them to recognize him.

"He's here then and he's been in my hotel."

"We've been in touch with his parents. Jill and Ned Dean are on vacation. Costa Rica. They were surprised to hear Gordon was in Las Vegas."

"Yeah, right. They probably put him up to it."

"How well do you know Shannon's brother?"

"We weren't exactly friends. Before Shannon died, I met him a few times but we were never chummy. He lived in Albany so we didn't see each other often. One or two family events. He's a consultant. Gordon's the guy you call when you need to downsize a thousand people. He helps companies with their dismissals."

"He used to," corrected Detective Bell. "Gordon Dean was downsized himself about a month ago. We spoke to his employer. He didn't take it well. They had to call police to escort him out of the building when he was let go."

"I see."

"Alex, did he blame you for Shannon's death?"

"Yeah. They all did. I tried to reach out to the family, to explain. They all made it clear they wanted nothing to do with me. Gordon had a few words for me on the phone about two weeks after she died. That was the last time I spoke to him."

"Until we can establish his whereabouts, I need you to be very careful. I can assign some plainclothes officers to the hotel."

"Okay. I guess that would be best."

"I have every expectation Gordon Dean will try to make another statement. His state of mind is a concern. We'll be looking for him but I want you to watch your step."

Alex stood. "Don't worry. Any funny business, I'll let you know."

Chapter Eight

Alex was just about to call it a day on Friday when his assistant buzzed him on his office phone. It had been a long day. After his visit to the police station, he'd been on edge. Everywhere he looked, he expected to see Gordon Dean materialize.

What did Gordon want from him? An apology? An admission of guilt?

As for apologies, Alex had tried. Right from the start, he'd tried. Neither Gordon nor his parents wanted to hear a word from him. He'd tried to explain what happened the night Shannon died, at least as much as he understood himself. They'd made it clear they weren't open to hearing his interpretation. In their eyes, he'd taken away their baby girl and they would never forgive him.

As for admissions of guilt, if that's what Gordon wanted, he'd be waiting a long time. Shannon's death had been ruled accidental. It was a tragedy but nothing about it had been premeditated on either of their parts. The police had made it clear Alex was never even a suspect, even though the rag magazines liked to imply he was one.

Maybe if he'd made more of an effort to get to know Shannon's family, this wouldn't be happening now. However, because Alex's relationship with Shannon had been tempestuous at the best of times, visits with the family had never been on the menu.

It had been hard enough keeping their life on an even keel.

He'd gone so far as to offer to pay for grief counseling for the Deans. They'd thrown his offer back in his face, as if it was an insult. He didn't like the idea they were still suffering but he couldn't make them accept his help.

And now Gordon was stalking him.

He felt for the man, he really did. It sounded as if he'd had a shitty year. If Alex had lost his livelihood, he probably would have lost his mind with it. His work was the only thing that had kept him going in those horrible months after Shannon's death.

Maybe, if he ran into Gordon, he could talk some sense into him. Maybe he was now in a position to accept his help.

The memory of Gordon's smile in the security footage unnerved Alex. It wasn't the smile of a man who was crying out for assistance.

It was the smile of a man who had nothing left to lose.

Alex hoped he was wrong, because all the sympathy in the world wouldn't stop him from protecting what was his.

It wasn't until his assistant buzzed a second time that Alex remembered he hadn't responded. "Yes,

Trevor?"

"Alex, I have a Ms. Hamill hoping to meet with you. She doesn't have an appointment."

"That's okay. Send her up."

As Alex walked toward the office elevator, his body tensed. Dana wanted to see him and he knew this meeting had to be some sort of reckoning. He was tired of dancing around her. He'd admitted he wanted her. If she was coming to see him, she would either tell him to take a hike or that she wanted him as well.

He'd thought about her today, hoping she hadn't suffered too much of a hangover. Did she have any regrets?

Did she miss him like he missed her?

Christ. He'd never been so on edge about a woman before. She had definitely done something to him.

Maybe this stalker situation was heightening his emotions. All he knew for sure was that he wanted to draw Dana close and never let her go.

He didn't have time to ponder his emotions. The elevator door opened and she took a tentative step into the room. "Oh, hi."

"Hi." Everything in the room lit up. It might be night time but she'd managed to bring the sun with her.

"You're right there. I was expecting some sort of office."

"This is my office but I also live here. It's an odd floorplan, I know. My predecessor's idea. I don't mind it, though. No one can get up here unless they get escorted by security or buzzed in by Trevor." He looked her up and down. She looked fresh and sexy in a white blouse, grey dress pants, and low heels, even though regret had placed some shadows under her eyes. "How are you today?"

"I'm all right."

"Really?"

"Okay. I've been better."

"Rough night?"

"Yeah, you could say that. A rough day too."

"Can I get you a coffee?" He gestured to the Keurig in the office seating area.

"I can't even tell you how much I would love a coffee right now. I don't want to keep you, though. I know you're busy."

"I'm never too busy for you."

Her eyelashes lowered.

As he walked over to the coffee machine, he realized he didn't even know how she took her coffee. There were so many things he didn't know, things that now seemed imperative to find out. "How do you take it?"

"Black, please."

Just like him. For some reason, it made him smile. He prepared a couple of coffees and handed one to her. They sat in the seating area, on either side of the glass coffee table.

Dana took a demure sip and placed her mug on the table. Whatever she had to say, she wasn't ready to say it.

"I tried to call you this morning."

"You did?" She whipped out her cell phone and rolled her eyes. "Sorry about that. I turned it off earlier."

"Too many telemarketers calling?"

"Something like that." She reddened. "I'm sorry I missed your call."

"It was nothing important. I just wanted to make sure you were okay after last night."

"That's nice of you." She looked around. "This is a cool office. Very streamlined. Not what I expected. Or maybe it is."

"I'm a simple man. My needs are basic."

"Yeah, right." Her huff held amusement rather than cynicism. "Basic."

He leaned back on the trim grey sofa, one ankle propped up on his other knee. "You're looking much better today."

"Oh, God, Alex. I look like crap. My eyes are red and puffy. I've had to hide behind sunglasses all day because the light hurts. My skin is sallow and I'm still not convinced I'm done throwing up. I had no idea I was such a pitiful drunk."

Was her skin sallow, her eyes puffy? He hadn't noticed. "You look good to me."

Dana shifted in her seat and swallowed a gulp of coffee. "I want to apologize. This is turning into a habit. I'm beyond embarrassed."

"You don't need to apologize."

"I ruined your evening and I'm pretty sure I got puke on your shirt."

"You didn't ruin my evening or my shirt. Far from it."

"But you saw me at my worst."

"That was your worst? You're going to have to do a lot more than that to scare me away." His throat grew thick. "Besides, I liked looking after you. I hated leaving you."

Her eyes grew big and wide.

Alex stood and walked over to the other couch, sitting next to her. "So did Anise lecture you?"

"Yeah. She's not used to seeing me go off the rails."

"Are you going off the rails?"

"I haven't embarrassed myself today yet, so there's hope. I know my sister means well. It's just hard to take."

"She loves you." He grinned. "And it never hurts to have a bulldog for a sister. We should all be so lucky."

"I finally told her about Tommy dumping me. I blurted it out at a bad moment and walked off. She's been avoiding me since."

"I'm sorry."

"It was my own fault. In trying to spare her any extra pain, I only caused more."

"She'll forgive you."

"We'll see." Dana sighed. "Do you have any brothers or sisters?"

"No." Alex paused. "I wish I did, though. My parents were in their forties when they had me. They'd both spent a lot of time concentrating on their careers and when they finally decided to start a family, there were problems. My mom's never talked a lot about it but she told me there were several miscarriages before I came along. After me, they stopped trying for other children."

"I can imagine. That must have been hard on your parents."

"I'm sure it was. To lose a child, at any stage…"

"Are you okay? You spaced out there for a second."

He grasped her hand. It felt smooth and cool in his own and he enjoyed stroking his thumb over her palm. "I'm all right. Really."

"I didn't mean to bring up a difficult topic."

"You didn't. Our little family might not be what my parents envisioned, but we were happy. I'm one of the lucky ones. I grew up loved and healthy and supported. If I'm fucked up in any way, it's my own fault, not my parents'."

"You're close to them."

He chuckled. "Yeah. In fact, my mother calls me at least once a week to ask me when I'm going to give her grandbabies. I've assured her at least six of the seven will be named after her."

"So you *do* want kids? You know, one day?"

"One day, yeah. Kids would be great."

Dana's face turned grey.

"Hey, are you okay?"

She reached for her coffee cup and brought it to her lips. When she sat it down again, it clattered. "Still a bit hung over, I guess."

"Listen, you didn't come here for my life story."

"I just really wanted to apologize for my behavior. I should go."

When she reached for her handbag, Alex grabbed her hand. "Don't leave. We need to talk. Please."

She set her handbag back down.

"I can't stop thinking about you."

She stiffened. "That's a shame. A busy man like you must have lots to do. I'd hate to get in your way."

"You're not. I like thinking about you."

"Alex, don't."

"Don't what?"

"Please don't start something I can't finish."

"Can't or won't? Because there's a difference."

"You're really putting me on the spot here."

"Maybe, but if there's one thing I've learned," said Alex, "it's that people appreciate honesty. They want to know where they stand. I never forgot you after that night at the tiki bar. And now…after what we shared last night, I don't want to forget you. Not for a minute."

"I didn't realize I'd made that much of an impression."

"Don't lie to yourself. We have a connection. You feel it too."

"It doesn't matter what I feel. We're from two different worlds. It wouldn't work."

"That's a copout and you know it. I want to unravel you, Dana. I want to get to the heart of you."

Long lashes blinked over big, brown eyes. The disbelief in those eyes hurt him worse than any rejection he'd ever experienced.

"You said something to me, something I can't stop thinking about. That you're broken. What would make you say that?"

"Drunken rambling, that's all."

"Boy, lying comes easily to you, doesn't it?"

"I'm not lying," she snapped. "It's just…you wouldn't understand."

"Try me."

"Look, it's not a good time for me."

"Ah. Okay. If it's convenient, I could circle back to you in another few months or so."

"Alex."

"There will never be a perfect time. I wasn't expecting you to come into my life either, but here we are." He leaned forward, bringing his face close to hers. "I want you."

"I—"

"I want to know what makes you tick, what makes you smile. And I really want to know what makes you come."

"Don't. You really shouldn't." Despite her protest, she didn't pull away. In fact, she leaned in.

"I don't play games. Don't play them with me."

"I'm not, but…"

"But what? You're not attracted to me? I think we already ruled that one out. But if that's the case, we can end this conversation now. I'll nurse my broken heart and you can go on with your life."

"Broken heart. Yeah, right. Alex, it's not that simple."

"Yes, it is."

He was pushing her, he knew it, but by the end of this discussion, she would be in no doubt as to his feelings. He could hold his cards close and act aloof. God knew he'd employed that tactic in the past. It had even worked several times.

He didn't want to this time. Something about Dana made him want to come clean, not just about his feelings, but about everything. Even in this short space of time, he found himself wondering about her activities and her thoughts. He wanted to know it all and he didn't want to wait.

He'd never been good at waiting.

How many times had Shannon called him "cold" and "unfeeling?" So many he'd begun to believe it.

Being with Dana, he felt anything but. When he was with her, his entire body warmed and mellowed. It was scary as hell, but he was willing to give it a try. He would make this work.

"Fine." She sat up straight. "I am attracted to you. Obviously."

He fought back a grin. "There. That wasn't so hard, was it?"

"Easy for you to say."

"And now," he said, touching a lock of her hair, smoothing it between his fingers, "we need to decide what to do about it."

"What if I don't want a relationship right now? What if I…just want sex?"

"Sex."

"Yes. Mind-numbing sex. What if it's all I can handle right now?"

Any man with half a brain would probably high-five him right now, but it wasn't quite the response Alex was looking for. Still, it was something. "Then I'll give it to you, until you let me give you more."

She let out a breath. "Good Lord, Alex. What won't you do?"

"Nothing. If it makes you come, I'll move heaven and earth to get it."

She shook her head. "I don't even know what to say."

"Just tell me what you want."

She steeled herself and looked him right in the

eye. "When I was with you, at Covet, I felt alive. I felt desired. Maybe it was the music. Maybe it was just the booze, but I want to feel it again. Doing what we did, knowing anyone could have discovered us, it was like all my senses came to life. Like a mask had been lifted off my face. I could smell for the first time, see for the first time. It sounds dumb."

"No, it doesn't. You deserve to feel that again."

"I want to."

His heart beat out of his chest. "Consider it done. Come to Covet tomorrow night. Alone. I'll make sure you feel desired."

"A booty call, huh?"

"That's not what this is. Let me be clear. This isn't just about hooking up. I want to get to know you, Dana, but if this is all I can have right now, I'll take it. I'll show you we can have it all."

"I see."

"I want to make your fantasies come true."

She paled and looked at her lap. "I'm not sure even you can do that."

"Give me a chance."

She stood.

"Dana. Will you come to Covet?"

She walked over to the elevator. He followed her.

"Answer me."

She turned and her face crumpled. "Alex, you don't want to get involved with me. You really don't."

Cupping her cheek, he murmured, "I know what I want."

When their lips met, it was electric. Sparks of light and energy coursed through his frame. Suddenly, the world was lit with her brightness and scented with her perfume. He wanted to drink her in and keep her close.

He needed her.

When she whimpered into his mouth, he knew she needed him too.

Deepening the kiss, he took control of her mouth. As his tongue tangled with hers, he dragged her up against his body. Her breasts strained against his chest. Her leg moved next to his. Alex's lungs expanded and yet he couldn't seem to get any air.

She was his air and he gobbled her down.

When they both seized a breath, she whispered his name. It was the most wonderful sound he'd ever heard. He wanted to hear it again and again.

She lay a hand on his pecs. "I need to go."

She was even more beautiful with her lips so swollen. He ran his thumb over her bottom lip, desperate to touch her in some other way before she disappeared. "Are you sure you can't stay?"

"I'm sure." She pressed the elevator button. "My friends are waiting for me."

He tasted her lip gloss. It might have been candy flavor but it tasted like manna. "Tomorrow night, then."

"It'll have to be late. It'll be Anise's last day in Vegas and I want to make the most of it. Hopefully she'll be talking to me by then."

"I don't care how late it is. Just come to me."

"Tomorrow night." The elevator door opened. She got in.

"One more thing."

"Yeah?"

"Don't wear any panties."

As her jaw dropped, the elevator door closed.

He rubbed his lip. She'd nibbled on it and it still stung. He didn't mind. He fucking loved it. She'd wanted him enough to put her mark on him, whether she realized it or not.

Dana might like to think there was no future for them, but she couldn't be more wrong.

If anything, they were just getting started.

***

As Dana rode the elevator, she tried to compose herself.

This isn't just about hooking up. I want to get to know you, Dana.

Alex Markov of Markov Development. New York nightlife trend setter. Hope of Las Vegas. Every man wanted to be him and every woman wanted to be fucked by him, or so she'd heard.

He wanted her.

Her. Little old her. Born in Henderson, Nevada. Educated in the public school system. Her mother Trudy was a teacher and her father Sam was a truck driver. They'd worked hard to provide a stable home for her and Anise but their daughters had had to work too. Dana had chased every scholarship and had studied her ass off to graduate top of her class. Now, she was at the top of her profession, but she was fully aware there were plenty of others waiting in the wings only too happy to see her fail.

She hadn't had everything given to her, like Alex had. She'd read his bio. The Markovs were both university professors, the famous kind. The sort that worked the lecture circuits. It was an understatement to say he had been raised in an affluent home. He came from money, probably old money.

He could buy anything, *anyone*, he wanted.

And he claimed to want her?

Rubbish. He was fooling himself.

"Let me guess. He wants a big wedding, a minivan, and two point five children too."

Still, she'd been swayed by all his talk about being attracted to her. What red-blooded woman wouldn't cave?

His touch had destroyed her common sense. Every hair on her body had stood on end. The earth had rocked under her feet and she knew it had nothing to do with fault lines. If he'd asked her to run away with him in that moment, she would have thrown on her comfiest shoes and torn up the pavement.

Somehow, even as she'd walked toward his admin office, she'd known she wanted to kiss Alex. In fact, she'd fallen asleep the previous night hoping she would once again feel his lips on her skin.

Her phone buzzed again.

Tommy: Dana, please. Just talk to me. There's something you need to know and I want you to hear it from me.

214

What did he want? He was driving her around the bend.

She didn't have a single moment to spare for Tommy. Right now, it was hard enough dealing with Alex.

Don't wear any panties.

Lord help her tomorrow night.

Alex had the potential to devastate her if she got too close. Dana couldn't afford that kind of heartache, and especially not now when her heart already seemed made of spider webs. It was fragile, and one breeze could send it spiraling into nothing.

She had to protect herself.

And yet, even as the warning bells sounded in her head, she knew she would go to him. She wanted to see what he would do. She wanted him to touch her and taste her and mark her.

She wanted him, period.

Discretion was the key. She'd already arranged to spend the entire day with Anise and the other ladies, and didn't want to spend it fielding questions about Alex.

When Dana had stormed out of the Fendi shop, she hadn't gone far. She'd loitered outside the store, waiting for Anise and the others to finish their shopping.

When Anise had come out of the store, she had walked up to Dana and put up a finger. "What happened between you and Tommy…I want you to know I'm sorry. But I'm not ready to talk to you right now and I hope you'll respect that."

Dana hadn't said a word.

Anise had left with Bea and Jessica in tow.

Knowing them, they would urge her sister to relent.

She knew her sister wouldn't stay mad forever. How could she? They'd pulled the same stunt, after all.

The elevator reached the ground floor and she walked on shaky legs toward the lobby. Bea and Jessica were waiting for her there. They had planned to catch a magic show at the Luxor that evening, although Dana already knew she wouldn't be able to concentrate on the illusions.

Anise was nowhere in sight.

"She isn't coming?"

"No," said Bea. "Give her time. She'll come around."

"Yeah," said Jessica. "I think the emotions are finally catching up to her."

"Should I go talk to her?"

"No." Bea shook her head. "She's okay. I checked on her."

"So, she'll talk to you but she won't talk to me."

"It's not that." Bea rubbed her arm. "Anise is just feeling sorry for herself. She told me she wants you to come out with us tonight."

"She did?"

"Yeah. It's been a turbulent week. You deserve some fun."

"Okay."

Jessica gave Dana a funny look.

"What?"

"Sorry. It's been driving me crazy since you came back from Alex's office." Jessica walked over and rubbed the area around Dana's mouth, like a mother wiping chocolate off her kid's face. "Your lipstick's smudged."

"Oh. Thanks."

"Someone's a good kisser," mused Bea. "I hope he's good to you. If not, your sister will cut him down like a lumberjack who just ran out of wood."

Dana giggled. She didn't doubt it.

***

The next day was a quiet one for Dana and the other women. Bea and Jessica both realized they hadn't picked up any souvenirs for their family members yet, so they headed off in separate directions to do some shopping.

Anise slept late, something she rarely did. Dana texted her before noon to see if she wanted to grab lunch, but her sister said she wanted some alone time. Something about nursing a headache. Dana texted her a few times.

Dana: Can I bring you anything?

Anise: I have some headache pills.

Dana: Are you still mad at me?

Anise: I'm not mad at you. I just want some time to mope.

Dana: I could mope with you.

Anise: Thanks, but I want to be on my own. Love you.

Dana: Love you too. Feel better.

Anise was still cooped up that evening and Bea and Jessica decided to call it a night and get started on their packing. After dinner, everyone hunkered down for the evening. After wishing them a good night, Dana headed to her own suite.

When she entered, she found a large gift box waiting in her sitting room. The rectangular box was wrapped in shimmery lavender paper and a massive silver bow sat on top.

Without even checking, she knew it was from Alex. The wrapping paper was too beautiful to be from anyone else.

Swallowing hard, she unwrapped it, taking care to fold the pretty paper. At home, her mother had always saved wrapping paper, in case it could be reused, and Dana had always done the same, hoping she was saving a tree somewhere.

Inside, a store sticker held the layers of tissue paper together. It said "Delilah." She recognized the store name. It was one of the upscale ladies' shops in the Vice shopping concourse. Dana had walked by it but had never gone in, knowing the items were far too expensive for even her shopping budget.

A tiny card lay inside on top of the item.

I hope to see you in this tonight.
Alex

She tugged at the layers of tissue, revealing a swathe of exquisite red fabric. Gasping, she removed the garment from the box and held it up.

The gown was ankle length and had fitted long sleeves. It might have appeared modest if it weren't for the fact there was a daring slit at the side. The slit went right to the hip. Some delicate ruching ornamented the top of the opening.

Alex had told her not to wear panties, but she didn't see how one could possibly wear them in a number like this.

It was the loveliest thing she'd ever seen, but she knew wearing it would take her right out of her comfort zone. To say nothing of the fact it cost far too much. She couldn't accept it.

The phone in her suite rang, making her jump. "Hello?"

"Did you get my gift?"

"Alex." She cleared her throat. "It's gorgeous, but I can't accept it. It's too expensive."

"You will accept it. Do you remember what I asked?"

"How could I forget?"

"Good. I want you to trust me, Dana. Can you do that?"

"Yes."

"This evening is going to be all about you. You're in charge."

"I get to call all the shots?"

"Every last one, but I'd like you to keep the dress. As for the rest of the night, I'll do whatever you want."

Any words she had dissolved at the tip of her tongue.

"When can I expect you?"

"Soon. I just need to freshen up."

"Good. Don't be long. I can't wait to see you." He hung up.

Dana stood still for a moment, fingering the fabric of the gown.

She could do this. There was absolutely nothing holding her back.

In the corner of her suite, the minibar hummed.

She knew for a fact the maid had restocked it with several new tiny bottles of Bailey's and wine.

"No." She'd been clear with Alex about what she needed from him, and she didn't need any liquid courage. "It's just sex. No emotions, no ties."

Determined to have the night of her life, she raided her shoe collection for a suitable pair of heels.

Chapter Nine

"So." Standing at the Covet VIP suite bar, Marissa sipped her Bloody Mary. "That woman you introduced me to. Dana. She seems nice."

Alex leaned his elbows on the bar and played dumb. "She is nice."

"You like her."

"You noticed?"

"I've always had a head for detail and I can see you're smitten."

"I didn't realize I'd made it obvious."

"To anyone else? Probably not." Marissa smiled. "But I know you. It's good to see you getting back in the game, Alex. You deserve to be happy."

"Do I?" He glared at his glass of water. The ice cubes floated around in the glass. He poked at one of them with the tip of his finger.

"Yes, you do. It's been too long."

"It's only been a year."

Marissa cocked her head. "Don't go there. I knew Shannon, and I know what she put you through, and it started a lot longer than a year ago."

Harsh memories made his eyes sting.

"I don't like to speak ill of the dead," Marissa continued, "but that woman had some major trust issues."

"I know."

Alex had tried to allay Shannon's fears. Anytime she accused him of sleeping around with a staff member or flirting with a woman in one of his clubs, he'd assured her it wasn't the case. He'd been devoted to her, and even after he'd recognized the relationship had failed, he'd still remained faithful.

She'd just never believed him.

Could he have done more? Probably, but he'd grown tired of defending himself, had become weary of the endless scenes and arguments.

She'd demanded his trust but had rarely demonstrated her trust in him.

Maybe that was why he craved it so much with Dana.

"Are you going to stick around tonight?" Alex asked Marissa.

"You know me. I may design nightclubs, but they're not really my scene." She finished her drink. "Besides, I connected with an old friend here in Vegas. I'm off to his place."

"Ah. A man. Interesting."

Marissa gave him a look. "I deserve to have some fun too." She stood on tip-toes and planted a kiss on his cheek. "Have a good night, Alex."

When the bouncer opened the door for Marissa, Dana was on the other side, standing with Viola. She exchanged a few words with Marissa. Dana then sucked in a breath and her eyes darted around the room, looking for him.

A rumble sounded from somewhere deep in Alex's gut. She'd worn the gown, although most of it was currently hidden underneath a beige trench coat.

She was nervous.

He strode toward her. "Dana, you look beautiful."

"Hi." Her gaze traveled from his grey trousers up to his pinstriped shirt. "You're not so bad, yourself."

Her face was flushed and her lips were parted. Gloss made them shine. Her perfume, that cloying mix of powder and fruitiness, teased him.

She looked absolutely edible.

He'd intended to bide his time, to drive her crazy with want, but he needed to taste her. Curling his fingers at the back of her neck, he took possession of her mouth. Needing to steal her every gasp, he nibbled at her lips. She yielded immediately, her hot tongue gliding against his in sweet urgency. Their kiss deepened as she placed her hand on his chest, trailing it down to his belt.

When they finally fell apart, he fingered her coat lapel. "Cold?"

"Not really. I've just never worn a dress like this."

"May I see it?"

She hesitated, but then allowed him to ease the coat over her shoulders and down her arms.

She was a vision in red. The gown hugged her body, a perfect fit. Tight nipples strained against the fabric. And that slit. It showed off her long legs to great advantage, drawing his eye toward the tantalizing crease at her hip.

Alex kissed the line of her jaw and whispered, "You are so fucking sexy."

A soft breath tickled his ear. Fighting his lust, he escorted her inside.

She nodded toward their nook, where one panel of the curtain was tied back in invitation. "I see no one has claimed our booth yet."

"That's because I reserved it."

"You thought of everything."

"Believe me, I've thought of nothing else." He led her to the bar. "Would you like a drink?"

"No alcohol tonight. I've had enough for a lifetime. Maybe just a sparkling water."

Alex motioned to the bartender and ordered her water.

Her nerves reappeared momentarily when she noticed how some of the other guests appraised her. His guests tended to dress to impress but everyone paled in comparison to Dana. The gown fit her like a second skin. Just looking at her made his throat itch and his palms sweat.

"Everyone's looking at me."

"There's a reason for that. You outshine them all."

"I don't know about that. It's just this dress. It doesn't leave much to the imagination." She grabbed her sparkling water and drank deeply.

"That's not true. It's not the dress. It's you. You're stunning."

"You're flattering me." Despite her scepticism, she stood taller.

"This isn't flattery. Dana, if you snapped your fingers right now, you could have anyone in this room."

"Oh, yeah? Even your fancy movie star friends?"

"I see at least five of them drooling over you right now."

"Drool. You're funny."

"I could call them over and ask them."

"I don't want them, Alex. I want you."

"That's good to know. I don't share well."

"Oh no?" She nibbled on her lower lip.

"No." Alex reached for her hand and kissed it, brushing his lips over each knuckle. "Your orgasms are mine."

"Possessive?"

"You have no idea." He gestured to their nook. "Would you like to sit?"

As they walked over to their nook, everyone turned to look at Dana. The way she moved in that dress was hypnotic. She was all legs and heat and perfume.

He held back the loose curtain so she could enter the nook. He let it fall back into place and was about to let loose the other side of the curtains to give them privacy but she stopped him with a word.

"Don't."

"You don't want privacy?"

"Not yet."

"Yes, ma'am." Leaving one panel tied back, he joined her on the couch. They had a view of one corner of the VIP suite and of the guests gathered there. From the couch, they could see one end of the bar as well.

When Dana crossed her legs, making that slit dance, he was tempted to banish everyone from the suite. Her legs looked so smooth. It took all his strength not to ease her back onto the sectional and slide between them.

But he'd promised her she was in charge of their evening and he aimed to keep his promise. "Dana, if at any point you become uncomfortable, I want you to tell me."

"I'm not uncomfortable. Maybe it's the gown, giving me visions of grandeur. I feel powerful. I haven't felt that way in a long time."

Alex's heart hammered in his chest.

She ran a finger along the slit of her dress. Even that simple movement had his stomach in knots of anticipation. All her gestures and actions intrigued him, even the most banal ones. The way she moved her hair off her face had him spellbound. Every time she crossed and uncrossed her long legs, he had fantasies of wrapping them about his waist or his shoulders.

Although there wasn't a dance floor in the VIP suite, it wasn't unusual for VIP guests to dance there. The music from the main part of the club was easily heard from this vantage point. As the DJ launched into a popular dance song, a number of the VIP guests started swaying. The beat was slow and sensual, rather than the usual amped up rhythms.

It wasn't long before some of the guests started grinding up against each other, exploring their own boundaries. Couples bumped hips. Hands gripped waists. There were a few long, deep kisses.

"I love this song." Dana closed her eyes for a

moment, humming a few bars. "Dance with me."

His throat tight, Alex stood and held out his hand, helping her to her feet. He pulled her into his arms. Her breasts crushed against his chest and her arms went around his neck. Gripping her hips, he held her close.

The fabric of her gown was so delicate, he could almost feel the softness of her skin through it. He kneaded her hips in time to the music and she swayed in his arms. When she dropped her head to his shoulder, he felt a shift, a yearning.

She yielded.

It seemed stupid. They were just two people dancing in a nightclub but suddenly, they were the only two people in the world.

She trusted him and he wouldn't abuse that trust for anything.

Lost in their dance, they moved, their bodies touching. His left hand rested so close to the top of the gown's slit. He longer to inch his fingers toward the exposed skin but bided his time. Instead, he lifted it to her hair and toyed with her curls. Kissing the length of her neck, he buried his fingers in her thick hair. With a light touch, he tugged and made her look at him. "Tell me what you want."

"I want you to touch me."

"Are you sure?"

"Yes."

Their first kiss of the evening hadn't exactly been tentative. The second one was even less so. When her lips met his this time, she closed her eyes and moaned. Alex trailed his fingers down her arms and back down to her hips. They were so lush and round. He could die touching those hips and he'd die a happy man.

Dana ran a hand up her exposed thigh, her fingers moving in a slow, circling dance of their own.

Alex's breath seized. He turned her so her back was toward the opening of the nook.

Anyone who looked in at them would only think they were dancing.

"Touch me." Her voice cracked with need.

He teased his finger under the fabric at her hip. Her skin there was so soft and he ached to drop to his knees and make the same journey with his lips. She sighed, relaxing into his touch. Giving in to temptation, he kissed the soft skin of her neck. She smelled so good, tasted so good. His cock was a painful rod between their bodies and she knew it. She wriggled her body against his, making him want to curse and shout.

The music pulsed long after the radio version of the song had ended. The DJ had chosen to spin an extended version of the sultry hit. It seemed the entire VIP suite throbbed with each beat.

Alex slipped his hand between Dana's legs. She was wet. Pure silk.

Her knees buckled but he held her in his other arm, guiding their dance.

"I've got you."

Dana rocked against his hand, transported. She moved aside the front of her dress to give him better access. Alex looked down and choked back a groan. She had the prettiest pussy, decorated by a tantalizing landing strip. He ran his finger along it, tugging on the tiny hairs, hoping she would be stimulated by the sting of mild pain.

"Yes," she said on a breath.

"You're so beautiful."

Alex caressed her over and over, basking in the sweet sound of Dana's moans. As she writhed, he eased his finger inside her body. She was tight and welcoming. She uttered a curse and he withdrew his finger, circling her clit. It was so swollen, so ripe, and her body seemed ready to go off. She was coming apart in his hands and he'd never felt so strong and virile.

She made him feel like a fucking god.

His cock throbbed. It ached for communion.

She was close. Her eyes were squeezed shut and her breathing was shallow. Determined to prolong her pleasure, her removed his fingers from her pussy.

"Oh, God." She frowned in annoyance.

He would have her orgasm, but not until he'd wrung every last shudder out of her.

"Tell me what you want, Dana. I'll do anything you want."

She opened her eyes. "Please. Make me come, Alex."

Alex circled his middle finger around her bud, giving it a long, luxurious sweep. He then captured her clit between two fingers, sliding his hand up and down her length. "Just like this?"

"Yes, *yes*."

Furious pleasure shot through his body just as she began to shake.

As Dana gave herself over to him, trusting him

in ways she'd never trusted another, something changed in him. All the doubt and guilt he'd carried around since Shannon's death seemed to ease. Old pains spiraled and churned inside him, seeking an outlet, an exit.

He'd never believed he could let those feelings go, but as he touched Dana, he began to wonder if he might be allowed some happiness after all.

Dana let out a cry.

"That's it, baby. Let it out."

No one would hear her. The DJ's song had long-since changed to a rowdier dance number.

She rocked and rocked against him as he fingered her. And as much as Alex claimed her body, she gave it willingly to him.

Even though a vicious orgasm laid waste to her body, he was the one shaken to the core.

"You're the most amazing thing I've ever seen. Ride my hand, sweetheart. Take it."

Just like that, she tightened. Her moans softened as she bit her bottom lip. She was biting so hard, he feared she might draw blood, but it still gave him deep satisfaction. He'd made her come in a way no one had ever done before. Pride and possessiveness made his chest swell.

Stroking her with a reverent finger, he helped her body calm. Everything grew still around them. He couldn't even hear the music from the club anymore.

All he heard was her heartbeat and the way she whispered his name.

Testing her, he continued to tickle the area between her thighs. How much could she take? He suspected his beautiful Dana could take a great deal. Although he lightened his touch, she pushed against him.

She burrowed her face against his neck. "Let's get out of here."

"I agree." He adjusted her gown. With her cheeks flushed, she was fucking radiant. Alex grabbed her hand. "Where would you like to go?"

"Your place." Dana stood up straight and wiped at the bead of perspiration on her brow. "Now."

***

Gordon Dean hovered in the darkest corner of Covet, waiting.

On his last trip to Vice, he'd noticed there seemed to be several new security people. Markov had called in reinforcements. He wouldn't have been surprised to discover some of them were undercover cops.

They'd be looking for him.

To be safe, he'd shaved his chin scruff and his head. With his shiny new pate, no one seemed to notice him. Feeling confident, he'd put on some nice duds and had tried his luck getting into Covet. Because he'd shown up nice and early, before the club kids dared to set foot in the place, he'd managed to get in.

He had been biding his time, nursing a drink no working man could afford. Fifteen bucks for some fruity cocktail that would probably just give him gas later. Each sip burned his throat because he knew his money would end up in Markov's pocket. Still, he tried not to glower. For tonight at least, he had to fit in so he could keep an eye on the man who was the closest thing he would ever have to a brother-in-law.

All around him, pretty people gyrated and laughed on the dance floor. However, it became clear early on in his evening not all the club patrons ended up in the same place. A select few had bypassed it completely, heading toward the back of the club.

He'd seen Markov go that way as well, and he hadn't come out yet.

Little by little, Gordon meandered toward the darkened hallway at the back. No offices, no johns. Just a shadowed corridor, leading to several locked doors.

He tried the final door. It opened to reveal a big guy. He had to be a bouncer, with those muscles and that face made of stone.

"Can I help you?"

"I was just curious about what was behind the door."

"Nothing for you, friend." The bouncer started to close the door.

Gordon put a hand on it. "Wait. What is this place?"

"VIP suite. No one gets in without an invitation."

"So how do I get an invitation?"

"Good night, sir. Watch your hand." He shut the door.

That was about an hour ago. He'd been sucking back ice cubes ever since. The bartender kept looking at him funny because he refused to buy another drink.

All he wanted was to confront Markov.

It was time.

Gordon had amused himself for a while by sending the anonymous letter to Markov and by his late-night paint job in the washroom, but he no longer found the pranks amusing.

They needed to talk. He had a lot of questions.

As if in answer to his prayers, Markov walked out of the back hallway, accompanied by a Black woman in a fancy red dress.

Shit. What he had to say to Markov needed to be said in private. He needed to get him alone.

Gordon retreated into the shadows. He didn't want Markov to see him yet, not with this woman on his arm.

When she turned to bat her eyes at the Russian, Gordon got a proper glimpse. She was damn sexy, especially with that hip-high slit in her dress. Distracted by the sight of her long legs, he almost missed what Markov said to her as they walked past.

"Let's go, baby."

Baby.

And little Shannon had barely been in the ground for a year.

The fucker.

They left Covet together. Gordon followed at a distance. Holding hands, they headed toward reception, stopping to kiss along the way. They couldn't keep their hands off each other. At one point, Markov pulled her into a quiet corner and tickled the exposed skin of her thigh.

If Gordon didn't hate the man so much, he might actually have gotten a stiffie from watching him paw her bare leg.

They quickly pulled apart, clearly trying to be on their best behavior. From there, they headed toward the admin area and the elevator that led to Markov's office.

Gordon grabbed a hotel map from reception and acted like a lost tourist. He continued to trail Markov. From around a corner, he watched as Shannon's ex swiped a card, giving him access to the elevator. Markov and his new girlfriend entered and disappeared from view.

So Alex Markov had a new woman in his life. That made things interesting.

Very interesting.

A couple of security guards stood about fifty feet away. One of them nodded in Gordon's direction. They headed over. "Anything we can help you with, sir?"

"Just looking for the nearest bar. This place sure is a maze."

The man peered at him and then pointed toward the rear end of the lobby. "The lobby bar is just over in that direction and there's another bar right by the casino."

"Ah. You mean the one I walked past?" He chuckled. "Clearly, I need that drink. Thanks for the help, guys. Have a good night."

Every hair on his body standing on end, Gordon walked away and out the nearest exit.

***

"Would you like to see any of those bracelets, sir?"

Bill Patterson gaped at the jewelry saleslady over the counter. "Come again?"

"I noticed you admiring the peridot charm bracelet. It's one of our bestsellers. I can take it out of the case if you'd like to see it up close."

Bill had only chosen that spot because it afforded a good view of the lobby. The small jewelry store stood at one end of the Vice lobby, not far from the administrative hallway. Pretending to appraise the various items, he'd seen Markov as he headed toward the elevator.

With his mystery woman.

"Are you shopping for a gift?"

Geez. Was the saleslady still babbling? "No. Just window shopping today. Thanks."

Bill exited the shop and wandered toward the admin hallway. He dared not enter the hallway for fear of being discovered. However, when a couple of security dudes stopped a bald guy to give him directions, Bill hurried past them toward the elevator.

He quickly pushed a button but the elevator wouldn't open. Only then did he realize this was Markov's private elevator. He'd heard the man lived on site and must have taken up in Liam Doyle's old digs.

Down the hall, the security guards finished talking to the bald man. One of them glanced in Bill's direction. "Sir! This area is restricted."

He waved at them. "Oh, right. On my way."

Bill looked over his shoulder and spotted an exit

door just beyond the elevator. It led into an alleyway.

The guards headed in his direction.

Bill raced to the door and pushed. Thank Christ it wasn't locked from the inside.

The security guards broke into a sprint.

Bill wasted no time and disappeared into the dark alley.

Chapter Ten

As the elevator door closed, Alex moved Dana against the back wall and kissed her hard. He kneaded her breast over her bodice and bra, pinching her nipple. Shards of sweet energy shot into all her limbs.

Grunting, Alex reached over to the control panel with his other hand and hit a button. The elevator came to a stop but the door didn't open.

"Is it stopped?"

"Yeah, but I can start it again at any time." He grinned.

"You should be careful, unleashing that Zeus smile. I might disintegrate."

"I think you're overestimating my power."

"Trust me. I know."

Alex caressed her cheek. "You have the same power over me. Do you want me to start up the elevator?"

"No. I'm in no rush."

Something ticked in his jaw. "Touch me, Dana."

She trailed a finger up and down his erection.

When it hardened even further, she massaged him there. Alex groaned and removed her hand. He ground his pelvis against her, letting her feel his sex at her core. His fingers dug into her ass and he nibbled her neck.

Everything in her was hot and wet and spiralling out of control.

Again.

It wasn't possible. Her body had never had such a reaction. She'd had some generous lovers in her time, had even enjoyed the odd multiple orgasm, but no man had ever stimulated her with such ease. One smile from Alex, one crook of his eyebrow, and she was pliable. She could indulge in a session of heavy petting with a Calvin Klein underwear model and she doubted she'd be as excited.

Every tick of her nervous system was because of Alex.

Granted, what they'd done back at Covet was unlike anything she'd ever done before.

It was more than titillation, though. He had put her in control. No one had ever given her that option. Every man she'd ever slept with liked to be in charge. Sometimes that felt good too, but Alex seemed to understand she needed to get some of her power back.

His uncanny intuition might be her undoing. His deference and caring would make it hard to walk away.

She had to walk away eventually. Didn't she?

This week had been a fantasy interlude but, in a day or so, she'd return to work and life would go on.

238

Suddenly pained, she stopped kissing him and touched his face.

His green eyes appeared darker in the elevator but they didn't twinkle any less. Although he was clean shaven, he'd missed a spot at the right side of his mouth. A few tiny golden hairs dotted the area over his top lip. If anything, they made him look a little less put together and appealingly human.

"Are you okay?"

"Never been better."

As she smiled, he ran his thumb along her lower lip, quietly considering her face. "I liked what we did tonight."

"Me too. I want more." Any worries about whether or not she and Alex could walk into the sunset together disappeared. She put her hands on his shoulders and pressed down.

"I like where this is headed."

"Be a good boy and get on your knees."

As Alex sank to his knees, the magnificence of the moment caught her off guard. Slightly disheveled but glorious, he turned up his face in expectation. The light in his eyes was that of a child about to receive a huge ice cream sundae.

She couldn't help giggling. "You like this dynamic, don't you?"

"You mean, do I like being bossed around for your pleasure? Yeah, I do."

"Good." She reached for the slit of her gown and pulled the fabric aside. "You know what to do."

With a devilish grin, Alex lay his hands on her thighs and crouched lower between her legs. As he flicked his tongue through her lips, warmth swarmed her body. Alex had a very talented tongue. It speared into her, awakening her body for the umpteenth time, and then gentled as he sucked. Over and over, he stroked her swollen pussy, as if he was the one who couldn't get enough.

Maybe he couldn't get enough. The idea astounded her.

Another astonishing orgasm lay on her horizon but Dana didn't want to come here. She wanted to be naked with him on a bed, where nothing mattered but their two bodies coming together.

She gave his hair a playful tug. "Start up the elevator."

With reluctance, Alex left his spot on the floor, stopping to kiss her clit, her stomach and her navel. "Are you sure? You taste like heaven. I could do this all night."

"I'll keep that in mind. Take me to your bed, Alex."

He stood and hit the elevator button again. For those last few moments in the lift, he gathered her into his arms and held her close. Warm and protected, Dana's heart beat somewhere under his. His pulse was just as erratic, just as amazed.

For the first time in a while, she wondered if there was a chance she might actually be able to claw herself out of the mire.

He doesn't know the truth. You have to tell him.

No. This was just sex.

And yet Alex had made it clear he wanted a relationship with her.

The elevator door opened. He held out his hand. "Ready?"

She nodded and took his hand. She followed him through his office area and into a spacious back hallway. He opened the door at the end and turned on the light.

A masculine sanctuary awaited her. Spare, like his office space, Alex's bedroom radiated calm. The floor was covered in soft grey carpeting and three of the walls were painted in the same soothing color. The wall behind his headboard was the showpiece. It was made of wood and painted a dark blue-grey. The bed was decorated in the same tones. With a metal frame and headboard and clean, white sheets, it invited her to sink into the mattress. There wasn't much in the way of artwork, but a couple of heavy sconces provided light. Off to the right side of the room, the doors to a large walk-in closet hung open. His suits and shirts were displayed in neat rows. At the bottom of the closet, his dress shoes, all polished to a shine, were lined up. A row of pristine designer sneakers sat directly above the dress shoes. The spaces between them were all so precise, Dana could imagine a butler measuring them.

She covered her mouth to stifle a smile.

"Excuse me, miss. Are you laughing at my closet?"

"It's so tidy. I just want to run over there and mess it up a bit. Maybe toss one of your shirts onto the floor."

Alex feigned shock. "You wouldn't dare."

She sashayed toward the closet, dragging her finger along his bedspread. "A little anal about organization, are we?"

He grinned. "You really shouldn't have said the

word 'anal.'"

"And why not?"

"Because it's giving me dirty thoughts." He reached her in a couple of long strides and wrapped her in an embrace. Palming her ass, squeezing each cheek, he took her mouth. After a kiss that left them both winded, he steeled himself and removed his hands from her body. "You have no idea how hard it is to stop kissing you."

"I think I have some idea." Dana rubbed her swollen lips. "Why did you stop?"

"Don't get me wrong. I'm dying to take control of this situation but I made a promise. I'm your humble servant, remember?"

"Right. Be careful. The power might go to my head."

"Tell me what you want," said Alex, his voice coarse, "and I'll do it."

"Anything?"

"Anything."

"Hmm, interesting." She sat on his bed. "Take off your clothes. I want to see you."

He began to attack his shirt buttons.

"No, Alex. Slowly. I want to enjoy this."

His lips compressed. "What about you? That dress needs to go."

"If you put on a good enough show, I might consider it."

Alex's nostrils flared but he laughed. She had a feeling once she relinquished control, not only would he seize it, he would take it and teach her a lesson.

His gaze never straying from her face, he popped

his shirt buttons through the holes at a torturous pace. Little by little, sections of his torso became visible. She'd always suspected he had rock hard abs under there, and when he finally removed his shirt, the proof made her giddy. She couldn't wait to run her fingers over the ripples of his abdomen. Golden hairs dotted his chest, just enough that she'd be able to inflict some punishment and tug them. He had a faded farmer's tan and for some reason, it struck her as amusing.

"Why are you smiling?"

"I didn't expect you to have a farmer's tan."

"I'll have you know this is a runner's tan. I wear t-shirts when I run."

"You won't be running anywhere tonight."

"Trust me. I wasn't planning on it." Alex pulled up a chair from the corner and sat down directly in front of her. He leaned over and untied his dress shoes, removing them and his socks. Barefoot and bare-chested, he leaned back in his chair and stared at her.

"What are you thinking?"

He spread his legs. "If I had my way right now, you'd be on your knees."

She tutted. "Oh dear, that doesn't sound like humble servant talk."

His knee began to bounce up and down. He was on edge and she'd brought him to it. The rush brought a huge smile to her face.

"You enjoy my pain."

"Shouldn't you be undressing, Alex?"

Like a great cat unfurling itself in its lair, he stood. His waistline was at her eye level and he knew it.

Dana batted her eyelashes. "I'm waiting."

He reached for his belt buckle with an unsteady hand. When he tugged on the belt, it was with more force than necessary. The rip of a couple of stitches on his pants brought them both into an even more heightened state of awareness.

Dana's heart raced like that of a doe being pursued by a wolf. Surely he could see the pulsing mass of erratic beats in her chest. It reminded her of the time her doctor had sent her to the hospital for an allergy test. She'd had a couple of mild reactions when taking aspirin and the doctor believed she might be allergic. The test, which consisted of taking aspirin in a controlled environment, had confirmed it. Her throat had proceeded to close. The specialist had administered a shot of adrenaline to eliminate her symptoms. *It will feel as if your heart is beating outside your chest, Dana. It'll calm down in a couple of minutes.* Sure enough, once the adrenaline was coursing through her system, her heart had felt as if it was pumping about a foot in front of her. In her dazed state, she'd even been tempted to reach out her hand to grab it.

Alex did the same thing to her.

He made her heart beat somewhere outside her chest.

He unfastened the trouser button and pulled the zipper down. When he removed his pants, it seemed as if all the air in the room evaporated. She breathed in and her breath formed a vacuum. Everything was silent. No one else existed but them. His playfulness had disappeared and hers did too.

All Dana knew in that moment was want. It was forceful and demanding and she couldn't have turned away even if she'd wanted to.

Zeus was about to reveal himself to the mortal.

Alex wore black boxer briefs. He hooked his thumbs in the waistband and slowly drew it down.

Slim hips gave way to powerful thighs and a needy, straining cock.

She licked her dry lips but it didn't help. He was too beautiful. It almost hurt her eyes to look at him.

He stood still, hands at his sides, awaiting her instruction. When his fists clenched, she realized she might be staring too long.

With difficulty, Dana stood and walked around him. Every angle was perfect. His back was a mass of lean muscle. His butt was high and rounded. His calves would make a quarterback cry in envy.

All of a sudden, she felt a little less in control.

Once again sensing her discomfort, Alex looked over his shoulder at her. "Where would you like me?"

Dana glanced at his bed. Four short posts stood at the corners. "Lie down. On your back."

He crawled on and lay down. His cock throbbed against his gut.

Dana walked over to his closet and chose four ties. "Spread your arms and legs."

Hesitating only a moment, Alex obeyed. Dana took her time and tied his ankles and wrists to the posts, looping the fine fabric over his skin. The knots might not be worthy of a sailor, but they'd do the trick. If he tried, Alex could disentangle himself, but he lay supine. Despite a tightness around his mouth, he appeared to have accepted his fate.

"Are you uncomfortable?"

"No."

"Have you ever been tied up before?"

"No."

"Do you want me to let you go?"

His somber gaze met hers. "No."

Dana swallowed hard. They were both crossing boundaries tonight.

She wasn't even sure what her end game was in tying him up. All she knew was the headiness of the feeling and the need to prolong it.

A tiny line of sweat beaded Alex's upper lip.

It was time to make him sweat harder.

Standing at the side of the bed so he could see her easily, Dana unzipped her gown and let it fall to the floor. Standing only in her heels and her flimsiest bra, she seemed even more on display than he was. His eyes darted all over, at her breasts, her hips, her sex. Determined to torture him, she unclasped her bra and tossed it into his closet. It landed in a silky heap on a pair of his sneakers.

His deep chuckle held a measure of danger.

"Did I just poke the bear?"

"Are you going to stand there all night long?" He pulled on one of his wrist restraints.

She waggled a finger. "Don't you dare."

"Dana, please. You're killing me."

She slipped out of her shoes and crawled up on the bed, kneeling between his legs. "That sounded an awful lot like begging." When she trailed a finger up his leg, he bucked.

"Fuck. I am begging."

She ran the same finger up over his abs and down the opposite leg, never touching him where it counted. "Oh, yeah? It hurts me to see a grown man beg for something he's going to get anyway."

His eyes darkened with want.

Leaning over, she dragged her tongue up his cock.

Alex groaned. "Fuck. Ah, yes, shit."

Thrilled with his reaction, she took him in her mouth, as deep as she could. From her peripheral vision, she could see him tugging on his arm restraints.

She wasn't sure this beast could be caged any longer.

In all honestly, she wasn't sure she wanted to keep him in his cage.

Dana licked and teased Alex until he threw his head back on his pillow in defeat. She took savage delight in dragging her fingernails up his legs, only to cup him tenderly. He writhed, thrusting his hips up to meet her mouth and every time he moaned in contentment, she withdrew and made him wait. His face grew pained and she took mercy on him again.

He was a rod of nerves and muscle, his entire body tensed. Aching for her own release, she rose up over him and whispered in his ear. "Condom?"

"Bedside table."

Stopping only to capture his earlobe between her teeth, Dana reached into the table drawer and found a condom. She unwrapped it and slowly rolled it on him. Even that made his eyes roll back in agony. Feeling a surge of power, she straddled his crotch and lowered herself onto him, degree by painful degree.

Alex let out a curse but then fell silent. His mouth opened and closed and he once more yanked on the restraints.

She ran her hands up his chest, tweaking his nipples. "Not yet."

With a smile, Dana rode him. As she rocked atop him, taking him deep into her body, he met her thrust for thrust. His thighs were like iron, the only way he could brace himself. She broke out into a sweat as well, moisture accumulating on her brow and lower back.

Delight coursed through her from head to toe. Awash in Alex, in his scent and in his submission, Dana neared another moment of bliss. She touched her breasts, transported by his pleasure as much as her own.

"Dana, please."

The pain in Alex's voice cut into her, reminding her of the pain she'd managed to suppress all evening.

Hollow, hollow, hollow.

She would never bear children, not with this man or any man. Her womb would never cradle another soul. She was alone, even now during the most intimate moment she'd shared with Alex.

He needed to know the truth. As much as she liked to pretend this was all about sex, emotions were now involved. She saw it in the furrow on his brow and in the way his hands strained to hold her. She recognized it in the unsteady trot of her heartbeat.

Would Alex turn her away, as Tommy had,

seeing her as inferior goods?

She must have stilled or whimpered because Alex asked again. "Please. Let me."

Her empowerment disappeared with his plea.

"You can trust me, Dana."

With a nod, she offered her permission. Dana extricated herself from his lap, in awe at the sense of emptiness it created, and began to untie the knots. When he was free, they both sat still for a second. She expected him to throw her down and fuck her senseless or paddle her ass until it was purple, but he didn't do either of those things.

Alex cupped her cheek and kissed both of her shuttered eyelids. "You're a warrior."

"No, I'm not. It was just a fantasy.'

"You're incredible. But now it's my turn."

Dana lay back and gave him her body, seeking transformation of some kind. Alex slid between her legs and entered her with a deep thrust. She closed her eyes when they misted, determined not to cry. She would not sully the moment with tears.

Alex drove her to the point of sweet madness, slapping her ass and scratching her skin. She knew he would leave marks but she didn't mind. She would be honored to wear those scratches.

When the hurricane razed the earth, she threw herself willingly into the storm.

As everything settled, their shattered breaths mingling, she realized he might not have transformed her body.

But he took her right out of it, and for now, she welcomed oblivion.

Come morning, she would have to face reality.

And she was terrified.

***

Dana had fallen asleep in his arms.

Alex had forgotten how good it could be to have a beautiful woman lay next to him, her body curled up against his in total trust. He'd certainly never anticipated how good it would feel with Dana.

Their night together had been an out-of-body experience. She'd claimed her power, taking utter control of their lovemaking, bringing him to the brink. He'd never come so hard or endured such sweet punishment. Now, she nestled next to him, sleeping like an innocent.

Humbled and excited for the first time in a long time, he traced the line of her jaw. It gritted under his finger. She moaned, grinding her teeth.

A nightmare.

Wanting to soothe her, Alex brought her closer to his chest and kissed her forehead. She smelled so good, of flowers and heat and of him. He'd left his stamp all over her body and wanted to do it all over again.

You're falling for this woman.

The thought should have been terrifying but it wasn't. He wanted more with her, wanted to see how far they could take things.

He definitely wanted her in his bed on a regular basis. They hadn't had enough time. Suddenly, he was obsessing over all the things they *hadn't* done during her week at Vice. They hadn't gone out for dinner. They hadn't shared a breakfast. She hadn't told him all about her childhood, her hopes and fears. He wanted to know what drove her, what inspired her.

Most of all, he wanted to be her inspiration.

Once again, she groaned and mumbled something. Under the sheets, her feet thrashed.

"Shh." He moved his lips down to her nose and capturing her flailing legs between his. "I've got you, baby. It's okay."

Her chest heaved, even as she slept. "Broken."

It wasn't the first time that word that slipped from her subconscious.

Nothing works inside me. I'm broken.

He'd brushed the comment off before, thinking it was the result of too many drinks. Clearly, it hit harder than any Golden Oblivion.

"Dana?"

"Hollow. So hollow."

Her cry broke his heart. Alex reached behind him and turned on the bedside table light to its dimmest setting.

Her face…it was changed by anguish. Her eyes were squeezed shut. Her mouth was contorted. She reached for her hair and pulled.

"Dana." He gently removed her curls from her hand. "Dana, wake up, sweetheart. You're having a bad dream."

When her eyes opened, they were filled with dark wonder. It wasn't the only emotion flitting there.

He saw shame.

"Alex?"

"I'm here." He gave her a soft kiss. "I'm right

here."

She began to cry.

Her tears. They sliced into him like knives. "Please don't cry. Tell me what's wrong."

She rolled over. "I should go."

"What are you doing?"

She sat up and began looking for her clothes. "I shouldn't have stayed." Seeing her bra at the bottom of his closet, her gown on the floor, her shoulders sagged. "Shit. I'd give anything for a pair of sweat pants and some granny panties."

"Hey. Come here." He pulled her back onto the bed and under the covers, even though she resisted. "Why are you doing this? I want you to stay."

"No, you don't."

"Yeah, so you keep saying. Thing is, Dana, you're the first woman I've brought to my bed in over a year and I let you tie me to it. That was a first, even for me. So, believe me when I say I want you to stay."

She fell onto the pillow, facing him. Every trace of his warrior woman was gone.

"Tell me what's going on. Why are you...*broken*?"

"I...how did you...?"

"You talked in your sleep, but you've said it before. I've been paying close attention. It's time to come clean."

"It'll change things, Alex. Between you and me. It'll change everything."

"Dana, if you can't be honest with me," he replied, keeping his voice gentle, "then things have already changed."

"No one knows. Only Tommy."

"You can trust me."

She sucked on her bottom lip and then released it. "I received a diagnosis a little while ago."

Diagnosis. It was the last word he wanted to hear coming out of her mouth. The word itself was vile, but it caused a whole other bunch of horrible words to shoot in front of his eyes. They blared in red, as if from a neon sign.

Cancer.

Multiple Sclerosis.

AIDS.

Measles. Mumps, Rubella. Even fucking leprosy.

His insides untethered. Cords of sinew and nerve unraveled, loosening every organ, every bone. Everything in him seemed to plummet as he considered the implications. When his voice did emerge, it sounded muffled, unsure. "What is it?"

"They call it premature ovarian failure."

"What does that mean?"

"Basically, it means I can't have children."

When the sigh of relief escaped him, he hated himself for it. The diagnosis was obviously hurting her and yet he couldn't help automatically comparing it to other conditions, never mind diseases. He just wanted to know one thing. Was it dangerous?

Did it hurt her?

Would it go away?

Okay, he had a lot of questions. At the same time, Alex was so grateful she wasn't sick. Or was she? He had no idea what this meant for her health. "I'm sorry."

"Me too."

"Does it mean you're sick?"

"No. Just barren."

Barren. Another terrible word. When he looked at Dana, the last thing he saw was something cold and devoid of life. What he saw was a vibrant, intelligent woman, one who was so lovely she made his head spin. He didn't ever want to hear her call herself barren again. "I take it you and Tommy had planned for a family?"

"Yeah. Him, especially. He loves children and wants to have a big family."

"Is that why he ended things between you?"

She nodded. "He called off the engagement a full thirty minutes after the doctor gave me the diagnosis."

"The little fucker."

"I wasn't enough for him. Full stop. He wants a wife who will give him babies, their *own* babies. In his view, he'd almost bought a lemon so it was time to return it to the shop."

"You're not a lemon."

"See, there's the thing, Alex. I've been trying really hard to tell myself that but it's hard to stay positive when the man who was supposed to love you forever tells you you're not quite right. In Tommy's eyes, I can't be fixed. No one can tinker with me and pimp this ride. This won't go away." She sat up, holding the sheets over her breasts. "I don't have all the same bells and whistles as other women. According to him, I'm the car with the wonky horn and a muffler that's dragging on the ground."

"Is he the one who compared you to a rundown car? Because if he is, I will find him now and make him apologize." When his voice started to echo in the room, he lowered it. "Or is this what you think of yourself?"

"Oh, I'm sorry. Did I choose the wrong metaphor? What should I compare myself to then? Other women? Okay. Other women are fertile. I'm not. Other women manage to have babies. Some of them don't even want children and they still end up having tons of them. I can't. I've seen some women *ignore* more of their children than I can ever conceive. And why? Because of some fluke. Because God or the universe or karma, or whatever the hell you want to call it, decided I didn't deserve the same choices. My fiancé walked out because he thought I wasn't enough of a woman. Because he thought I was defective. Unable to create life. Broken." She gestured at her belly. "My line ends with me."

At the end of her tirade, tears poured down her cheeks.

Alex didn't think, didn't wait. He sat up and enfolded her in his arms, and let her cry until she had no more tears.

"That night at Joe's, you took me out of myself. For a while, I managed to forget everything. I thought I was functioning. Then I saw you again and all those feelings came back, the need to just forget. At Covet, you helped me feel pretty and desirable again. When you touch me, I feel good about myself. It's why I keep coming back."

Alex's throat scratched. He cleared it. "You

shouldn't need me to feel good about yourself. There's plenty to feel good about."

"I appreciate that and I know what you're saying. I really do. I've never felt this way before. I know I have a lot going for me and maybe one day, I will get past this. That's why it hurts me so much to feel so stuck. The only time I can shut out Tommy's voice is when you're inside me. I'm sorry. I know I just wanted to use you for sex."

"Would it be terrible if I told you I didn't have a problem with that?"

Her laugh was quiet, small, unenthusiastic. "I'm just so tired."

"I can only imagine." He kissed her temple, lingering on her soft skin. "And your sister doesn't know?"

"I didn't want to upset her."

"You have to tell her. She goes home tomorrow. You *all* go home tomorrow." The idea made him want to vomit, even if Dana did live in Vegas. He liked having her under his roof. He wanted to keep her there.

"I know. Before checkout, I'll talk to her. It was a mistake to keep everything bottled up."

"Don't blame yourself. You've been dealing with a lot of stress, and on your own."

"I feel better when I'm with you."

"I'm glad."

"But this has to stop, Alex. It's not fair to you."

"With all due respect, you don't get to decide what's fair to me."

"We have to nip this in the bud before emotions get involved." She pulled her chin into her chest, as if retreating.

He touched a finger to her chin and made her look at him. "Too late."

A year ago, he wasn't sure he even had any emotions, other than the circling black fog that surrounded him.

Dana had poked a hole in the darkness, whether she knew it or not. She'd let the light in and now he didn't want to cover it up ever again.

She lay back down on a sigh and he lay with her. As he reached his arm under the covers to hold her, he realized she was stroking her stomach, absentmindedly rubbing.

Other women are fertile. I'm not.

Horrible memories of Shannon's last hours encroached.

For once, he didn't fight them.

When he made the decision to leave New York, the Deans had accused him of running from the truth, from justice even.

If only they'd known he was running from memories and shame.

Somehow, they'd followed.

Alex had always been the sort of man who managed his feelings, but there were times when the lack of closure ate into him. Was there something more he could have done to salvage their wreck of a relationship?

He'd never know now.

The Dean family had seen to that. They'd swooped in, claimed their blood relative and excluded Alex from any of the funeral arrangements.

Leaving him with nothing but memories that ate into him. Memories that cut so deep, he'd been forced to up sticks and leave his home.

Leaving him alone, aching for the family he would never have.

In his darkest moments, he'd realized how much he wanted it.

Now he knew the truth about Dana. Did it change things?

He couldn't lie to himself. Despite his unorthodox work life, he'd always planned on having a family. He and Shannon had discussed it in their happier days. He'd even envisioned it. One of his favorite fantasies used to be holding his little girl's hand, a daughter who looked just like her mother.

When Shannon began to doubt his fidelity, those fantasies stopped.

He'd forgotten how badly he wanted to make them a reality.

And now, here he lay, sharing in the aching vulnerability of a woman who would never give birth. His heart broke for Dana and he hated the fact Tommy had given her no time before dropping his bombshell. The man just panicked. Nothing else made sense, unless Tommy was just a mean bastard. If that was the case, he doubted Dana would ever have fallen in love with him. A part of him understood Tommy's misgivings, but if Alex had been in his place, he liked to think he wouldn't have reacted the same way.

He wanted to believe he was stronger than that.

If you loved someone and she loved you back,

shouldn't that be enough?

She felt inferior to other women. Few things had saddened him more.

She believed there was a hole inside her. He didn't think for one moment that he was capable of patching it, but she'd said herself he helped her feel better. He helped her feel desired.

He could do it again.

Maybe this wasn't about planning futures. They should be taking things one step at a time. Right now, all he knew was he wanted Dana. He knew it as well as he knew his own reflection. But she obviously had lots to consider and he probably did too.

"Dana?"

"Yeah?"

"Do you even want children?"

"Truthfully? I don't know, but I never wanted to rule out the possibility. I never wanted to have it taken from me."

"I realize this is just my opinion, but I think you might need to decide what it is you want. If you can sort that out in your head, maybe this diagnosis won't be so painful."

"You're probably right. I need to figure out what I want." She snuggled in deeper. "Do you mind turning out the light?"

He reached over and turned it out. He lay awake, eyes wide open.

She'd trusted him with the knowledge and he owed it to her to respect it. Was she just using him for sex? Frankly, he didn't care. He just wanted her in his bed and he'd wanted it from day one.

The future would resolve itself.

Right now, he just had to tread carefully, for her heart and for his. She didn't need any extra complications and neither did he. This thing with Dana was powerful but he had no idea how it would end, and he didn't want to hurt her in the process. She'd suffered enough.

As for him? Maybe he needed to give her some space to come to terms with her new reality. It might also give him a chance to figure out what he wanted.

If he was smart, he'd insist they maintain a friendly relationship. No touching. No longing. And no more nights at Covet.

It was probably for the best.

Friends.

He could do this.

Even as his sensible brain reiterated the plan, his fingers curled against her back, hugging her tighter.

Friends.

Yeah, right.

Chapter Eleven

Before dawn, Alex accompanied Dana back to her suite. Although dressed in that sinful red gown again, she appeared younger, more fragile. She'd draped her beige trench coat around her shoulders and she clutched it around the neck, as if warding off a chill.

The penthouse level hallway was quiet and so were they. She hadn't been talkative when they were getting dressed and he didn't know what to say. He hoped his presence would be enough.

When they reached her door, she turned to him and removed her jacket, slinging it over her arm. "Well, I guess this is it."

"It doesn't have to be."

"You know as well as I do, it does." She touched his chin. "I should have stayed far away from you, Alex Markov."

"Why should you? You're a dynamic woman. Last I checked, no one was trying to wall you up alive in an old castle."

"There's an idea."

"Dana…"

"I'm joking. I am capable of humor from time to time." She flattened her hand on his chest, slowly dragging it downward. "Last night was…"

"It was the best I've ever had."

"Yeah, for me too. Until I messed it up."

"You didn't mess anything up. I want…I want to try."

"I don't think that's wise."

"Fuck wisdom. Wisdom can kiss my ass."

His words almost got a smile out of her but that hint of a grin disappeared when they heard the shuffling at the next door. It opened. Anise walked into the hallway, dressed in the hotel slippers and bathrobe. When she saw them in a clutch, and Dana in that dress, her mouth fell open. "So, I guess you two are a thing now?"

Alex said "yes," the same time Dana said "no."

They gave each other a look and then Dana turned to her sister. "There's something I need to tell you."

Anise's eyes widened. "If you tell me you just eloped with that man, and in that dress…"

"Get inside and sit down." Red in the face, Dana unlocked her suite door and nudged Anise inside. She held the door open for Alex. "Would you stay? Please."

"Of course."

She shut the door behind him.

Anise crossed her arms and sat on the couch. "I'm waiting."

Dana took a deep breath and sat on the couch opposite her. Alex risked Anise's wrath and sat next to Dana. Anise looked him up and down and rolled her eyes.

Dana sat up tall. Alex grabbed her hand and held it. She squeezed it. "I never told you why Tommy broke up with me."

"I know," said Anise. "I've been trying to figure that one out."

"We found out I can't have children."

"Wait. What? You can't have children?"

"No."

"But…how? Why not?"

"I have a condition called premature ovarian failure."

Anise's eyes welled up. "Are you sick?"

"No. I just can't conceive. Tommy couldn't deal with it, so he left. I couldn't bear to tell you, not with everything going on between you and Roman."

"Oh, honey." Anise flew to her, so Alex got up from his seat and let her sit next to her sister. "I'm so sorry."

As the sisters embraced, he perched on the armrest of the other couch. He licked his lips, amazed that Dana's taste and scent still lingered all around him. She'd been trying so hard to warn him away when all he wanted was to keep her at his side. Now that he understood why, he wanted to keep her even closer.

He was an idiot. To think he'd attributed her sorrow to losing Tommy when she'd lost so much more than that. And yet it was Tommy's rejection that shaped the way she viewed herself. He'd made her feel like damaged goods.

Alex wanted to damage Tommy. He wanted to

pulverize him.

In a moment of weakness, when Dana had fallen asleep in the early hours, Alex had pulled out his cellphone. He'd sought out Dana's Facebook profile. The search had left a pit in his gut. She hadn't updated her profile in months and her status was still listed as "Engaged." Her page was littered with pictures of her and Tommy.

Although Alex had taken perverse delight in picturing Dana's ex as an ogre, the truth was quite the opposite. Tommy Parker was a handsome white man with a shaved head and a twinkle in his eye. In every photo, he was either kissing Dana or had his arms around her. There were images of them hiking together, biking together, going on a trip to Amsterdam together. They had a history, one full of laughs and funny faces and little heart emojis.

It had sickened Alex and he hated himself for feeling that way, especially because if the photos were to be believed, Tommy looked like a good guy. The sort any man would want as a friend.

But that didn't change the way Alex felt. He hated Tommy for hurting her, for thinking she was anything less than perfect.

The woman in those Facebook photos didn't resemble the woman sitting in front of him. Dana's shoulders were hunched. Her skin was pale. Her voice was soft and low as she spoke to Anise.

Alex's ribs scraped against the pulsing organ housed inside them.

He wanted to be better than Tommy.

He wanted to be better for Dana.

"I can't believe it," said Anise. "I hate what

Tommy did to you, but are you sure you can't salvage what you had?"

"I'm sure."

"Why should she even try?" Alex couldn't help putting his two cents in. "Tommy had his chance. He blew it."

Anise ignored him. "He loves you, Dana. You know he does. He just made a mistake."

"Right," replied Dana. "And I bet if I asked Roman, he would say he still loves you too."

"It's not the same thing."

"Tommy betrayed me. He might not have done it with his dick, but he still did it."

"He was hurting. He overreacted. I'm sure this is hard, but you have options. You can adopt."

"Tommy wasn't even interested in discussing that option."

"I just think you're being hasty. If your relationship can still be repaired, you should give it everything you've got. Trust me."

"My relationship can't be repaired." Dana threw up her hands. "*I* can't be repaired! Don't you get it?"

Anise reared back as if she'd been slapped.

"That's enough," said Alex. "This is upsetting Dana."

"And what do *you* know about Dana?" scoffed Anise. "You've known her for days."

Alex sighed. "That's not exactly true."

"What is he talking about?"

"I ran into Alex the night Tommy dumped me. He listened," Dana explained. "He didn't know everything then, but he supported me when I needed it."

"How convenient." Anise shook her head. "And how exactly did he *support* you? Oh, wait. I can figure that out. By the way, sis, you might want to put some panties on next time you go out."

"I said, that's enough." Alex couldn't contain his anger when he glimpsed the mortified expression on Dana's face. "What's your problem with me, anyway?"

"My problem," Anise said slowly, as if he had trouble understanding, "is you fucking my sister when she's vulnerable. Do I have to spell it out? Dana doesn't belong in your world."

"And what do you know about my world?"

"I know enough."

"Stop it, both of you." Dana held out her hands.

"We know *nothing* about you, Alex," Anise continued. "How do I know you'll treat my sister with the respect she deserves? I've read the papers. I know what they say about you. Your last girlfriend ended up dead!"

From out of nowhere, a football launched itself at Alex's head, or so it felt. He stared, unable to come up with a response. Shame coated his esophagus. Thick and acrid, it made him want to hurl.

"Get out." Dana pointed at the door. "I mean it, Anise. Get the hell out."

Only then did Anise realize she'd gone too far. Abashed, she tried to make excuses. "Dana, I just want you to see the full picture. I realize Tommy hurt you, but you shouldn't hold grudges. He's a good man, steady and loyal. You can come back from this as a couple." She turned to Alex. "Look, I appreciate you might care for my sister, but she needs stability in her life, not fantasy. Tommy can give her stability. I know him. He'd do anything for her."

"Except the one thing she needed most."

"Anise." Dana's voice was tired. "Just go. I'll talk to you at checkout."

"But Tommy…"

"Please do not mention his name to me again. If you say it one more time, I will disown you as a sister, I swear to God."

Tommy. Alex was so exhausted of hearing the name Tommy. It offended him. It was the name of a boy, not a man, and Dana needed a man.

Dana walked over to the door and held it open. Anise made her way over, sighing the whole way. She paused at the door and leaned in to kiss her sister. Dana stood still, letting her, but didn't look Anise in the eye.

"Call me if you need anything," said Anise, and then she left.

Running his hand over his face, Alex paced the living area of Dana's suite. It took him a few seconds to realize Dana hadn't closed the door yet. She was still holding it open. For him. "You want me to leave too?"

"Not really, but I'm tired, Alex. It's almost morning. Maybe we should call it a night."

Despite the fact the door was hanging open, he could have sworn it had been slammed in his face.

Calm down.

She just needed some time and some space.

He could give her that. He *had* to give her that.

"Sure." Alex joined Dana at the door. He kissed her once, and then again. Leaving was harder than he thought it would be. "Are you sure you don't want some company?"

"I'm sure." She didn't meet his gaze. Her walls had gone up again. "Thanks."

"I'll talk to you tomorrow."

"Alex, don't. You know as well as I do this is the end. Anise is right in one way. It's time for me to go back to reality."

He cupped the base of her skull and kissed her harder, sliding his tongue into her mouth until she whimpered. "I will talk to you tomorrow."

Touching her lips, Dana closed the door.

When he heard the click of the lock falling into place, something snapped inside Alex.

She thought it was over. On some level, she thought he needed saving.

From her.

Even worse, she saw him as a bit of fun. A lark. A fantasy. Like her sister, Dana believed they were incompatible, and his wealth and position was only the tip of that iceberg.

Anise believed Dana needed stability.

He'd never been very good at providing that for others. Did he even know the first thing about stability? He'd certainly never given it to Shannon.

You care more about your friends than me. You spend more time at Champagne and Liberty than you do with me.

You know I love you. My work is just that. Work.

No, Alex. You get off on watching all those

strangers flitting around you. And you know why? Because it's safe. Because you don't have to get involved. You might like to play the conductor but you've never composed a piece of your own. God forbid you engage that cold heart of yours.

Maybe it was time for him to face reality as well.

In many ways, he was cold. He'd cultivated that reputation in business, believing it served him well, never realizing the chill had settled over areas of his personal life.

In creating his fantasy clubs, he'd built a world where he could be king. The best part about being a king?

No one got too close.

He didn't allow anyone to get too close.

But Dana had found a way to cross his moat, even with all its snapping crocodiles.

She brought him heat and pleasure and made him want.

And yet he was scared. What if his frost began to infest her too?

Shannon had been a good woman, despite her insecurities. He'd hurt her in the end.

Would he hurt Dana?

She thought she was bad for him.

In truth, he was probably bad for her.

***

The next morning, Dana headed to the lobby early, with Anise and the others in tow. Their flight left before noon and she wanted to go home to her own bed, her own walls and floors. She would definitely miss the luxury suite at Vice, but staying here had put too many wild ideas in her head. She'd been avoiding her problems, ever since that crazy night at Joe's Tiki Bar, and it was time to meet them head on.

The dream was over. She needed to heal in her own surroundings.

In the lobby, Dana took turns saying goodbye to Bea and Jessica.

"I had a great time," said Bea. "Even if I didn't make any money at the casino."

Dana laughed. "I think that was a given."

As Dana hugged Jessica, she whispered, "You'll keep me posted on the baby?"

"You bet. Thank you."

The ladies grabbed their suitcases and headed toward the door.

Dana stood in front of Anise, her head high.

"About *he-who-can't-be-named*," Anise said, "I still think you're making a mistake."

"Anise, I realize you just heard the news, but you need to remember I've been living with this for a while."

"I can't believe you told Alex Markov about your breakup before you told me."

"Do you really want to go there?"

"I guess not." Anise reached for her hand. "Can we start over? We used to be so close. We told each other everything. I don't remember why that stopped."

"I guess, somewhere along the way, we just grew apart."

"I don't want that with my sister. I want to be

270

able to share everything with you, the good and the bad. Maybe we could try to be more open with each other. You know, checking in regularly. That sort of thing."

"I'd like that."

"Do you want me to be there when you tell Mom and Dad?"

"No, it's okay. I'll call them when I get home."

"What about Tommy?"

"We're through." Dana made a face. "He's been texting."

"Why?"

"I don't know. I guess I should call him. Can't avoid him forever."

"Dana. I know it might sound like I was defending Tommy. I wasn't. After my own experience, I would never want to see you saddled with a man who doesn't value you." She gestured around the Vice lobby. "I just don't want you to get swept away by all of this. It's not real, not any of it."

Not *him*, is what she really meant. Alex wasn't real.

Only, when he was deep inside her, whispering her name like a prayer, he'd felt all too real and tangible.

Like a mirage in the desert, Alex appeared across the lobby. For a moment, Dana thought she recognized the man from Joe's. Alex wasn't wearing one of his nice suits. He had on some shorts and a t-shirt, as well as a pair of his designer sneakers. His face seemed pale, his expression wary. He spotted her and Anise and stopped in his tracks, hanging back so they could finish their conversation.

Anise nodded in his direction. "I guess you'll want to talk to him now."

"I should say goodbye."

"Well, he can wait for a minute while I hug my sister." They embraced and Anise kissed her on the cheek. "Call me tonight, okay?"

"I will."

"Thank you for arranging this week, baby girl."

"You're welcome, old woman."

"Ouch." Anise grinned. "That hurt." As she walked toward the door to meet with Bea and Jessica, Anise pointed two fingers at Alex, and mouthed, "I'm watching you."

Sighing, Alex walked over. "Your sister hates me."

"I don't think it's you, specifically. I think it's more what you represent to her."

"And what do I represent?"

"Someone who'll hurt her little sister."

He drew closer. "And what does little sister think?"

Dana ignored his question and fingered the edge of his t-shirt. "What's with the outfit?"

"I was going to go for a run."

"Ah." He was definitely pale, and now that he was standing closer, she could tell he hadn't showered since she saw him last. Although he had bed head, it suited him in ways she dared not contemplate. "Did you get any sleep last night?"

"No."

Leave it to Alex to give it to her straight. "I

didn't sleep much either."

"Dana—"

"Alex, I want to thank you. For everything."

A storm gathered in those green amber eyes. "But?"

"But it's time for me to go home."

"When can I see you again?"

"That's not going to happen."

"I see. You got what you needed and now you're done. Is that it?"

"You know that's not the truth. I have a lot on my plate. I need to take some time for myself. A relationship just isn't in the cards right now."

"You said I helped you feel better. Those are *your* words, not mine."

"I know."

"Whatever comes next, you don't have to do it on your own."

"I'm trying hard to do the honorable thing here. You said yourself you'd like to have kids one day. Why on earth would I let myself get attached when I can make a clean break now?"

"You're already attached."

"Well, then, I'll just have to detach myself." She sighed. "Alex, this shouldn't be so hard."

He stepped right in front of her and reached his arm around her waist. His forehead lowered to hers. "The fact that it's hard tells me you don't want to go, and I don't want to let you go."

Dana closed her eyes and fought temptation. She lay a hand on his chest, intending to push him away, but she only melted against him. "Don't."

"See?" His minty breath fanned over her face.

"You can't leave. Don't leave."

Summoning all her power, Dana pulled herself out of his grip. "We're done."

His mouth hardened. "I'm not asking for forever, Dana. I'm just asking you not to write us off."

"That's the problem right there, Alex. If we do this, any of this, eventually I'll want forever. And I can't bear for you to look at me with regret a year from now. I have to be careful who I let into my world from now on. I can't have another Tommy in my life. One was enough."

"I'm not Tommy."

"No. You're better, and that's exactly why I can't get any closer to you."

Alex was quiet, seemingly stuck for a response. She took the chance to flee. With a firm grip on her luggage handle, Dana hurried toward the entrance of Vice. She didn't look back.

She kept expecting to feel a firm hand on her arm, but it never materialized. Only as the doorman grabbed her suitcase did she glance over her shoulder.

Alex remained where she'd left him. He stood absolutely still, shoulders back and hands at his sides. She would have seen his frown from a mile away.

Charming, youthful Zeus was gone.

The angry, vengeful god had taken his place, insulted by the actions of mere mortals.

***

Pulling his baseball cap low over his face, Bill

leaned against one of the pillars in the lobby.

He now had a name. Dana Hamill.

As soon as he'd spotted the Hamill woman this morning, he'd recognized Markov's elevator companion. When she'd checked out of the hotel, he'd sauntered close, pretending to talk on his cell phone. He'd been able to get close enough to hear her conversation with the checkout clerk.

"I'd like to check out please. It's Dana Hamill." She'd handed over her key card.

"And was everything to your satisfaction, Ms. Hamill?"

"Yes. Thanks."

When she turned to look at him, Bill raised his voice. "Is this where I can book a tour to the Hoover Dam?"

The clerk said something else and Dana Hamill stopped gawking at him.

He had a name. That was really all he needed.

Once she left the hotel, Bill remained for a few minutes longer, keeping an eye on Markov. The man clearly had a thing for the lovely Ms. Hamill. When she left, he looked like a puppy dog who'd just been kicked. Markov had stood still for a few moments after she'd exited and had then marched down some other corridor.

Bill did a quick Google search and located the woman's information, including her place of work.

He would have to pay her a visit soon. It didn't take a genius to figure out Markov was sleeping with her, and in Bill's experience, people revealed a lot of secrets while under the effects of the afterglow. What sorts of secrets did Markov share

as he and Ms. Hamill shared a pillow?
He'd find out.

Chapter Twelve

No one told him running in Las Vegas was a bitch.

An avid runner, Alex had thus far been working out on the treadmills in the executive health club at Vice. Today, after his conversation with Dana, he'd wanted to hit the pavement the way he used to do in New York.

As soon as he headed outside, he realized the folly of his ways. Nobody ran in Las Vegas. They meandered, usually with their arms overloaded with shopping bags, or even while carrying the odd pitcher of beer. With sidewalks and escalators that directed foot traffic into the various casino hotels, it was impossible to run without knocking tourists over.

He certainly couldn't blame the tourists. Without them, he'd be nothing. He just wished more of them had stayed home that morning.

Frustrated, Alex headed onto Park Avenue and circled the arena a few times. The scenery was uninspiring, concrete block after concrete block.

Next time, he would have to drive somewhere off the Strip to find an adequate place to run.

Not that he cared right now. Today, he just wanted to push his body.

To punish his body.

I have to be careful who I let into my world from now on.

Dana equated him with Tommy and he couldn't blame her. The greatest love of her life had let her down. Why would some Vegas hookup be any different?

And yet she'd said herself she thought he was the better man. He wanted to be the better man but he'd never be able to prove it if she didn't give him a chance.

Alex had asked Dana for honesty but he hadn't come clean either, not about everything.

His secret shame burned a hole in his chest. The flames stung so much he dared not even think about it for too long. Shannon's death, and the haze of forgetfulness that surrounded it, tormented him on an almost constant basis. The humiliation of having his name bandied about in the rag magazines had driven him deep into a hole.

But no one knew the worst part. He, alone, carried that burden.

Some days, he wondered if it might kill him.

"Jesus." As he approached Vice from behind, he bent over to tie his shoe. "You are so fucked up."

He knew his sense of guilt was playing with him again. When he was angry, it got the better of him. It would pass. It always passed.

But he did have to make some decisions. He'd

suggested Dana decide what she wanted out of life, as far as children.

He needed to do the same.

His heart pumping, sweat dripping down his back, Alex walked into the alley outside the administrative hallway. The alley was empty, as usual, and he welcomed the peace and quiet. The only people who used it were employees on their smoke breaks.

It was dark there, even in the daytime, but he just wanted to do a short cooldown before heading back to his apartment. Walking slowly, hands on hips, he paced the alley.

It might actually be a bit too dark there. He'd get some lighting installed so his staff didn't have to smoke while looking over their shoulders.

One more item on the to-do list.

Alex rolled his head to stretch out his neck muscles.

Only then, did he notice the shadow in the furthest corner of the alley.

He froze.

The shadow spoke. "It's been a long time, Alex."

"Gordon? Is that you?"

Shannon's brother emerged, clean-shaven and his head shaved. His lack of hair made him appear slimmer, almost gaunt in comparison, and nothing like the hairy, beefy man Alex had known. This man could walk right into Vice, past the undercover cops, and no one would connect him to the Dean family.

Even in the low light of the alley, Alex could see Gordon held a crowbar. His fist was tight around its base, his knuckles straining.

"You should probably put that down, friend."

"*Friend*. That's hilarious."

"The cops are looking for you."

"I know."

Alex took a step back.

"Don't even think of running."

Alex opened his arms wide. "You want to hit me with that thing?"

Gordon slapped the crowbar against his other palm. "I haven't decided yet. Truth is, I've been thinking about this moment for a long time. It's been playing in my head on a loop, only with different outcomes every time. Sometimes I shoot you. Sometimes I stab you. But most of the time, I pound your head on the floor, making you bleed the way Shannon did."

"You know as well as I do, Shannon's death was an accident."

"Don't you say her name!" Gordon pointed the crowbar. "Don't you *dare* mention her name. You don't deserve to speak it." He choked back a sob. "My baby sister shouldn't have died like that. She shouldn't have died at all."

"You're right." Alex blinked back his own tears. "She shouldn't have. I would do anything to bring her back."

"Liar! The last conversation you had with her was an argument. You told the police she suspected you of cheating. My sister was no fool. You *must* have been cheating."

"I never cheated on her, not once. But we had our problems."

"So you got *rid* of your little problem, didn't you? Tell me, Alex. You were at some fancy resort. How much did you have to pay to get one of the locals to polish her off? How much was her life worth to you?"

"I did not pay someone to kill Shannon. I cared for her."

"Cared for her, huh? You just didn't love her."

"I didn't anymore! Is that what you need to hear?" Hot tears slipped between Alex's eyelids. He wiped them away. "I tried. God knows I tried. The truth is, Shannon and I were over long before we got on that plane. I couldn't take it anymore. The constant snipping, the accusations. You want to know something, Gordon? I *wanted* to fucking cheat! I dreamed about it, about going to Shannon and laying it all out in front of her. She never believed I could be faithful so why was I trying so hard? But no, I didn't. Because, deep down, I couldn't hurt her like that, not when other men had already done it. She never trusted me, no matter how hard I tried to help her heal. When I took her to Bermuda, it was one last attempt to save what we had. There was no need for me to try to kill her. We were already through."

"I don't believe you."

"You know what? I don't fucking care. I have danced around you and your parents long enough. I tried so hard to be respectful, to offer support, and all you people have done is drag my name through the mud. You wouldn't let me come to Shannon's funeral, wouldn't even let me grieve her!"

His entire body coiled, Alex finally let his

despair manifest. On a wail, he punched the brick wall. Pain exploded up his arm. He crumpled to the ground, cradling his bloody fist.

In his moment of weakness, as he huddled against the wall, Alex expected to feel the whack of the crowbar. He might even have welcomed it in the anguish of that moment.

Gordon dropped the crowbar and kicked it toward the dumpster at the back of the alley. He stared at his hands, horrified.

All was still in the alley. Although sirens blared down the Strip, the soundtrack of Las Vegas, they weren't for him. The cacophony faded and all Alex heard was his breath and Gordon's breath as they both struggled with their thoughts.

He dropped to the ground next to Alex and reached for his hand.

Alex pulled away.

"Let me look at your hand. I'm not going to hurt you." When Alex offered him his arm, Gordon inspected the wound. "I'm no doctor, but you might have a fracture. You should probably get this checked out."

"Isn't this what you wanted? For me to feel pain?"

"I don't know what I want anymore, Alex. My life is so messed up. It seems like yesterday my dad was telling me Shannon had died, and now here I am, in an alley with you and your broken fist. I don't remember how I got here. It's a blur."

"I know. It's been a blur for me too."

Gordon wiped his eyes. "My car's parked around the corner. I can take you to the hospital."

"You mean, dump my body?"

"No body dumping today, I promise." Gordon stood and held out his hand. "Let me help you up."

Alex hesitated, but then extended his left hand.

***

"Welcome back, stranger? How was your Vegas stay-cation?"

"Great, Phil." Dana smiled at her boss and set her briefcase down next to her desk. She should have known he'd want a debrief the minute she got through the door. "Really great, thanks."

She wasn't even sure why she'd come in this morning. She'd taken today off, an opportunity to recover from her week with the girls. However, as soon as she'd walked into her condo early that morning, she changed into some work clothes and had walked right out.

It was too empty. She didn't want a day alone at home. She wanted to be at work, surrounded by deadlines and distractions.

"Did you like Vice? Pretty swanky, huh?"

"Yeah. I got bumped to a penthouse suite."

"No kidding? Your sister must have been over the moon."

"It was really nice. We definitely, um, took advantage of all the amenities."

"Wow." Phil stood at her desk, slurping his coffee and smiling. "So, is it true what they say? What happens in Vegas and all that jazz?"

"You're the head of the convention and visitor's association. I'd assume you know all about that."

He chuckled. "I've had my moments. Not anymore. The wife keeps me on a tight leash nowadays."

"Now, now, Phil. Remember what I taught you? We don't say *the wife* anymore. Pam has a name. It's good to use it." There may have been a slight sharpness in her tone, but she didn't rein it in. Phil loved it when she talked this way. In fact, he'd told her one of the reasons he'd hired her was because she didn't pull punches. He might be old school and it sometimes slipped out in conversation, but he appreciated her frankness.

"One of these days, I'll learn, kid. And by then, they will have hung me out to dry. You'll be running this show then." He nodded toward her laptop. "What does your day look like?"

"Busy. I'll be touching base with Leon Corcoran from the Shriners this morning to finalize details, and I have calls set up with the teachers' federation and the auto convention folks."

"Do you think you can squeeze in another little project?"

The last *little project* Phil gave her was a convention of seven thousand accountants. She fully expected the same this time. Not that she was complaining. She wanted to stay busy.

Busy was good.

Busy wouldn't allow her to dwell on a certain pair of eyes and the disappointment she'd seen in them.

"Sure. Who've you got for me?"

"Last week, I met with the head of the Mystery Writers Association. I convinced them Vegas is where they need to be for their annual conference in two years' time. I talked you up. They want you to handle all the details."

"Great. Sounds exciting."

"It's the first time they've brought the conference to the Strip, so I want you to pull out all the stops. We need the best shows, the best restaurants, the best hotel."

Best hotel. One stood head and shoulders above the rest.

"They want Vice."

Her heart sank. "Oh, yeah? Vice is awesome, but maybe I should reach out to my contacts at the Bellagio or the Venetian. I have a solid relationship with those hotels. I know I can get a good price for them."

"Really?" Phil made a face. "I thought you said you liked Vice."

"I do. I just don't have the same connection with the executive team there."

Liar. She had a connection, all right. Just not the sort Phil would have condoned.

"Hmm. Well, I'm going to need you to establish that connection right away. They asked for Vice and I promised them Vice. Oh, and see if you can get them into that new club there. What's it called again? Covet! That's it. Get them into Covet. If anyone can pull it off, you can. I've sent you an email with the contact details for the mystery writers. And before you ask, no, her name isn't Miss Marple." Laughing at his own joke, Phil walked back to his own office. "I'll be in meetings all day. Text if you need me."

Dana sat in her chair and stared ahead. She'd known she'd have to contact the people at Vice sooner or later. It was the most sought-after hotel in Vegas.

It wasn't as if she had to deal directly with Alex. He was the owner. He wouldn't get involved with her convention. He had people to do that sort of thing for him.

Still, if she wanted to, she knew she could text him and tell him about the convention. She could keep it professional. No doubt, he'd respond in kind. After all, no hotel owner worth his salt would turn away that sort of business.

Professional.

Sure. She could see it now. They'd be all handshakes and small talk.

She wouldn't swoon and he wouldn't look at her as if he wanted to eat her.

Right.

For the purposes of maintaining a clean break, she'd hoped to avoid dealing with Vice for a while. If she didn't have to think about Vice or Covet, she wouldn't have to think of Alex.

A clean break.

A dull throb formed over her temple but she couldn't afford to think of that either.

Determined, Dana fired up her laptop and started to work.

***

"You got off lucky." In the hospital parking lot, Gordon held the car door open for Alex.

"I guess I did." Alex got in, taking care not to jostle his right hand. It still hurt like a sonofabitch. Served him right for getting emotional in front of his stalker and punching a wall.

His wounds had been cleaned and ice had been applied to keep down the swelling, but he'd be wearing a splint for a few weeks. He also had a few weeks of rehab to look forward to.

Gordon got into the driver's seat and shut the door. "At least your injury sounds kind of badass. A 'boxer's fracture.' Who knew?"

"They should call it an 'idiot's fracture.'"

"You're not an idiot, Alex."

"I hit a wall."

Gordon hung his head. "I guess I sort of drove you to it. Listen…I'm sorry about everything."

"Yeah. Me too."

"I've never seen you express any emotion. It was easy to believe you didn't feel any."

"Do you still blame me for Shannon's death?"

"I think I just needed to blame someone, so I blamed you. We shouldn't have kept you from the funeral. You needed to grieve. You never got the chance, and that's on me and my folks. I'll talk to them when I go home. You know, if the cops don't lock me up for defacing your hotel and coming at you with a crowbar."

"I'm sure I can talk to the cops."

"You'd do that?"

"I'm tired, Gordon. I don't want to fight with you and your parents anymore. I just want to put my life back together."

He nodded.

"Besides, you never actually came at me with the crowbar. You just sort of waved it in my general direction."

Gordon chuckled. "If we're coming clean, I should probably admit I never would have attacked you. I just wanted to scare you into some kind of confrontation. Like I said, my life is messed up."

"I heard you lost your job."

"Fifteen years with those bastards. I knew a reorg was coming. I just never guessed it was coming at me."

"That's a lot of experience. Shannon used to talk about your work. She was proud of you." As an idea formed in Alex's head, he prayed he wouldn't regret it later. "What if I could find you something in my HR department? Would you be interested?"

Gordon's jaw dropped.

"It would be a trial, of course." He grinned. "I'm not a total idiot."

"That was the last thing I expected you to say."

"Frankly, it was the last thing I expected to hear coming out of my mouth."

"That's generous of you. Thanks, Alex. But I can't work for you."

"Too many memories?"

"That, and I have to rebuild my life. This grief, it's been hard, harder than I ever would have imagined. There are so many things I didn't say to my sister when I had the chance. I need to start fresh. But I appreciate your offer."

"So, we're good?" Alex extended his left hand to shake.

"I want to be. I'm tired too." He shook his hand.

288

"I hear you."

They sat for a while in the car, both of them staring ahead. After a while, Gordon stuck his key in the ignition and turned it. "Would you...it's going to sound stupid."

"What?"

"Would you like to see where Shannon's buried? Next time you're in New York, I could take you there. Only if you want to, of course."

"I want to. I'd like that very much."

"It's a nice plot. You know, with trees and shrubs nearby."

"She would have liked that."

"Yeah. Okay, we'll do it." Gordon revved the engine. "I guess I should take you back to your hotel."

"Where you are staying?"

"Oh, my God, don't even ask. It's a total shitbox."

Alex laughed. "Let's see if I can't find you a better room."

"I don't want to impose, Alex. After all, I did come all the way to Sin City to, um, cause you bodily harm."

He held up his bad hand. "I found a way to do that without your help, remember? Let's go."

***

It had been two weeks since Dana's departure from Vice.

She wasn't coming back.

The cold realization had stricken Alex late one

289

night and had moldered in his gut ever since. He'd held out hope for a couple of days after his encounter with Gordon, figuring she'd go home and realize they were good together.

He hadn't heard a word from her.

After injuring his hand, he'd hung out in his apartment, working from home for the most part. It had given him time to think.

He didn't want to lose her but he also didn't want to pressure her.

Two days ago, he'd caved and texted her. Just a short message to let her know he was thinking of her.

Alex: I hope you're doing okay.

Forty-eight long hours had elapsed. She hadn't replied.

"What did you expect?" He rifled through the papers on his desk late one night. "She made her intentions clear."

He'd thrown himself into his work, as much as he could with the injury. There were still areas of the business he needed to learn, but he could only absorb so much at a time. Just this week, he'd met with the heads of catering, finance, and the hotel spa. His inbox had exploded accordingly. That was his own damn fault. He'd asked to be copied on certain communications. While he appreciated the distractions and the challenges, he also wanted to tell everyone to fuck right off and leave him alone.

Tonight, he was supposed to host another private party at Covet.

It was the last thing he wanted to do.

He was expected to schmooze the in-crowd. All the while, their booth would stand sentry in the corner, a reminder of what he and Dana had shared. The red velvet curtains would mock him. He wasn't sure he could bear to see anyone else sitting in the space. It would feel like sacrilege.

He checked the time. Like an automaton, he finished up his work, not bothering to put his laptop away. A few papers lay scattered on his desk, as well as two used coffee mugs. He didn't care.

Taking care not to bump his right hand, he retreated to his bathroom. The doctor had assured him his thermoplastic splint could be worn in the shower, but it was removable, so he'd gotten in the habit of taking it off to shower. Showering, itself, wasn't easy, but he was getting the hang of washing his hair using only his left hand. He'd never be ambidextrous, but he was getting things done.

After showering, Alex put on some fresh clothes. Out of habit, his gaze landed on his rack of ties, but he'd forsaken them the past couple of weeks. He hadn't even bothered to tidy up his closet. A pile of dirty clothes sat on the floor.

Dana would laugh if she saw it.

Once again, he thought of her. This time, he was tormented by the memory of her riding him in bed. Her sweet body, slick with sweat. Full thighs, gripping him hard. Her breasts bouncing as she took him deeper.

So beautiful.

He needed to get her out of his head. She'd clearly forgotten about him.

Finished dressing, he headed to Covet.

Alex didn't say a word to anyone as he strode through the club toward the private rooms in back. As soon as he entered the VIP room, several acquaintances hurried over to greet him. He let himself be led over to one of the couches. A waitress brought him a Coke, even before he could consider what sort of drink he'd like.

He didn't turn it away. He drank it down.

Someone started talking about a movie premiere, but five minutes later, he couldn't remember which one.

For that, he'd have to care.

He sat in the same seat for an hour, barely participating in the conversations around him. It was all the same to his guests. They might defer to him but, at the end of the day, they didn't care about him either. It was more important for them to be seen in his company.

Out on the pool deck, people frolicked. Celebrity guests laughed, their heads thrown back, their brilliant white teeth lighting up the room. Connections and liaisons were established. Love affairs began and ended.

There was a time when he enjoyed being among these people, when the fantasy turned him on.

Tonight, he couldn't have cared less.

At the end of the hour, a woman approached. He knew her well. Rose Harding was a starlet. Her latest film had been a hit at Sundance. A beautiful brunette, clad in a form-fitting purple gown, she had the eye of every man in the VIP suite.

But she sat next to him.

"Hi, Alex. Long time, no see."

"Hi, Rose."

"Congratulations on Covet. This is the first chance I've had to visit."

"Glad you could make it."

"Me too. I needed to get away from work for the weekend."

"Trouble?"

"Not really, but my new leading man has shit for brains. He's driving me crazy. He's never acted a day in his life, but he's prettier than I am. He makes Brad Pitt look like Quasimodo. You watch. He'll be the toast of awards season."

"Poor you. Life's hard, isn't it?"

"Don't tease." She grinned. "You have no idea what I deal with on a daily basis." She nodded at his splint. "How did you hurt yourself?"

"I punched a wall."

"Ooh. I never pegged you as a violent man."

"I'm not."

"And what made you want to punch a wall?"

He shook his head, not wanting to get into it.

"There are only so many reasons a man would cause harm to himself. Guilt, shame, love. Or maybe the lack of it. So which one is it?"

Alex stared at the pool deck.

"Ah, so we're not talking about it. That's okay." Rose scooted closer and turned her attention toward the pool as well. "I love what you've done with the pool."

"Thanks."

"It's a beautiful night and the water looks inviting. I see your splint is removable. Care to take a dip with me?"

"I don't feel like swimming."

"Who said anything about swimming?"

Alex looked at his lap.

"There's something different about you tonight, Alex."

"Same as I've ever been."

"No, there's definitely something. You look...lonely."

"Look around, Rose. I'm surrounded by friends." His flat voice didn't sound convincing.

"Of course, you are. And you know as well as I do the loneliest place in the world is often a crowded room, where everyone is watching your every move."

A male guest at the bar held up his glass, in a silent toast to Rose. He looked her up and down as he drank.

"They're watching you tonight, not me."

"Boring." She rolled her eyes. "Talk to me, Alex. Tell me why you have that whole Byronic hero thing going on."

"I don't."

"Now, now. I recognize a tortured hero when I see one. Didn't anyone ever tell you? Women love damaged goods. Ask any woman here and she'd offer to take you home so she could fix you."

"Is that what you want? To fix these damaged goods?"

"Not at all. I mean, don't get me wrong. The dark circles under your eyes are mighty appealing, but I'm not tender-hearted enough to think I can repair you. I'd really just rather fuck you."

294

There was a time when Alex might have been shocked by her candor.

Not anymore.

The man at the bar started walking toward them. Alex inclined his head. "You're about to get a similar offer."

She clicked her tongue in disdain. "I don't feel like playing with the plebs tonight. I'd rather spend some time with my gorgeous host. I hear you live onsite. I don't suppose I could see the master's chambers." She put her hand on his thigh.

Alex met Rose's gaze. Desire shone there, clear as day.

Rose Harding was exactly the sort of woman the world expected to see on his arm, the sort of woman *Dana* expected to see on his arm. Talented and sexy, Rose oozed confidence. She traveled easily through his world, accustomed to privilege and excess. She spoke her mind and took what she needed.

It would be so easy with Rose. They'd be an item in no time. He could already see the headlines. *Hotelier and actress set a date.*

He'd partied with Rose for a couple of years now and they'd talked at length. He knew her as well as he knew any of his patrons. Certainly, he knew enough to understand there wouldn't be any concerns about children or the lack of children. In fact, she'd broken up with her last boyfriend because he'd wanted a family and she didn't. She was perfectly content acting and partying. Hell, a woman like Rose would be gone on movie shoots half the time. To some, that would be ideal. They could do their own things and would meet up periodically to smile for the cameras on the red carpet.

The perfect relationship for his cold heart.

If he had an ounce of sense in his head, he would grab Rose by the hand and never look back.

"I'm going to share a secret with you. I've had a crush on you for a long time," she whispered in his ear. "Take me to your room. You could do anything you want to me. And I do mean *anything*."

I should have stayed far away from you, Alex Markov.

Dana seemed so far away right now, she might as well have been in the North Pole.

What was she doing right now? Was she thinking of him or had she managed to banish him completely from her thought processes?

The hand on his thigh crept higher. He gently removed it.

"Maybe I didn't make myself clear." Rose cocked a perfectly-groomed eyebrow. "I did mention the fucking, right? Lots of fucking?"

"Yeah, I got that."

"So, you're brushing me off?"

"I'm afraid so."

She sat up straight, her head quirked at an odd angle on her long neck. "Interesting."

"There's still the guy at the bar."

"Him? Do you see his outfit? I don't think so."

"I'm sorry." Only he wasn't.

"Hmm. I don't think I've been rejected since high school. This is a novel feeling. I'm not quite sure what to make of it."

"I think you'll struggle through." He stood and set his glass down on a table. "Have a good night, Rose."

Alex turned from the starlet's wide-eyed gaze and walked out of Covet.

As he headed back to his apartment, he wished he could talk to Shannon just then. Despite knowing he'd never cheated on her, it couldn't have been easy for her to see him in this environment with people like Rose. It wasn't so much that Rose was a bad sort, but she never heard the word *no*. So few of his customers ever heard the word *no*.

Shannon had come to the club with him many times. How often would she have heard hushed conversations about him? How many times would she have had to tolerate other women making passes?

He may not have acted on them but they still happened.

And he should have done more to reassure her.

He had another chance now with Dana. He wouldn't screw this one up.

Chapter Thirteen

When the phone rang that weekend, Dana thought it was her parents again. Ever since telling her folks about her diagnosis, her mom had been bombarding her with emails and phone calls. Most of them referenced articles about "fixing" infertility. So far, Dana had received articles telling her to cook with coconut oil, to drink more water, to avoid stress, and to minimize her exposure to household chemicals.

It was driving her up the wall.

She answered the phone. "Hello?"

"You're alive."

Tommy. Damn. In her quest to bury herself in work, she'd forgotten to get back to him. Okay, in truth, she may also have avoided him on purpose a few times.

"You haven't returned any of my calls, Dana."

"What do you want? I'm busy."

"I want to talk to you."

"Why? Haven't we said everything there is to say?"

"No, actually. Look, it's important. Can I swing by? I never had a chance to give you my copies of your key anyway."

"Don't worry. I had the locks changed. You're good."

"Dana, please."

"Can't you just tell me this important piece of information over the phone?"

"No. I'm downstairs in the foyer. Will you buzz me in?"

"Shit, Tommy. I don't need any of your drama."

He was quiet for a second. "Please."

"Fine. You get five minutes." Rattled, Dana ended the call and hit the buzzer that would allow him into the condo. She checked her reflection in the foyer mirror, although she had no idea why. She'd stopped worrying about how she might appear to him.

The knock on her door shocked her into awareness and readied her for a fight. She wasn't sure what Tommy wanted, but figured it couldn't be good. She whipped open the door. "Well?"

The Tommy who stood outside her unit looked so much different than the man she'd left behind in the hospital cafeteria. For one thing, he was hunched at the shoulders, clearly nervous about being there. There were some dark circles under his eyes.

Who cared? She had dark circles under her eyes too. She hadn't been sleeping well lately, despite being back in her own comfy bed.

"Can I come in?"

She held open the door and Tommy walked

inside. "Feel free to leave your shoes on. You won't be staying long."

"Boy." He took up a spot near her couch, but didn't sit. "You really hate me, huh?"

"I don't hate you, but I've decided it's perfectly fine for me not to like you."

"I get it." He gestured toward the couch. "Do you mind sitting with me for a second?"

Dana sat. Tommy sat at the opposite end of her couch. The last time they'd sat together there, they'd watched a romantic movie, sharing a bowl of popcorn. Afterward, they'd made love. She banished those memories.

"How was your week at Vice?"

"Could we not do this? The whole small talk thing? I'd prefer if you just told me the reason you've been texting me every day for the past couple of weeks."

"Okay." He inhaled deeply. "I, um, I'm *with* someone and I didn't want you to hear about it through the grapevine."

"I hardly think that's news, Tommy. I figured you'd meet someone at some point. In fact, I haven't exactly been sitting here by my lonesome—"

"She's pregnant, Dana. Tiffany's pregnant."

"Pregnant? But that would mean you…"

"I'm sorry." He paused, letting the news and the dates sink in. They hadn't been apart long enough for him to find a new girlfriend and impregnate her via traditional timelines. Tommy Boy had gotten a head start.

"How far along is she?"

"Five months."

"Five months, huh? Wow."

"I'm sorry, Dana."

"You cheated on me. This just gets better and better."

"It was a moment of weakness on my part. That night I went clubbing for my brother's stag…it just happened."

"Oh, no. You don't get to use the old 'it just happened' excuse. I remember you coming home that night. You weren't drunk. You knew what you were doing."

"Like I said, it was a moment of weakness."

"Oh, my God. That day in the hospital cafeteria…you already knew. Didn't you?"

He was silent. Red in the face and silent.

"You already had an exit plan. My diagnosis just gave you the out you needed."

"I'm sorry. You deserve so much better."

"And what about Tiffany? I almost feel sorry for her. Does she even realize how she fits into your plan of convenience?"

"I don't expect you to forgive me."

"Forgive you? Tommy, you're lucky if I don't slaughter you where you sit. You sicken me."

"I guess I deserve that. I feel badly, Dana, but I hope you understand this is actually a good thing for me. I'm excited about the baby and Tiffany's a good woman."

"Hmm. Did Tiffany know you had a fiancée when you slept with her?"

More silence.

"Right. Well, I hate to burst your bubble, but that

means Tiffany's not such a good woman. And you know what? You *suck* as a man!" She stood, shaking in outrage. "Get the fuck out of my home."

He stood.

"Don't ever call me, Tommy. Don't ever text me. Don't send me baby photos or invite me to any wedding showers. I hope you rot in hell."

"But…"

"And you know what else? I feel *sorry* for that child." She pointed at the door. "Fuck you."

Tommy exited without another word. Dana slammed the door behind him.

When she finally roused herself from her spot in the foyer, she walked into the bedroom and lay down on her bed.

The phone rang. Her parents trying her again, no doubt.

She didn't answer.

***

The clock on Dana's bedside table said two a.m.

Two in the fucking morning and sleep wouldn't come anywhere near her.

She rolled over in bed and squeezed her eyes shut. The minutes crawled. Hunger and thirst alternately plagued her, causing her to toss. She tried rolling onto her stomach. Whenever she couldn't sleep, laying on her belly seemed to help. For some reason, in that position, sleep always overwhelmed her.

This time, it didn't.

On her stomach, her cheek to the pillow, she was

too conscious of the ache inside her. Laying still, her hearing muffled on one side, she became aware of her heartbeat. The steady pulse grew louder in her head, echoing in a void.

She was a vacuum. Tumbleweeds rolled around inside her, scratching the walls of her womb.

Kicking off the covers, Dana launched herself out of bed and began pacing in the dark. When she stubbed her big toe on the corner of a table, she shouted. "Fuck!" Grunting, she fell back on the loveseat opposite her bed, clutching her toe. "Fucking piece of fucked up shit. Fuck you. Fuck. *You.*"

Startled by her own outburst, Dana reached for the closest light stand and flicked the switch. She caught her reflection in the mirror hanging opposite.

A haunted woman stared back at her, one she didn't recognize. Her tired eyes, so dark and lined with shadow, made her look older than her years. The lines around her mouth seemed deeper. Pain was etched in every crease.

Dana hated that woman. She hated Tommy. She hated fucking Tiffany.

He just had to go and cheat on her with a Tiffany. She'd never met a single Tiffany she liked. It started in grade two when Tiffany Atkinson pulled her hair in class, initiating a cycle of bullying. It had all gone downhill with the Tiffanys since then.

Now, as darkness put a chokehold on her room, she wanted to unburden herself.

She wanted to talk to Alex. More than anything, she craved his company.

Which wasn't possible.

She couldn't be that person, and certainly not after leaving his last text unanswered.

If she ran to him now, for sex or solace or whatever the hell she needed, it would be just plain wrong.

Because he wouldn't turn her away.

Or would he?

Walking gingerly on her sore foot, Dana walked into the kitchen. She opened her fridge and reached for a bottle of spring water hiding at the back. Right next to it was half a bottle of white wine she'd forgotten. She had opened it up a few weeks ago when a friend came over for dinner and must not have finished it.

Right now, it looked eminently more drinkable than spring water.

Dana hauled the bottle out of the fridge and walked over to her sink. She didn't bother to grab a wine glass, or even a plastic cup. She unscrewed the lid and lifted the bottle to her lips.

All at once, she remembered that first night at Covet, when she'd drunk so much she couldn't even find her own purse.

All her breath rushed out of her lungs.

She poured the contents of the bottle out into the sink and watched the liquid disappear down the drain.

Fighting tears, she grabbed her cell phone from where it was charging on the kitchen counter.

No new messages. Of course.

Alex's last text was still at the top of her message feed.

Alex: I hope you're doing okay.

She wasn't okay. In truth, she probably hadn't been okay for a while.

Would he still care?

Feeling like a fool, Dana tapped out a quick message. She wouldn't ask for help and didn't want to come across as needy. She would ignore the fact that she'd never needed him more and would simply acknowledge his text. She should have done it the moment he'd sent it.

Dana: I'm sorry I never replied.

There. Just an apology. He could do with it whatever he needed to do. She wasn't asking for anything, wasn't begging to feel his touch on her body, no matter how much she wanted it. The message might be coming through at two in the morning but that didn't mean it wasn't sent in the spirit of politeness.

It was simply an expression of her regret and she didn't expect a response.

But she got one, less than two minutes later.

Alex: It's okay. You're up late too. Can't sleep?

A question. If he didn't want to talk to her, he wouldn't have made an open-ended statement.

Dana: No.

Alex: Are you okay?

Dana: Been better.

Alex: I can come over. We can talk.

Dana: You mean you still want to talk to me?

A pause.

Alex: Dana, I'd be happy just to breathe the air around you right now.

Shivers made her skin prickle into goosebumps.

Maybe talking wouldn't be so bad. They were both adults and liked each other. Who said their time together had to be about sex? Surely, they could contain themselves.

Although the thought of Alex's hands on her body made her want to sing. When he touched her, she felt youthful and free and jubilant.

She needed to feel it again.

Dana: I'd love to see you.

Alex: Tell me where you live. I can be there in no time.

She glanced around her messy condo. Shoes were strewn in the hallway and dirty dishes were piled on the counter. Not exactly like the pristine environment in Alex's apartment. It might very well give him a case of the hives. Besides, her condo seemed far too empty. She didn't want to be there, not tonight.

Dana: I'll come to you.

Alex: I can send a car for you.

Dana: No, it's okay. I'm all right to drive. I'll just throw some clothes on.

Alex: I'll be waiting.

Dana: Alex, I want you to know this isn't a booty call. I'm not trying to use you.

Alex: No booty call. Got it. Am putting my booty away as we speak.

In spite of herself, she laughed.

Alex: Just come.

She signed off and threw on some clothes, the jeans she'd discarded earlier and a clean t-shirt. Finger-combing her curls, she headed to the washroom and brushed her teeth. Slipping into a pair of ballet flats, she grabbed her purse and keys and headed into the corridor, locking her condo behind her.

She reached Vice in ten minutes, but it felt like thirty. She left her car with the valet and headed inside. Even at this time of night, or morning, the casino was a hive of activity. Tourists played every casino game. Some were dressed in eveningwear and others wore casual clothes. One woman even had pajama pants on. As Dana walked by, she saw a security guard discreetly approach the woman, reminding her of the dress code. The annoyed tourist was forced to abandon her slot machine and walked away, presumably to change.

If there was one thing they insisted on at Vice, it was a classy atmosphere.

Although the lights and commotion were programed to distract, she continued toward the admin hallway. Tired, she stumbled a few times on the thick carpet.

She must have looked stunned, because one of the employees came over and asked if she was lost.

She shook her head. Although she didn't say it out loud, she'd never felt so lost in her life.

"Alex."

She didn't realize she'd mumbled his name until it was out of her mouth.

Everyone comes to Vegas looking for something.

She was looking for him, even though she might not have a hope in hell of having a long-term relationship with him.

The admin hallway was dark and quiet. The casino might never sleep, but it seemed the admin staff members were allowed their rest. There were a number of offices in the hallway, all locked up. At the end of the corridor was the elevator that led to Alex's office. Its silver doors were shut tight, making it seem like an insurmountable barrier, a symbol of what she had with Alex. The doors might slide open here and there, but at the end of the day, if she didn't have the right access, they could be closed to her for good.

Not tonight. As Dana approached the elevator, it

swung open for her.

She should go home and get over herself. Lots of people had partners who cheated. She didn't even love Tommy anymore. In all honesty, she'd stopped loving him the moment he'd retreated from her in Dr. Batra's office.

Go home. Don't involve Alex.

She couldn't leave. His allure held her in place. She was a willing captive, hoping for a glimpse of her captor.

More than anything, she was tired, so tired, and she just wanted to talk to him. Was it so wrong? Perhaps talking wasn't what drove her out of bed. The pain inside her had grown, had started snarling like a beast, and it could only be eased by his touch.

Dana longed for Alex to touch her again.

Here, in his domain, her loneliness didn't cut quite as deep. Here, she could breathe. Filling her lungs, she entered the elevator and backed up against the wall.

So tired.

For a second, she pretended she was in Covet, numb with pleasure.

Numb, through and through.

Willing herself there, Dana closed her eyes.

***

Alex held his breath as the elevator rose to the fourth floor. What on earth would have possessed Dana to reach out to him in the middle of the night? Not that he minded. She could text him round the clock and he wouldn't have a problem with it.

309

The elevator door opened. Dana leaned against the wall, her face creased in pain.

He flew to her. Her mocha skin was grey.

She opened her eyes. They were the shadowed eyes of a woman at the end of her tether.

He held out his arms and she fell into them.

"It's okay." He stroked her curls and kissed her head. "It's going to be okay."

She raised her head. Her lips parted. So kissable.

No. She left him, wanting a clean break. He could comfort her, but they couldn't do this.

Dana had made it clear she didn't want him in her life.

Get a grip. She's not yours. Remember?

"Your hand. Alex, what happened?"

"It's okay. I'll tell you about it later. What happened to you?"

"Tommy."

Fuck, how he hated that name. Without even knowing the story, Alex wanted to wrench the man's arms from their sockets.

I'll kill him.

He forced himself to take a deep breath.

"Let's go inside. I'll make you a coffee."

They walked into his office and she took a seat on one of the couches.

"No coffee, please. I can't sleep as it is. Caffeine probably isn't the best idea." She shrugged her shoulders. "*This* is probably not the best idea."

"What?"

"Being here. With you."

"Never mind that." He turned on the coffeemaker and it gurgled to life. "You don't mind

310

if I make myself a cup? I could use the caffeine."

"Go ahead."

Small and soft, her voice put a vise around his heart. As he waited for the cup of coffee to brew, the vise tightened, squeezing all the vitality out of him.

Swallowing hard, Alex grabbed the freshly brewed coffee. He sat next to her and waited, giving her as much time as she needed to unburden herself.

"So," she began, "I saw Tommy."

The imaginary vise turned into a massive millstone, grinding Alex's heart into powder. "Okay."

"He cheated on me while we were together. They're having a baby."

Alex *would* kill Tommy. He might even toss him under that millstone. "I'm sorry."

"This shouldn't hurt as much as it does."

"Give yourself some credit. You're only human."

"It doesn't matter. I should be able to rise above it. This isn't like me. I don't sit around the house, pining for men. I move on. It's what I've always done. I don't understand why I'm so stuck."

"Dana." He gentled his tone. "You're not pining for Tommy. The man's a shithead and doesn't deserve you, and you know it. This has never been about Tommy."

Her eyes welled up.

He put his coffee down and curled his arm around her shoulder. "Sweetheart, you need to talk to someone about your condition."

"I can't. Alex, I just can't."

"You have to."

"I feel like I've lost myself. I've never been the sort of woman who picked out baby names before she picked out a husband. I've always rolled with the punches. But now, I can't help feeling this is somehow my fault. That I failed somewhere along the way."

"You didn't do this."

"Didn't I? I don't know. And even if I didn't cause it, I'm drowning under the weight of it. It's always there, Alex, at the back of my mind. It's like a monster, clawing at me. Every time I find a distraction, I feel the scratch of its nails on my back. Reminding me. Torturing me."

Her description tortured him.

"Some days, I think it might kill me."

"No." He pulled her into his arms. "You're too strong for that. Besides, I won't let anything happen to you."

"I'm not sure I deserve your friendship."

"I'm not offering friendship, Dana. You know that."

She gazed at him. Once again, her face was so close, so touchable. And yet she was vulnerable in the worst way. He shouldn't want her, but he did. He wanted to take her into his bedroom and fuck the sadness out of her. He wanted to fuck her into a state of unending bliss.

"Look." With trouble, he put some space between them. He couldn't think when she was so close. "I'm not trying to pressure you, and I know you believe you're making some sort of noble sacrifice by staying away from me, but let's not kid ourselves. We care about each other. We want each other. I'd like to be at your side for this, but not just for this. For everything. And I think if you give us a chance, we can work through these feelings together."

She stood and paced. "What if I'm not enough for you? What if you change your mind?"

"Listen to me." Alex reached for her. "Anyone who thinks you're not enough on your own is a damn fool. And as for either of us changing our minds, we'll never know if you're not willing to take that risk."

"I can't."

"Nothing in life is guaranteed. Children, marriage, jobs, health, sanity. None of it. But whatever we're given, I'd like to share it with you."

"How can you know? It's too soon."

"I get that. I've just never felt this way before."

Wonder made her dark eyes appear twice as large. "I'm not sure I'm ready to make promises."

"I don't expect any. Let's start out simple. We agree not to label this and we take it one day at a time. We can even keep things platonic. Just don't shut me out."

"Platonic, huh?"

He grinned. "Sure. Why not? I can do platonic. I'm an easy-going guy."

When she smiled back, the horrible millstone rolled away. "Yeah, sure. Something tells me you can do platonic and easy-going as well as you can do messy."

"Yeah, well, I've been doing messy pretty well lately."

"Really?"

"There are three shirts sitting on my closet floor right now. I'm almost filthy." He chuckled. "I'm just asking for a chance to be there for you."

"I'd…like that."

Not only did the millstone disappear, it took the vise with it. Alex's heart expanded like a balloon, filling his veins with heat again. "Good. So, it's too early to go out. Do you want to watch TV?"

"No, thanks. I'm already worrying about how I'm going to make it through the work day. I'll be a zombie."

"It's Sunday. Do you always work the weekends?"

"No, but I just got a new convention. I wanted to get a head start on a few things."

"Oh, yeah? Which convention?"

"The mystery writers."

"I heard they were coming to town. Congratulations on landing it."

"Thanks. I usually do my own legwork, but this one sort of landed on me. My boss made the initial contact." She made a face. "They want to stay at Vice."

"Awesome. Consider it done."

"You'd be okay with that?"

"Why wouldn't I? I'm glad you told me. I'll make sure we treat them well."

"I can't be seen giving Vice preferential treatment. I work with every major hotel on the Strip. They all pay hefty membership fees to belong to the convention and visitors' association. I have to be careful about conflicts of interest."

"You said yourself they want to stay at Vice. You would have booked it, whether you knew me or not, right?"

"Yeah."

"Then I see no conflict here."

"Thanks, Alex. I didn't want to impose, you know, after everything."

"It's not an imposition. We'll give them the VIP treatment, I promise."

Another smile. Everything inside him lightened and soared.

"On one condition. I want you to talk to someone."

Her smile drifted away.

Alex placed a hand on hers. "I know it won't fix things, Dana, but it might help. Please."

"Okay."

Alex turned on some soft music and they sat together. They didn't talk, just basked in each other's presence. She cuddled next to him, her head on his shoulder, and he put his arm around her. It felt so good just to rub her shoulder and offer some comfort.

Her head grew heavy and bobbed a couple of times. He loved that she was comfortable enough to fall asleep with him. He started to doze next to her when she startled awake.

She shook her head. "I should go. I have a lot of work to do."

"But you're exhausted."

"I know but I have no choice."

"You'll be working from home?"

"Yeah. I have to update our online delegate

website before I send the link to the mystery writers. We have a few new member restaurants and I need to get them added to the site. They've paid for the privilege so they get more exposure with convention delegates."

"I was hoping to hang out with you today, you know, in a platonic way."

"I would like that, but—"

"How would you feel about getting away from the Strip altogether and doing your work in a nice, peaceful environment?"

"Sounds great. Where is this haven?"

"My home."

"But you live here."

"I have another home. When I first arrived in Vegas, I rented a house in Summerlin. I decided to keep it, you know, so I have a quiet place to clear my head."

"Only you, Alex Markov, would keep a house on the side to help you clear your head." Her laugh was music, so bubbly and happy, it might have been composed by Mozart.

"I like my casino pad, but it's not exactly homey. It's important to have a retreat."

Dana's lips continued to curl upward in a silent tease. It would be so easy to claim those lips right now, to lick at the corners and nibble their fullness.

But he didn't.

They were having an actual friendly conversation, one in which neither of them was declaring the intention of fucking the other. He wanted to sleep with her and he knew she wanted to sleep with him.

It probably wasn't what either of them needed.

Alex kept his lips to himself and swallowed his sigh of sexual frustration.

One step at a time.

"Okay, Alex. I'd love to see your retreat. Do you mind if we stop at my place first, so I can get my laptop?"

"Sure. I'll get my driver to take us, so neither of us falls asleep at the wheel. Sound good?"

"Yeah." Dana's voice was quiet, pensive, but the smile hadn't left her face. "Sounds good."

Chapter Fourteen

Dana had figured Alex's home away from home would be something special.

What she didn't expect was a Mediterranean-style estate.

She'd seen a few nice homes in her time. After all, her role at the tourism association involved a fair amount of hobnobbing. She'd been a guest at numerous wine and cheese parties, weddings, and open houses. Her long-term clients had invited her to many exquisite functions.

This was just a whole other level of exquisite.

Perhaps it only seemed that way because Alex's apartment at Vice was so spare and basic. It made this custom-made home seem even more luxurious. Under the bright sun, she could see all the details that proved the house was well maintained. There wasn't a single patch of dead grass on the green lawn. Not one chip marred the brickwork. And the floor-to-ceiling windows sparkled.

Before getting out of the car, he leaned over and whispered in her ear. "I know. It's a bit much, but I like it."

She gestured toward the courtyard and the elegant arch at the doorway. "Who wouldn't?"

He smiled. He got out of the car, grabbed her briefcase with his left hand, and held the door open for her. "Ready?"

"Probably not, but I'm coming anyway."

Alex spoke to his driver, Pierre, and let him know he wouldn't be needed for a while. The man waved and drove away.

As they walked to the front door and passed through the archway, Alex tried to sling his right arm over her shoulder. Upon remembering his splint, he huffed in annoyance, and lowered it. "I can't wait 'til this thing is off."

"You never told me what happened."

"It's a long story."

"I have time."

"How about I make you breakfast while I tell you?"

"But your arm."

"I'll manage. Are you hungry?"

"I could eat."

"All right, then. Let's eat." He unlocked the front door and allowed Dana to pass through. "Make yourself at home."

The foyer led directly to a living room that was awash in light, thanks to another set of enormous windows at the back of the house. Through these windows, she spotted a gorgeous pool, the sort often featured in landscaping magazines. She hurried forward to take a closer look. A number of decorative boulders and shrubs dotted the edge of the pool. At the far end, the boulders were built higher and water spilled from the highest point, creating a waterfall. It created a curtain-like effect, making her think of their nook at Covet.

Alex walked up behind her. "What do you think?"

She turned to him. "I've never seen anything like it in someone's backyard. It's amazing."

"I guess it's nice. I don't spend a lot of time out there, though." A muscle ticked at his jaw. "Where would you like me to set up your laptop?"

"Oh, um, wherever it's convenient."

"There's a seating area in the kitchen. You could start your work there while I cook for you."

"Are you sure I can't help?"

"No. I want to do it, and I don't want you to be stressed about your work."

"Okay," said Dana, relinquishing herself to the lunacy of this situation. "I'll work in the kitchen. Let me know if I can open any jars for you."

"Will do."

Alex showed her to a bright kitchen with all the latest appliances and neutral granite countertops. He even had one of those refrigerators that made coffee. She closed her gaping mouth and took a seat in the breakfast nook. Plugging in her laptop to the nearest outlet, Dana clicked on her document and reviewed what she needed to do.

It wasn't long before her attention strayed back to the chef.

Although normally of a serious disposition, Alex lightened up in the kitchen. She caught him humming as he prepped his ingredients, and almost laughed when she realized what he was humming.

"Wake Me Up Before You Go-Go" by Wham.

He bobbed his head, unaware of her appraisal. He moved slowly, taking care not to use his right hand if it could be avoided, and never once asked for help. She almost got up a few times to take over, but knew he would only shush her and send her back to her seat. With tentative movements, he mixed up a few ingredients in a blender. He closed the lid, held it down and shimmied to the music in his head.

Dana had to put a hand over her mouth so she wouldn't laugh.

At that point, she didn't even bother to pretend she was working. "It's not fair that I'm toiling over here and you're having fun with George Michael."

He looked over his shoulder. "You heard that, huh?"

"Oh, yeah."

"If you tell people, I'll deny it." He winked.

Who was this new Alex?

As he fiddled with the blender, she offered her help again. "I'm worried you're going to hurt your hand."

"I'm fine. Awkward, but fine. You worry too much."

"I have been accused in the past of smothering people."

"Who said that?"

"My sister."

"No comment." He was trying not to roll his eyes, but she caught some movement at his lashes. "You just sit there and relax. I've got it covered."

While he finished with the blender, he prepared some coffee. After rummaging in the fridge, he produced a plastic container filled with chopped up green pepper. Returning to the stove, he sautéed the peppers. His blender ingredients then went in the pan and he pushed them all around with a spatula. After a couple of minutes, he put the whole thing into the oven.

Pouring out two mugs of coffee, he joined her at the table and placed one in front of her. He returned with the other for himself. "There. Let me know if it's strong enough."

"I'm sure it is." She took a sip of the delicious concoction but then set it down. "This is weird."

"The coffee?"

"No. This situation. Alex Markov cooking me breakfast in his home."

"Yeah, for me too. I don't cook for anyone, but it's because most of my meals get delivered or prepared in the Vice kitchens."

"So, I'm special?" she teased.

"You are," he replied, without a hint of a tease in his voice. "I want to do this for you."

"Ah." She sipped her coffee to escape his gaze. "Are you going to tell me what happened to your hand?"

In a few short sentences, he relayed the story of Gordon Dean. When he told her about the crowbar, a chill skittered down Dana's back.

The thought of anyone hurting Alex took her to dark places.

"And this man is still in Vegas?"

"Yeah. I vouched for him, of course, so the

322

police have dropped the case. I don't want Gordon to suffer. He made a couple of mistakes. I'm not pressing charges. He'll be heading home soon, but I think he just wants to come up with a plan first."

"And what if that plan involves coming back for you?"

"He won't. We talked it through."

"Alex, this man and his family have held a grudge for over a year now. He flips sides out of nowhere, and you believe him?"

He averted his gaze.

"One minute, Gordon Dean was threatening you with a crowbar. The next minute, he's taking you to the hospital? I don't understand. Why did he change his mind?"

"I broke down in front of him. I think it shocked the hell out of him. Gordon realized he'd taken things too far. He's even going to talk to his parents and get them to back down."

"How nice of him."

A glint shone in his eyes. "Are you worried about me?"

"Of course."

"Don't." He covered her hand with his for a moment and then went over to the stove. He opened it and used a fork to poke at the omelette. "Eggs are ready."

"Great."

Too bad her stomach was turning over.

Alex plated the mixture and delivered it to the table. "Now, be open-minded."

"Why?"

"They're not real eggs. I'm vegan."

"Vegan? How did I not know this about you?"

"Well, we haven't really spent our time together eating."

As his voice trailed off, he met her gaze. Hunger flitted through his eyes and it had nothing to do with the faux omelette.

"I guess you're right." Her tongue thick, Dana attacked the dish and put a forkful into her mouth. "Mmm. These are good. Different, but good." She ate some more. "So, what made you go vegan?"

"Mostly health reasons."

"Mostly?"

"After Shannon died, I indulged in a lot of things that were bad for me. I realized I'd been consoling myself with a lot of rum. Getting wasted was never my thing, but being numb was."

Dana understood that temptation.

"Being in the public eye, with so much scrutiny coming at me, I knew I had to maintain some sort of control over my behavior. But I kept to myself a lot, drank a lot. One day, I grew tired of looking at my sad face in the mirror. I cut down on my drinking, started eating different foods, and hired a personal trainer to help me work out. My trainer suggested the vegan diet, so I tried it. I function better this way. With my work, I need a lot of energy and this helps."

"That's great. I admire you for making such a big change."

He smiled, sipped his coffee, and polished off his own vegan eggs. "Thanks. If you don't mind, I'm going to change into some shorts. I'm hot in these jeans."

"Of course."

"I'll be right back." He disappeared through a doorway. Within seconds, she heard his footfall above her.

Dana finished her breakfast, marveling at the egg-like texture and taste. She typed out a couple of notes on her document but the floor creaked above her as Alex moved around his bedroom.

Somewhere over her head, Alex was stripping out of his clothes.

He would be unzipping his jeans, dragging them over his hips, stepping out of them. His gorgeous thigh muscles would be on display as he chose a pair of shorts.

Cruel memories pounced. Specifically, one of him tied to his bed, his legs splayed. She'd run her fingers up those long legs as she'd nestled between them…

Dana groaned.

This day might not end up being so relaxing, after all.

When she heard Alex's footsteps coming down the stairs again, she held her breath and stared at her computer screen. As he entered the kitchen, she glanced up.

Why was it that the sight of him in workout gear should stimulate her just as much as the sight of him in one of his sexy suits?

He wore a simple outfit consisting of black gym shorts and a sleeveless shirt, along with a pair of running shoes. Everything about him was long and lean and hard. His biceps flexed as he scratched his back. His strong thighs gave way to solid calves.

You might want to stop staring at his muscles now.

"How was the omelette?"

"Great, thank you."

"Can I get you some more coffee?"

"No, thanks. I'm good." She let out the breath she was holding and it sounded a lot like a sigh.

Alex walked over and passed a hand over her hair. "You look shattered."

"I am. It's hard to concentrate."

"You need to rest."

"You're probably right."

His half grin made her belly flip-flop. "Wanna see my bed? You know, for sleeping purposes?"

"I can rest on the couch."

"Don't be a martyr. If you want to get any real work done today, you need some sleep."

"You don't mind?"

"Dana."

"Okay. In that case, I would love to see your bed. For sleeping purposes, of course."

"Come on."

She locked the screen on her laptop and shut the lid. He held out his hand and she took it.

Holding his hand was such a simple pleasure, his skin sliding against her own, and yet it brought her such joy. As their palms touched, Dana felt protected and cherished.

It made her greedy for more.

He led her down the hall and up a curving staircase. They didn't speak on the way to his bedroom and she barely took note of her surroundings. She saw flashes of color and art hanging in the hallways, most of it in calming and neutral shades like the rest of the house, but she didn't notice many details.

She was too concentrated on Alex, on the way he moved and the way he smelled. The more she got to know him, the harder her attraction was to fight. She just wanted to run her hands over his shoulders and down his back. She wanted to feel him inside her again, to watch his face as he came.

What would he look like next time? Would he grunt in ecstasy? Would he bite his lip? Would he close his eyes or maintain eye contact?

You need to stop dreaming about his O-face.

They turned a corner into another hallway and walked through an open double door. The first thing that greeted them was a king bed. She grinned upon seeing the grey color palette on the sheets and walls.

"Why are you making that face?"

She pointed out different objects around the room. "Grey, grey, black, navy, grey, grey, greyish brown. Hmm. I'm seeing a theme."

"I like what I like." He pulled aside the sheets for her and shifted his balance from one foot to the other. "So. These sheets were just changed. I'm sort of a fanatic about fresh sheets."

Dana didn't know how to respond. Alex was being charming and accommodating, almost awkward. He disarmed her. She'd had an easier time when he was intense and serious.

He opened one of the drawers in the closet, pulled out a couple of his t-shirts, and set them on the bed. "If you're more comfortable wearing one of these, feel free. Or if you prefer staying in your clothes, that's fine too." He rubbed his chin. "I'm not trying to tell you what to wear to bed."

"I know."

He pointed to a closed door. "The bathroom is in there. Help yourself to anything you need. In the second drawer, you'll find extra toothbrushes and toothpaste. There are towels stacked near the vanity. If you need to freshen up and have a shower, go ahead. Not that you're not fresh, of course."

She laughed. Okay, he needed to stop being so adorable or she was going to jump his bones.

He reached for her hand and played with her pinky finger. "I just want you to feel at home."

"Thanks."

He sighed and released her hand. "Anyway, I'll be in the gym, working out. It's down the hall from the kitchen, if you need to find me."

"Don't worry. I left bread crumbs."

"Ha ha. Are you trying to say my house is too big?"

"I'm just kidding. It's beautiful. Extremely large, but beautiful."

"I guess it can feel a bit lonely when I'm here on my own. It's a lot less lonely with you here."

For a few moments, neither of them spoke. Tension throbbed so hard in her head she wondered if the room had a pulse.

"Well," he finally said. "You get some rest. Take all the time you need."

"I appreciate it."

He walked to the doors and began to close them, but popped his head back in the room. "Dana?"

"Yeah?"

"I just want you to know…I don't think you're broken. I think you're perfect."

Goose pimples claimed every inch of her skin.

Alex slipped outside and shut the doors.

Alone in his bedroom, she did a slow turn and examined every corner of the room, avoiding his hulking bed. She could only ignore it for so long. Exhaustion forced her shoulders into a slump and those sheets looked so inviting.

Unable to resist, Dana undressed, leaving her panties on. She held up both of the t-shirts he'd set out for her, a plain white tee and a fitted black one. They both smelled fresh and clean.

She spotted the t-shirt he'd just discarded, hanging over the back of a chair. She reached for it instead and brought it to her nose.

Closing her eyes, she breathed in. It smelled like him, like his deodorant and traces of his cologne.

She put it on instead of the clean ones and brought the collar to her nose once again.

What am I getting myself into here?

"A bed," she reminded herself. "Nothing more. He's just offered you a place to crash. Get over yourself. This isn't goddamn Romeo and Juliet."

Dana got into bed and pulled the covers atop herself. Turning to his closet, she counted yet another armada of suits. "Grey, grey, blue, black, grey, grey. Ooh, a tuxedo. Grey, grey…"

Smiling to herself, comforted by his luxurious sheets and his nearby presence, her eyelids began to droop.

The memory of his voice lulled her into sleep.

I think you're perfect.

***

"Aw, man." Wade Kennedy groaned as his cousin told the cab driver where to go. "The Golden Nugget? Seriously, Benny?"

"What?" His cousin Benny shrugged. "It's a Vegas institution. You promised to show me whatever I want when I visited."

One day off this week, and Wade was stuck in another casino. God forbid Benny might want to check out the Hoover Dam or ride horses at a ranch. No, his cousin wanted the Golden Nugget.

At least Wade didn't have to worry about escorting drunks out of this casino.

As the cabbie headed toward East Fremont Street, Wade stifled his next series of groans. Benny was right. He had promised, and it wasn't often his cousin got to visit. If he wanted to waste his time, losing money he couldn't afford on the slots, who was Wade to argue?

The cabbie dropped them off near Fremont and they walked the rest of the way. Sheesh. Even in the daytime, the Nugget managed to look bright and garish.

At least when he was working at Vice, Wade didn't have to shield his eyes from all the gold fittings.

"Do you mind if I hit the casino?" asked Benny, already pulling out his wallet.

Before Wade could answer, Benny was across the lobby. "Be my guest."

Benny got comfy at a slot machine. Wade stood next to him but was bored out of his skull within minutes. "Hey. I'm going to go look around."

Benny, absorbed in his game, just waved him away.

"Try not to miss me." Wade headed off, in search of a coffee shop. Something told him this was going to be a long day.

As he marched through the casino, it was hard for Wade to turn off his security instincts. Over to his left, he spotted a wobbling woman who'd already had too much to drink. Over to his right, he saw someone fall asleep at a slot machine.

"Not my problem."

Smelling coffee, Wade turned a corner. As he approached a craps table, he ran into a familiar face.

"Hey, Pierre." What was Alex's driver doing here? He was wearing his uniform. "Aren't you on the schedule today?"

Pierre looked up, startled. "Oh. Hi, Wade. Yeah, uh, I drove Alex out to the Summerlin house. He's with a friend for the day."

"Really? Which friend?"

"Some lady named Dana."

"Oh, yeah! Dana. Rico Maximum's pal."

"What?"

"Never mind." At least someone was enjoying his day off.

"Anyway, Alex gave me a few hours off. I'm just killing time."

"Right." Wade nodded at the table. "You gamble much?"

"Nah. Just having some fun." Pierre's eyes flitted around the table. "What about you?"

"I don't gamble. Probably a good thing,

considering where I work. It's my day off anyway. My cousin's visiting. He wanted to come here."

"Cool. Well, have a good one."

"Yeah, you too."

As Wade walked away, he tried to ignore the warning bell sounding in the pit of his gut. If Alex wanted to release his driver from work for the day, who was he to argue?

Some shouts went up at the craps table. He looked back, just in time to see Pierre pound the table in frustration.

Someone just lost big.

Unsettled, Wade went in search of his coffee, with every intention of making it a double espresso. When he walked back the same way, Pierre was still grousing.

Wade took up a spot behind a pillar and watched Pierre for a while. With every loss, the driver grew more agitated.

So much for just having some fun.

Sighing, Wade made a mental note to talk to Pierre the next time they had a quiet moment.

After years of working in casinos, he knew how to spot a compulsive gambler. And he was looking at one right now.

***

"Can I see what you're working on?" Alex crept up behind Dana.

"Sure. Have a seat."

He joined her on the kitchen bench. She smelled good, like faded perfume and bedding. There was a

332

faint mark at her temple, from where the pillowcase had bunched up under her head, and he wanted to kiss it. Resisting, he left a bit of space between them.

He was glad she'd fallen asleep. She'd slept for a good couple of hours. He'd used that time to squeeze in a run on the treadmill and had grabbed forty winks on the couch. After she'd vacated his room, he went upstairs to take a shower, only to notice she'd slept in his discarded shirt.

It wasn't hard to figure out why and it made him happier than he'd been in a long time.

Dana had been hard at work for the past hour and he'd stayed out of her way, but his curiosity was getting the better of him now.

She clicked on an icon and a website appeared. "This is the delegate website that I maintain for our clients. I tailor it for every convention, based on what their interests are, where they'd like to eat, that sort of thing. Of course, I have to ensure all our customer companies are represented in some way, but very often, convention reps will tell me if delegates have particular needs. I try to organize the data in a way that makes sense for each group."

Dana handed Alex the mouse and he perused a couple of the pages. She had placed a vibrant "Welcome to Las Vegas" page at the start. With links to YouTube and succinct blurbs from travel magazines, it caught the eye. Unlike so many of the advertisements for Vegas, it wasn't focused solely on gambling. It included images from theater shows, fine dining, and a sumptuous hotel room.

"Hey," he said with a smile. "That's a Vice

room."

"Of course. It's the hotel they want, so I included it. The rooms at Vice are outstanding. I want them to feel indulged, right from the get go. I have stock photos for every hotel on the Strip, but what's the use of including a picture from the Luxor if they aren't going to stay there?"

"I like the images you used. That's a nice collage of the bedding and the marble in the washrooms. I didn't realize we had those kinds of stock photos."

"You don't. I took some of my own shots when I was there. I hope you don't mind."

"Not at all. These are excellent."

"Thanks. I've always thought a good picture should engage the senses. Look around any room at Vice and you'll see the most amazing textures. Silk, marble, metal. It seems a shame not to show that off. That's why people want to stay at your hotel. It's a feast for the senses."

She was good at her job. Very good. "Show me more."

As Dana reached for the mouse again, their hands touched. A spark of electricity made her gasp.

Alex fought the urge to clear the table with his arm and lay her on it.

She cleared her throat as she clicked on another page. "Well, my contact has told me which cities the mystery writers are coming from, so I've put together a "Getting Here" page, which will show how many miles are between them and Vegas."

"I like it. The page has good information, without being cluttered."

"Thanks. There are pages for dining, shows,

sports, and of course gambling. I have a page on what to do in the surrounding areas. I've even made up some digital postcards so delegates can send them to family when the time comes. See? You click on the back of the card, write an email address and a message, and voila! It's sent, without ever having to buy a stamp."

"You love your job, don't you?"

"Yeah." She sat back. "I really do."

"It shows."

"Thanks, Alex."

"I can see that'll make it very hard for me to steal you away."

"From my work?"

"No. From your job. Come work for me, Dana."

"What?" She shoved his good arm. "Get out."

"I mean it. You already know my conventions team. I'd have no trouble putting you in charge of them. You'd be doing the same sort of work, only for Vice, Sin, and Luxe."

"Alex. You're joking."

"Do I look like I'm joking? What do you make right now?"

"That's a personal question."

"If I don't ask it, how will I know what to double?"

Her mouth fell open. "You want to *double* my salary?"

"I don't mess around."

"I should warn you. I'm not cheap."

"You're worth it." His gaze dropped to her lips, her kissable lips. He leaned in.

Dana scooted out the other side of the bench.

"Alex, I'm flattered, I really am. But you've made it clear you're interested in me, you know, as more than just an employee."

"True."

"So how do you reconcile that with offering me a job?"

"Easily. There are plenty of couples out there who work together."

"Yeah, but how many of them slept together before the work started?"

"Are you trying to confuse me with facts?"

She leaned across the kitchen bench and kissed him on the cheek. "Thank you. You're sweet and it's a very tempting offer, but I really do love my job. I get to talk to people from all over the world, sharing the best that Vegas has to offer. Visitors trust me to help them sort through the maze of attractions on the Strip. They may be here to work, but I have the privilege of making sure they have fun while they're at it. I get to put smiles on people's faces every day, and I can't envision a day where I don't get to do it."

"That sounds an awful lot like fulfillment."

"What do you know?" Her face grew pensive. "I never really thought of it that way."

"And I wouldn't dream of messing with that."

"I appreciate your offer."

"Fair enough. It doesn't mean I won't try again, though."

"And it doesn't mean my salary won't have gone up by then." She hummed in amusement and sat back down. "I hope you have deep pockets, Mr. Markov."

Alex grinned and let her get back to work.

***

By nine o'clock that night, Dana knew she should really be getting home. Tomorrow was a work day for both of them, and she'd trespassed on Alex's hospitality long enough.

His Summerlin "retreat day" had done the trick. She'd managed to do far more work than she would have done at home. In her condo, she would have found ways to avoid her laptop. Eventually, errands and chores would have dragged her away. At Alex's place, she could forget all those things and concentrate on her job.

Of course, now she had all sorts of chores to catch up on before she went to bed. She hadn't even done any grocery shopping for the week ahead.

They had enjoyed a long, leisurely dinner in each other's company. Alex had ordered in. Something made out of eggplant and chick peas for him. Steak for her. She'd felt guilty eating meat in front of him but he didn't make an issue out of it. He'd offered her some of his dish and she'd been surprised at how delicious it was.

Alex surprised her in many ways.

They sat around the kitchen table now, enjoying the last of their coffees. Neither of them had said anything for a while. Alex kept looking at her, desire darkening his gaze. No matter how much coffee Dana drank, she couldn't seem to quench her thirst.

She didn't want to go home. They may not have

done anything exciting today, but it had been the best day she'd had in recent memory. Just being with him in his space was comfortable, natural.

Alex put down his coffee and loosened his splint. He prodded the skin underneath.

"Is your arm hurting?"

"It gets sore at the end of the day. I'm dying to take this thing off."

Dana got up and moved her chair in front of his. She sat before him and held out her hand. "May I?"

Alex removed the splint and extended his arm.

"Where is it sore?"

"Near my elbow."

She held his arm carefully, bracing it on her knee. "I won't touch the fractured area, but I can rub your elbow for you."

"That would be nice." He frowned but not in anger. His expression was too full of heat.

Making slow circles around his elbow, Dana massaged his arm. As soon as she touched him, Alex let out a long breath. She drew closer, spreading her legs so his knees could sit between hers. As she kneaded his skin, their heads fell together, foreheads touching.

Alex closed his eyes.

His nose tickled hers. His breath landed on her cheek. Her womb clenched, wanting to take him in as deep as it could.

She moved her fingers up his arm, luxuriating in the bulges at his biceps and triceps. Caressing her way up to his shoulder, she continued. Because he wore short sleeves, she was able to enjoy almost every inch of warm skin. When her fingers dipped

338

under the collar of his shirt to touch his back, Alex moaned.

"Dana." Her name was followed by a quiet curse. "Stay the night."

She let go of his arm. "I want to, I really do, but—"

"No." He cupped her cheek. "Don't overthink this. This doesn't have to be hard. Just say what you want."

Each of her breaths was shakier than the one before. "I want you."

He bit his bottom lip and smiled.

"What about your arm?"

"We'll be careful."

His lips at her neck caused all thought to fly away. Dana closed her eyes, brushing her chest against his, and let him worship her skin. With his tongue, he traced a path along her jaw, back to her mouth. As his lips met hers, he clutched at her bottom with his good hand, urging her closer, digging his nails into her jeans.

As they kissed, his hand journeyed between her legs, toying with the denim seam. Jolts of pleasure shot through her limbs, liquefying her. She writhed in her chair, trying to ride his hand, but the jeans proved a horrible barrier. She couldn't get close enough.

"Time to take these off, angel."

She nodded.

"I can't undress you with my arm the way it is." He shook his head. "I wish I could rip your clothes off."

"Let me do the work."

With difficulty, Dana stood and removed all her clothes. Once she was naked, she moved between Alex's legs. He licked at her nipples, nibbling each one in turn, and held her by the bottom. His left hand caressed her ass cheek, plumping and squeezing its fullness, grazing the area between her legs.

As her juices coated his fingers, Alex marvelled. "Fuck. You are so beautiful."

His talented digits prodded, spreading her moisture. On a gasp, Dana opened her eyes.

Just outside, the tempting waterfall by the swimming pool beckoned.

"Alex," she whispered. "Let's go outside."

He looked up from her breast. His eyes were hooded, like a drunk man searching for his next mouthful of wine. Upon seeing her intention, they darkened. "Is that what you want?"

"God, yes."

His head dipped in a solemn nod. "Sure."

She helped him undress, taking care not to hurt his arm as she removed his shirt. She bent down to untie his shoes, conscious of his gaze. After removing his sport socks, she hooked her fingers in his shorts and boxers and pulled them both down.

An enormous erection sprang before her.

Already on her knees, Dana took advantage of the moment and licked him from base to tip.

Alex touched her chin and encouraged her to stand. "If you do that, I'll be a goner."

She stood and he led her to the pool deck. Testing the pool water with her toes, she sighed at its heat.

"Don't worry." He stepped onto the steps and held out his left hand. "I keep it warm."

Stepping gingerly, she joined him in the pool. The water lapped at her knees, thighs, and the valley between them. He dove into the water, coming up dripping, and held out a hand. Although she knew her puffed up coils would pay her back later, she threw caution to the wind and dove after him. Together, they swam toward the waterfall.

The pool was lit, and it seemed they moved through a blue sea. Once they reached the waterfall, they dove under it, entering the nook from underneath the cascade. A bench was carved into the pool's side and they sat there. It did indeed feel like their nook at Covet, only here, they could sit and listen to the gentle water coursing.

Alex sat on the bench and Dana scrambled atop his lap. Clutching at her with his good hand, he let the right one sit off to the side. Their mouths met in a frenzy. She ground down over him, dragging her core over his girth.

"Shit," he said between kisses. "The condoms are inside."

In that moment, Dana didn't care. She certainly couldn't get pregnant. Still, it was probably best not to get too carried away. "We can go inside soon."

"It might have to be very soon." Alex closed his mouth over her nipple and sucked.

They rocked and rocked under the waterfall. So hungry for him, Dana almost slid his length inside her a few times. She was so wet and ready and her body had a mind of its own. Her thighs shaking with her lack of control, she ran her fingers over his rippled chest, amazed at the patterns created by the lights around the pool.

Alex never took his eyes off her. He gazed at her, seemingly enrapt.

She was falling for him.

The realization caused her to cry out. How had it all happened so fast?

She didn't want to fall in love. Not yet. She didn't trust her heart.

Mistaking her cry for one of pleasure, Alex slid two fingers inside her. "Come for me, angel."

With the heat of the Las Vegas night enveloping her, and Alex's stronger heat filling her, Dana came. It was unavoidable. One touch from this man and her spirit shot into the sky, a phoenix taking flight.

She needed to cage that bird and control this situation.

"I love doing that to you." His tongue flicked at her lips. "I love holding you and feeling your body shake."

"You're very good at this."

"It's not me, Dana. It's us. Together. We're good together."

"The sex is amazing."

"It's not just the sex and you know it. This isn't just about me making you come. Any idiot can bring a woman to orgasm." He frowned and swiped at a few droplets of water that trickled from his hair into his eyes.

"Are you okay?"

"The pool...I should have stayed inside."

Oh, no. The pool. Of course. The papers had

reported Shannon had died by the side of the pool at their resort. "Alex, I'm sorry. I didn't think."

"Believe it or not, the pool is one of the reasons I liked this house. I just haven't used it until tonight."

"Let's get out."

"No. I can't hide away forever." He took her hand and placed it over his heart. "Dana, this past year, it's been hell. Knowing what some people think of me. There have been times when I haven't even wanted to show my face. The shame...it's unbearable." He blinked and tears appeared in his eyes.

"Oh." She kissed his eyelids, wanting to take his sadness away. "You have no reason to feel ashamed."

"Don't I? I destroyed Shannon."

"No, you didn't."

"I might as well have. I may not have bashed her head on that resort floor, but I initiated the chain of events that got us there."

"What do you mean?"

"It all started when I opened my clubs in New York. The funny thing is I met her there. She was one of my first customers. We got to know each other. She was beautiful and fun and it seemed right, but from the beginning, I sensed she was clingy. It didn't bother me at first. I liked having her around, but it got intense. She didn't like me talking to other women at the clubs and used to hang on my arm, watching their reactions to me. I wasn't flirting with anyone else. I've had girlfriends cheat, and I made up my mind I would never do it. But Shannon never trusted me, not really."

"Why not?"

"Same story as everyone else. She'd been cheated on herself, several times. I didn't blame her for being suspicious and I promised her she didn't have to worry about me. But as my nightclubs became more popular, the clientele began to change. It wasn't just New York club kids anymore. Celebrities were starting to call. I added VIP suites. We started getting a lot of attention."

"You were growing your business."

"To Shannon, those movie actresses and popstars were just more women she couldn't compete with. She stopped coming to the clubs and would ask me a hundred questions when I got home, grilling me on who was there, who I'd spoken to. It got on my nerves, and little by little, I started to spend more time away from home. I didn't want to have to account for all my actions."

"Of course, not."

"My circle of friends expanded. All of a sudden, I was rubbing elbows with some very influential people. I won't lie. I found it exciting."

"Anyone would. Look at your friends, Alex."

"Friends, right. The thing is, these people who come to my clubs, they're not really my friends. They use me as much as I use them. My clubs became a place for me to forget, a place to escape. A place to, well, covet what I couldn't have."

Just as Covet had become that place for Dana.

"Some mornings," Alex continued, his voice quiet, "I wake up and I hate those people with everything in me. Shannon recognized that but I wouldn't listen to her. She got tired of competing with fakes and losers, and I don't blame her anymore. After she died, my business seeped into my life. I've kept everyone at arm's length. No real connections meant no pain. Deep down, I think I might be the biggest fake of all."

"Oh, Alex. You're not a fake. You've been nothing but real with me."

"I want to be that for you. I want to be everything you need me to be, and not just because I couldn't do that for Shannon. Because you mean a great deal to me and I think you might be one of my only real friends in the world."

It broke her heart. Although surrounded by adoring people, Alex felt utterly friendless.

"But there is one thing my fake friends have given me. Because they never get too close either, they've pretty much accepted me as I am, which is something I don't always get from the rest of the world. My reputation doesn't bother them. They don't care what the press labels me. If someone calls my past sordid, they embrace it. When Shannon's family blamed me for what happened…"

"What *did* happen?"

"That night in Bermuda, Shannon and I had an argument, a bad one. She accused me of flirting with the waitress at dinner. I'd finally had enough. I called her insecure. I called her a lot of things. She said I was cold, unfeeling. And you know what? In that moment, I was. I stopped caring. I stopped trying. I had brought her on that trip to try to fix our relationship but she couldn't see that. She couldn't see past her jealousy. We'd both had a bit to drink that night. She took off, saying she wanted to clear her head." He choked on his words. "And I let her go. I should have chased after her. I should have made her stay in our room, but I was so fed up. So *sick* of feeling guilty for nothing!"

"But you stayed behind."

His shoulders slumped. "They figure she must have stumbled in the dark. And like I said, we'd been drinking." Alex gazed, unseeing, through the waterfall toward the pool deck. "Shannon must have wandered to the pool. She fell and hit her head on a concrete ashtray pillar. A resort employee found her the next morning when he went to clean the pool."

"I'm so sorry."

Alex's face twisted. "She died that night, because of me."

"Alex, honey, no." She grabbed his face and kissed him on the lips. "No, no, no. It's not your fault."

"It might as well be. That night I met you, at the tiki bar, I had just moved to town and was feeling sorry for myself. I couldn't stop wondering if things might be different if I'd followed her. Whether any of it even mattered at all."

"You were there to forget everything. Just like me."

He nodded. "But my demons won't let me forget. If I'd been better to Shannon, she might still be here today."

"Alex, you listen to me. You are a very good man, and even if Shannon was still here today, you might still be having the same arguments. Sure, you might have gotten married, but that wouldn't have fixed anything. It might only have added to your stress. What happened to Shannon was horrible and sad, and I'm so sorry for her, but you need to stop beating yourself up. You can't live this way. It'll kill you."

"There are people who believe I'm guilty."

"Oh, yeah? Well, fuck those people! No one asked them."

He laughed through his tears. "I like you."

Dana wrapped her arms around him and got as close as she could to him. His pain, and her anger at the people who doubted him, made her shiver.

"You're cold. Let's get out of this pool."

"Good idea. I want to lay in your bed again, but with you."

"Careful, sweetheart." Alex whispered into her hair. "I might just have to keep you there."

Chapter Fifteen

As Gordon checked out of his shit motel, he glanced out the front office window. There was another car parked next to his.

Weird.

So he wasn't the only one who'd shelled out cash to stay in this dump.

Grabbing his luggage, he headed outside, glad to be breathing fresher air.

A man got out of the car next to his and leaned on it, waiting for him.

Gordon headed to his driver's side. "Can I help you?"

"You Gordon Dean?"

"Who's asking?"

The man extended his hand. "Bill Patterson. I'm a reporter."

Gordon slung his suitcase into the back seat. "No comment."

Patterson hurried around to his side of the car. "I'm not here to bother you. I just have a few questions about Alex Markov."

"Everyone always does."

"And with good reason."

"I'm not interested in talking about Alex."

Patterson leaned against Gordon's door.

"Look, buddy. I have a long drive ahead of me. Do you mind?"

"I've spoken to your parents, you know. I know how they feel about Markov. And I just want you to know it's a crying shame that man is walking the streets. After what he did to your sister, no one would blame you for wanting to get back at him."

"What the hell? You know nothing about what I want."

"You sure about that? I've been following your case very closely. Your sister was a good woman. I can see the effect her death, her *murder*, had on everyone around her. Your parents are wrecks. You know this, Gord, my man. They've never gotten over the injustice."

"Shannon wasn't murdered. It was an accident."

"Did Markov tell you that? You don't really believe it, do you? If you did, you never would have gone after him with a crowbar."

Gordon's face was on fire. "How would you know that?"

"Like I said, I've been sticking very close to your friend Alex. He may have tried to pull one over on you with his 'woe is me' act, but I can see him for what he really is. A liar. He's responsible for your sister's death and he should pay for it."

"You don't know what you're talking about."

"How long do you think it took her to die, out there by that pool? She was all alone in her final moments and the last thing she ever got to hear was Alex, telling her to take a fucking hike. What do you think went through her head as the blood was spilling out of it?"

"Shut the fuck up about my sister."

Spittle gathered at Patterson's mouth. His eyes were red. "That's no way to die!"

"You're drunk. I can smell it on you."

"This isn't about me. This is about justice. Men like Markov get away with everything. Don't you think it's about time someone made him pay?"

Gordon shoved the man. "Leave me alone. We're done here."

"Look. I don't want to make you feel bad. I want to help you get some real closure. Just consider this for a minute. Whatever happened between Markov and your sister that night, he's still responsible. Let's say, for the sake of argument, it was all just a horrible accident. Don't you think Markov should have been at her side? He let her leave, instead of chasing after her. Doesn't that bother you?"

"No. Maybe. I don't know."

"If you ask me, it's pure negligence, and he should pay for it."

"You don't get it. Alex has suffered too."

Patterson brought his hands to his cheeks in an expression of mock horror. "Oh, poor Alex! Little rich boy must be having such a hard time."

"It's true. He has had a hard time."

"Not as hard as some people. Not like Shannon. Not like their baby."

"What baby?"

Patterson's eyes narrowed. "Oh, didn't you know

about that little detail? I'm not surprised. Very few people do. But I just got off the phone with your parents and they were very forthcoming. The doctors told them Shannon was pregnant at the time of her death."

"But...they never told me."

"Nope. Didn't want to hurt you, I guess."

Tears flooded Gordon's eyes. A baby. His sister's child. Snuffed out, before it even had a chance.

"Sorry to be the one to tell you, Gordo. Your sister was four months along with Alex's child. And that prick knew it the whole time."

"He never said."

"You mean your good buddy Alex didn't tell you the God's honest truth? Shocking. Well, I don't have the same issues. You see, this is just the sort of information the world needs to know, and I'm going to be the one to tell them. Alex Markov caused the death of his own child."

Gordon's stomach pitched. As bile shot up his throat, he turned away from his car and vomited onto the asphalt.

Patterson backed away. "Turns the stomach, doesn't it? Can I get you anything?"

"Fuck off!"

"You know, you should be thanking me for being up front with you. I'm the only one who has. If you have an issue, you should take it up with Markov." The man got into his car, took a flask from the glove box and drank the contents, wiping his mouth with the back of his hand. He then drove away.

Ten minutes later, his head throbbing, Gordon realized he was still standing alone in the parking lot.

All the bitterness Gordon had carried around for the past year resurfaced. Swallowing the last crumb of bile, Gordon got in his car.

Unfortunately, he had no idea where to go.

***

As Dana was on the phone, confirming room numbers with her mystery writers contact, a little instant message speech bubble appeared on her computer screen. The message was from the receptionist.

There's a special delivery out here for you. You're going to want to see this!

Dana bit her lip. It had to be from Alex.

Because it had been a busy week for both of them, it had been a few days since she'd seen him. After their time at his Summerlin house, they'd returned to the Strip early Monday morning. He'd had his driver drop her off at her condo in plenty of time for her to freshen up before work. They'd kissed, lingering at her door, like teenagers who couldn't let each other go.

On Monday night, they'd had dinner together. They'd talked about all the tough topics. Religion, politics, family. She'd been pleased to learn they had a lot of the same thoughts. The evening had ended with a groping session on her couch, but they'd both put a stop to it before it got too far. They were too conscious of letting themselves get carried away. As Alex had said, "I want to show you we're more than just sex."

Of course, he'd said that while his hand was on her breast. She'd taken great delight in pointing that out.

She'd suggested they take a timeout for a few days. Her work week was a busy one and she'd promised to take her mom to a couple of appointments. Alex had agreed. His week would be busy too.

Every night away from him tore a hole in her.

Even though he'd never slept in Dana's bed, the piece of furniture seemed bigger, emptier, without him. It was as if she'd already earmarked a spot for him there, on the left side, next to her alarm clock.

She finished her conversation with her client, checked her lipstick for smudges, and walked to reception.

Dana was greeted by the largest, most colorful bouquet of flowers she'd ever seen. It was so big, the delivery man struggled to look around it. There were lilies, and roses, and so many blooms she didn't even recognize. With greenery that spilled over the vase, it would make her desk groan under its weight.

"My Lord," she murmured.

"Someone's well liked," said the receptionist, Jane, her eyes twinkling.

"It's a bit heavy," said the deliveryman. "How about I bring it to your office for you?"

"That would be helpful. Thanks." Dana led the

way back to her office. She cleared off a corner so the man could set it down.

"I don't think the desk is a good idea," said the man, touching the falling greenery. "This stuff will get in your way."

"You're right. There's a little table behind you."

The man lowered the bouquet onto the table.

Dana reached for a little card that was tucked next to some red roses.

I miss you.
Alex

Warmth spread across her chest. She missed him too. This was moving so quickly, but it didn't make her want him any less.

The deliveryman cleared his throat.

"Oh." Dana slipped the card onto her desk. She'd forgotten he was there. "I'm sorry. Do you need me to sign something?"

The man took a step toward her. "Not at all. I just have a question for you."

"Okay."

"How does it feel to sleep with a murderer?"

"What?"

"I'm talking about your new boyfriend, Alex Markov. Tell me something. When he's fucking you, do you ever spare a thought for the woman he killed?"

Any heat Dana had been feeling was immediately replaced by icy cold. "Get out of my office."

"How do you justify it? Is it because Markov's

354

rich? I bet a lot of women would be willing to forgive him his sins for a chance at all that money."

Dana moved behind her desk. "I said, get out."

"I just want you to have all the facts. You seem like a nice lady. Markov, on the other hand, is slime. He hurts people. Badly. And he doesn't give a shit who he hurts as long as he gets what he wants."

Dana pressed a button on her phone and buzzed the receptionist. "Jane, call the police. This man is harassing me."

There was a flurry of exclamations on the other end as Jane assured her she was dialing 9-1-1.

"I won't stay." The man twisted one of the rose blooms on her bouquet, breaking it off in his hand. "But there are things you should know about charming Mr. Markov, things I'd be only too happy to tell you. Things the world will know about very soon."

"The police are on their way."

He tucked the rose into his shirt pocket, like some sort of creepy boutonniere. "Remember what I said. If you're smart, you'll stay far away from Alex Markov. I'd hate to see you on some other pool deck some day, with your brains smashed out."

With a wink, he hurried out of her office and down the hall.

Dana knew she should be taking note of the man's appearance, of the finer details, but as she picked up her cellphone to click to the notepad, her fingers could only type out one command. She texted Alex and asked him to come to her office. She didn't want to alarm him, but when her fingers typed out a hasty message about being threatened, she clicked "send" without even reading it first.

As co-workers began to call her name, flooding into her office to check on her, she tried to breathe.

***

"Drink some water." As the police officers left Dana's office, Alex held out the bottle of water on her desk. His hands shook as he held it out for her.

Patterson had come for her.

He would pay.

When the plastic bottle buckled under Alex's grip, he loosened his grip.

"I'm not thirsty."

"Maybe you should take the day off." Dana's manager, a man named Phil, patted her on the back. "Hell, take the week, if you'd like."

"No."

"Dana," said Alex. "Listen to Phil."

"No. I have work to do. I'm not going to hide away just because some crackpot reporter decided to take a shot at me."

When Dana had provided a description of the man to the police, Alex had recognized the similarities between the flower deliveryman and Patterson. The paparazzo had probably bribed the real deliveryman to hand over the flowers so he could get to Dana. The cops were going to follow up with the flower shop.

Alex waited a breath and regulated his voice. "That crackpot knows where you work. He knows where I live. He's been watching us."

"The police are on it, Alex, and you've already spoken to your security team. What more do you want me to do?"

"I want you to take some time off until they have their hands on Patterson. He's out there right now. The man is clearly obsessed with hounding me, and now he's trying to hurt me by intimidating you."

"Taking some time off is not a problem," agreed Phil. "I'll cover your desk, Dana. I'll handle your customers myself."

"So I'm supposed to stay at home, twiddling my thumbs?"

"Actually, yes," said Alex. "That would be great."

"Alex, I can't. I just took a week off. In this business, if I don't look after my clients, they'll find someone else who will."

"Your clients are devoted to you." Phil sat on the edge of her desk. "You know that as well as I do."

"And I want them to stay that way."

"What if you worked from home?" suggested Alex.

"And what if it takes the cops a while to find Patterson?" Dana argued. "I can't be at home the whole time. I have meetings and business lunches to attend."

"Then work from my home," he countered. "I can give you all the space you need."

Dana glanced at Phil. Alex knew she was uncomfortable about advertising their relationship, but the ship had already sailed on that one.

"No." She shook her head. "Thank you, but I don't want to uproot my life and my work."

This woman was driving him nuts. She'd been pale and jittery when he'd arrived, and had fallen into his arms the moment he'd been shown to her office.

He'd been fighting a major case of the jitters himself. As soon as her text had appeared on his phone, glowing at him in the semidarkness as he viewed a PowerPoint presentation in the Vice offices, his heart had bottomed out. The very idea that someone would harass Dana made his gut turn over. He'd raced out of the meeting, to everyone's astonishment, stopping only to leave a quick message with his assistant. He hadn't bothered to page his driver, Pierre, and had run into the executive parking lot, preferring to drive himself. It was amazing he'd arrived in one piece.

Patterson had gone too far. It was one thing to stalk Alex, but if he thought he could stalk Dana, he had another think coming.

So why was she pushing back on this? He'd explained everything that the dirt bag had done so far.

"Okay." Alex calmed his racing pulse. "How's this? You work from home. *Your* home. I'll keep you company. We'll keep a couple of my security guys outside your condo, just in case. You'll have my fleet of drivers at your disposal, to take you to any meetings you need to attend."

She hesitated, clearly tempted, but when she opened her mouth, Alex knew it was to object.

He turned to Dana's manager. "Phil, could you give us a minute?"

Phil nodded and left her office.

Alex grabbed Dana's hands. "I'm trying hard to stay calm here. So, in my calmest voice, I'm telling you these are your options. I know what you're thinking. I have no right to tell you what to do."

She huffed.

"But I'm telling you anyway because the thought of anyone hurting you scares the shit out of me."

"Alex."

"If you insist on working, you either work from my home or I work from yours. Either way, you're stuck with me."

"I know you're worried."

"You're right. I am. Patterson found a way into your office. I'm not letting you out of my sight, Dana."

He'd been lax with Shannon.

He wouldn't make the same mistake again.

She stroked the skin at the edge of his splint. "What happened to taking things as they come and not rushing our relationship?"

"Shit happens. We adapt." Cupping her cheek, he drew her in for a kiss. "I'm sure the cops will find Patterson right away. In the meantime, humor me, okay? Just with this one thing."

"Okay." She smiled. "But you stay in my condo."

His shoulders relaxed and he pretended to grimace. "Your place, huh? I saw your hall closet. Not very *feng shui*. We need to talk about that."

She punched him in his good left arm.

Chapter Sixteen

Alex moved his things in late that afternoon. A few of his things, anyway. Dana couldn't help grinning when he walked into her condo with only his laptop bag, a small piece of luggage, and a garment bag that held a few suits. Of course, he lived right down the street. If he needed anything else, he could literally walk to Vice or send his driver.

He set a leather toiletry bag on one of her bathroom shelves and popped his toothbrush in the holder next to hers. "See? Low maintenance. You'll never even know I'm here." He grabbed her around the waist, pulled her close, and began to nibble her earlobe.

"Right." She squirmed as his breath tickled her skin. "You're practically invisible."

"I know this is weird, and I'm not trying to force my way into your home or your life. I just want you to feel safe."

"I know."

"We can still take things easy." His left hand

360

trailed down her back, over the curve at her waist, toward her hip. His voice softened. "Nothing needs to be rushed."

Desire pooled in Dana's belly. "Sure. We'll keep things casual."

"I can even sleep on the couch."

"No need to go to extremes." She danced her lips over his jaw, toward his mouth. "It's not as if we haven't slept together."

"This is true. And there would only be one set of sheets to fix in the morning."

"Sleeping together is just more efficient."

"I'm all about efficiency." His hand crept up to caress her breast. "As long as you're sure."

"I'm sure."

With one hand, Alex began to unbutton her shirt. "You should probably give me the tour of your bedroom. You know, so I don't bump into anything in the night."

As he teased her shirt from her shoulders, her skin rioted with delighted goose pimples. "Of course. We wouldn't want you to stub your toes."

She led Alex to her bedroom. He removed his splint and set it on her bedside table.

"So," she said, laying back on the bed. She wriggled out of her work skirt and tossed it into a corner of the room. "This is my bed."

"Looks sturdy." He removed his shirt and dropped it on the floor.

"Oh, it is. You should probably test the mattress, though. You'll want to make sure it's firm enough." She dropped her gaze to his pants zipper.

Alex pulled the zipper down. "It's firm. Trust

me."

Dana held out her hand and drew Alex onto the bed. He rolled onto his back and she climbed on top of him, making sure she didn't bump into his right hand. Clad only in her panties and bra, she slid up and down his length. "Rock hard, actually."

Their mouths joined. Alex cradled her head and tugged on her curls as he plunged his tongue into her mouth. Her whimpers were met by his moans. The temperature in her bedroom skyrocketed, or so it seemed.

Dana surrendered to the heat.

Were they getting ahead of themselves by shacking up? Probably.

Did she care? Not at the moment.

***

"Thanks for meeting with me, Pierre." Alex welcomed his driver into his office and gestured to the chair opposite his. "Have a seat."

Pierre looked around the office, as if expecting someone else to pop up behind a potted plant. Fiddling with his jacket buttons, he sat down. "I was surprised you wanted to see me."

Alex sat at his desk. "I know your shift just finished and you're probably eager to head home. I've been in touch with Payroll. I understand you asked for an advance on your pay."

"They told you?" Pierre paled for a second, but immediately schooled his face into a mask of annoyance. "I can explain. There was just a bit of a mix-up with one of my bill payments this month at the bank. I was just hoping to avoid some red tape, that's all. I'm sorry they bothered you with that, Alex. I don't understand why it had to be escalated."

"It might have something to do with the fact you've asked for three advances lately."

"Three? No, that doesn't sound right."

"I've got copies of the emails you sent to Payroll." Although radiating what he hoped was calm from the waist up, Alex's nervous tic manifested under the desk. He put a hand on his knee to stop his leg from bouncing up and down. "You're one of my drivers, Pierre. I want to make sure you're okay."

"It's just a temporary cashflow problem."

"I understand."

"Do you?" When he caught the harshness in his tone, Pierre shook his head. "I'm sorry. I shouldn't have said that."

"It's okay. I am concerned, though. Several team members have come forward recently, saying you asked them to lend you large amounts of cash."

"Ah, man. A twenty here, a twenty there. We're not exactly talking about big bucks."

"Those aren't the figures I received."

Pierre's mouth opened and closed a few times. "Are you firing me?"

"No. I'm offering to get you some help."

"I don't need any help."

"You've been seen gambling at the Golden Nugget."

He let out a nervous laugh. "So that's what this is about. You're ticked because I didn't gamble at

Vice."

"That's not it at all. Do you deny you were gambling?"

"Is this because I ran into Wade? Is he the one who ratted on me? Because I told him I was just blowing off some steam."

"There's a difference between blowing off steam and addiction."

"Addiction? I'm not addicted to anything. Ask anyone who knows me. I'm a straight shooter and always have been. Jesus, I've never even touched a cigarette."

"Which is why I want to offer you my support. I know this can't be an easy thing to handle. Less than twenty percent of compulsive gamblers seek treatment."

Pierre rolled his eyes. "Oh, boy. Someone's been doing his homework. You've got statistics on your side."

"Pierre, you have an addiction. As your boss, I want to help you kick it."

"Do you really think that little of me? Do you think I'm like those losers out there in your casinos, the ones who don't know when to call it quits?"

"No one is calling anyone a loser."

"Because I can stop anytime I want!"

"You were seen at the Golden Nugget five times this week alone."

"What I do on my own time is my own business."

"Three of those times were during your shifts."

"Alex, come on. You've always said you don't expect me, or any of the other drivers, to be your

364

shadow. I can't believe you'd insult me like this."

"This isn't an insult. Pierre. We work in the world of Vegas casinos. A place like this has a lot of temptation. You're only human. That's why I'd like you to take a paid leave and get some counseling. I'll cover the cost and your job will be waiting for you when you get back."

"I don't need counseling. I just need a bit of cash. Maybe if you spotted me the money…"

"That's not going to happen."

"Oh, I see. Don't want to make a dent in your enormous wallet? Just can't spare the change today? I see how it is."

"That's not it. If you had a legitimate need for the money, I'd give it to you, no questions. But I'm not going to fund your habit." Alex pulled out a brochure and handed it to him. "There's a local organization called New Horizons. A friend of mine has recommended them. They can help you with your addiction."

He tossed the brochure into the trash basket at the side of Alex's desk. "Yeah, right."

"Pierre, please. I can't make you go to counseling, but would it hurt to check them out, maybe attend a meeting or two? Be sensible."

He turned his head.

Even though he wanted to shake the man, Alex remained calm. His Human Resources manager had warned him Pierre might fight back. It wasn't unusual to find gambling addicts working in casinos and one of the first things Alex had insisted on learning when he took over from Liam was how to address the issue with empathy. "How about I get you a coffee and we talk about next steps?"

"Next steps?" Pierre stood and backed away from the desk. "You want to know what my next step is? My next step is paying off my creditors. Care to help me with that?"

"I've made it clear I won't throw money at your problems. It won't help anything."

"Well, then, Alex. It seems I have no fucking *next steps* with you. I can't believe you'd treat me like this." Pierre headed to the office elevator and pounded the button.

Alex followed him. "Like I said, I just want to help you."

"And how long will it be before the rumor mill starts turning? Give it a couple of days and everyone in this joint will avoid me like the plague. No, thanks, *boss*. I'll take care of myself. I don't need your help." The elevator arrived and Pierre got in. "I'm done here."

As the door closed, Alex considered racing down the emergency stairs after him, but decided not to. Pierre was pissed. He was in no position to accept help, not yet anyway.

It was a good thing Wade had come to Alex with his concerns after spotting Pierre at the Golden Nugget. HR had already reached out, and Wade's observations had allowed Alex to connect the dots.

He would call Pierre tomorrow. Maybe then he'd see sense.

He'd done a good thing here today, probably the hardest thing he'd ever had to do on the job. The outcome had been disappointing, but hopefully Pierre understood someone was on his side.

Alex sighed. If it was such a good thing, why did he feel so rotten?

***

When the familiar three knocks sounded on her unit door, Dana looked up from her work. She smiled as Alex walked in. "Alex, I gave you a key. You don't need to knock."

"Just trying to respect your space." His half grin didn't reach his eyes. No sign of Zeus anywhere.

She pushed away from the table and went to him, running her fingers through the hair near his ear. "Hey. Are you okay?"

"Yeah."

"Rough day at work?"

"You could say that. I had to deal with an employee who's addicted to gambling. I just feel bad for him."

"That is rough. Come on in."

He removed his tie and took off his suit jacket, hanging them both on a chair in her living room. After undoing his top two shirt buttons, he wrapped her in his embrace and kissed her. "Mmm. Something smells good, something other than you."

Dana led him to the kitchen, where a couple of pots sat on the stove. "I was inspired between meetings. Do you want to talk about the situation at your work?"

"I probably shouldn't. Confidentiality and all."

"I understand. Well, let's see if I can distract you with food, then." She lifted one of the pot lids. "Vegan curry. It's got cauliflower, cilantro and quinoa. And we've got steamed asparagus on the side."

"You made all of this?"

"Yeah. I'm not a great cook, and I've never cooked vegan food before, but I've been doing some quiet research since you've been here. I know we normally order in, but I had some time and I wanted to make you something nice."

He leaned in and sniffed the curry. "It smells incredible."

"It's ready whenever you are."

Alex stared at her for a moment, his gaze bright with wonder. He paced the kitchen a couple of times and then plunked himself down on the couch.

Dana went over and sat on his lap. "Are you sure you're okay?"

"I like this. Being here with you."

"You haven't tried my curry yet."

"I mean it, Dana. I know I'm just staying here temporarily, and I realize your condo isn't my place, but I get excited coming home to you."

"You mean you like me being your domestic goddess?"

"You know what I mean. I like being in the same space as you, breathing the same air. Sharing the same bed, the same utensil drawer, the same closet."

"I like it too."

She dropped a soft kiss on his cheek, but he captured her mouth, seducing her with the velvet glide of his tongue. His left hand curled around her hip, his fingernails digging gently into her jeans.

"You make me look forward to the future," Alex

said between kisses. "I want you in my future."

It was still hard for her to envision where she would be in a year's time, never mind beyond then. Still, she didn't argue about it anymore, not even with herself.

Alex had helped her start looking forward too.

"You really need to try my curry before you make any rash decisions." She eased off his lap and grabbed his left hand, leading to the kitchen. Dana grabbed a fork from the utensil drawer, lifted the lid off the pot and speared a piece of cauliflower. She held it to Alex's lips.

He ate the cauliflower, his gaze on her. As he chewed, his smile widened, restoring her Zeus to her. "It's delicious."

Dana stifled a giggle of happiness. She liked making Alex smile like that.

She didn't want a day to go by without seeing that smile.

***

Pierre Dubois checked his bank balance on his cellphone.

Where had it all gone? He was sure his funds would have lasted longer.

Of course, he had been spending a lot of his time free time at the Golden Nugget. Even more so since Alex canned him.

He didn't can you. He made that clear.

It didn't seem to matter.

This was Alex's fault. The day he'd offered to help, Pierre had gone right out, despondent. He'd headed for the craps table at the Nugget and had won big. His elation had been all-consuming. He'd continued to gamble and had promptly lost his last dollar.

What was he supposed to do, accept Alex's help? Because of him, Pierre was in this mess. If Alex had bothered to provide a bit more stimulation on the job, Pierre wouldn't be forced to look for stimulation elsewhere. And there was so much stimulation on the Strip. How was he expected to avoid it?

Being a driver for Vice had sounded so glamorous. Carting Alex around Vegas, as well as the odd celebrity, had seemed like a dream come true.

In reality, there were long stretches of boredom. It wasn't as if Alex needed him on a constant basis. What was he supposed to do? Sit on his ass and stare at the wall until the big man decided he needed help getting from Point A to Point B? Maybe get the Escalade washed one more time? If he buffed it any further, the paint would peel off.

Convinced he'd made a mistake, he checked his bank balance one more time, but none of the numbers magically changed. He was officially in the red. His rent was coming due. He owed big time on his credit card, and his ex-wife kept emailing him about his inability to keep up with support payments.

It didn't matter that Alex put him on paid leave. No matter what he did, his paycheck always ended up in someone else's pocket.

One big win would help so much.

But he needed cash to place a bet.

Sweating, he walked up the Strip. Vice loomed before him, the taxi bay alive with activity as customers got in and out of cars. Alex's palace. The entitled golden boy probably loved sitting on his throne, passing judgment.

His cellphone rang. He was tempted to let it go to voicemail but when he realized the phone company would likely cut off his service soon, he figured he'd better answer. "Pierre here."

"Is this Pierre Dubois?"

"Yeah. Who's this?"

"My name is Gordon Dean and I need your help."

Dean. Why did that name sound familiar? "What kind of help?"

"I have a little problem with Alex Markov. I need some information."

"Problems with Alex? Get in line. And by the way, my help doesn't come free of charge."

"If you give me the information I need, I can pay you."

"You'll have to be more specific."

Dean told him what he wanted, giving him a figure.

"I'm going to need you to transfer some funds before I say a word." He gave Dean the email address attached to his bank account. Within seconds, he received a notification that funds were being transferred. Four figures worth of funds.

"Well?"

It was just an address. Pierre wasn't hurting anyone. And with the money Dean had just transferred, Pierre could return to the Nugget and win everything back. He gave him the address on Dean Martin Drive.

"Thank you," said Dean.

"Hey, it was nice doing business with you, Gor—"

Dean hung up.

Pierre ignored the burn of guilt in his stomach and headed toward the Golden Nugget.

Chapter Seventeen

It had been over a week and the cops still hadn't found Bill Patterson. When police went to his apartment, they'd found it empty. The landlord said Patterson had just picked up and left.

Not knowing the paparazzo's whereabouts made Alex sweat at night. He could handle unpleasant confrontations, but Dana didn't deserve to be treated with the same lack of respect.

Nevertheless, there had been no other incidents that week. Alex had shared Dana's space and her bed, traveling to Vice whenever he needed to. She'd worked from home as well, availing herself of his drivers when she had to meet with clients. Despite Pierre's departure, there was no shortage of staff to drive them around town. He employed a number of drivers, as many of their high rollers appreciated shuttle service from time to time, so there was always someone available to help Dana with her transportation needs.

Aside from concerns about Patterson, it had been an incredible week. Alex and Dana had coexisted beautifully, caught up in the excitement of a new relationship and unrelenting sexual hunger. Alex couldn't get enough of her. Having her fall asleep in his arms every night was a pleasure he never wanted to deny himself again. Waking up with her was even better. There was nothing as sweet as rolling over to see her face on the pillow next to his.

She had a cute morning routine. As she slowly woke up, she mumbled and rubbed her eyes. She would stretch her legs, sliding her toes up his shin. Upon whispering his name, she would open her eyes and look at him for the first time each morning.

On their third morning together, emotion put a stranglehold on Alex.

He'd fallen in love with her.

He knew exactly when it had happened too. There had been one evening when they'd been working from home. He'd stared at the same email for some time, caught up in concerns about Patterson. For one moment, Alex had allowed himself to imagine how he'd feel if something bad happened to Dana.

The turmoil of that moment had made him realize he would always put her safety ahead of his.

That evening, he'd lured her away from her work by kissing that spot on her neck, the one she said drove her crazy with lust. He'd spent the night worshiping her from head to toe.

They made love every morning, while their bodies were still hot from the sheets and their dreams were tangled with reality.

It was bliss. It was everything he'd ever wanted.

Alex didn't want to leave her condo. It already felt like home. He almost wished the police wouldn't find Patterson.

But at the same time, he knew that wasn't an option. He needed to know the man wouldn't cause any more trouble.

Now, on a quiet Saturday morning, Dana emerged from the bedroom. She was dressed in cute little shorts and one of his t-shirts. She borrowed Alex's shirts a lot. Every time she did, he swore his heart pumped harder.

"I like your outfit," he said, as he checked his texts.

"This old thing?" She waved at the shirt. "I went shopping at the Markov Emporium."

He put his phone down, walked over, and kissed her on the top of her head, fingering the sleeve of his shirt. "I wish you'd told me you're a kleptomaniac. I would have packed more shirts."

She gasped in mock indignation. "I don't have a problem. I just like wearing your shirts. They smell like you."

He crouched in front of her. "That's a good answer."

His cellphone buzzed on the table with a couple of incoming texts.

"Someone's a busy man."

"It's probably just Trevor. He's been on my case, reminding me I RSVP'd for an event next week. He's been texting me the details."

"Oh, yeah? What event?"

"A benefit for a breast cancer awareness charity. With everything going on, I forgot about it."

The cellphone rattled on the table again.

"Boy," said Dana, "Trevor is one persistent guy."

"Tell me about it. He's probably triple checking that I have a tuxedo ready to go."

"Tuxedo? Nice." Dana waggled her eyebrows. "What does a girl have to do to wrangle an invitation to this benefit? I know someone who might like to see you in a tuxedo."

"Oh, yeah? Would that someone be you?"

"I'd love to go with you."

Her dark eyes shone with such sweetness, such openness.

Only he hadn't been open with her, not completely. His unsaid words scratched like wadded up sandpaper in his throat. She was the one person in this world who deserved his truth, even though the rest of the world seemed to think they were entitled to it.

And she was the one person who might be hurt if he kept it from her any longer.

"Dana, there's something I need to tell you."

Once again, the cellphone buzzed.

She giggled. "It's Saturday. Doesn't poor Trevor get a day off?"

Alex stared at the phone, as an undefinable dread settled in his core.

"Why don't you check your messages and then we can talk." She walked over to the door of her unit. "I'm just going to see if the Saturday paper has arrived yet."

Buzz buzz buzz.

Trevor might be efficient, but there was no way

this was about a tuxedo.

Dana opened her unit door and leaned over to grab her rolled up newspaper. She slid the elastic off and began to unfurl the pages.

Alex reached for his phone. The texts from Trevor screamed at him.

Trevor: We have a problem. Call me.

Trevor: Alex, it's important. Are you there?

Trevor: Don't come to Vice. There are reporters everywhere.

Trevor: Patterson finally surfaced. His paper ran a story about you early this morning, a bad one. You need to see it.

Trevor: Alex? We need to come up with a plan to confront these lies.

Trevor: Are you getting my messages?

One final text from Trevor contained a link to Patterson's article. Alex clicked on it.

Hotelier Alex Markov's secret love child...dead!
The Deans.

They'd finally talked. They'd always said they would.

Blackness swirled around Alex's head, cloaking him in confusion and dismay. In that one second, the temperature in the room seemed to drop. His skin came alive with goosebumps, and for one moment, he thought he could see his breath in front of his face.

All his breath dissipated as soon as Dana turned around, holding up the front page of the paper.

"Alex?" Her eyes were wide with alarm. "What's going on? The newspaper…they've printed some vicious lies."

"They're not lies."

"But…" She dropped the newspaper. Its pages scattered on the floor. "A baby? Dead?"

He stood and walked over to her, holding out his hands. "Let me explain."

She pulled away.

His Dana pulled away.

Shannon, his constant companion since that horrible day, laughed. *You did this to me, Alex. It's all your fault.*

"Dana, please."

She was a statue, completely unmoving. The only sign she still breathed was the moisture at the corners of her eyes.

"I was just about to tell you."

"Really? Interesting timing." She pointed at the newspaper. "Patterson is saying you were responsible for the death of your child."

Alex sank into one of the living room chairs, defeated. It wasn't often he allowed himself to visualize the stark room in the King Edward VII Memorial Hospital in Bermuda. He dared never picture the doctor's face, his eyes so full of sympathy. He did so now and allowed the painful memories to wash over him, taking him back to that awful moment, the one that changed everything.

I'm sorry, sir. We couldn't save her. And I'm so sorry we couldn't save the baby.

Baby?

The doctor's brow had creased. *Shannon was pregnant. Again, you have my deepest condolences.*

"Alex?" Dana whispered. "Tell me."

Although it hung like a weight, he lifted his head to look at her. "I didn't know. Shannon never told me. They figured she was four months pregnant with my child, but she never said a word. The fucking doctor was the one who told me I could have been a father."

Moving with trepidation, Dana sat on the couch across from him. Not next to him.

He was losing her. She wouldn't forgive him this lie of omission, not after everything she'd been through.

"Only three people knew, outside the hospital staff. Me and Shannon's parents. I don't even think they told Gordon. At least, he's never mentioned it. When Shannon died, the baby died. The Deans always threatened me with exposing the truth about the baby. It's been hanging over my head all this time. Patterson must have finally gotten to them. I knew he would."

"Why didn't you tell me earlier?"

"Because I can't take the shame." He threw up his hands. "Don't you get it? I should have been there, but I was passed out in our room. While Shannon bled to death, while my baby slowly died, I was pissed out of my gourd!"

Tears poured over Dana's cheeks.

"It's haunted me ever since. Do you have any

idea how many nights I lay awake, wondering if the baby was a boy or a girl? Do you know how many nights I drank myself into a stupor, needing to forget? But I can't forget. I see the baby everywhere. It's little face, its tiny fingers. I've even created a whole fantasy world around it. I swear some days I can see its hair color, eye color. I can hear that baby laughing and crying. Only none of it's real. Because of me, Shannon is dead. Because of me," he said, his chest heaving, "my child is dead."

After his outburst, neither of them spoke. Too ashamed to face her, Alex surrendered to his grief and let his aching head fall to his knees. He covered his head with his good arm and wept.

A few minutes passed but he didn't look up. When he heard some shuffling, he finally forced himself to blink away his tears and wipe his snot and look at her.

Surely, she was getting up to walk away.

From him.

Only she hadn't.

Dana crouched in front of him and rested a gentle hand on his arm.

"I understand if you want to call things off. I'm so sorry I didn't tell you when I had a chance, Dana. I just couldn't bear to think about how it might make you feel."

"No." She wiped her tears away. "*I'm* the one who's sorry, Alex. I'm sorry for all the pain you've endured. And I'm so sorry that I showed you anything other than compassion just now. That headline, it came out of nowhere, and we've been so happy. I just wasn't expecting to read that."

"I know. It's been killing me inside because I always knew this day would come. I was the only one the doctor told about the baby, but I told Shannon's parents out of respect. It just made them angrier. I begged them not to say anything to anyone. Her death was already a circus. But they lost their grandchild that day, and they've never forgiven me. I've never forgiven myself."

"Now you listen to me. I don't care how Patterson twisted the truth. I know you, and I know you would never hurt another soul."

He dared to caress her cheek, so relieved she didn't push him away. "Now that it's out, I can handle the world hating me, but I could never handle you hating me."

"I don't hate you, Alex." She smiled through her tears. "I love you."

"You do?"

"Yes, you silly man. I know it's far too soon for me to even be thinking it, never mind admitting it to you. It'll probably give my sister a heart attack, but I'm willing to deal with her because you mean the world to me. You told me I was enough for you, Alex, so here I am. Offering myself to you, if you'll have me."

"I'll have you." He stood, pulling her up with him. They embraced and he ran his hands under the t-shirt she'd commandeered, resting his forehead on hers. Her skin was so soft, so soothing. The greatest comfort he'd ever known. "And I love you too."

She cupped his face with both her hands and kissed him with butterfly softness. But when she opened her eyes, there was a fierce determination in their depths. "We will handle this, *together*. Do you hear me? I'm not going anywhere."

"I hear you."

"And when I get my hands on that slime Bill Patterson, I'm going to scratch his fucking eyes out. I hope that man has cashed in all his Lotto tickets because he's about to meet his maker."

Alex laughed. God, he loved this woman, and couldn't wait to plan a future with her. He slid a hand up to her bare breast and cradled her softness.

If Dana could forgive him, maybe it was time he learned to forgive himself.

Dana loved him.

Screw the rest of the world.

***

"I still think you should sue that bastard," Dana declared, as they left her condo unit. "Patterson published confidential information, information given to you in confidence by a doctor. Surely, that goes against some code of ethics, even for the paparazzi."

"I'm not sure they have a code of ethics." Alex chuckled.

He was relaxed today. Too relaxed.

It made Dana nervous, considering they were about to visit a memorial.

Patterson's attempt at destroying Alex's reputation had backfired, and in spectacular fashion. The paparazzo had expected Alex's dominion to implode once the news got out about the baby, but in truth, Alex had received nothing but messages of support from the community. He'd been inundated by words of sympathy on Twitter and Facebook. Since the day the headline broke, tourists and residents of Las Vegas had been leaving little bundles of flowers and teddy bears outside the Vice doors. Now, four days later, there was a sizable pile. Every evening, the TV news channels showed footage of new people paying their respects outside the casino.

Even the other reporters had left. On the day of the story, the press had inundated Vice, looking for comments from Alex. According to Trevor, even the reporters had given up and gone elsewhere.

The story was basically dead.

Alex and Dana had spent those four days at her condo, quietly working from home and spending time together. They'd grieved each other's situations, talking about feelings they'd never shared with any other. Dana felt stronger each day, and Alex seemed to as well. More importantly, they both felt accepted and loved.

This morning, she awoke to find him sitting up in bed, a gentle smile playing on his lips.

"I'm ready," he'd said.

Dana was pleased for him, even if she wasn't quite ready to take the high road with the paparazzo. "Maybe just a little lawsuit? Something to make him sweat?"

"I just want to let it go. Patterson wanted to get a rise out of me. He didn't get it. That's got to be eating him up. Every last detail surrounding Shannon's death is out there now. There's nothing more to tell. His huge scoop blew up in his face. I'm good with that."

In fact, the backlash against the reporter had been so intense, he'd had to go into hiding himself. That was after the police visited him and issued a stern warning about harassing Dana.

She locked her unit door. "You're better than I am, Alex. If I ever see that scum again…"

He grasped her by the waist and spun her around, claiming her lips. "Have I ever told you how sexy you are when you're acting badass?"

She extended her fingers like cat claws. "Does this look like acting?"

"Rawr." Purring like a great cat, he nuzzled her neck, tickling her until she broke down and laughed.

When their laughter subsided, she stroked his face. "Are you sure about going back to Vice to see the memorial? You don't have to."

"Yes, I do. People were kind enough to leave flowers. It's the least I can do."

"I'm proud of you."

"When everything has blown over, I want to do something to give back to the community. For so many years, I've been putting all my energy into my clubs. I want to do something more, something worthwhile."

"I've been thinking of doing the same thing."

"You have?"

"Yeah. I've always been defined by my career, and lately I've been letting my lack of choices define me. I need something more in my life, an activity that will still give me fulfillment, even if I change careers one day." Dana lowered her eyes as she contemplated the idea that had taken root in recent days. "I was thinking of putting together a benefit event, something to do with infertility awareness. I'm sure so many people struggling with it feel alone and misunderstood. I'd like to help those people."

He grasped her hands. "Angel, I think that's amazing."

"Amazing enough that you might want to lend me a hand?"

"I'd like nothing more."

Excitement fluttered in her chest. "Because between your contacts and mine, we could make a real difference."

"Let's do it."

Holding hands, they headed downstairs in the elevator and toward Dana's condo lobby. It was all Dana could do not to skip the entire way. She'd never been so eager to put a plan into action before and couldn't stop smiling.

One of Alex's drivers was waiting out front to take them to Vice.

As they made their way to the door, Alex stopped in his tracks. "Damn. I forgot my wallet upstairs. You go ahead and wait in the car. I'll be right back."

"Okay." Dana patted him on the butt. "Don't be long, Zeus."

Winking, Alex disappeared back into the elevator.

Still grinning to herself, Dana rummaged through her purse to make sure she had her own wallet and approached the Vice Escalade.

"Dana Hamill?"

"Yes?" She looked up.

A man stood at the Escalade, aiming a gun at her. Next to him, Alex's driver lay on the ground, unconscious.

"Oh, my God."

"Get in the car," said the man. "Now."

"Is he…"

"Dead? No. I didn't shoot him, but I'll have no problem shooting you." Using the gun, he waved toward the SUV. "Get in."

Alex. She looked toward the lobby, but of course he wouldn't have arrived yet. The elevator in her building was notoriously slow. As for the security guard, he was nowhere to be seen, and was likely on his rounds.

She couldn't get in the car. No one would know where she was.

Hell, she didn't even know who this person was.

The man took a step. "Ms. Hamill, I haven't really decided if I want to hurt you or not. Please don't make that decision for me."

"Who are you? At least tell me who I'm getting in the car with."

"I'm Gordon Dean."

"Gordon, please. You don't have to do this."

"Get in. Don't make me say it again."

As much as she wanted to stall for time so Alex would find them, she also didn't want him to confront a man with a gun. Alex might be strong, but he was no match for a firearm, and Gordon's sad face was lined with desperation.

He was at the end of his rope.

"You've suffered a great loss. I've lost people too. Maybe we could talk."

"I'm done talking."

From down the walkway, a couple approached the condo. They were far enough away to be oblivious to Dana's situation, but it would only be a matter of seconds before they became aware.

"Where are we going?"

Gordon grunted. "For fuck's sakes, lady. Get in the car!"

Dana glanced back one more time.

Alex appeared in the lobby. Smiling, he waved his wallet.

And then he saw Gordon, and the gun.

His eyes widened in terror. Calling her name, he broke into a sprint.

"Now," shouted Gordon.

Stifling a cry, Dana got into the Escalade's front seat and slid over to the passenger side. The man got in next to her, shut the door, and turned the key in the ignition.

"Dana!" Alex banged on the back of the SUV.

Gordon tore away.

Once more, Alex started running, but it was no good.

They veered into traffic and headed for the highway.

Chapter Eighteen

It didn't take long for Gordon to become agitated. They hadn't been on Interstate 15 for more than a few minutes before he was banging his palm on the steering wheel.

She didn't dare reach for her phone. Alex would have called 9-1-1 for her anyway.

Alex.

The fear in his eyes had just about destroyed her.

She couldn't let it. She had to stay calm and keep Gordon as calm as possible as well.

He said himself he didn't know if he wanted to hurt her.

There was a way out of this. She just had to find it.

"So," she ventured, "where are you taking me?"

He didn't respond and just stared ahead.

"I've always hated this route. Nothing to see. Unless you like gravel at the side of the road, of course. The mountains in the distance are nice, though."

Gordon was silent.

Dana decided to follow his lead. He still held the gun in his right hand, steering with his left. If she annoyed him enough, he might strike out and hit her.

They drove past the Sloan Canyon National Conservation Area. Dana knew for a fact Nevada Highway Patrol had a tiny office near the rest stop up ahead.

Would Gordon know that? He wasn't from around here.

They might very well be driving into a trap. Once he realized it, would he lash out?

Call her crazy, but Dana wasn't ready to go out in a blaze of glory.

"I'm, um, I'm sorry about your sister. I've heard some good things about her."

"Who told you that? Alex?"

"Yes."

"That's bullshit. He couldn't wait to get rid of her."

"That's not true. He tried to make things work. He loved her, but sometimes love changes. People change."

"You really believe that, lady? People don't change, not for anyone."

"Maybe not, but circumstances change. Gordon, in your heart of hearts, do you honestly believe Alex wanted to kill your sister?"

His eyes watered.

"I've gotten to know him. He doesn't have a violent bone in his body."

That would change if he ever caught up with them.

When he caught up with them.

Alex would kill Gordon for doing this.

Mile after mile of road stretched before them. From this vantage point, it looked like the road to nowhere. The odd car or truck passed them on the other side of the road. Dana flirted with the idea of grabbing the wheel or banging on the horn but she doubted either option would serve either of them well. And with that gun between them, she dared not make any rash moves.

"Alex told me you waited for him in that alley with a crowbar."

His laugh held no joy. "Yeah. I decided to upgrade my weapon."

"You could have hurt him that day. No one would have known. No one have seen. You could have gotten away with it. But you didn't. You made the right choice that day."

His knuckles tightened on the steering wheel, showing white tips.

"You can still make the right choice here, Gordon. You can just drop me off at the side of the road. I won't tell a soul."

"Bit late for that, don't you think? Alex saw us." He shook his head. "No. I need to see this through."

"And what exactly does that mean?" Dana tried to hold her voice down, but now she was getting pissed. "What's your end game? Shooting me in the desert? Is that how you want to hurt Alex? Or is this our Thelma and Louise moment? Because if you're searching for a cliff, I can check Google Maps for you."

"Shut up."

"No, I will *not* shut up. Do you even know where you're going?"

"I said, shut the fuck up."

Dana opened her mouth to speak again but another noise caught her attention.

From somewhere in the distance, she heard a faint wail. It was so far away she couldn't tell if it was behind them or in front of them.

Sirens.

Help me, Jesus.

She could not allow this to turn into a stand off.

Forcing calm into her being with a series of quiet breaths, she brought the conversation back to the one thing that seemed to give Gordon pause.

Shannon.

The man was grieving.

"I lost my grandmother a while back. She was more like a second mother to me. There are days when I feel like everything is okay and I function like usual. But then, out of nowhere, I'll get hit by a memory. It always seems to happen at the worst times, the inconvenient times. I'll remember her smile or the way she used to sneak me extra desserts when we visited. She loved butterscotch ice cream and she knew I loved it too. When my parents weren't looking, she'd always give me and my sister an extra scoop." Her voice caught. "I can't even look at butterscotch ice cream in the damn grocery store anymore."

Gordon glanced at her, his eyes red and full of tears.

"Grief is horrible, isn't it?"

He nodded.

"We're never the same after we lose someone. They leave a mark. It's like a fingerprint burned into our skin. And even though no one sees it, we still feel the imprint. We feel the burn."

He let out a cry. "She was my baby sister. I was supposed to protect her."

Dana wiped her eyes. "Shannon loved you with all her heart, and I have no doubt you always made her feel protected. But Gordon, what you're doing here…she wouldn't want this for you. She would want you to get help."

"I don't know."

The sirens grew louder, closer. Dana wasn't sure, but she thought she spied parked cars up ahead.

Police officers?

"You can't bring Shannon back, but you can do one last thing for her. Pull over, Gordon."

His speed dropped.

Several police cruisers veered up behind them, keeping a distance. Sure enough, another set were parked up front. Officers stood outside the cars, aiming their weapons.

"Think of your parents. They've suffered enough, and so have you. If you surrender, they'll go easier on you."

"No one's going easy on me." He laughed. "We both know that."

"Please." She didn't like the look in his eyes.

With a sigh, he pulled over. Reaching across her, he opened her door. He wiped his eyes with the back of his hand and smiled. "I'm sorry, Dana. Go."

"But—"

The tendons in his neck strained as he hissed,

"Just go."

Dana scrambled out of the SUV, her hands in the air. Despite the tremors in her legs, she ran toward the police cars in back. "He has a gun!"

When she heard the single shot, she dropped and covered her head.

But the shot hadn't been intended for her. Gordon had turned his weapon on himself.

Somewhere in front of her, feet scuffled. The gravel kicked up as a couple of officers helped her to her feet and brought her to a waiting ambulance.

Sirens.

So many sirens.

And yet she couldn't shake the sound of that single gunshot. It reverberated in her head, over and over.

Alex emerged from one of the cars, his face drained of all color. He flew to her and she collapsed in his arms. Together, they fell to their knees.

"I'm sorry," he whispered. "I'm so, so sorry, my angel."

Comforted in his arms, Dana wept.

Epilogue

One year later

Dana had never walked a red carpet before.

Of course, this one was turquoise.

In planning the Tranquility Ball with Alex, she had tried to come up with a life-affirming theme, and it only made sense the carpet should echo that theme. She loved the turquoise carpet. It stretched before them like a peaceful river, representing waters she no longer feared to enter.

She still had to make it down the carpet. Considering every news outlet in Nevada had sent reporters, ones whose cameras were flashing at an alarming rate, the task was daunting. She'd attended some charity lunches and the odd benefit concert, but none of those events had ever involved strutting one's stuff on a length of rug, smiling for the cameras.

As their limousine approached the Fashion Show Mall, Dana whistled. The shopping area had been closed for the event and pale blue lights shone around the entrance, welcoming guests to the ball. On either side of the carpet, photographers stood at the ready. Tourists craned their necks, hoping to catch sight of celebrities.

It wouldn't be hard. Alex had reached out to every VIP he knew and they had all come out to support them. Even from inside their car, Dana could see them up ahead on the carpet. Hollywood actresses posed with athletes and politicians. Everywhere she looked, she saw manicured hands on jutting hips, and perfect angles. These were people who understood how to work a camera. Several of them had stopped to talk to reporters about the foundation she and Alex had created.

The Tranquility Project was getting a lot of buzz.

Every dollar from tonight's event would go directly to funding programs for those struggling with infertility and related diseases, and Dana couldn't be happier.

She glanced at her date. Alex looked amazing. Clad in a designer tuxedo, his hair cut short and his face clean shaven, he outshone any of those people on the carpet.

He couldn't stop looking at her.

He reached for her hand and kissed it. "You look beautiful."

She'd splurged for the occasion, treating herself to a fancy updo and a strapless black gown. Although tight around the bodice, the skirt billowed with a design of appliqued red roses. It was the prettiest dress she'd ever seen and it made her feel like a prom queen.

Forget prom queens. She felt like a princess.

"I may have to wear this dress for the rest of my life."

He leaned over and dropped a soft kiss on her cherry-stained lips. "There might be moments when I have to pry the dress off you. Do you think you can bear to let it go every so often?"

"Hmm. Let me see." She kissed him again, sighing into his mouth. "I think I'll manage."

"I love you."

"I love you too."

There may have been a time when she'd doubted her heart, but that time was over. She loved the man with everything in her and it only grew stronger every day. She knew it in the quiet moments, when he held her in his arms and played with her hair. She knew it when he trailed kisses down the length of her body, whispering in awe that she was the most remarkable thing he'd ever seen. To Alex, she was the woman he treasured. To her, he was just Alex, the man whose past no longer had control over him.

They still had bad days, of course, and the last year had been a journey full of triumphs and rocky moments. In many ways, they were both still grieving their losses, but they now knew they had a safe space in which to grieve.

She had finally caved and accepted a job with Alex's company. By the time he made his third job offer, she figured she might as well stop fighting. He wasn't about to give up. It made sense for them to work together and she was still doing the same sort of work, just from a different angle. Phil hadn't been happy to see his protégée go, but he'd understood. She was thrilled to be part of the Vice team and loved getting visits from Alex in her cushy new office. Thank God the door had a good lock on it, because no one on her team needed to know what they got up to in that room.

A sturdy desk was a wonderful thing.

Dana wasn't sure what the future would bring. They'd set a date and her family was now looking forward to another wedding, even Anise. In fact, Anise had accepted Alex wholeheartedly.

Hearing her sister had been held at gunpoint helped any old grudges dissipate.

Now she just had to discourage her sister from texting them all day long with her suggestions for flowers and tuxedos and wedding marches.

Life was good and she cherished everything she shared with Alex.

Dana knew the day would come when she and Alex would make a decision about whether or not to adopt, but right now, neither of them saw a need to make any changes. They were happy. No matter what the future held, they would embrace it together.

As their driver opened the back door on his side, Alex took a deep breath. Releasing it in a long stream, he stepped out of the limousine.

Photographers turned in their direction. There were flashes everywhere, blinding Dana as she took his hand.

"Alex! Dana!" Several paparazzi called their names.

One day, she would get used to his surreal life, but it probably wasn't today.

Alex drew her to him, kissing her on the cheek. "Ready?"

"Ready, but can you do me a favor?"

"Anything."

"Show me Zeus."

Alex laughed, his lips curling into the broad smile she cherished.

"There. Now, I'm ready."

They stepped onto the turquoise carpet and posed, as a hundred camera flashes recorded the moment.

THE END

ACKNOWLEDGMENTS

When I originally wrote Vice, Vegas Sins 1, I had intended it as a stand-alone romance. However, Jennifer O'Neill and Lori Whitwam of Crave Publishing encouraged me to return to Las Vegas and expand the story into a series. I'd like to offer my heartfelt thanks to Jennifer and Lori for showing such confidence in my work and for the kind support.

Thank you to my wonderful editor Toni Rakestraw. You always manage to teach me something new and valuable, and I'm so pleased I get to work with you.

In tackling this novel, I knew I had to do a lot of research. I also wanted to ensure it was seen by eyes other than mine. I'd like to thank Anise Eden, Rosemary Rey and Gryffyn Phoenix for reading my manuscript and for offering so many words of wisdom. I could not have done this without you.

There were several other writer friends who helped me as I worked on certain elements of this story. I had lots of questions for lots of people and I truly appreciate the feedback and honesty of their answers. Thank you to the wonderful writers in All The Kissing, in particular Gwynne Jackson, Zoe Ashwood, Michelle Geel, Madi Dearson, Allison Temple, Savannah J. Frierson, Tara Watson, Anne Terpstra, Madison Diaz, Belinda McBride, Kristine Yarwood, Stephanie Arrache, and Jill Keller.

Thank you to everyone in the Crave Publishing team for always making this so easy and such a pleasure.

Last, but not least, I must offer my continued thanks to my readers. Your support means the world and I hope you enjoy this story.

ABOUT THE AUTHOR

Rosanna Leo is a multi-published author of contemporary and paranormal romance. Winner of the Reader's Choice 2015 in Paranormal Romance at The Romance Reviews, Rosanna draws on her love of mythology for her books on Greek gods, selkies and shape shifters.

From Toronto, Canada, Rosanna occupies a house in the suburbs with her long-suffering husband, their two hungry sons and a tabby cat named Sweetie. When not writing, she can be found haunting dusty library stacks or planning her next star-crossed love affair.

A library employee by day, she is honored to be a member of the league of naughty librarians who also happen to write romance.

Facebook:
https://www.facebook.com/rleoauthor1

Twitter:
https://twitter.com/LeoRosanna

Goodreads:
http://www.goodreads.com/author/show/5826852.Rosanna_Leo

Pinterest:
https://www.pinterest.com/rosannaleo/

Instagram:
https://www.instagram.com/rleoauthor/

Bookbub:
https://www.bookbub.com/authors/rosanna-leo

Amazon author page:
https://www.amazon.com/Rosanna-Leo/e/B007X5P4I8